# ATENIA

# ATENIA

JAY REQUARD

Cover Illustration: Simon Underwood (www.lizardbrainart.com)

Book Cover Design: Lucy Gray

Interior Layout: John G. Hartness (falstaffbooks.com)

Editor: Tim Marquitz (dominioneditorial.com)

ATENIA

Print Edition ISBN: 979-8-218-17910-6

E-book Edition ASIN: B0C2T9BLGK

Published by Look-far

New York, New York

First Edition: April 2023

Visit my website: jayrequard.com

*This book is dedicated to every tyrant in the world who think they are worthy of deciding on the dignity of anyone outside of themselves. A day comes when it ends.*
*So it will be for you.*

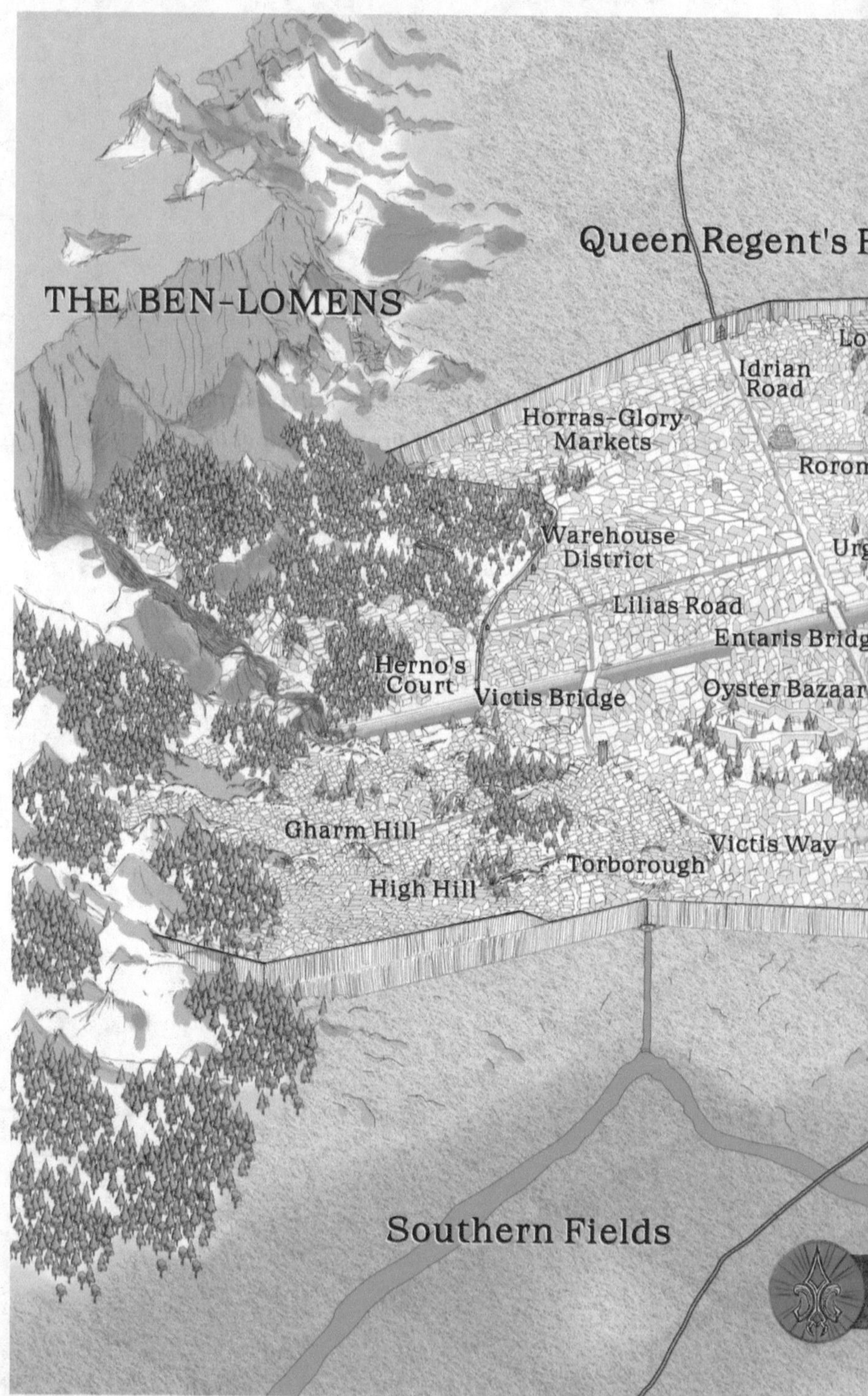

THE BEN-LOMENS
Queen Regent's R
Idrian Road
Lo
Horras-Glory Markets
Roron
Warehouse District
Urg
Lilias Road
Entaris Bridg
Herno's Court
Victis Bridge
Oyster Bazaar
Gharm Hill
Victis Way
Torborough
High Hill
Southern Fields

N
W E
S
THE VEARDEN RANGE
Bhadran's Wood
Bhadran's Line
Mt. Ectis
Tomb of the Veards
Snail's Way
w Hill
The Colis
Gallows Square
Military District
The Franc
ned by Queen-Regent
Veard on behalf of the
Dusk Age 2712 (DA)

# PART I

# THE INVASION

None ever thought Atenia would fall.

Then, Solomon de Veard III, a fine king for a dusking age, vanished into a peace that disappeared with him.

The sun had not crested the horizon when silver horns blasted from Atenia's spiraling fortress, high on the spike of stone the Veards settled long ago. Woken by the call, many of the citizens closest to its foot had massed by the time knights rode out of the lower gate, glittering in the peeking dawn upon their powerful mounts. The steeds armored in finery to match the purple-plumed warriors, they tore through the streets, shouting commoners back inside their homes and threatening the use of their swords.

The few men and women who protested were quickly arrested. Some of the elders, many of them parents to the knights, met with the sentries in a plea for calm.

"What has happened? Why have the horns been blown?"

"The king is dead," was all the curt warriors said. "Dawn rises in Atenia."

"But what of the queen-mother Marta? What about princess

Fransica?" some dared asked to scornful glances and sneers by the mounted men. "Have they called back the prince from his sojourn below the Southern Sea?"

"The king is dead," they repeated, cold and short to the citizens' creeping panic. "Dawn rises in Atenia."

The dawn had waved its farewell when the horns resounded from the citadel a second time. Another set of calvary descended to Atenia's forested streets to reinforce the first, this time commanding citizens to leave their homes and march toward the royal square. Eager to the promise of an explanation, thousands of families from every corner of the valley put on mourning clothes and crowded the white gates an hour later.

The morning dragged with the rising heat of the early summer. Sweat and restlessness surged by the time the trumpeters called their attention.

A thin woman with a golden coif flattened by a crystal diadem rose to the parapet of a balcony high above the craning heads of her subjects. Gowned in a simple dress that showed off her tanned shoulders and long, elegant neck, she gazed down.

And smirked.

For a long, droning pause, Princess Fransica de Veard searched below in a mad quest for something, or maybe someone. Her red-painted lips remained parted in a wolf's smile, revealing her teeth.

A man came to her side. Taller than her by a head and slight of build, his hair thinned at the top of a large, rounded head. An amber beard failed to cover a dishonest mouth and weak chin. His eyes lacking luster due to long nights by candlelight and the smoke of ritual incenses, Fransica's sorcerous husband Niklon whispered in her ear. He touched her throat with a bare hand once and stepped out of sight.

She spoke, the volume of her voice amplified by her husband's spell.

"My people of Atenia," she said in a somber tone not

matching her gleeful expression. "It is with great burden I come to you. In the passing of the night, our king, Solomon, third of his name, went to his rest."

A dread quiet spread among the people below, interrupted only by the stamp of hooves and the scrape the knights' armor. Lined before the gates that closed the high wall encircling the royal citadel and its sharp, towering peak, they kept their lances skyward.

"In normal circumstances, the crown would pass to the rightful heir," she continued, at perfect ease, "but there are no rightful heirs to Solomon."

The crowds below gasped in unison.

"Long has Atenia grown rich and wealthy, a house of splendors for all who live within its walls. These walls...these cages," the princess said, raising her enchanted voice. "For within this cage you call home, I have long suffered the assaults of my father. Long was I put to the side, neglected for greater ambitions. Solomon was no king, no father, no man worth his name!"

The gasps turned into shouts. Some in shock, some in outrage, but all in doubt.

The knights before the palace gates maintained their steeled vigil.

"Worse, he sired a devil!" she shouted, high and hard. "Never again will the name of my brother—my molester—be spoken! Never again will my violator be heralded! He is cursed, a wretched criminal from here until his dying breath! And after! Never again will I hear his name nor feel the touch of his hand, let alone the sight of his evil!"

The shock of the accusations none had thought possible, of a faraway and absent prince, quaked through her subjects. Men gaped in horrid astonishment while their wives shuddered and shouted about a knight far afield not only for Atenia but the whole of humankind.

One whom they cherished.

"A new dynasty emerges to lead Atenia to true glory and honor," Fransica shouted, the volumizing spell crackling her words. "My son, my only true heir in blood, now becomes King Tobias de Veard, first of his name, Scion of Atenia and prince of the Lomens! Because of his age and the work needed to heal the scars inherited from his dastardly forebearers, I will serve as queen-regent upon the throne until he becomes of age."

The proclamation thrust the citizenry into a riot. Demands for answers were shouted at the self-appointed regent. She stared in disinterest at the hundreds upon thousands she had been sworn to serve, or at least had been before the dawn, raged on the earth. Scanning where the people wedged in front of the gates and all the way back to Urghenna Street, a forested plaza named after a long-dead ancestor, a sneer flared her blue eyes and delicate nostrils.

Women rushed their children away while the youths and elders marched on the line of knights. The warriors lowered their lances and directed their horses forward, halting the unarmed populace in their tracks.

"From this day forth, my son's reign shall be total," Fransica boomed across the sky. "Any who dare defy the House of Veard shall face death!"

The knights broke straight into the protesters. Innocents screamed in terror no matter if they fled or stood to defend themselves. The calvary ran them down, regardless of age or dignity, leaving bodies cooling in the daytime breeze. Blood flooded the cobblestones. In the span of a few minutes, the lines of whole families splattered on the pavements.

"Dawn rises in Atenia!" the new tyrant declared.

Fresh banners, once adorned by a yellow bear in the midst of a blue stream on a black field, were replaced during the fray by a standard of three petals bound at the base, a peach-pink symbol on navy. Horror echoed through the city as these flags were flown until Fransica's law was made real.

Weeks later, after the commoners buried their dead and sorrow lessened into cold acceptance, the queen-regent convened the city elders and local politicians with the promise of a sumptuous feast.

***

The lower gates opened to the long twisting path known as Snail's Way, lit by so many torches the wise-whisperers later noted how the pale walls glistened leagues away in other provinces and kingdoms, a beacon on many horizons. The citizens summoned for the feast ascended the steep, sloping route.

Manned on both sides by archers spying from the high ramparts, none put away their bows or lifted arrows off their strings. A vanguard of knights, feathered and flared in the new pink and navy flashings, cordoned off the upper gate to the citadel, forcing the visitors into a tight queue. Escorted to the opened doors of the palace, none were allowed a moment of rest, herded under gruff orders. Pressured by halberds waving and pointing them in the direction of the feast hall, only under complete compliance did the guard relent, the butts of their weapons stamped in the plush cream carpet running throughout the sterling keep.

As promised, an elaborate meal had been laid out, steaming and ready to eat. Atenia's wary folk assumed places on the benches. Plates were filled, and ale brimmed a multitude of cups, heartily sipped without worry or thought of danger. Bowls of fragrant cabbage and squash pottages spiced with cumin and coriander were ladled alongside savory stews of lamb's heart, dishes of pig loin and bacon, and bowls of dark beans sweetened in a sauce of sugar, tomatoes, and tangy vinegar. The aromas eased the distress of their rude entrance, though a few stayed wary.

"What of the queen-regent?" the elders among them asked, hesitant to feast without the ruler's presence or consent. "What of King Tobias, or the king's father? Should we not wait? Is Marta coming?"

"No, please, eat!" the servants bade with practiced smiles. "Our lady told us to let her guests enjoy themselves as they would naturally."

Musicians joined the soiree, garbed in flashy suits stitched to the Veards' new navy and pink heraldry. Bountiful notes of the flutes, harps, and sweeping drums drove the party, the initial rudeness of the guard a total afterthought.

Bellies filled and mouths drank deep as Queen-Regent Fransica, alongside her consort Niklon, entered without great pomp and circumstance or any sort of announcement. They appeared behind their table like ghosts.

The citizens finally noticed their liege had entered, which brought their celebration to a clattering halt.

The queen-regent, between the table and her throne, waved off her subjects. "Please, my beloved folk, enjoy yourselves! As you would! Atenia speaks through its people, and you speak now with your merriment." Her smooth, powdered smile seemed fixed, almost in rictus. "As you would!"

Slowly, solemnly, her subjects lowered back onto the benches. The musicians picked up their song from where it had left off, springing and light. Servants brought fresh platters of sausages, livers, eels, and garlic-buttered mushrooms. Supping on the delicacies, all were aware of their monarch and her husband, who had taken to shaving his large head but leaving the scruffy red beard. He dressed in a fine jacket of dark purple, which glittered at the sleeves with diamonds to match the stones in his wife's arched diadem. He ate heartily while she studied those who had come from the city below, seeking something on their faces. She never looked to her plate nor asked it to be filled.

A messenger ran into the feasting hall and approached the royal table.

Niklon rose to receive him. Whatever the man relayed into the sorcerer's ear was quickly relayed to the queen-regent, who responded with a tight nod. Her confident stare rose to the entrance as two trumpeters stepped through, lifted their silver horns to their lips, and blew a melody of trilling notes.

An old woman, bent by the gold and emerald crown on her head—the queen's proper circlet—slowly entered the room. Though they had been unprepared for the queen-regent, the subjects of Atenia were ready for Marta de Veard, saintly wife of the disgraced king. Garbed in a simple-made gown to match her understated presence, she plodded on her cane. Accompanied by Sir Harras, the newly crowned champion of Atenia did not seem pleased to serve her.

The citizens stood in unison, every single one of them willing to perform the task.

Her venerable mother was not halfway to her seat, oddly stationed at the end of the grand table and far from her daughter, when the queen-regent contested the reverent quiet. "What is wrong?" Fransica asked aloud. "Has something happened under your tables? Sit, sit! As you would!"

Awkwardness in lamplight and shadow danced on guests' faces. Some dropped into their seats on the order, only to push themselves back up before bobbing again in confusion. Others stayed where they stood, agape as they wondered at which matriarch to heed.

Marta offered a kind wave, a silent signal for them to sit.

An hour passed in a muted supper. Men restrained their drinking while the women in the hall tried to make pleasantries with Fransica. Not hiding her contempt, she met them with false smiles and a stare beyond whoever addressed her, as if bored with the air they inhabited. The musicians tried to brighten the feast, but no matter how fast they plucked their strings, blew their melodies, or patted the goatskins, little surmounted the disinterested aura of their ruler.

To the relief of the listless revelers, the servers brought out creme-cakes, raspberry tarts, and the cinnamon rolls known throughout the kingdom as a royal favorite. The sugary treats were served with hot cups of tea and a mulled mead heavy in floral herbs and lovely esters, capping the final course. Marta enjoyed herself finally, getting up to leave the high table and visit folk whom she had called her friends over a long life. The break in edict roused some familiar happiness. Her welcoming charm spread through the hall.

The distinctions in temperament could not have been more apparent. The queen-regent fumed at her mother, gripping the arms of her pearled dining chair until her knuckles whitened.

Leaning to whisper in his wife's ear, Niklon instructed her on something out of earshot.

Nodding a few times while she nuzzled her head to his velveted shoulder, Fransica straightened. "What wonderful days we see," she declared, loud enough the room turned her way. Beaming at their undivided attention, she took the peach-pink napkin off her lap and dropped it on the royal table, signifying the end of the meal.

"You know," she began, "I worried if the kingdom would hold after my dread predecessor met his end. I know, sometimes, confusion can find its way into our hearts, but if we listen to what causes the confusion, we will find the truth. To see you all here, supping, drinking, living like the days are as they always were..." She sighed with a pitying smile. "To think you all sat through it beforehand, knowing you cheered evil. I'm glad so many of you see past yourselves to this happier moment. I endured it for you all."

The mood in the feast hall plummeted like a stone kicked

from a cliff. Some turned baleful, fearful gazes to the sorcerous Niklon, but the focus centered on the queen-regent as she struck again.

"Don't you think so, Mother?" Fransica almost sneered at her behind a sugary smile as she fixed her quarry seat among the insulted rabble. "Isn't it good to know the truth now? Isn't it wonderful to see me thrive despite everything done to me?"

However Marta answered every person in the room never repeated what was said on fear of execution. A few days later, the "loveless" queen-mother vanished from Atenia's history, right beside a dastardly husband and monstrous son.

# 1

# THE WRAITHS

Haidra tried to shut her mouth, anything to steady her rapid breath or the pounding in her chest. She struggled to strike the flint to the stone at the correct angle, fingers too numb to grip the gray chip properly as she scratched against the iron nail she had found in the dirt. The night air, cold and stinging, bit at her bare face as she worked to light the torch between her knees, half-sunken in the wet grass. The sun had not come yet.

"Please, Crook, please," she whispered to the shepherd guarding the living, hoping the archers on the palisade did not spot her. She had covered her dark hair in a black shawl, smudged her face in coal ash and stinking mud, and dirtied her clothes to not stick out against the edge of the northern fields where the queen-regent's grain was grown. No thought on the starvation she was about to inflict on her neighbors, she scraped and scraped and scraped until a spark leapt onto the oiled cloth.

A wisp of acrid smoke, a shred of hope, she struck until the small points of light became a sputtering flame. Scooting back so the torch did not burn the inside of her dress or legs, Haidra snatched it up by the other end and ran for the wheat. The stalks caught the moment she stuck the red coal into their lengths. The fire spread in an instant. Columns of black smoke sprouted at multiple places throughout the field.

The reality of what she had done caught.

She had kept her promise to him, her father, to the ruin of everyone else.

Haidra dropped the torch and covered her mouth with her hands. "Oh, no."

Watching in horror as two season's worth of hard work charred to the root, her shock broke when a horn sounded in the distant hills to the north. Unsteady on her feet, Haidra stumbled away from the fire, toward the palisade gates she had slipped through earlier. Surprised by the lack of guards rushing to meet her, she arrived at the entrance to Atenia's northern walls as the first line of spearmen appeared. Armored in shining mail and capped in conical iron helms, they leveled their pikes forward.

Hiding in one of the bushes to the side, Haidra followed the direction of their focus to the highway road. Her eyes adjusted to the gloom.

Three black points charged down the strip of road. Unable to discern any details of the riders' garbs, strange spots of illumination bobbed in front of their hoods. Closer and closer, the distance eaten up by the seconds, she gasped.

The lights in the riders' hoods were their burning eyes.

"Spears at attention," called the gate sergeant, sword out as he walked in front of their formation. "First line, kneel! Second line, at the ready!"

Of their thirty, fifteen took a full-step forward and knelt on one knee. They placed the butt of their pikes beneath them, anchoring the poles to allow better leverage of the points. The last fifteen raised their weapons high in both hands, up by their temples.

A lifelong witness to violence in the streets between her neighbors and the law, Haidra braced for the impalement.

A flash in the distance broke her expectation.

Ahead of the three riders drove a wedge of light, its illumined point flush to the dirt road but throwing up dust like the marauders behind it. Grim voices above the crackle of the flaming fields, the three riders moved their hands in unified gestures. The wedge shot ahead of them.

"Hold!" called the sergeant. "Hold!"

Magic smacked into them with a thunderclap. Light exploded as the whole troop collided into walls, the earth, and farther distances, while those who remained on their feet reeled out of formation. The sergeant fell to his knees, his sword a crutch.

The riders neared. Two men and a woman by their obvious frames, they wore matching shirts of blackened mail with steel gauntlets and greaves fitted to strong, sinuous limbs. The two men came armed, one raising his ax high while the other, at the point of their trifecta, wielded a shining longsword. The sorceress among them stood on her saddle, a shade from the depths of Haidra's worst nightmares.

The three wraiths won the charge, running over a trio of men as they cleaved into the stunned soldiers beside them. The sorceress launched from her horse with a graceful flip, landing among the survivors. Her comrades let their horses carry them forward a bit more before they slipped off. Haidra watched in amazement as the woman with burning eyes unleashed a rapier and small target. Without hesitation, she pierced the sergeant's throat. Using her small shield in quick defense, she withdrew and went at the next spearman.

The three wraiths tore into the guards, felling them by sword, ax, and rapier.

The bloodshed entranced Haidra as decapitated heads cracked the dirt, the choking screams of the less fortunate men silenced by hard, heavy hackings. The black spirits slew without word, strain, or mercy.

An alarm sounded farther down the palisade to the east.

The wraiths broke apart, the ax-slinger collecting their horses while the sorceress and swordsman roved the gate area.

"Where is he?" the swordsman called, tall and broad in the shoulders. "Where's Arverin?"

"That's my dad," Haidra whispered without thinking.

The sorceress searched the opposite hedgerow from where Haidra hid, the glow of the blazing fields making her seem shaped of soot. "Maybe the archers spotted him when he was lighting the fields." Her red gaze wandered to the wheat, its smoldering line now halfway to the other side of its borders. "We should try to find his children. I think he had a daughter."

"I'm his daughter," Haidra said aloud this time.

The two wraiths faced her, the red points within their hoods fixing like real eyes. Neither raised their weapons.

The sorceress spoke, "Come out. We won't hurt you."

Stepping from behind a dense shrub despite every doubt, arms over her chest for the lack of knowing anything better to do, Haidra revealed herself to the creatures. They stood statue-quiet among the dead, which she dared to look at in horror. The stench of their offal soaked in the burning air, making the sight of their exposed guts worse. The heat of the wheat field, its smoke, blew upon the night wind to leave an overpowering scent of burnt bread.

"Who are you?" the wraith with the longsword asked.

"Arverin," Haidra answered quickly. "Arverin the mender. I'm his daughter," she said, trying not to stammer. The black robes of the wraiths writhed at the hems, the ragged bits snaking on their own accord.

"What's your name, girl?" the swordsman asked, harsher this time.

"Haidra," she said, swallowing so her guts did not come up. "My name is Haidra."

"I'll carry her on my horse," the sorceress replied, "but we need to get to cover. The entire city will be on high alert."

The taller wraith made for the inside of the palisade gates. "Good."

The third of their number, the ax-slinger, recovered their black horses. The slight details of their garb sharpened the longer Haidra had to study the trio. Clearly in possession of a single head, two arms, and two legs, the lack of tails proved she dealt with something like a mortal, removing her worst fears of whatever lay underneath.

The swordsman said something to the ax-slinger in a foreign tongue familiar to her ear. Heard in the markets near the bakery where she worked and spoken by the desert folk from below the Southern Sea, she knew it was Eaith, the traders' speech from Arbikk.

The sorceress appeared, ushering Haidra to the side of her black beast.

"Quickly up," she said, not unkind like the swordsman but with an equal authority. Haidra did not argue as she put her foot in a stirrup. The sorceress provided a small lift of support with her strong, thin arms. She deftly leapt into the saddle, positioning in front of Haidra with perfect ease. Taking the reins, she squeezed her lithe legs into her horse's flanks.

"Which way?" the swordsman asked.

Haidra pointed south to Idrian Street, the main road through the city and the only way she knew to make sense of. "Down that way. To the third street on the left, and then we go through the alleys to get to my house."

The sorceress shifted her head to the left in her hood. "What happened to your father? He was the one who was supposed to meet us here."

The question quieted Haidra, her scattered thoughts falling

into clear, violent clarity. She remembered climbing through the window of their hovel, knees scraping on the sill. Her father tried to wrestle a sword in a knight's hand, already bleeding badly as he kept the intruder at bay.

His shrieks echoed inside her heart.

The swordsman spoke, "Answer, girl."

Haidra tried to speak, to say what had happened, what she had witnessed.

The sorceress sighed at her fellow wraith. *"Lady Haidra."*

The swordsmen said nothing for a few seconds, then tried again. *"Lady Haidra,* where's Arverin?"

"I don't know," she said, too scared to answer with the truth. "I don't know what happened to my daddy. The guard came and..."

"Then we cannot take you home," the swordsman said. "Did your father have any friends who kept his secrets?"

"We can go to Mr. Ecktor's house," Haidra answered. "He's a cobbler in the rebellion. My father said he was involved."

"We'll need your help getting to this cobbler," the sorceress said, both a firm order and gentle request. "We need to get there if we're to keep you safe."

Arms tight to the sorceress' waist, gnawed by exhaustion, Haidra mustered a nod.

The entire night mashed into slums, darkness, the noise of stray animals yowling, infesting Low Corner, and of blood and her father's frantic eyes. The city's damnable gloom, stinking and persistent, blunted the sourest bits. Alongside the pain came a strange pride, steeped in the odor of the burnt kernels saturating the night air.

One last chill mustered before the sun's coming, waking her to the truth again as the singed scent spread.

She had done it, and she ruminated in pride and horror.

For her dad, the fields burned.

She had done it.

2

# WORM ON A HOOK

Littered with trash and puddled by emptied chamber pots, the alleys of Low Corner chattered to the song of thriving rats. The sorceress directed her black horse down the cobblestone decline caked in mud and slop dumped from the windows, all shut to block the constant drone of the palisade horns and the quarter's smells. The other two wraiths walked ahead, leading their beasts by the bridles. Taken to the alleys, Haidra led them to Ecktor's house after multiple pauses and detours, the wraiths stepping onto the next road or turning the corner every time a cadre of knights rode past.

An hour later, they reached the right street. Morning cut hard shadows.

Stopping at the right stoop halfway up the hill, the sorceress let Haidra off her saddle first. "Go let them know we're here," she said. "We'll wait."

Haidra balked at the order. "But—"

The swordsman interrupted, "We don't want to frighten them, Haidra."

Her name spoken aloud by the tall wraith did not freeze her this time, but Haidra nodded before facing the door of the cobbler's house. A two-story row of wattle, beams, and thatching, the boarded service-windows shut with heavy slats bore the scratches of more than one robber's attempts.

Taking a deep breath, she knocked four times.

The sorceress stepped out of the way with her horse. The other two flanked the door, out of sight of whoever came to it and on lookout for the next patrol.

No one answered.

Haidra knocked again. "Ecktor?"

Someone shuffled behind the door. Waiting for a long second, the view-slot slid open.

"Who's there?" asked a woman's frantic voice.

She knew it. "Melana? It's me, Haidra!"

"Haidra?" the woman almost shouted on the other side.

A bar scratched wood as it was pulled back. The door popped open to reveal a young woman close to Haidra's age, her reddish-brown hair hidden by a blue-black scarf. Ruddy from tears, she stood in the doorway for another long second. "Why are you out here? The entire lower city was put on lockdown this morning!"

"I know," Haidra said, trying to sound steady. Friends since they were little, her and Melana had grown up playing together before the realm ordered them to work, as it did every child once they turned seven. Seen only a few times as they grew into teens and Haidra's time at the bakery, the small notion of familiarity lowered her guard for a brief second. "They came for Arverin."

Melana drew a hard breath. "Oh, Haidra. Is he…?"

"I don't know." The shudder came, a surprise to her entire body. Haidra squirmed. trying not to cry, not to think back to when the mender grabbed a sword's naked edge. "I don't know."

"Oh, Haidra." The cobbler's eldest daughter reached out with a delicate hand and laid it on her shoulder. "You're covered in soot."

"I set the fields on fire."

The wraiths flanking the door froze. Their cinder-bright eyes shifted to her.

Melana drew her hand back, as if touching poison. "You... you're one of them. Like my father!"

"Where is he, Melana?" Haidra scraped her wet cheeks with the back her hand. "It's really important I find him."

"They came and took him this morning." Melana's tone hardened. "He was escorted to the guard station with the promise he'd be hung before the queen-regent's husband by sunset. I hope he kicks, and good riddance on your father! I hate you and every single dirty traitor! Go! before I call to come and get you too!"

The door slammed shut a few inches from her face, stunning Haidra as it rattled on the stone frame. Quickly, the swordsman stepped in, put an arm around her shoulders, and guided her away in the direction of the sorceress, who kept their horses in the next alley.

The wraiths convened.

"Go ahead and loose them. They'll find a way out," the swordsman said to the sorceress.

Following the order, the sorceress brought the horses by their bridles, wrangling them despite their powerful bulk. She placed her gauntleted hand, shining in spiked steel, on the face of each. The strange lady whispered to them in Eaith. Each beast glossy black with well-kept manes and tails, they nuzzled her palm before they trotted off, deeper into the alley before they clopped out of sight.

"Do you know which guard station they would have taken Ecktor to?" the swordsman asked.

Shamed by Melana's words, Haidra refused to raise her eyes from the ground. She rung her dirty hands, trying to ignore the stink of ash in every pore, a new layer of skin to remind her of what she had done. Her father screamed in the back of her mind.

What had she done?

The sorceress spoke to her, "Haidra."

Something in the wraith's light, echoing voice compelled her to look up. Haidra startled as she did.

The flaming embers in the three wraiths' eyes disappeared, revealing mortal pupils and blue-green irises familiar to her and common to Atenians. Alert but kind, their faces were matched by strong aquiline noses she innately recalled but could not place, golden complexions tanned by life under a constant sun she had seen little of. The swordsman was the oldest among them, a strapping man in his forties with the looks of someone younger if not for the age and bitterness in his eyes. The second, shorter only by a few inches, was in his late-teens and only a few years older than Haidra. Both wore long beards on their faces dyed dark and red, which only highlighted the gallant lines of their features.

"It's all right," said the sorceress. Her pleasant copper face closer in relation to the older swordsman than the young ax-slinger, her bright white eyebrows and deep chestnut lips noted a heritage farther south of Atenia. She could not have been a summer older than Haidra's sixteen.

"You're not—" Haidra said, starting to put reason to what she saw.

"It'd help if you kept thinking we were," said the swordsman. "Do you know the guard station that woman mentioned?"

Haidra finally nodded. "It's a mile up the street. They'll march them at noon to Idrian's Way as they always do, and up to the palace gates so everyone sees."

The ax-slinger glanced to the swordsman, speaking for the first time. His voice was pleasant, another unexpected detail. "Too exposed. We have to take the station."

The swordsman nodded his agreement. "Moon, go south

along the street with Haidra. Bon and I will follow on the roofs. Call when ready."

The sorceress gave a curt tip of her head as the two wraiths departed, following their horses down the same alley they exited.

Reaching forward, the sorceress held Haidra by both arms and looked into her eyes, piercing deep down inside. "Haidra, I need you to listen and listen carefully. I understand you might be very scared. That makes all the sense in the world. I imagine you might be very sad and angry, too. *I'm* sorry for that. But we're here to help you and your people. Your father was going to help us." She let that truth hover over them before she continued, "We need your help if you are brave enough to give it. We're going to help free Atenia. You can be a part of that. However..."

The sorceress leaned forward so her face took up all Haidra's vision.

"This is your last chance to get out. If you want to help, come with me, but if you want to run you need to do it now. Time to pick your side."

FOLLOWING the sorceress up the hill, they approached the edge of a small square. Barren of any traffic, the jail in the north-western quarter crowded outward toward the center, its two iron gates guarded by corresponding lines of infantry. On the small towers of wood and stone sculpted into the visage of growling bears smoothed by erosion, four archers spied from their perches.

The sorceress used her arm and pushed Haidra flat against the wall as they cornered an alleyway. "Give me a moment."

Wordless for fear of gasping if she spoke, Haidra nodded.

The sorceress whispered a series of words as she brought a

hand to her bare face under her hood. A shadow manifested in the space between her nose and palm. Two fiery eyes opened, the illusion remade of the terrifying spirit and her hell-bound glare. Drawing her armored hand down to her chest, a layer of darkness rose from the billowy, black folds of her cloak, writhing with the quality of bound smoke.

She looked at Haidra with those glowing eyes and drew her rapier. Flipping the slender blade in her hand, she offered the hilt. "I need you to provide a distraction."

The image of her father's hand ripping against the sword clashed with the safe handle shown by her weird companion. Haidra did not reach for it. "I don't want to kill anybody."

"You don't have to do that right now," said the sorceress. "I just need you to hold it and walk out into the square."

"And have them kill me?"

The wraith paused in a deep breath and shook her shifting, shrouded head. "No, no," she said, voice echoing in her hood. "You will be safe by my spell. Trust me."

"A spell?" Haidra understood how magic existed in the world, and even knew a few words she once heard at a circus the queen-regent put on for a son none had ever seen. A sorcerer from far to the north, "one of the decent ones,' her father had said, floated one of her friends high above the ground at the fair, using voice and gestures alone. Now, she had seen it used fully to its worst effect at the gates of the city.

"Yes, and one of protection," the sorceress added. "Please know I would never place you in harm's way unless I was sure about it."

"Oh, well, thank you," said Haidra, not heartened by the shaky oath. A second study of the rapier's hilt, its riveted handle of polished whalebone sandwiching the steel tang and wrapped in soft brown leather melded to her palm as her hand closed around it. The weight of the weapon, light and nimble, delighted in her grip.

"Don't lose it," said the sorceress. "You let go and my spell will not work. Then you're in trouble."

Haidra squeezed the hilt tighter, the curve of the core forced into the grooves of her palm. "What about the archers?"

"Don't think about them." The sorceress placed both hands on Haidra's shoulders and spun her around to face the square. "Walk. Don't stop until you reach the gates."

"But—"

"Go!"

Shoved out of the alley, Haidra stumbled a few steps before she righted, walking quickly toward the jail. Before she had time to look at the archers a shower of sparks blotted her vision. She blinked to clear the blindness and discovered herself ensconced in a sheet of illumination coating her skin like oil. Hot iron filled her nostrils as electricity sizzled on the gleaming, sluicing surfaces.

Another arrow thudded off her chest with barely a touch of pressure, disintegrating in another gout of hot sparks. Then another, and another, all of them destroyed by light and flame.

She followed the volleys, locking eyes with the stunned bowman who had last fired upon her, tall in his pose. Two citizens of the same country, they gaped in complete confusion before the next gout of sparks ended their contact.

Cognizant of her true shape within the shielding illusion, Haidra cried out in wonder as a new distortion formed. Fire covered her body completely, orange-red and licking. Warm and scentless, to her astonishment it did not burn. As she advanced, she noticed the ground seemed farther away. A foot taller than she was, every inch of the illusionary guise pocked and blistered, blackened and oozed. The cheeks and forehead of a new face in front of her own, burning away to reveal the skull underneath.

Whatever horrid creature she had become cried out.

"The wraiths of Veard walk," the ravaged mouth uttered

behind stained teeth. The hoarse voice boomed, "The wraiths walk!"

Unable to see the archers in the towers, the guards on the ground unified in front of Haidra as a pair of knights trotted out of the gate to her left, bearing lances.

The swordsman and ax-slinger appeared at the sides of the horsemen and leapt, bowling the armored warriors out of the saddles. They crashed on the rough concrete. The black ax cleaved a coned helm apart, sending blood spurting, while the swordsman slashed his prey in a parting stroke. They split in the midst of the disarray, the older headed into the jail.

A loud *boom* followed his invasion, rattling the walls.

The younger wraith swung his ax upward toward the rampart, near one of the archer nests, ascending in a remarkable feat of levitation. His edge bit into a wooden beam as he vaulted to the top of the wall connecting the two towers. Archers on both sides struggled with the decision of where to fire first, upon her illusion or the wraith as he climbed to the right and reached the men inside. The four men dead after a few savage moments of hacking, he dropped behind the tower's partition as the other position loosed a volley on him.

"The wraiths of Veard walk," Haidra's illusionary shield screamed. "The wraiths walk!"

More explosions rocked the station. Guardsmen shouted within the crumbling barracks of block and wattle.

Through the din of hell, Haidra somehow kept walking for the gate where the dead knights lay, their horses already escaping into the streets. Able to draw focus on a few objects amid the explosions, Haidra awed as the ax-slinger jumped the gap between the archer nests. The body of the sentry who had fired shafts for her heart moments before tumbled over a second later, thudding hard on the pavestones.

She held out the rapier the sorceress had given her, as if she was Atenia's mother-goddess Imna, drawing water with her wand to slake the earth's early thirsts. She had considered the possibility she might wipe away the infantrymen in front of her when the sorceress appeared at her side and yanked the rapier free. She attacked the disordered spear men as the ax-slinger on the walls descended to join her.

Without the steel, the illusion dissipated in time for Haidra to witness the full carnage.

The youngest of the two demons danced violently among the spearmen, who fumbled with their long weapons as their faces were stabbed through. Blows of the ax-slinger lopped off limbs by the second. Left out in the open, all Haidra could do was watch as the creatures she had let in slaughtered the guards to the man.

The swordsman emerged with a cadre of the townsfolk, one of them close by his side.

The sorceress broke from the heap of bodies she had made with the ax-slinger, headed for Haidra. "Get over here," she called to her.

Oblivious to everything else, Haidra jogged to meet them.

The freed prisoners huddled close to the three wraiths and their companion, made up of many of the most prominent craftsmen and merchants in the Low Corner and Urghenna's Mall, all of great respect as Haidra considered some of the surprising faces that appeared. Some recognized her immediately, freezing or shying from her glance.

The only one who did not break when they found each other was Ecktor, a well-built but balding man with big hands for a cobbler. He walked beside the swordsman, unaffected by the presence of the demonic figure.

"Hello, Haidra," Ecktor greeted in a kind, sad voice. "In it now, aren't ya?"

# 3

# THE CHILDREN OF MARTA

Totaling sixteen, the freed members of Atenia's merchants and craftsmen led the three wraiths and Haidra to a warehouse in the east of Low Corner's depleted slums, farther than Haidra had ever gone and near the wall separating the city from the royal forest of Bhadran's Wood. They covered the windows on the bottom floor with planks and locked the doors with chains. A few men retrieved a small barrel of oil and enough lamps so each of the conspirators had a light to warm their hands and illuminate the large space of hard-packed dirt and cold, musty air.

The wraiths' eyes glowed red and hellish in the dim room. Their weapons held to their chests in a regimented stance, they seemed sprouted from the shadows behind them.

Ecktor stepped forward with his lamp and set it at his feet. Its light made his jowls and cheeks thicker, heavier. "Those who need to rest should do so now. I ask those who started this to remain."

One by one, eleven men slowly lowered their lights to the boards and paced toward the stair leading to the next level of the warehouse, promised rest in the form of stiff cots and fresh bowls of meaty stew. Already the smell of the cooking fire upstairs carried boiled carrots and onions, the fish savory in its broth bubbling out of sight.

Five remained behind, including Ecktor. Their faces defined by where the lamps cut away the shadows, they met the grisly stare of the wraiths, too exhausted to be frightened.

"You're lucky we arrived when we did." The sorceress stood in front of Haidra. One hand on the throat of her rapier's scabbard, the other hidden behind the small steel target she carried, she spoke for the three terrors. "It seems like things did not go as planned."

"You can bloody well say that," one of them groused.

"We were betrayed. The knights killed many as we were rounded up, so who knows?" said Ecktor, smoothing his bushy mustaches. "At least we're not dead yet, Lyndon."

"But you haven't explained who they are yet, Eck," said one of the five, an older woman dressed in a blacksmith's smock. "You made promises about someone coming to save us, but you didn't say who." She hesitated before glancing at the swordsman, peering at his weapon with pointed interest. "You didn't say devils."

"They're not devils any more than the Children of Marta are traitors to Atenia." Ecktor cast a nod toward the three wraiths. "But they do deserve an answer, my...my lords...?"

"We are the wraiths of Veard," said the sorceress, "but we are not lords, my friends, nor do we wish to obscure our natures."

Taking her hand off her rapier, she pulled back her hood to reveal her frost-white mane and dark face, the demonic glamor disappearing in a small glitter of magic. The two men with her unmasked as well, revealing their bearded faces and, to the relief of all the rebels present, their humanity.

The sorceress spoke, her hazel eyes piercing in the lamps, "I'm New Moon, and I came at the behest of his crown prince Aron Toliv of the northern coasts of Arbikk. We are his sentries sent to assist the Children of Marta in their rebellion against the maddened queen-regent and to restore Atenia to justice."

"You mean you're invading," said the same blacksmith, exasperated.

"No more an invasion than to assert the rights of the dead," said New Moon, confident against an elder . "Prince Aron seeks to lay claim to Atenia through his contract with the late Jhean de Veard, fallen prince of Atenia and rightful heir to the throne. Before death in exile, Veard bequeathed his rights to his friend, who in turn has come to see that the rights of every citizen be renewed."

Another of the five Children of Marta spoke, a young man who kept his hands in his pockets, "And what would this prince receive in the balance?"

Ecktor made sour face toward the questioner. "Fhilip."

"Did you not speak to them before now?" New Moon asked the cobbler.

"No, he did not," said the blacksmith.

"It wasn't just my idea," said Ecktor, throwing his hands up at all of them. He wrenched in Haidra's direction and pointed. "Arverin was the one who plotted all of it!"

The room's attention fell on Haidra, who tried as hard as she could not to flinch under their focus. Thankful to not be by the lamps, which hurt her eyes, her gratitude doubled when the wraiths did not turn with the rebels.

"The disagreements among you do not matter," said New Moon, undeterred. "Aron is bringing his army from the north in two days. You all now have a choice: you may either accept the support he has offered, along with the many benefits I have previously mentioned, including justice for you and your families, or you can all go upstairs, eat your soup, and wait for the siege to begin. We will do what we have to on our own."

She stepped forward, nearer to the light so her beautiful face appeared clearly. New Moon bore her stare into each of them, her words weighed in fate. "There's something else to consider. Once Aron's artillery begins to land, nothing will be spared. Not your homes, not your shops, and not you. Perhaps if you consider our support and help us complete Arverin's agreement, we may find a way to spare as much as we can. We await your decision."

Dumbfounded, the five leaders of Atenia's nascent rebellion gaped at her response, flummoxed before they came together. Looking over their shoulders every so often at the dark trio, they murmured and whispered. The wraiths watched in perfect stillness.

The odd one out, Haidra found herself letting her gaze wander to ignore the need to fidget with her hands or feet, tapping her toes like she did when anxious. To her left stood the two male wraiths, the swordsman ahead of the ax-slinger, positioned in much the same way she was behind the sorceress, who reminded Haidra more and more of the swordsman the longer she compared them. Sly to the chance one of them spotted her, she checked within the hood of the wraith wielding the ax.

Tan like his sister, a light brown beard covered a strikingly handsome face of full lips and high cheekbones, holding up a set of aqua eyes that stole her breath. Catching Haidra, he smiled at her before she whipped her eyes forward.

Doing so in time to see the Children of Marta break their informal conference. Ecktor stepped forward again.

"We accept," the cobbler said. "It seems we have no choice in the matter really, now that..." He stared at the floor for a long second, measuring his words. "Is Jhean de Veard truly dead?"

"He fell in battle in Arbikk," said New Moon. "He fought mightily to reclaim his name and honor, but many would not look past the dreadful lies his sister spread about him. Crook called him home in the end."

"Aye," said Ecktor, faraway. "Aye, good."

"The poor bastard," said the blacksmith, embittered in the oil lamp's low light. "We'll never know if he was innocent or not."

"Don't matter now, didn't matter then," said Philip. "Never got anything good from those royals anyhow. Burn them in their beds, for all I care."

"You weren't there, youngin'," said Ecktor. "You don't know what you throw away so easily. He was... Now he's dead, so what will we make in his place? Did he have children? Did he do the crimes Fransica said he committed? Who was in the right?" The cobbler licked his lips to moisten them against the warehouse's cold. "Now we will never know."

Philip spat a glob of saliva on the packed dirt floor. "Good fucking riddance."

"With Aron's army approaching from the north, we need to neutralize the palisade," New Moon said, commanding their attention. "What numbers you can gather will be appreciated. We will perform reconnaissance on the northern walls and discern the best way to take them before our force arrives."

"Taking the walls is one thing, but who will hold them?" asked Philip, scoffing. "We don't even have weapons or armor after the raid this morning."

"Then what needs to be done is clear," the sorceress said, unmoved by the rebel's attitude. "How many soldiers can you gather before sunrise?"

Ecktor and the blacksmith glanced at each other.

"I can get you twenty men in the next hour, a few hundred if I have a day or two," the blacksmith said, the corner of her mouth wrinkled by her frown. Her light brown eyes went from the wraiths to Haidra and back. "But Philip is right. It's all for nothing if they can't defend themselves."

"We'll settle that," said New Moon. "Gather your twenty and bring them to us before dawn. Until then, you should go eat and rest with the others. You've all been through quite the day."

"Wait," said the blacksmith, not moving when her brethren

did. "We know who you are, Lady New Moon, but who are the other two warriors with you? Neither of them has spoken during this meeting."

"These wraiths are my kin, lady," said New Moon. "They do not speak because they have chosen me to speak for them, but they do carry names. The man with the sword is Black John, and the one with the ax is called Bon the Bloody. I simply call him Bon."

The younger of the two men bowed his head respectfully. Hazel-eyed like the sorceress, he could have been an Atenian now that Haidra had a better view of his bronze face, and the five Children of Marta knew this too when they saw him.

The blacksmith, wily and wizened to the brutal ways the realm's subjects lived studied that bearded face intently until, unable to find what she sought, broke for the wide staircase to the warehouse's second level.

Ecktor stayed. "Haidra."

Startled to have her name called, the mender's daughter cleared her throat. "Yes, Mr. Ecktor?"

"I..." The cobbler, a man she had known since she was little and had been good to her, chewed the words in his mouth. "I don't know how to tell you this, but—" He huffed, summoning a depth to his words when he spoke, "He fell bravely. The knights slew him, Haidra. I'm sorry I have to be the one to tell you, but you deserved to know."

She wanted to tell him, to yell it in his face, to let him know there had been a witness.

To her wonder, Haidra remained placid, the news flattening her mouth to a wordless line. Gazing at the cobbler, she blinked a few times and said nothing.

Discomforted with her silence, Ecktor bowed to the three wraiths and retreated for his meal.

A sinking in Haidra's chest grew as every part of her face tightened in preparation to weep. No tears came, no matter how desperately they were wanted. Staked to where she was, nothing brought the release she craved in the lonesome, sad moment.

New Moon turned halfway in her direction. "When was the last time you ate, Haidra?"

The question broke down the last wall. "I ate with my daddy." Everything disappeared after a sob dropped her to her knees. Haidra crumpled inward, heaving, until the darkness of sleep and misery conquered the waking nightmare.

4

## A DAY TRIP

Haidra dozed on the pallet of old musty blankets, her face swollen from crying. She rolled to the right, flat on her back, and stared up into the triangle-honey-combs of the warehouse's ceiling. Particulates of its dust on the bridge of her small nose, her eyelashes, shaking her head only gave her a headache that failed to remove any of it.

Opening a dry mouth, barren of the spit needed for a good swallow, she woke completely when Black John whispered, "Start them here and here, away from the main irrigation. They were dry enough when I scouted a few weeks ago, but it might have rained."

Holding a hand ensconced in white flame above the map, Bon the Bloody nodded at the instructions. Hood pulled back to reveal his shock of honey brown hair matching the mane of the older swordsman, Haidra lingered on the ax-slinger's handsome face, trying to remember every detail in the weird illumination. New Moon stood across from him, holding the map out in her hands.

The oldest warrior towered over them both, his back to Haidra.

"I'll need a few men if I'm to cause a real ruckus," New Moon said, glancing up at Black John. "Perhaps Bon lights the fields after I'm done."

"It means you'll have to be first. And faster," said Black John.

"She can do it," Bon said. "It will give the fires more urgency. Probably make them think more of us have arrived."

"Both provocations have to draw the attention of the royals completely if I'm going to meet my end at the armory in Gallows Square." Black John reached out and took the map from New Moon, rolling it into a thin tube before folding it in half. He stuck the soft piece of vellum into his ragged cloak. "Make them big enough they'll have no choice but to pay attention."

"Then I *will* need the men," said New Moon.

"All right," Black John replied. "Stop nagging."

"What about her?" New Moon asked.

Haidra shut her eyes and rolled over, facing a dusty corner of the warehouse.

"Well? What about her?" asked Bon. "She goes or she stays, right? It's her choice."

"She has to go with someone," said the sorceress. "She showed some real pluck at the guard station. You two couldn't have done what you did without us, and I couldn't have if she hadn't been brave and dumb enough to walk out there like a sitting duck."

Haidra screwed her face at the backhanded compliment.

"Well, you're speaking up for her," said Black John. "What would you like?"

"Have her go with Bon to the fields," New Moon replied.

"Oh, no, no," Bon rebutted. "I see what this is."

Black John sighed. "Stop playing. And wake her, Bon. The Children of Marta should be here soon."

Bon shook out his hand to banish the white flame, the polished steel gauntlets of sharp ridges and spikes glittering bright before they dulled. He leaned over and retrieved his black ax from the floor. "I'll be lucky if they can even get me to the bloody fields."

Moments later, the soft thump of Bon's boots closed on Haidra. She played at dozing, hoping she wouldn't startle.

"Haidra," Bon whispered.

She startled anyway, flailing in her twist of blankets, before she ended on her knees. Embarrassed, she craned her head up.

Bon had drawn up his hood and enchanted his face with his illusionary mask, red eyes lost in the void. While not as frightening as before, it was a disappointment to meet first thing in the morning. Outside the eastern windows, dawn had crept over the Vearden Range, warming the world.

"Sorry to wake you," he said, an enchantment distorting his voice lower than its natural tone. "We have some clothes for you and breakfast when you're ready. Moon will come get you in a bit. We're going to south today."

"South? To where?" Haidra asked, half-playing dumb.

"You'll see when we get there." Bon turned away from her, his footfalls muffled by his writhing cloak sweeping the floor boards.

Haidra hobbled to the corner the wraiths had used as a campsite of bedrolls and a small fire they had built in a scorched fire bowl. Hung above the last of its coals, a small black iron pot rested above the heat by a hook and stand. A dense soup of chicken, roots, and oats congealed inside, nutty-smelling and savory. A rough spun shirt and hide leggings were laid out atop a pair of good boots. She recognized them from Ecktor's shop stall, presented carefully on a fresh bedroll apart from the others.

Using one of the wooden spoons beside the cooking pot, Haidra spooned herself mouthfuls, the lack of salt and the chewiness of the chicken small hurdles for the sheer joy of a full stomach. After five or six tastings, she shed her flaxen apron dress and the undershirt she had worn underneath, sweat and soot cracking in the fibers. She left everything where it fell. The new clothes rested well on her well-proportioned chest and hips, the hide neither too tight around her thighs or the shirt too stiff against the soft flesh of her breasts. Binding her honey-brown hair into a bun at the back of her head, Haidra waited in the quiet before the sorceress appeared.

"Come with me, Haidra," New Moon said. "We're leaving."

She followed the sorceress out a door in the northwestern corner of the warehouse to an open lot at the intersection of two deserted streets. Somewhere in northeastern corner of Urghenna's Mall, built on the last steppe lowering to the northern half of the city before the foothills terminated at the west-to-east flow of the Ursin Canal, the Children of Marta had returned with the promised score and two canvas-covered wagons, each led by a pair of horses hitched side by side.

New Moon spoke with Ecktor and the blacksmith, whom Haidra learned went by the name Aleaus.

"We can spare that number," Aleaus said when Haidra was within earshot, "but we need to know you'll get us those weapons. And we'll need good ones! Steel. And new. That should be there in the armory at Gallows Square."

"We have lived up to our ends so far." New Moon stared up at the blacksmith, who was taller than her by more than a few inches. "Whatever help you can provide would be gladly welcomed. It will take more than the three of us, including our magics, to hold off the Atenian guard once we attempt our escape."

"We'll do what we can, but we're still putting out the call after everyone heard of the raid. Many didn't expect us to be alive, and some might think it a trick by the royals," said Aleaus. "I might be able to scrounge some archers."

"I know where I can find some," said Ecktor, "but we need to check our caches. If we waste these arrows now we won't have any later."

"Have faith," said New Moon before she departed from the small meeting with no farewell, leaving both stupefied. She acknowledged Haidra with a light nod as she passed, reaching out with some fingers to brush her forearm.

"Follow me and don't look back," she whispered.

Haidra turned on the spot and followed the wraith's shadow. They found the other two by the first wagon, along with the twenty rebels they had been given for the day's mission. Already, Black John had divided them into their groups: five for him, six for Bon, including Haidra, and nine of the fastest and strongest among them for New Moon. The Children of Marta's leadership escaped with their small escort of men armed with cudgels, quickly ducking into the alleys already stinking of urine for the day. Dew added an acrid mold to the stink, but none paid attention as the arcane warriors in their fiery masks evaluated them one by one.

"Of the nine gathered before me, which one of you knows the quickest, safest routes to the northern palisade?" New Moon asked of the mortal men assembled for her scheme.

One of the boys in front lifted his hand.

"You shall lead the way for us. Do not fear, for my magic will protect you all," the sorceress said. "Lead on."

New Moon and her nine marched northward into the slums as Black John took his five and loaded the first wagon. Ordering one of the older rebels to drive to Gallows Square, the tallest wraith crawled into the covered wagon bed and laid down as the rest of the men took their places on the benches, their legs concealing him. The wagon took off a minute later, leaving Haidra alone with six rebels and Bon.

The ax-slinger watched as the older swordsman rolled into the distance. "All right," he said, wiping his armored hand down the front of his face to banish his illusionary mask. He looked to his troop, giving a sincere smile, including Haidra, who found herself smiling back. "Let's get underway. Who here knows how to get to the southern end of the city without too much of a fuss or running into the guard?"

Of the six, four women and two men, one of the latter raised his hand. Graying at the temples with brown hair on its way to receding, and half a foot shorter than Bon, the old man cleared his throat. "I know a way that takes us through the back streets a few blocks from here. The city's guard doesn't use them much anymore."

"Excellent," said Bon, jovial in a manner unbefitting his appearance. "What's your name, my friend?"

"Talic, my Lord." The old man coughed a second time. "I'm— I *was* a guardsman. Long ago. I know how to get around."

"Well, Talic, that will do nicely," Bon replied. "And no need for that 'lord' nonsense. No crowns about these parts, right? Haidra, you ride with Talic on the bench. The rest of you in the wagon with me."

Without waiting, he went to the back and opened the folding gate. He promptly crawled in and sat on the floor, his back against the wall separating the cabin from the driver's bench. Hesitant at first, the rebels of the Children of Marta filled the benches before they were off, in search of new terrors to wreak on their homeland.

TWO HOURS LATER, the sun had risen halfway toward noon, leaving the cool day cheerful if not for the tense, hard mood of Atenia and her citizens. The streets were full as always. Even under the fifteen year-reign of King Tobias I and his mother's tyranny the markets had grown, children were birthed, and from the far kingdoms of Torsdaina and beyond had come migrants to build lives within the domain of a kingdom still ascendant despite of its dark reputation. Young boys and girls, dirty from play in the mud-packed roads of the poorer sections Talic drove through, ran alongside the wagon as it rolled southward down Idrian's Way.

Dozens of knights and infantry manned the guard stations on the street corners and in the trading dens under threadbare awnings, a dramatic shift in their usual presence, though they made no great show of their numbers. None paid Haidra and the old man attention, taking them as country farmers or merchants, going to or from the markets. Trying not to seem anxious on the bench, she often shared an uneasy glance or grin with Talic, who remained quiet as the southern walls neared.

A knock on the wall separating them from the passengers in the cabin broke their nervous silence.

"Hey, Haidra," Bon called from inside. "How much farther?"

Surprised to be addressed so casually, Haidra focused on the ramparts of their destination. "Um, let me—"

"Twenty minutes, give or take," Talic said as if speaking to the air in front of him. The old man gave her a small, quick nod.

"Right," Bon replied. "Thanks. Let me know when we're past."

They approached the last intersection of the city on the south side of Idrian Street sandwiched between the wealthy High Hill in the west and the military compound south-southeast of the royal citadel. To nobody's surprise, the southern gatehouse buzzed with more than forty spearmen while three knights oversaw a checkpoint, halting every person or cart. Splitting traffic into two lines, one filled with people on foot and the other a growing queue of wagons, each undergoing intense inspections.

From where she sat, Haidra could see the infantrymen walking around to the bays, ordering the drivers to open them up. "Uh oh," she sighed under her breath.

"Shush," said Talic, as calm as he had been the entire ride.

The reins of the two roans in his hands, he righted himself into a straight posture while doing nothing to slow the horses until they reached the wagon line.

Reclining as much as she could on the bench, Haidra whispered, "Bon?"

"Shush," he said from inside.

Talic signaled the horses onward when the next wagon moved ahead. Before they stopped, the guards swarmed, spears and swords out as they hurried the driver off his bench. Drawing the attention of citizen and soldier alike, everyone watched as a footman held the young man to the side. The knights and other spears tore through his cart, tossing out food and belongings.

Like everyone in Atenia had done since she was little, Haidra simply watched.

Over as quickly as it started, the infantrymen dismissed the young man with a curt warning, without time to pick up what they had smashed and thrown. The emptied cart rumbled through the gates, far lighter and poorer.

Shaken in her seat, Haidra looked to Talic.

The old man stared ahead, dauntless as he struck the reins to signal the horses forward.

Unable to run, Haidra felt her breath shrink in her chest, tight as she tried her best to present a calm façade. Talic brought the covered wagon to a halt when one of the knights on a brown charger raised a mailed fist.

"Halt," the rider ordered, even after the wagon had stopped. Approaching Talic's side, he offered both Haidra and the old man a passionless expression, his mouth already sunk in an irritated frown. Snorting, he waved one of the spearmen to the wagon's rear. "What's your business?"

"Already sold out at Horras market," Talic said, the lie smooth and certain as he spoke. "Just taking my daughter and workers back to the farm for the day."

"Farmers, eh?" The knight leaned over in his saddle, glaring hard at the old man before his gaze shifted to Haidra. "Why are you so nervous, sweetheart? Your pa lying to us?"

Unable to speak in a clear answer, Haidra shook her head.

The knight growled. "What's that? Speak up, girl! I asked you a question!"

"You're scaring her," Talic said, eyes still fixed on the gates ahead.

"Did I say you could speak?" High in the saddle, the knight spat into the space between his horse and the wagon. "Open the bay," he instructed the spearmen waiting in the back. "Let's see these workers."

Haidra closed her eyes when the latch holding up the back door slid free, almost jumping when the chains snapped taut. Expecting the end in a few moments—either her freedom or life —a long second passed before the burn in her lungs forced her to open her eyes and breathe. Confused, checking on Talic showed even the old man had turned to see what paused their bullies.

"Nothing back here, my Lord," one of the spearmen said. "Just the same crap."

The knight gathered a wad of saliva in his mouth and spat again. "Get out of my sight," he told Talic as he guided his horse to the next wagon. Stunned and wordless as they drove forward, Haidra withheld an exhale of relief until the gates disappeared behind her, which the old guard shared with her.

# 5

# TINDER

Neither Haidra nor Talic spoke until they cleared the portcullises of the southern palisade, leaving behind the noisy city for the bucolic quiet of wheat fields that stretched from the walls all the way to the banks of the river Franc, Atenia's golden hill sloping down to its sparkling line.

The view calmed Haidra to let out a loud breath she had held too long.

"You did good, kid," said Talic.

Haidra nodded to him before she twisted on the bench, knees on the seat as she drew open the curtains of the wagon's canvas cover. To her shock, the first face to meet hers was Bon's. The wraith smiled up at her, his head resting against the wall on her left.

The other four rebels had moved to the farthest end the cabin allowed. The terrified expressions on their faces added more confusion to the scene.

"How did you do that?" she asked.

"Magic," Bon answered.

Unsatisfied with the answer but too worn out to inquire

more, Haidra faced ahead and huffed, once in relief, and then a second in a failed attempt to banish the exhaustion. Her neck ached, pain across her shoulders. She clutched the lip of her bench, squeezing with all her might until the nerves in her hands numbed. She checked the road as Talic turned toward the southwest, along the wide highway that would take them to the other city-states along the continent of Torsdaina's southwestern spur.

"Where do you want to go, Bon?" Talic asked.

"Oh, just turn off somewhere you like," he replied. "We'll have to get out and push anyway."

Talic grunted an affirmative. A few minutes later, he turned the horses to the right, along a path bordered by two irrigation trenches. Haidra followed his eyes to an opening at the edge of an immense wheat field, a lane the fieldhands had cut to make their harvest easier while also taking the early hay. He directed the two roans down its muddy way a quarter mile, well out of view of the roads.

"This looks good," the wraith said. "Stop so we can all get out."

Talic reined the horses to a stop. Quick to escape the confined space, the four rebels leapt out, eager to put a respectful distance between themselves and Bon. Exiting with a gracious tact, the hooded man shouldered his dark ax as he took in the sunny sky, following the clouds northward to Atenia's white walls already cast gray by the sun's slant. He brought his attention around as Haidra and Talic appeared from the front.

Bon levered his ax at the wagon. "Let's get the cover off and shred it. I'll take care of the ribs."

They stripped off the cloth shell, exposing the banded wooden staves that shaped its roof. One of the women had brought along a small shearing knife hidden in her skirts, a poor weapon in a fight but excellent at slicing the old canvas. Haidra assisted her and the two other women in the task while Talic and the other man, Rigen, watched the opening in the wheat. Bon took his ax to the staves, breaking them into kindling he piled in the bed. When they finished, he directed the canvas scraps, many of them long, stringy lengths fraying at the edges, dumped atop of the wood.

"Haidra, you know how to lead a horse?" Bon asked.

"Yes, Lord," she answered before she winced. "I mean—"

"It's fine," Bon replied. "You and Talic untie the horses and get them ready. The rest of you come help me roll the wagon into that field," he said, directing them toward a southerly expanse dipping sharply from its crest.

The reddish-brown horses, one an old gelding and the other a mare, were loosed from their harnesses and tack, though Talic left the bits in their mouths. After the animals were calmed and relaxed, Bon led the rebels in rolling their stripped cart into the middle of a depression at the bottom of the slope, his surprising strength accounting for most of the effort.

After wedging the wheels tight with rocks and barring the wooden spokes, they regrouped higher up the hill.

"What now, sir?" asked Jana, who had brought the shearing knife. She wiped the sweat from her round face with the corner of her sleeve. "Surely we don't intend to stay here?"

"Well, that depends," said Bon, bouncing his ax's haft on his palm while holding the handle in the other. Contemplative as he spun about to face Atenia again, he breathed deep and exhaled the yeast sweetening the air.

"On?" Talic asked, a bit annoyed as he buffed the sweat off his face with the hem of his shirt.

"Ah, we'll know when we see it," the wraith answered.

"What does that mean?" Rigen asked in his high-nasal voice.

Bon chuckled at the question. "Just find a good place to sit and wait."

Confused by the lack of direction, the Children of Marta, nonetheless, took the opportunity to rest, plopping down at the edge of the field where the high wheat covered their locations but allowed a decent view of Atenia's southern bounds. Allowed a moment of peace, some lay ensconced in a waving blanket of yellow-gold stalks, their fibrous riches budding at the ends.

Left alone, both Bon and Haidra found themselves separated from the rest. The wraith tended to one of the horses, softly rubbing the mare's neck and nose to gain her attention.

Haidra watched, unsure of when and where she was.

"Hey, girl," called Jana, seated in the soft dirt a few yards from her. She signaled for Haidra to come over with a flick of her head. "I hear you're Arverin's daughter," said the cloth-maker. "I'm sorry to hear what happened. He was a good one."

Crossing her arms over her chest in the cool breeze blowing from the northwest, her flesh goosed under her clothes as she tried to smile through a shiver. She tried her best to recall his face without pain or suffering upon it. "Thank you," she said, quiet as she approached.

"Did you know about all this?" the strange woman asked, using her right thumb to rub the callouses in her left palm.

"The rebellion?"

"Yeah," said Jana. "Your pa joined not long after your ma died."

The mention of her mother, Etta, surprised Haidra. "He never told me."

"Ah. Probably trying to keep you safe."

"May I ask you something, Miss Jana?"

"Of course."

"Why did he do this? Why are you all doing this?"

In her late thirties, with a mop of mousy brown hair, Jana combed a tress out of her cerulean eyes and across a delicate forehead. "You know how your ma died?"

"A cadre of knights ran her over in the streets. Told him it was an accident."

"The Veards say everything is an accident when it comes to

them, the bloody bastards and their bastard friends," Jana replied, each word more bitter than the last. "It wasn't an accident, just those knights not giving a damn about who was in the road. Your pa remembered a time when they weren't allowed to do that. There was a time, not long before you were born, when the sworn did not act this way, or they wouldn't have been allowed to be that way if old Solomon or Marta had lived past their damned daughter. I remember Marta. Sweet lady." Caught in the memory, she shook her head at something in the dirt beside her. "I think your pa wanted to have people remember when Atenia was like that: sweet and good. It's why we've named ourselves after her."

"But Queen Marta betrayed King Tobias and—"

"Atenia's sweet and good with lies, too, Haidra," Jana said. "None of that was true."

"Then, why?"

"Because scared people are scared and will do anything not to be that. Whatever reason the others have is their own, but I'm not someone to live under a boot no matter who's wearing it. Simple as that."

Too tired to react, Haidra looked to where Bon stood guard. A black-robed outline against the shimmering carpet of wheat, he faced north, trained on the city as he massaged the mare's jaw. The gelding waited beside her, eager for some tenderness as well.

"What happened back at the gates? How did they not find him?" she asked, flicking her head in the wraith's direction.

Jana's cool demeanor blunted at the question.

"Miss Jana?" Haidra asked again.

"He just...vanished," she half-whispered. She tried to hide a glance in Bon's direction. "One minute he was sitting there, eyes shut and still, and the next, he was gone!"

"Gone?"

"He weren't there, girl. Or at least not for anyone to see.

When he reappeared, it was like smoke had blown into the cabin, or maybe his shadow. I don't know."

Haidra probed the back of her teeth with her tongue, a habit she performed when thinking. Again, to Bon, the powers he and his black-clad friends possessed was a strange contrast to their humanity, which made her wonder aloud what she had only kept silent to herself.

"Do you think they're really human?" she asked.

Jana laughed but would not answer.

<hr>

AN HOUR HAD PASSED by the time Haidra found the courage to approach Bon, ensconced in the wheat field after he sat down. Both legs crossed and hands on his knees, he had stuck his black ax into the earth, using its pointed shod at the end of the handle to stand it upright. Intimidating whether it was in his grasp or not, the weapon turned a blacker hue, as if devouring the sunlight upon it.

But armed or unarmed, aloof or merry, there remained a gentleness on Bon's tanned face, his deep-lidded eyes taking in every detail of the southern ramparts. He didn't look her way when she came within a few feet, the thigh-high stalks quiet in their constant rustle against her hide leggings.

"Hi, Haidra," he said, not breaking his northward stare.

"My Lord—I mean, Bon—how much longer do you think we might have to wait?"

"Eh," he replied in a little grunt, shrugging his shrouded shoulders. "Moon will get it done, but she'll get it done when she does. I actually like the wait. Better this than that."

"How so?"

He craned his head back to look at her upside-down, his hood falling with it. Once again reminded of the resemblance to the older wraith, Black John, their eyes met and held for a breath she wasn't sure she took.

Those hazel pools glistened in curiosity. "You've seen a lot now, haven't you?"

"Enough," she replied.

He grunted in consideration. "And war?"

She dimmed. "Not as much."

His smile waned as he righted his gaze upon the city. "I've been in two. So has Moon. She'll get it done."

Haidra understood, though she gave no reply.

"Are there other places in the city to get a view like this?" he asked. "I'd like to do more of this, if I can get the time."

She could not help but smile at the idea of the dark-clad warrior lazing in the light, taking in the sights. "A few places, if you know where to look."

"Perhaps I'll need help finding—"

An earth-shaking boom echoed from the north, on the other side of the city's hill. Columns of smoke rose thick and black against the blue firmament. From the depths of the billowing cinders appeared a woman's face. Her burning eyes opened to sprouting hellfire. Her features familiar yet foreign to Haidra, the illusion separated her full, shifting lips to reveal blackened teeth and a fiery throat.

She spoke in a screeching voice wrapped in death.

"It ends!" the great face screamed across the day. "It ends! I have come again, Fransica! I have come again!"

Bon sprung to his feet. "Tell the rest to escape and get one of the horses! Hurry, Haidra!"

He wove his hands in an intricate pattern, chanting arcane words. A small ember of magical fire, wine-red and throbbing, materialized. Bon looked back at her again and threw his head hard, the last order to flee. He cast the burning jewel toward the wagon.

"It ends!" the burning woman screamed.

It plunged into the heap of oiled canvas. Great plumes of smoke dragged against the gentle breeze before the fire shot high, consuming the heap.

Haidra sprinted to the edge of the wheat field, the heat of the magic chasing her. Already the charring kernel darkened the day, no matter how much the sun shined. She ran from another crime, complicit in hungering her neighbors.

Talic, Jana, and the rest rushed to meet her.

"Go," she shouted. "Get back to the city and hide! Flee!" She reached toward Talic and the red mare. "Talic!"

"It ends!"

In no need of a great explanation, the former guardsman handed her the reins before he escaped. Frightened by the screaming visage above the city, the roan pulled against her when she tried to bring her along. The giant beast reared and let out an equine shriek, chopping the air above Haidra's head with her hooves.

"It ends!"

She almost let go when Bon appeared beside her in his illusionary darkness. He lifted her in his strong arms and onto the saddle-less mare, who calmed at his steely touch. He leapt up next, seated in front as he grabbed the reins.

"Hold tight to me!" he said in his deepened voice. "Hold tight!"

# 6

# BLOWOUT

"It ends!"

Clinging to his back, Haidra buried her face in Bon's cloak as he charged up the small embankment. Their mare heaved, foam flying from her mouth. Jarring as her face scraped and knocked against the hidden mail under his black coverings, she looked up, desperate to breathe.

The apparition of a woman's face in the thick columns of smoke had yet to cease screaming, her wails overriding all other noise.

"It ends!"

The guards of the southern palisade gate faced the wrong way when the wraith and her blew past, the mare knocking two spearmen on the ground. Haidra braced for the arrows. None fell, but the tension in her back stayed as she kept her arms wrapped tight to Bon's torso.

"It ends!"

He directed their mount around carts and throngs of rubberneckers who had turned northward on Idrian Street to watch the huge mouth threaten certainties the years had set in them. The reaction doubled when the poor souls aware of the black rider in their midst caught sight of him, paying almost no attention to the young woman behind the nightmare figure. Women screamed as men shoved them and the children out of the way, no matter how much room they were given, unwilling to fall under striking hooves.

"My ax," Bon shouted, his distorted voice acute amongst the terrorized masses dodging from them. "Haidra! You have to get it!"

Giving herself space between her chest and his back, she was shocked to find the broad, bearded curve lay only a few inches from her head. She grabbed the black weapon at its throat and pulled, somehow removing it from a hidden holster. Bon quickly claimed it before the awkward weight or the mare's bounding caused her to drop it.

"It ends," the burning woman in the sky screamed. "Bhadran's spirit turns toward home!" Then, like a folding ray of sunset snuffed by the horizon, she disappeared in a blink.

"Get ready!" Bon raised his ax high to strike.

Haidra hugged against him and shut her eyes. She felt the blow cleave and skip against something, movable but firm. Fresh rounds of screams opened her eyes again to find the ax-slinger's weapon coated in fresh blood. Daring to look back, a group of Atenians surrounded a beheaded knight fallen from the saddle. Some tried to give the body space while others looted it.

The scene disappeared as Bon drove them toward Entaris Bridge, running north-south through the city's center, where the uphill leg of Idrian met the Colis, a curving ascent used to access Gallows Square. Whipping past more frightened folk, the lane cleared as the intersection came in sight.

Another miraculous thing happened when, clattering through the nexus, rumbled a large wagon. Recognizing one of the troop transports used by the queen-regent's navy and pink bannermen, a motley group of four men and women had latched to its boarded sides. Its heavy load rattled the cart. On the driver's bench a fifth man steered the two draw horses while, posting one foot on the seat, Black John drew back on a horned bow.

Arrows flying from his string scattered black light, catching one of the two horsemen on their tail. Booming when the point found the armored chest, the rider dumped off his saddle, leaving his partner to continue the chase.

Bon coaxed one last burst of effort from the flagging roan as he sidled her and Haidra next to the wagon. He placed his armored mitt atop where her hands clasped upon his chest.

"Jump," Bon shouted as he broke her grip. "Let go and jump!"

"You're crazy," she shouted.

Black John appeared at the wagon's side. Having discarded his bow, he reached out with taloned fingers. "Haidra!"

Haidra threw herself toward the swordsman. Snatched out of the air and guided to a spot between two of the rebels on the wagon's outer wall, he never loosened his grip on her arm. Terror driving her greater instincts, she found immediate handholds.

Bon vaulted from the roan's back and landed beside the taller wraith. The pair faced the knight still trailing them as the mare halted and was left behind.

"Oh, shit," the driver on the bench screamed. "Brace!"

The wagon struck a clatter of iron and bodies. Wheels crunched bones before something or someone knocked into her. The tearing force too much for her hands, Haidra landed hard on the street, rolling until the constant beating of the pavestones broke her momentum.

Stinging from head to toe, she tried to post on hands and knees. The effort dropped her face-first to the ground. Blood ran from her nose, oozing heat and iron from a cut in the left nostril. Her weight slumped her onto her back.

Six Atenian infantry men pointed their spears down at her.

The knight chasing the wagon wheeled his horse about to make a return. Another of the Children of Marta had fallen from the wagon's side. Before he could rise more spears ended his escape in a few hard thrusts to the face and chest. She did not see the body fall as more mail-clad soldiers clustered and blocked the sun. Dozens of eyes upon Haidra, the bullies smirked down in wolfish anticipation.

Until one of them glanced up.

"Oh, shit," the guard whispered, the point of his weapon only a few inches from her face. The unified distraction of her captors only made her follow their gaze.

Black John and Bon the Bloody charged to rescue her.

As the wagon of stolen weapons and armor rumbled into the distance, the black invaders assaulted the Atenians without fear of their numbers, red-eyed and enveloped in night. Unable to move for the dozens of mashing boots, Haidra curled on her side and covered her head with her arms.

The first wraith she saw near her as she opened her eyes, Bon, cleaved into the immediate circle above her. Smashing apart the man atop of Haidra, hot gore rained on her face, running thick into her scalp. The corpse landed beside her. His great roar, thunderous as a bear, shuddered in her bones.

Black John entered her vision on the left.

Jumping from the pavement, his great frame bowled the oncoming knight off the saddle. The armored rider crashed to the ground with the wraith atop of him, quickly dispatched by the long length of steel stabbing into his open-faced helm.

Her saviors clashed around her in moments beyond her worst nightmares. Every man died under a weapon's stroke as her father had, lifeless and wide-eyed, leaking like him too. The wraiths decimated the Atenian contingent, hacking apart formations of spears in great swings.

Bon lunged over Haidra on his second pass to defend her. He met one of the spearmen that had been smart enough to draw an arming sword in lieu of his longer weapon. Batting the small blade to the side before halving the man's skull at the forehead, he searched about the ground to find her.

"Get up," he roared when he located her in the mess. "Get out of here!"

"Bon, incoming!"

Bon wrenched in the direction of Black John's voice. "Flee, Haidra! Flee!"

Processing the words, she rolled to her hands and knees, willing herself beyond the pain of her fall. All effort went into rising, only for her to almost trip when a cadre of knights approached from the north on Idrian Street, backed by two full columns of infantry three men wide and sixty deep. They carried longer poles.

The lead knight spotted her in the midst of fleeing. He raised his sword from atop his horse to order his fellow's mounted advance.

"Elim Marta! Elim Marta!"

Citizens of Atenia raised up on both sides of Entaris Bridge's embankments. A mix of bows long and small, hundreds of shafts rained death on the royal forces on both sides as the wraiths collected Haidra, guarding her between them as they hurried to the north end of the bridge.

"Elim Marta!" the Children of Marta resounded in the language of the Lomens, the dead queen's people formerly nested in Atenia's glacial range before the crown expelled them. They peppered the distraught guard, some of them their own kin. Slowly the knights, hiding under their shields and protected by their plated coats, gathered their troop when the volleys ended. Dozens dead and dozens more wounded hampered an advance or retreat, relegating the royalists into a tight schiltron, spears out in wait for the charge they were trained to expect.

Instead a slow, gentle song echoed as the rebels ended their rallying cry.

New Moon appeared on a northwestern rooftop of a villa, a ball of dark fire growing in her hands. She flung it into the middle of the Atenian soldiers, consuming them in boiling magic.

"Faster," Black John said as he ran ahead.

Bon plucked Haidra off the ground and threw her over his left shoulder, main hand free to wield his ax. The smooth pauldrons under his mantle dug at her stomach. The sensation worsened as he quickened to catch up.

At constant risk of vomiting what breakfast resided in her guts, Haidra let exhaustion claim whatever was left of the burning, bleeding scenes around her.

# 7

# A MEETING OF SHADOWS

**B**ut—"

"But nothing," Black John said to New Moon in his deep baritone, reverberating through the wall by Haidra's head. "You went too far."

Bon broke in. "Father, she—"

"And don't you start," the elder wraith was quick to chide. "You two get away with too much as it is."

Haidra laid on her side in the empty bedroom, wide-eyed as her left shoulder and hip throbbed—the side she slept on before the fall from the cart—and listened since the moment she heard three wraiths talking. What began as whispers flowed with tension, the exchanges between them in her native Torsii and Eaith from Arbikk, the latter more fluid and breathier. She heard the anger in Black John's voice, the frustration Bon spoke in response, and the consoling but defiant tone New Moon struck to mediate it.

Haidra was certain the younger wraiths were Black John's natural children.

The fact hammered away the last doubt she had about whether she trafficked with evil creatures. More worrisome, the handsome face of the younger man beguiled her no matter how much she tried to think of something else other than Arverin, and she tried her best to avoid the latter. Yet something about Bon's face seemed starker to her now, but no matter how hard she searched, the reason refused to surface.

"It's what you taught us to do," New Moon said in a calm, collected tone. "She's probably up there losing her mind. Isn't that what we wanted? To unbalance her?"

"In stages. At places and times we agreed to with Aron. Now there will be questions, and obvious ones as well," replied Black John. "It could create distance between us and the rebels."

"What of it?" said Bon in the same placating tone as his darker sister. "They won't turn away our help."

"I don't care. We're here to do a mission not put on performances. Understood?"

Black John's steel-shod boots clinked gently as he exited into the hallway, his tall frame hunched in the folds of his black costume. He stopped at the doorway to the bedroom Haidra lay within, rested atop a thick pile of reindeer furs they had brought for matting. Going without sleep, which she imagined sorcerers did, they had created more than a suitable bedding once she had wrapped herself in a bed roll.

He stared into the room, his bare face revealed by an oil lamp somewhere in the hall of the empty house they had claimed for the night. A profile cut by the warmth, his gentle but pointed nose reminded her of the man on the side of an old coin her father had kept.

Black John's voice startled her. "You might as well come speak with me, Lady Haidra. Don't tarry." He stalked down the rest of the hall and descended the stair to the basement-kitchen.

Caught where she lay, Haidra blinked to end the burn in her tired eyes. In the clothes she had worn to the fields, the dry sweat in the linen tunic and hide breeches cracked and rubbed on a grimier body. The smell of her odors had faded in the mental fog, replaced by the iron of blood and earthiness of human shit. And smoke, bready before it crisped in ruin.

Shaking herself from her vexing, she stuck her cold feet in her boots, whining when her toes meet the gummy moisture in the toe box. On wobbly legs, she found her balance immediately when the bruises on her left side flared with every move.

By the time she hobbled to the top of the steps in the abandoned home, deep tannins found her nose, heady and rich. Peeking between the spokes of the banister as she limped down the stair, she found Black John in a chair by the fireplace. His sword lay beside his seat, sheathed in its black scabbard. An iron tea kettle hung by a hook over the rebuilt blaze in the hearth, and on the heated stones rested a dark blue teapot. A thin trail of steam drizzled out of the spout.

He had lain out two earthenware cups.

The wraith had drawn up his hood and cast his glamor, red eyes of malevolence in the void. "I can see you, hear you," he said. "Come pour the tea."

Haidra slowly came down the steps and stopped at the bottom. "Pardon me, lord. I did not mean to sneak."

"I do not hold it against you," he said, "but let's do away with pretenses. You know what I am, and I know you're smarter than you pretend. Why keep up this performance?"

"What performance?"

The segmented bits of steel armoring each finger joint on his bright gauntlets glittered in the firelight as his hands tightened on the arms of his chair. The man within the hood sighed. "Lady Haidra."

"You're the one wearing a mask." Tired of being tired, scared, Haidra forced herself to look at Black John, dead in his hellish eyes.

"Do you know why?"

"Because you're very familiar," she said. "I don't know where I've seen you, but you look like one of them."

"Like who?"

"Those who live up there."

He paused, measuring her for a lingering moment. "Pour the tea."

The perpetual sense of *stuck* pervaded Haidra when she approached the iron tea pot and picked it up by its wooden handle. Filling both earthenware cups with a black brew, she set the pot back down with a small clang and slosh.

Black John held out a barbed hand. "You can sit there by the fire if you like."

Despite her bravado from before, the gentle suggestion sapped Haidra of it as she handed him a cup of tea then sat on the hearth's warming stones. He cradled it in a wide, heavy palm, paying no mind to the scalding heat she was forced to balance on fingertips alone until she set it on the floor to cool.

Steam wafted into the void of Black John's hood. "I knew your father. I came because he asked me to."

"That's not what you told the Children of Marta," she said.

"I told them the truth," he replied. "There is a prince on the way, but it was your father who started all this."

"How?" Haidra asked.

The wraith sipped from his cup, his face invisible behind the illusory shroud. "His father found me. Your grandfather, I'm guessing."

"I never knew him." Haidra's answer surprised her because, in truth, she remembered seeing the doddering old man when he came through every few years, ranting and raving about the wider world outside of Atenia everyone was too worn to care about. The constant grind, paid little from the crown's coffer, deadened the imagination. Arverin had worked his hands raw every day of her life, certain to make the exact number of fish-nets needed so the tax collector, usually a knight, did not take more than he owed. A homeless man like her grandfather never lived with such worries, but rarely any meaningful presence.

Her thoughts flicked back to that coin her father kept.

"Drink while it's warm," Black John said. "It will help your side."

The reminder of the sharp ache up her body ceased her mental digging. She sipped a mouthful of warm, florid tea, tasting of mint and peels and cinnamon and something else she did not know. To his word, a strange relaxation melted into her bruises, alleviating the pain. She took another mouthful.

"He told me what had happened here," the wraith said. "How it has gotten worse."

"From what?" she asked.

The wraith stared at her from his chair in silence.

"I know who Marta is," said Haidra, the tea soothing her raw throat. "She was Fransica's mother. 'The Good ol' Queen' my father called her. I was little when she went away. I know who your daughter—"

Black John firmed in his chair.

Haidra dared to continue. "She dressed me up in magic as The Burnt Lady." Then, for some reason, she blurted, "I still dream about her."

"What do you dream?"

"I think I remember the day..." She glanced down at the cup in her hand, now cool enough to hold. Raising her gaze to her host, she frowned at him. "This stuff is too good for what it does."

"Some spice to heal, some spice for the truth," he said, terse. "Why do you remember the Burnt Lady?"

"Because she didn't deserve it." The brew's potency revealed, Haidra quaffed another mouthful anyway.

"We need to come to an agreement, Lady Haidra. There are things at work that need to be done if I'm to free Atenia. I'm without real insight into the Children of Marta. They are your neighbors, but nobody claims you except for us. But you also know them. You know this city and its people. All of these things may become boons to me but only if you stay alive. Understand my meaning, Lady Haidra?"

"Fairly enough, Lord," she said.

"That, too, stops here. The only reason you know so much is because you have had the unfortunate honor to bear witness. If you wish to remain, you must swear not to speak to a soul about anything you've seen or heard when it comes to myself or my children."

The face on the coin. She had forgotten his name. "I swear."

"We're done, then. You can go back to bed."

"Don't you want an answer?" she asked. "Why I'm here?"

"I knew the answer the moment you set the wheat fields on fire," he said. "Where my interests lie now is what you can do—here and now. The rebels are successfully armed but, so far, they've done nothing to make me think they're worth much in a real fight."

"We're not soldiers," said Haidra.

"But they are at war. As are you. To win at war you need every advantage you can muster, even ones made of deceit and duplicity. And always cruelty. The queen-regent and her forces are adept at these things. You must become so as well, Lady Haidra." She could almost imagine him smiling in his hood. "You're a soldier now."

He took a few more sips, leaving Haidra to her silence.

Sitting on the edge of the hearth, the fire's warmth flooded every aching nerve. A slight buzz crowned her head, fueled by the magic tea. "I have a cousin. He's a guard on the northern palisade."

"Go on," said Black John.

"His name is Lerrod," Haidra said. "I knew about the guard shifts because he told me not too long ago. He's still stationed there unless something has happened."

"Did he know about your father? About the rebellion?"

"I don't think so. He would have been there if he did. At least I hope he would have."

"Do you think he'd even consider betraying the crown?"

"I don't think he knows about Arverin," Haidra said. "But I'm sure he'd have something to say if he did."

Garbed in a paint-stained apron and dark woolen dress, Haidra peeked around the corner as New Moon tried to pull her back into the place, standing her straight so she could finish tying her tresses into a loose queue. The wraiths had already smudged her cheeks in soot to mix with fresh sweat during their march through Low Corner. A chilly midnight murk had left the city quiet, with only the sound of the wraiths boots and Haidra's floppy ghillies laced too tight to her shins accompanying the yowling cats in the refuse piles as they hunted vermin. Stray dogs barked in the distance, some near, others echoing in the mists.

Damp by the time they found the northeastern stair to the palisade's most easterly tower, the wraiths and Haidra watched in the shadows. The guards near the first bank of stone steps, six in all, kept two of their men posted at the foot. The other four ranged about in boredom.

Haidra pointed at the man standing to the right of the bottom step. "That's Lerrod."

"I see him," said Black John.

"There's more men in the tower up the steps," said Haidra. "And there is an alarm bell on the battlement at the top."

"Can you get him to come over here?" Black John asked.

"I don't know." The sudden folly of her plan revealed, Haidra considered the idea of speaking aloud, to quit now, when Black John beat her to a decision.

"Go ask," he said. "Moon, Bon, find points above to watch

her. Be ready to provide a distraction if I have to go in to get her."

Haidra found her voice. "Wa—"

Black John's children parted, the sorceress dashing around the corner to their right while the ax-slinger doubled back the way they came, disappearing into the maze of muddy lanes. Left with the swordsman, she gaped in surprise as he drew his blade.

"Go on," the wraith said. "I'm watching."

Summoning her courage, Haidra marched toward the torch-lit steps. At the edge of the orange radiance one of the spearmen spotted her, leveling his weapon from his shoulder.

"Halt in the name of King Tobias," he shouted as the other five converged.

Lerrod stopped their advance. "Haidra? Hold a minute, boys! Haidra, is that you?"

Impressed by the fact the men had stopped on her cousin's order, she stepped forward to show her full face in the light. "Lerrod? Oh, thank goodness! I've found you!"

"You know this wench, Ler?" one of the guards asked.

In his late-twenties and clean-shaven, Lerrod shared her gold-brown skin and chestnut hair, the same cheek bones of her father, but there the similarities ended. Hard-eyed and grim, the tall warrior had given his life to days of marching, absent in their lives save for the few high holidays Atenia celebrated, which had not happened in many years.

He did not smile when she looked to that dour face. "What are you doing here?" he asked, harsh and accusatory. "I'm on duty."

"My father is dead," she said aloud. "Please, Lerrod. I need your help!"

"Oh, gods, this," said one of the guard. "Lerrod, get her out of her. Go— Just get her going and come back to your post."

The shock of her news, the way he barely flinched when the other man snapped at him, clued Haidra to her cousin's hesitance. Wordless, he nodded over his shoulder to the senior guard before motioning to Haidra to lead them away. She retreated with no fear of the unlit alley.

"What do you mean Uncle Arverin is dead?" Lerrod asked in a much softer tone than he had met her with.

"He's dead," she said, almost bitter at Lerrod for not knowing, and at herself for the hollowness in saying it now. "The crown killed him."

"What?" He bent until his nose was at her eye-level. "What do you mean by that, Haidra?"

"You heard me! Killed him three days ago. Right in front of me."

Backing away, he searched her features. "But…he was just— Not Uncle Ave," he said in a sinking voice. "He just…he just did nets!"

"Cousin, I—"

"These fucking royals," he said, tears filling his eyes. He heaved. "These fucking royals."

She shushed him. "Shh, Lerrod," she whispered. "You don't want your friends to hear."

"Oh, fuck them," he said. "Gods, I'm so tired of this."

"Then," she said, trying to peer around him in case the guard heard, "please, Lerrod. Please help me."

One of the guards in the corner shouted. "Lerrod! Hurry up! You're on duty."

"Fuck you, Gerrit!" Lerrod turned and ripped the dark navy sash from his shoulder, casting it to the earth. "I fucking quit you rape-supporting bastards! Down with the Veards!"

"Lerrod!"

"And fuck you, too, Franc," Lerrod roared back at the other voice as he shooed Haidra to depart. "We all know you hate them, too!"

To her surprise, the guards did not follow the deserter.

He trailed behind Haidra at a respectful distance before he

spoke. "So, what kind of help do you need, girl?" he asked, "Stop here."

Already discomforted by his eyes on her backside, she turned toward him, hands folded in front of her. "Lerrod, the knights who killed Arverin did so because he was part of a rebellion. He was working against the crown."

Nothing registered on his mean face.

Haidra spoke a little faster. "He was tired of those rape-supporting bastards like you are, and he—"

"Was he part of the raid on Gallows Square?" Lerrod asked in interruption. "Are you aligned with those ghosts?"

"What ghosts?" Haidra asked, faking honest curiosity.

"Don't bring me where no one can see us and lie to me." He took a step forward, forcing her to take two in retreat. "The ghosts of Jhean de Veard, his mother, and father are back from the dead, come to claim Mad Queen Franny and the rest of her awful kin. We're all going to burn for them royals and their sins, ain't we?"

"I haven't heard anything like that," she responded. "We have help coming, Lerrod. Listen, there is a prince in the north who is bringing a great army to free us. He'll bring down the Veards, once and for all!"

"More foreigners?" Lerrod asked, less coarse.

"No," said Haidra. "They're here to help us—real Atenians. Our friends, our neighbors, the people who built this city. The Children of Marta. Arverin was among them."

"And he knew about this prince?"

She nodded, hoping he saw it in the dark.

After a pause, Lerrod spun in the opposite direction, toward the easternmost tower of Atenia's northern palisade. "What will you need?"

"The northern palisade. A way in would be helpful."

"My old man and yours loved old Queen Marta," Lerrod

said. "All this still happened. Your daddy is still dead. She is, too."

"And now it ends," said Black John from the darkness.

Before either Haidra or Lerrod could look in his direction, the dark red eyes awoke in fresh flame, the bloody light glinting off his upraised blade. Only a foot behind Haidra, Black John towered over her and her cousin, looming like the deepest of shadows.

Bon and New Moon appeared from the ether, flanking Lerrod. The ax's curve rested on his back as the rapier's edge pressed across his chest. Frozen in place, the deserter opened his mouth to scream when the sorceress grabbed him by the jaw, seizing him to silence.

"Please," she said. "Don't."

# 8

# ROLL CALL

A royal decree wax-stamped by Tobias' own hand was issued with a full calvary who paraded up and down the entire length of Idrian Street the next day. Hordes of infantry flooded the roads and byways of northern Atenia about the Ursin, stationed on every block in Low Corner in the east all the way to the Horras Market and Hernos' Court in the west. Most caught outside were arrested on the spot, slammed into the ground for the crime of emptying a chamber pot or a clean breath of air. By sunset, the poor and homeless were herded south over the two bridges connecting the city's upper half with its lower, most never to be seen again.

Some would later say many a poor man, woman, and child hung from the gibbets in Gallows Square, forgotten among those already lost to the Veards.

As the creeping night blued under a moonless, starry sky, the commanders of the Children of Marta ducked out the back doors of their waddle and thatch huts, from the rows of rickety old townhouses near the wall of Bhadran's Wood, sneaking the small squalid squares their generations had built. Dodging the guards, twenty-five leaders of individual cells met in an audaciously risky location near Entaris Bridge in Urghenna's Mall, a north-embankment estate in full sight of the citadel.

It's three levels abandoned many times over, the hearth on the attic floor lay empty and cold of a real fire, but not its heat. A pair of glass orbs rested on the iron grate set upon the bricks. Within the crystal balls floated two contrasting points, one white and slowly winking and the other a healthy orange which seemed to flicker like a candle in a breezy window. Brought together, the conflicting powers forged a gentle dance, blending in something akin to firelight. To the amazement of the rebels gathered, real warmth flowed out.

Their backs to the illumination, the three wraiths took their places before their allies.

Haidra had been ordered to the spot beside Black John. The painter's smock thrown away in one of the empty sleeping chambers below, she had let her hair loose, leaving the dirty locks lank on her shoulders. She spotted a few familiar faces like Ecktor, the blacksmith Aleaus, and shared a nod with Talic when the former guardsman arrived. Lerrod joined out of a favor to the wraiths, who had promised the man a clear role in whatever they had planned after he had revealed the shift-pattern of the guards at the gate.

When all were seated on the long wooden benches they had hauled up from the bottom floor, New Moon addressed them.

"We will remember your bravery in coming here," the sorceress said, her writhing, shifting shape silhouetted by the weir-lights. The shade of her hood left her dark face and silver mane obscured as she and her kin went without their illusions. "We shall keep this meeting brief so you may return to your homes as safely as possible but remember that speed and silence are essential from this moment forward. No one can know of this plan once it is spoken."

None replied in a room full of traitors.

"I assume the arms we furnished for you from our successful raid have not only been distributed smartly among your soldiers, but further solidifies our commitment to your cause," New Moon continued. "Many of your neighbors, friends and family, took great risk to help ensure you now wield steel instead of wood, girted in mail instead of homespun. At this point what is required is a complete and total trust for what comes next."

Haidra tried to catch the reaction on every face. Again, consigned to the ones she knew, only the face of Lerrod showed any unease. The former guard tried to sit still among the strangers, a lonely island like she had once been.

Once.

The belonging she had discovered in that moment steeled her. Haidra posed proudly, the only resolute member of flesh and blood among magic and mail.

"Prince Aron Toliv should only be a day's march from Atenia," New Moon said. "We need all soldiers who are properly armed and armored with a bow, arrows, a shield, and side weapon to report to points we will show you on a map. Before dawn we will convene at these places, and on a signal you will not mistake, storm the eastern tower of the northern palisade. From there we will claim the gatehouse. We will hold it until Aron arrives."

A few like Ecktor and Aleaus whispered to their seconds or the nearest to them. Others furrowed their brows and quietly shook their heads or simply stared at their cloaked allies. Nobody attempted to leave.

Haidra checked on Lerrod again. Her cousin had not lifted his gaze off the boards under his feet, deep in thought.

The whispers peaked and died. Ecktor stood up from amid the cell-leaders, adjusting his belt for the heavy wedge and hunting dagger tucked in its band. "We can provide three hundred fitting your needs, but no more. This commitment calls in most of our forces. If you were to fail this rebellion would fail, too."

"That will be the risk of every battle going forward," New Moon replied. "Now, depart from this place. Rest and ready to fight for your freedom."

Disturbed by the sorceress' confidence, the Children of Marta unfroze from their places. Awkward, the leaders of their individuals cells exited without a nod or well-wish, even to Haidra. Lerrod left as well.

Bon padded over to one of the benches the rebels had left. "Thank Uma," he said. "It was getting harder by the second to look at them."

"They are brave," New Moon said, exhausted. "That's something."

"We need to get you gear," Black John said.

A second passed before Haidra realized the elder warrior had addressed her directly. On the spot, she searched between Bon and his sister for any clue of what their father meant. "My lords?"

Both children shushed her.

"We're not like that," New Moon said.

"You'll need armor and a weapon by morning," Black John told Haidra. "Otherwise, we'll have to leave you behind."

"We'll find something," New Moon interjected, waving off the worries of her father. "Haidra, will you go check on the door downstairs and make sure it is still locked? The patrols will be coming through again soon and I wouldn't want to give them the chance to barge in unannounced."

"Of course, my— Moon."

She headed for the wide staircase to the house's second level. Filled with dozens of lamplights they had set out in the inner hall of their makeshift camp for the night, the only item in the master bedroom was a large, black trunk New Moon had mysteriously produced. The lone chamber with its windows not tacked over with boards to hide their occupancy, she lingered a bit to look at its brass lock and glossy ebon panels. She finally tore away from it when she reached the next stair to the main level where Lerrod had been assigned to sleep for the night.

Haidra spotted the open front door before she made it down the steps. Laying ajar to the darkness outside, she did not have to guess when she ran down the steps in time to see her cousin dart into the shadow of the nearest alley across the way.

Reasons skittered through her mind why Lerrod had betrayed her so quickly, or his fellow Atenians, for fear of the sway of the Veards. Whatever they were lived with the same doubts that had plagued her until the queen-regent's knights broke down her father's door. For her cousin, she surmised, the choices fell harder for a man who had lost nothing but might lose as much as anyone else if the rebellion's plans fell into place. The difference between a patriot and a traitor, never easy to discern, disappeared in a few moments to greater worries.

Gaping in shock, she wondered what to do in the moment: Warn the wraiths or give chase?

Who was she to chase down a guardsman?

The choice was made for her when Bon landed beside her, his booted feet pounding the hardwoods as his back and knees bent in perfect time. Standing tall beside her, he snatched her by the arm, dragging Haidra alongside him to the hunt.

"After him," the ax-slinger said. "After him before he rouses the guard!"

SHE KEPT CLOSE to Bon as he dashed ahead of her. Over his broad shoulders she spotted Lerrod ahead of them, taking a hard corner between two more empty homes. The reasons why he had fled vanished to a weird recollection, her faraway cousin's expression during the meeting with the Children of Marta formed a stone deep in Haidra's stomach.

He had seen all their faces.

He had seen her at the front of the room.

A shower from a few hours before had left the streets muddy and puddled, exploding bright in her eyes when Lerrod's feet splashed them apart. Ax drawn at his side, Bon rounded the next corner and disappeared. Unarmed against a man twice her size and slowed from fatigue, Haidra brought herself to a halt in hopes the distance and darkness would veil her from Lerrod's sight, perhaps giving her a chance to rest.

Such hope ended when he looked back and saw her immediately.

"Please, don't," Haidra said.

Lerrod resumed his escape toward the west and Idrian Street.

Haidra took after him, no longer willing to be left behind, or saved by sorcerers and happenstance. Her determination receded when she gained on her traitorous cousin. Halfway to the next junction of alleys which opened to Idrian Street beyond—where he could summon the royal forces—Lerrod faced her in anticipation.

He brandished a dagger.

Her dad had taught her to fight like every father and every mother had instructed their daughters to while living in Low Corner, where the eyes and hands of a guardsman strayed too often or desperate men stalked their trail. In no way a soldier, Arverin had forced Haidra to keep two things in mind: She could always run away, but if fate forbade it, it was better to die in their faces than be taken, used, or worse. Useful in a few past scraps, she had thought herself a decent fighter, like her dad in toughness and guile.

Like the mender had until the royals came for him.

Haidra met him, too terrified of what would happen if she

allowed herself to stand there like Arverin had against the knight. She launched into him below the knife, shoulder colliding with his stomach, holding on in shock when he collapsed backward. The back of his head smacked a patch of mud. Both hands went flying, the dagger with them. The blade skipped with a clatter, landing a few feet out of reach.

Haidra rose first, but Lerrod kicked her legs out at the shins, driving her into the ground again, hard to her stomach and chest. She crawled for the dagger again.

Lerrod's full weight fell atop her back. She felt the rough hair on his arms as they snaked around her neck, sliding across the hollow of her throat.

"Fucking traitor-bitch," he growled in her right ear. He freed one of his arms and snatched one of her wrists, the wringing strength cutting the feeling from her fingers. "Fucking traitors like you killed your daddy!"

Fighting her head free, Haidra looked to where the dagger lay. A few inches from her outstretched hand, she dug her fingers in the mud and pulled, twisting from Lerrod's other grasping hand near her throat. Her middle finger brushed the grimy pommel.

"No, you don't, you little—"

Lerrod's words were stolen as Bon batted him in the face with his ax's flat. The edge still catching the man's cheek, he rolled away groaning as blood speckled the wet stones beneath him, running on his clothes. He kicked away from the looming specter that had descended from a roof.

Haidra did not hesitate for the dagger a second time. Diving to grab hold of its hilt, she rolled to her knees and lunged at her brutish cousin, thoughtless until the iron slipped the flesh under his sternum. Fueling a manic strength, she drove deeper into his heart, confused and captured by its terrible power.

Lerrod's life drained away in a jerking death-throe before the body stilled.

Hand drenched in hot blood, she let go, leaving the weapon lodged in his chest.

Bon dropped to his knees at her side, the ghostly mien banished to reveal his kind face. Ax cast to the ground, her gathered her face in his warm palms, the metal ends of his gauntlets poking her temples and scalp. "Haidra! Haidra! Are you all right?"

She fixed on those hazel eyes, not wanting to look at Lerrod.

"Haidra! Haidra, did he hurt you?"

One of Bon's jolts restored reality. She turned away from him, toward her cousin. Head lolled to the side, Lerrod's dead eyes reflected the dim light on a puddle's surface not far from where he sprawled in the gutter.

"I'm all right," she said, first at a whisper, and then louder when the wraith holding her in his arms asked Haidra to repeat it. Neither oblivion nor exhaustion claimed her full awareness of what she had done.

---

Bon stopped her outside the front door of the manor, a hand on her shoulder.

"Are you certain you're fine?" he asked for the sixth time in the last hour.

The question seemed funny to Haidra, though nothing about it was laughable. She had expected shame the moment the dagger's point pierced her cousin's heart, or to arrive when she helped Bon cover the corpse in a manure pile in one of Urghenna's forgotten streets. Blood dried on the front of her dress, indelible against the dark green fabric no matter how many times she had tried to massage it out using rainwater during the trudge back.

"I'm really okay, Bon," she said. "I had to do it."

"Killing isn't something someone just does, Haidra." He faced her on the manor's concrete walkway. "It still hurts, even when we have to. Us and the dead."

"I'm fine," she said, more as confirmation for herself than him. She nodded a few times before she met his gaze. "I wasn't going to make it through unless I... It had to be done."

"All right," Bon replied. "No more argument from me."

"All right," she echoed for the lack of a better conclusion.

She knew why she had killed Lerrod. It was for the same reason why he had tried to flee, the consistent motivation shared by all people forced into struggle, whether they were a knight cutting down a net-maker or rebellious archers slaying their countrymen. She killed Lerrod because she was scared and didn't know anything better in the moment.

The knowledge made her wonder what the knight who had slain her father had endured in the act. The question around this did not relieve the grief of Arverin's murder, but it firmed her shaking hands and squared her shoulders in preparation of the next round of it.

After barring the manor's entrance they climbed the first flight of steps to the second level and discovered Black John and New Moon seated around their magical brazier, moved from the attic's hearth to a squatting fire bowl. Reset in the center of the floor, the two glass globes heated the iron kettle rested on their crests. The swordsman's open tea pot, blued steel and pocked in small silver mounds, waited by one of the bowl's iron feet.

Black John rose from his stool as they entered. "What happened?"

"Lerrod broke cover and was running for Idrian Street," Bon said. "We chased him down."

The older wraith turned on his daughter. "I told you. I told you there was reason to worry!"

"And yet they are both here, and Lerrod is not." Her silver hair glimmering in the fiery orb-light, she crossed her legs under her and rested both hands on her leather-capped knees. Her eyes remained closed in meditation. "I imagine things did not go poorly?"

"We took care of it," Bon said. "We were able to—"

Haidra interrupted. "I killed Lerrod."

The admission woke New Moon.

Black John seemed to grow in the ruddy light, bearing down on his son. "Are you all right, Lady Haidra?"

"I am. Yes," she answered, trying not to add a *milord* to the end. She watched his eyes go to her stained clothes. The discomfort of his gaze returned, but not for any lurid reason other than a cold sadness shared between her and Black John, much more than before.

"Moon, Bon, go look in the trunk," he said before he returned to the fire bowl and its warming magic. "Find her some mail to replace that dress. Might need to mount one of the spearheads for her, too. On a short shaft."

"I'll get them," Bon said, clearly relieved as he broke from Haidra and returned to the hall.

"Adorable," New Moon sang after her paler brother. "Haidra, why don't you come sit by the fire? There's going to be a chill tonight."

"We'll need that tea, then," said Black John in his full gloom. "Dawn is not far."

# 9

# THE WALLS OF ATENIA

The taste of the tea, of peel and the bite of cinnamon on the back of the dark leaves, lingered long after Haidra had left the manor with the wraiths for one of the three meeting points they had organized with the rebellious Children. Out of their mysterious trunk they armored Haidra in a light mail shirt which sat comfortably on her shoulders and back despite its heft, a pair of leather riding gauntlets New Moon swore Haidra not to lose, and a bladed spear they mounted on a six-foot shaft. Walking hard to stay apace of the three, she breathed through her mouth more than she liked, leaving her throat dry.

The three summoned their guises. Burning eyes in endless night, they traveled smoothly through the shadows as they approached the gathering point. A cluster of forty rebels lined the alley, leaving the wraiths room to spy out the infantrymen near the northeastern tower Lerrod had guarded.

Restlessness from a long shift in the freezing dark had broken the watch. The spearmen amongst them sat on the steps, waiting for relief. The night sky above glittered in scant points of starlight, drawing more than one exhausted eye.

"Storm on my signal," Black John said, drawing his longsword. Bon followed suite with his black ax, New Moon her slender rapier. "Don't stop until you take the tower. Once we send a second signal, hurry to man the ramparts between you and the gatehouse. Understood?"

Haidra glanced around her. Many of the rebels, wearing stolen mail and the rounded helms common to the city's guard, bobbed their heads in frantic agreement.

"Moon," said Black John.

Suddenly reminded of the sorceress' presence, many, including Haidra, turned to find her busy in a quiet incantation. Swinging her arms like one casting water from the pail, a dense green mist shot out from the alleyways for the guard post, thick and waist high. A fog of confusion gripped the spearmen shouting in distress.

"Forth," boomed Black John, his sword leading the way. "For Marta! For Marta!"

"For Marta," the rebels of Low Corner replied in chorus.

Three hundred rebels surged from the narrow lanes between the surrounding buildings. The wraiths slew the first spearmen found in the conjured fog, the sudden screams in the emerald miasma ended by stroke and stab. Others chased down the few that tried to flee. Haidra kept herself behind New Moon and Bon as the two waded through the battlefield. Every royalist dead by the time the two younger wraiths reached the stairs, they ascended without hesitation.

A few steps ahead of his sister, Bon dodged to the left side. "We're seen!"

Trying to balance in the moving flow of rebels and not take up too much room with her spear, Haidra checked in the direction of the tower.

Doored on the western and southern sides and at least three levels high by the rows of windows she counted, a contingent of guards clustered at the western end, working to open the lock while the reinforcements ran from the central gatehouse. More than a dozen, she estimated, part of her wondered how many waited in the tor as a loud horn blast echoed from its top. No matter the number, nothing quieted the fraying at the end of every nerve, her skin tingling in terrified anticipation.

"It's time," New Moon said to her brother as they neared the door on the south side. "Go! I'll cover you!"

Bon shouted arcane words as he leapt from the top of the stairs to the parapet by the western door where the enemy massed. The air seemed to explode under his feet, an invisible floor launching him high to cover the distance. Black ax in both hands, he landed in front of the first runner to the gatehouse. Stunned by the black spirit flying out of the night, the Atenian did not have time to scream as his skull cleaved in two. Shoving the body off the wall, the ax-slinger cut into the next man, then the next.

Keeping her eyes on Bon as long as she could, Haidra ripped her attention away to focus on what lay ahead of her as New Moon kicked in the door. The banded slabs of nailed and framed wood shattered under the blow, which would have stopped Haidra in her tracks if the sorceress had not immediately skewered the man behind it. Jerking her rapier free of his chest, New Moon charged inside. Haidra went in behind her, spear up so she did not wound her in error. Any thought of staying out of the way disappeared as she entered the tower's central floor, the foundation of a large stair twisting up the inside of the cylindrical wall.

New Moon went right, somehow producing a dagger in her other hand as she dueled two spearmen. The sorceress negated their reach and left one of them dead at her feet.

But there were more foes. Many more.

Before she could guess their number two appeared in front of Haidra, spears leveled. Without hesitation this time, she thrust at their faces, skewering the one on the right. The shock of it spread to the man beside him, who dropped his weapon. Pulling back, her shoulders popped when she freed the weapon and thrust again, always at the face like the wraiths had taught her. Unable to free her barb when it caught in the mail of the second guard's metal coif, he closed his hands around the shaft as the point dug deeper into his destroyed cheek. He slumped to the ground, taking the weapon with him.

The three behind the two she slew had their spears readied. New Moon dueled new threats as well, her back to Haidra in that dire second.

Prepared to die, Haidra braced for a fatal, final agony when the Children of Marta flooded through the tower's southern door behind her. They attacked around her from all sides, knocking her to the floor in their haste to kill the royalists. Crunching into a ball, arms ups to guard her head, hot blood splashed on her back and shoulders.

Groaning in disgust, a thought to move out of the way was cut short when the body of a rebel dropped atop of her. Struggling to breathe under the convulsing dead, she shoved her blood-drenched arm against the corpse, enough to raise her head. The melee of stomping feet on the wooden floor and the clash of steel continued unabated until, suddenly, shushed. She pushed herself up and rolled the dead man off her.

New Moon appeared at her side and lifted Haidra to her feet, setting them both aright before she whipped her rapier out the side again, less blood on it than before. "We have the tower." A few more quick huffs and she calmed, quicker than Haidra could in the same span. "If the boys are doing their job, we should be able to open that door," she said, nodding toward the western exit to the gatehouse.

"But that'll let them in, Moon. We'll have to keep fighting," Haidra said, dazed from the first skirmish. She searched for her spear, spotting it still fixed in the face of the last man she had killed. Her stomach twisted before her throat constricted. "Oh, Crook…"

The morning's breakfast of beans and eggs mixed in the lake of red on the boards.

New Moon rubbed Haidra's back. "I'll get it." She put her boot on the dead man's jaw and grasped the spear's shaft. A quick jerk up slid the point out while the body flopped a bit. Fresh gore drizzled off the steel.

The moment Haidra thought additional vomit was a certainty one of the rebels sent up to the tower's nest pounded down the steps with arm-loads of unstrung longbows and fresh quivers, his friend behind him to guard his back. A rebel carrying his sword and a half-shattered shield, life trickled down his nose from a cut somewhere in his helmet.

"The one of you—with the ax—is doing a good job out there, but there's still a few," the man with the broken shield noted. "Want to let them in?"

"Ready when you all are," said New Moon, holding out the spear for Haidra to reclaim it.

Her guts calm, Haidra accepted it as the Children of Marta split their forces, appointing a team of ten to man the tower above while they continued the push. Aligning in front of the heavy wood-and-metal door on the western side, the rebels prepared for the enemy flow. Haidra assumed a place on the left column, her spear low and forward.

The young boy opening the door gave no signal as he loosed the latch. The slab swung in and slammed against the stone, rattling on its hinges as five royalist infantrymen fell backward through the opened portal. Swords and axes chopped down, killing a pair of them flat on their backs. The standing soldiers fared no better.

Rushing outside, Haidra discovered the parapet carpeted in the dead and dying.

In the middle of the slaughter, Bon the Bloody earned his

dreaded name. Pressing a royalist against the wall with one hand, he cut to the knee first, then the ribs, before he stepped away to smash the spearman's head with his ax. He followed with a chop to the spine of a wounded foe nearby.

Haidra did not shudder, this time, as she watched.

"Come on," Bon shouted to the Children of Marta. He led the way to the northern gatehouse. "He's already ahead of us!"

To the shock of Haidra, Black John had scaled the inner wall of the palisade to the gatehouse's battlement. He dropped the men he killed over the sides to the ground below. New enemies climbed the wooden stairs leading to the cramped rooftop. His sword a brand of shimmering light, he cast it to and fro like a fisherman, capturing a life every time.

From the northwestern tower at the other end of the palisade sentries blew their horn to alarm the city.

Attempts at surprise nullified, the two young wraiths and the Children of Marta broke down the gatehouse's eastern entrance. Bon waded in, creating a path of carnage which halted the flow of fresh men manning the inside stair to his father. Bolstered by other brave rebels with axes, better in the confined space than a spear or sword, they hacked their way to the other door. The walkway slicked in gore, Haidra stepped carefully behind New Moon when they passed under the threshold with the rest of the group.

The rebels barred the entry points after the last guard fell. Several rushed downstairs to drop the portcullis gates, lowering them with a bang.

"Make sure the chains are locked," Bon shouted to whomever would hear him in the chaos. He caught his sister's attention and waved for the sorceress to make the rest of the climb to the top of the gatehouse. Haidra went after them, up the stone steps, among a handful able to follow.

They found Black John alone atop the gatehouse, perched on the southwestern corner. Longsword steeped in blood, the senior wraith stared off in the direction of the Veard's high citadel. Torches and braziers burned in its windows and on its faraway balconies, shining bright to cast off the usual gloom. Horns blasted from its heights, answering the alarm.

"Get everyone outside and find me a runner ready to brave the northeastern tower and back. We need to spread out evenly," Black John said above the constant drone. "We have little time."

# 10

# HORN SONG

Atenian horns blasted ringing notes throughout the city as a great force of two hundred knights on horses braided in the finest pink and navy flashings led a battalion of infantry to the northern palisade's gatehouse. Trotting down paved lanes cleared of citizens locked in their homes by the queen-regent's order, crested helms shook on every hoof beat, out of time with the sway of a thousand spears in silent formation. An effective psychological tactic, fear goosed Haidra's arms as she watched the knights halt the mass.

Five splits in the line opened. Along the center of Idrian Street ran archers in their pink-trimmed harnesses, spreading into a staggered wedge of kneeling men.

"Arrows at the ready," the head knight shouted over the horn blowers far-off in the citadel, who did not cease their noise.

The archers below picked a shaft from their hip quivers and placed them on their strings in unison. On the commander's next order, they launched hundreds of arrows up at the wraiths perched atop of the gatehouse.

"Short," Bon said in a bored, drawn voice.

True to his word, the shower of missiles missed by dozens of feet. Iron heads tapped the wall below, unable to be seen in the night as the shower of broken shafts on the street echoed in different places.

"The second one won't be," said Black John as he dragged his son down beside him. Tucked behind the battlement overlooking the city to its south, the three hunkered under its inward-facing lip with six rebels. Haidra wedged herself as deep as she could beside New Moon. The sorceress seated in her meditative pose, tranquil no matter how awful the racket.

Grunting as he waited beside his father, Bon brought his knees up toward his chest and cast his ax in front of his feet, the black weapon clanging on the ground. "I know, I know. First to gauge, second to score. They'll batter us after that."

"How long are we going to be up here?" asked one of the rebels.

"Until they run out of arrows," Black John said to the woman. Nestled in his cloaks, he nodded to the blankets he had instructed them to bring. "Find what rest you can and stay warm. We don't know when they might decide to throw up the ladders."

Haidra heard one of the Children of Marta mutter whether or not the wraith "was serious?" The next volley of arrows ended any more protest. At a safe distance and angle that the shafts bore little threat other than intimidation, her bedroll provided shelter against the night's chill.

Hours passed as the royal archers peppered the gatehouse. The cold air deepened and Haidra's breath fogged from her red, runny nose. Wrapped in the brown threadbare blanket with its musk and moth-holes, she shivered awake every time she nodded off, teetering back and forth between an aching sleep and small rouses of terror caused by clattering arrows.

"Why don't they just blow up the gate?" one of the rebels asked sometime later. "It's what I'd do if I wanted to end this."

The man spat a glob from the back of his dry throat. "We should have blown this place up."

"That would be a fool's errand," another one of the rebels voiced, a familiar and frank tone Haidra thought belonged to Aleaus the blacksmith. "What good is a palisade with a hole in it when this prince's army shows? For anyone?"

The first rebel began to say something snarky as a horn blew a short note. The twang-thrum and rat-tat of the archers' endless fire ended their banter.

The three wraiths broke from cover before the next signal by the knights. New Moon leapt upon the battlement and threw her hands skyward, evoking a name at the end of each incantation she completed.

"Agnu," she intoned, hellfire eyes blazing bright in her hood. "Agnu!"

Her open hands spewed curtains of flame.

Haidra was thankful whomever they fell upon died out of sight. The conflagration halted the horns of the Atenians, replaced by the cacophony of voices, frightened horses, and a thousand footfalls. A smell quickened into the air, the sweet-sick of burning flesh. Far different than the char of wheat-kernels, it snarled and twisted her stomach.

New Moon waved her hands in different patterns, her chant a variation on the first. A ball of fire manifested. She hurled it far ahead of her. It exploded with a boom that dimmed the stars in brief passing.

The sorceress halted her magic in time for Bon to catch his sister as she fainted. He ducked below the battlement's lip, cradling her in his arms.

Black John was there immediately to draw the rebel's focus, his longsword thrust toward the steps down to the gatehouse. "Haidra, tell everyone to get their bows! One of us will be down to lead the volley!" He ascended the gatehouse's separating wall, a black shape looming over the killing field his daughter had created at Idrian Street's northern mouth. Using his free hand, he traced into the air, shouting the same incantations as his daughter.

Frozen while she watched the wraith summon more flame, reality claimed Haidra when someone snatched her arm.

"Get going, girl," Aleaus screamed, shoving her onward. "Go! Go!"

---

Lost in the mash of men and women, mail scraping those unlucky to be barehanded that night, a longbow and quiver of nine arrows found their way in Haidra's hands. Given to her by Talic, he shared a nod before he disappeared in another direction.

Bon came down the stone steps from the gatehouse's battlement, black clothes and black weapon stained a dark, dry red. The illusionary mask gone, his hazel eyes searched the room. He looked for her, Haidra for him, almost rising on her toes before they caught each other.

"Listen to me," he called, addressing the rebels. "Listen! We will exit through that door." He pointed at the door leading to the western wing of the palisade, toward the tower they had not taken. "The best archers among you need to aim for the knight's horses. The horses! Don't try to kill the men in the saddle. The rest of you not so good at archery just need to fire. Shoot the best you can as long as you can. If we see them ready for a volley you need to duck down, but it will probably not come to that."

"Why not?" asked his audience.

"Oh, they'll throw up ladders by then," said Bon in his nonchalant way. "We'll be fighting."

Another boom of magic quaked the earth, rattling dust from the gatehouse's interior walls and supports. It was met by blasting silver horns, but in disarray, bereft of the usual cadence.

"Now," shouted Bon. "Remember, the horses!"

The closest rebel wrenched the western door to a flashing night full of smoke. Dragged into the charge, Haidra kept her feet under her and the bow in her hands as she hugged the quiver to her chest. Out in the sulphureous air and allowed more room thanks to a wide rampart, the Children of Marta quickly fell along into lines of two or three, each group taking a post at one of the crenelations that would allow them to shoot behind cover.

The flagstones beyond the gates of Atenia had been blasted into craters of broken stones laid down at the founding of the kingdom. Fire guttered in patches. Among the pits roasted the dead unlucky enough to be caught in the wake of the wraiths' spells. The fireballs New Moon and Black John flung had left gapes in the infantry's line.

Atenia's archers had retreated under the direction of the knights to allow the footmen to fill them. On their shoulders were hefted tall, thick siege ladders.

Bon shouted over the clamor, "Nock arrows!"

Beyond a measure she would fail to remember later on, Haidra figured out her quiver's loop in time to get it around her head and shoulder. Drawing one of the arrows, she fumbled it onto the rest near where she grasped the bow in her right hand, fighting with her left to align the notch to the string.

"Fire when you hear the strike of my ax," he shouted as he rushed behind her, checking on every group. "The strike of my ax!"

Tight and hard, the bowstring bit her fingers and thumb as she pinched between the goose fletchings. Everything lined up, but the sinew did not give at first when she pulled back. Haidra breathed past the pain like Moon had tried to teach her in a few minutes that morning, bracing her right arm as long as she could. She raised her bow.

Bon's strike rang against the stone like a bell.

Pulling to her chest, Haidra aimed the arrow's point toward the mass of infantry in the distance and loosed. She did not see where it landed once it flew, lost in the night's hot murk. Other arrows shot too high disappeared along with it, but a few managed to raise the squealing cries of the horses and the crash of men thrown off the saddles.

Haidra fished the next shaft with an aching hand. She posed herself as she did before, the notch on the string.

The ax rang a second time.

Bracing and pulling with all her might, she fired into the dark. Sweat ran into Haidra's eyes but, undaunted despite the misery, she fumbled a third arrow onto the string.

The ax echoed thrice.

Horses cried in the night, sad sounds which pierced her being. Haidra loosed two more arrows, never knowing if any of the ones she fired had done anything worth their waste. Hands numbed to the bone, arms wracked, she considered failing to heed the next call until the royalists blew their horns in cascading notes.

"Take cover!" Bon shouted.

Dropping everything, Haidra spun, putting her back to the wall and let the weight of her mail pull her down. She clenched her eyes shut and prayed to Crook, again, not to take her life by an arrow.

The royal forces launched five storms on their section. Hundreds of shafts broke on the ramparts. The rest flew over to land in the fields she had burnt days ago. She tightened into her ball and waited for the royals to capture her—hopefully kill her before whatever else they had planned—when inhuman roars broke the daze.

Black John's voice echoed on the air, the wraith out of view.

The potent words he spoke, dark and weird, roused Haidra to look over the rampart's edge. Several of the rebels popped their heads up as well in grim curiosity.

She counted six dead horses in the haze, three of them pinning their riders while the others had been finished off in the rebels' hails. Among the dead and wounded crawled awful monsters, gluttonous worm-creatures slithering about on clicking legs. Opening helminth mouths to scream acid and bile, they wiggled over bodies and whipped their barbed tails at any soldier nearby, forcing their disjointed line back. The knights in the lead, many of them ordered to the front seconds ago, fought to steady their mounts and ranks.

Each of the worms swelled like a rotted bladder, their membrane-skin thinning to the barest margin before they popped. Instead of gross, slimy viscera, intense rays of rainbow light strobed in every directions. Knight and infantry turned away from the miasma of colors, thrown into renewed panic. New worms, no more real than the first wave, crawled from under the dead.

"Get your bows down! Weapons out!"

Bon appeared from the end of the rebel line as his father's illusion ended, storming through to gather them. Haidra and the others did not hesitate to answer. The stragglers crowded after them.

"Gather arms," he shouted. "Prepare for the ladders and ready to fight! We have moments before they're upon us!"

"What do you mean?" asked an ignorant doubter. "What of those beasts? Surely the damnations are doughty enough to battle an entire army!"

"Then why would we need you here, dummy?" the wraith snapped back. "Hell only lasts so long against blood, bone, and iron. They will set up their ladders, climb up here, and kill every single one of you if you stand around. Get your weapons! It is time for you to stand for Atenia! The real Atenia! Show Fransica and her tyrants that you will not be stamped out for cruelty and lies! Today is the day you set generations after you free! Fight for them as you would fight for you! For those you love!"

Restored by the wraith's encouragement, the Children of Marta fell in behind him.

Tearing her attention from the field one last time, Haidra spied the sky in the east. The stars had disappeared.

Dawn was on the way.

---

SOLDIERS FINALLY CORNERED a devil-worm that dragged itself too far, working up the courage to stab its pus-slick flesh after it belched toward them. The iron head of the spear passed through air.

In the blink of an eye the illusions vanished.

Fueled by rage at their own idiocy, the knights rallied the infantry and pressed on the walls. Teams of oxen brought by conscripts in the south were chained to the inner portcullis gate in preparation to break it. High ladders made of stripped tree trunks nailed with boards for the rungs teetered high in the air, ready to crash down on the long edge of the inner rampart. Four in total, the flanking strategy of the gatehouse was obvious.

Black John split the Children of Marta in two. "Keep the ladders down," he said to Bon after dolling him his portion. "When the two go up on your side, call for the withdrawal. New Moon will try her best."

"And then what?" Haidra heard Bon ask.

"Then we wait for Aron. He should be close." Black John stared hard at his son from behind the wraith's terrifying visage.

The two shared a moment Haidra wished she had had with Arverin. Blinking the tears away, she fiddled with the straps of her shield, tugging until their tightness bit the flesh of her forearm. Instead of love she found anger, hot and stinging in the moment the knight's sword opened her father's hands. She fixated on that hate, pushing aside exhaustion. Life or death no longer mattered next to grief.

The horn for the infantry advance sounded outside.

The wraiths led the Children of Marta out both sides of the gatehouse, taking to the wall as the first ladders caught the edge of the ramparts. Haidra went out the eastern side with Black John.

Spearmen drew arming swords and climbed. The swordsman conjured the blood-red crystal as his son had in the southern fields and set the nearest ladder ablaze. The three royalists on it caught fire and plummeted as its full length lit.

"Line up and protect the door! Hold yourselves together," the towering wraith boomed in his haunted voice. He placed himself at risk first, always steps ahead of the fastest rebel. He skewered the first infantryman at the top of the farthest ladder. Stepping aside to let the dead fall where he made them, he parried a second attacker's thrust and opened him across the throat in riposte.

Soon, the Children of Marta fought their long-awaited foes, fellow citizens transformed into the bitterest enemies. Some of the less experienced died against the better trained soldiers and basic swordplay, but the violence in every pass of the wraith's longsword evened the rebel's odds.

In the midst of the melee, one of the spearmen stumbled past Black John's deadly wave, tripping over his feet to land on hands and knees.

Right in front of Haidra. She did not think as she swung a hatchet into his cheek, crushing in the side of his face.

The rebels kept their line tight. The wraith slew four out of every five men daring to climb onto his killing field, leaving the survivor to be finished by whatever rebel stood closest, but the

Children of Marta fought in a valiant fashion. Haidra later remembered she had killed two men by herself.

More kept coming. One by one, then two by two, and then too many.

The fall of the third and fourth ladders on the western side of the northern gatehouse crashed in the hearts of every rebel. The tide turned as the royalists forced their way up. The wraith, crowded to the point of stepping back from the ground he had held for valiant minutes, slowed his counterattacks. One rebel died, then four when a trio of spearmen stabbed their part of the line down.

"To the gatehouse," Black John ordered. "Fall back!"

Heeding the order, the rebels fled inside. Bon's troop had already retreated, crowding the flights going up and down the inner stair where New Moon joined him. Jammed tight, all pressed the doors on both sides, the closest responsible for the first line of defense and the first to die once the melee started.

Black John, a giant among the men, held his sword high. "Hope!"

Red eyes upon them, a spell fell over the rebels when they locked his burning gaze with theirs, but without fear of the hero they saw before them.

"Children of Marta, you need not lose hope," Black John said. "Never has Atenia seen greater heroes stand against the darkness! You have battled and won. I did not order the retreat because we were broken. In battle lives are lost and those who died did so bravely! I ordered the retreat because I saw the sun break the horizon from where I stood, and I knew you no longer needed to struggle."

Their peace broke as axes bit the outside of the iron-banded doors. Only minutes separated them from their destinies.

"Hope," Black John called above the hacking of wood and bolt. "Like the revered mother whom"—the man beneath the wraith shuddered— "listened to you all the days of your life, and who's name you've taken for your own, have hope Atenians! Listen to the world and it will tell you we have not lost yet!"

On the order, they said nothing, basking in the bravery Black John placed in their hearts where there had been none for too long. Beyond the loud, breaking blows on the doors, they bent their heads to listen. A few looked to the portholes.

True to the wraith's word, the land brightened to morning.

And horn song in the north.

## PART II

# THE SACKING

Years bore the shame in silence, a failing effort to forget how everything changed and what happened afterward. Some simply denied Marta de Veard's disappearance out of the pain it caused, wondering if countless generations had venerated a family of monsters. The seasons cycled on as they were meant to, gold rusting the trees, snows piling, and ends budding before the summers ended with the old chill.

Life went on in Atenia.

The only true change any noticed was King Tobias' knights.

Fear had its advantages. The cobbled streets of Atenia's sprawling metropolis grew to be free of crime, but the poor grew poorer, thrown out the gates to endure the wilderness no matter their age or ability. Soon, word came from the merchants in the Horras Market and the Oyster Bazaar of the old forests stinking of rot again, and in the shadowed dales and high rounded hills sightings of dangerous beasts became common.

Into the fourth year of Tobias I's reign, a decree was made that every able-bodied male older than ten was to be conscripted for the construction of new spires at the citadel. From the slums of Low Corner and flats of Urghenna's Mall emerged the hard-nosed scrabble, the poor intent on proving themselves as deserving of considerations as their kings and queens once paid.

The gates of Atenia were opened to them. Knights with their squads of infantry herded laborers together into tight blocks up Snail Way's steep, twisting ramp. The walls were manned every five feet by a trio of longbow archers, ever a foreboding presence that heightened the growing unease many felt as they crossed under the high gate at its apex. The home of the Veards, once bright and towering, loomed in a shadow sunlight seemed unwilling to meet. Men grabbed other men by the arms and pointed at shapes they thought they saw out of the corner of the eye. A gentle confusion held their minds.

Halted before a stage built before the palace doors, the workers waited long minutes before a foreman appeared to the sound of silver horns not heard since the night the queen-mother vanished. The doors, inset with new gold on once-austere oak, opened in a flourish.

Niklon descended the long, sloping staircase out of the palace's strange darkness. On his right and left flanked five men and one woman. The pointed hoods of their silk white robes obscuring their faces, each wore the mask of a white dragon carved of scrimshaw, decorated in rows of raw pearl and powered in mica.

The queen-regent's consort did not dress like his followers, allowing his face to be free to the mid-morning breeze on a gray day. He treated the workers with a thin smile one gave guests they wanted to see depart.

"Ah, good citizens of Atenia," said Niklon, two fingers to his throat to amplify his voice. "The Queen-Regent Fransica, finest of her name, has commissioned the construction of two great spires in veneration of her son, Our Goodly King Tobias de

Veard I, to be added to the citadel. Because of their dire importance to the kingdom and his kingship, they must be built by the time of next year's solstice."

A murmur of shock spread among the workers. Many of them used to hard labor knew the demand was impossible to accomplish. Before any could ask about how they would be compensated, as kings had done in the past to reward such monumental tasks, Niklon marched back into the palace with his serpent-masked retinue. The stunning departure ignited a furor of shouting and calls for the queen-regent's husband. The knights and infantry that had escorted them closed when some of the elders tried to ascend the palace's granite steps.

"You will be told of your compensation," one of the pink-frilled riders declared. The spearmen prodded the citizens into place. Backed into their herd, the workers were marched to a nearby pit to start the dig.

The first foundation was set by a month's passing, yet the crown made no payments.

The citizens spent their days rising to dig, tamp, and brick the towers' bases, shuffling themselves back to their shacks every night, their bellies less full than the day before no matter how much bread and gruel the overseers fed them. The markets, expecting a flush of coin from the employed, shuttered windows and boarded doors as fresh deliveries were left to rot, unsold in merchants bins.

By the end of the fifth week, the local foremen convened a committee as they had done in previous generations. Their company, ten in total, approached the lower gates by themselves that early morning.

One of the knights trotted forward to rebuff the contingent. "What's this? Where are your lads to build the tower? It is past dawn's light!"

"We've come to bargain for our compensation," replied the workers' chosen representatives. "The former king, may he and his demon-spawn rot, nonetheless paid us fair wages for our services, and it has been a full turn of both moons. Without a proper pay to feed our families, pay our landlords, and go to Horras, how can we work? We ask to see the queen-regent."

Scoffing at the request, the knight wheeled his horse around and rode through the lower gates, up the ramp to the palace. The party waited a long, nervous hour, their eyes never falling away from the archers looking down from their high perches.

When the rider finally reappeared, he did so with fresh companions:

Nine more knights on horseback.

Lances shining in the winter sunlight, the point of their formation addressed the committee. "Summon your people to work," the knight said. "They will be fed and so will your families their proper dollop. Don't tarry!"

"But when?" asked the workers brave to insist on their rights. "They need to eat now. The merchants need to sell their wares. When?"

"When the queen-regent makes time, you damned peasant! Now, gather the workers!"

The ten citizens of Atenia refused the order. They were hung by their necks in Gallows Square an hour later.

With the seasons, acceptance of the Veards' iron rule fell hard on Atenia. Low Corner thinned in places as those families, unable to afford even hovels, left for the wilderness, adding to the growing unrest along the trade routes. Across the continent the name of the kingdom grew to one of scorn for the clusters of homeless wandering in different lands, doubled by the reputation of cruelty unable to be hid behind barrier walls and the heavy policing used to separate the rabble from the traders still bringing goods to the city's otherwise-bountiful markets.

The crown and the class which held it up had heavy appetites.

Sections of High Hill, where the gentry lived, blossomed into the shining center of civility of the city. All parts south of the Ursin Canal were beautified as more laborers were conscripted to build walls separating the temple district at the foot of the Ben-Lomen glacier from the rest of the northern quarters, including the Horras Market which now homed nefarious characters. More than one man fell to thuggery as the next generation of women either chose tough lives with them or whoring for the guards.

Cruelty carried the greatest currency.

Where the free lands of Torsdaina once saw Atenia as a jewel of hope, those fed on war and vices flocked to the calls of Fransica's growing army. Sellswords from the continent's eastern coasts grew exponentially by the year. Another great project was unleashed in new fortifications south of the citadel. Much of the forests in the city, once famed for its integration of the natural world, were felled to complete the construction. Soon the only trees left to be found above the Ursin remained in the walled climes of Hernos' Court, who soon disallowed visits to the temple by the commoners after several robberies. The poor became poorer, the rich grew richer.

In the midst of her tenth year as queen-regent, Fransica announced a celebration to mark the occasion.

Rarely seen and only by the wealthy during the sacred feasts marking the seasons and their midpoints, the mysterious queen-regent ordered the Colis to be opened to the entire populace so its gentle curve could serve as the grounds for her games. Home to those families considered too low for Atenia's highborn, earning their money through crafts and trade, the young lords and ladies situated just above the canal woke one morning to the squadrons of infantry sent to banish them alongside the other newly homeless, pushing them north over Entaris Bridge.

Washed and scrubbed by legions of servants suited in pink and navy, the southern streets glistened. Tents were erected next, massive enclosures which housed circuses, gambling halls, and entire eateries dedicated to feeding revelers at all times.

Great choruses sang beside an army of musicians. Spread throughout the city starting at the four corners of the palisades, to the center where the Colis forked from Idrian Street on route to the citadel's rise, the populace stood in wonder as glorious music was played with the rising of the sun.

The gates of the Veard's high fortress opened. The queen-regent's personal champion, Sir Harras, led his procession of one hundred knights in their polished armor out first. In their saddled columns, two by two at the shoulders, they pranced to the view of tens of thousands of onlookers from the south, the only people able to afford partaking in the festivities. Then came a block, three wide and as deep, of flower-girls who spread rose petals as they sang, a fine departure from the constant militarism endured by the average citizen.

Songs throughout the city, often mismatched and off-key, fell into perfect harmony the moment the queen-regent Fransica and her consort Niklon emerged in their open carriage. Ornate with its mother of pearl runners and pink lacquered boarding, its luxury compared nowhere near its riders on the white velvet benches.

Without their son, never seen before or after his ascendancy, the couple dressed in matching fabric of a dark, almost-black navy. Niklon sported a single piece of luxury, binding his robes closed with a lavish girdle of precious stones enclosed by a silver dragonhead pin. He did not smile or frown, even to the smaller children at the front of the parade-watchers waving little hands at him. Dour in expression, perhaps sullen, he leaned in the corner of the carriage and stared lifelessly.

The complete opposite in every way, Fransica soaked up the expected applause and cheering. Standing many times in the compartment to be seen in her finery, her gown was tailored to reveal her smooth shoulders, long neck, and a peek of her breasts while accentuating what contours she had in her hips. The garment dripped in strands of diamonds and pearl. A diadem of blood rubies and emeralds shaped into her favored heraldry—three plucked petals bound by an iron ring—sat upon her head to glitter in the sun. A gross display of wealth almost every man, woman, and child would never see again after that day, she kept perfect poise to maintain its upright balance.

The parade rolled off toward the temples in Hernos Court on the glacier's western foothills, the streets thronged with tired subjects eager to demonstrate their devotion.

Until Fransica's procession reached the end of the Colis.

From the north end of Entaris Bridge, a young woman emerged.

Wearing a red dress trimmed in stripes of gold along the skirts, her hair fell down her back in a waterfall of white starlight matching her perfectly trimmed brows. An Arbikkean by origin, she flared her golden eyes at the oncoming line of knights led by Harras, unflinching as onlookers watched in confusion thinking this foreigner had gone mad. Resolute on the spot she had picked, she kept her dark, empty hands by her sides.

Trotting to lengthen the parade so as many subjects possible could see the queen-regent, Fransica's champion raised a gauntleted hand to signal a stop. His face covered in sweat from the heat inside his helmet, Harras brought his black steed to the center of the bridge, turning his horse to the side to block the way.

Hand on the golden, rubied hilt of a sword that had replaced the legendary High John the Conqueror, the Veard's timeless longsword, he licked his teeth as he studied her. "You will move, lady, or you shall be arrested," he said in plain Torsii, the common language of Torsdaina. "Move now."

The white-haired woman glared up at the knight.

Harras switched to Eaith, a central language on the continent below the Southern Sea. "Did you hear me, woman? I ordered you to move."

When she spoke, she did so with a light accent. Her Torsii came smooth, simple, but carried the weight of a larger world than his. "I have come to proclaim the innocence of Jhean de Veard."

The mere mention of the name sent the crowd reeling. No one spoke it, and unlike the old queen before her daughter became regent, most tried their best not to think of the damned figure because of the promised pain of death.

The open violation of Fransica's most sacred law, one which none had broken since the day she declared it, shook Harras atop his horse.

"What did you say?" the knight asked, stunned.

The white-haired woman repeated, louder this time to the crowds. "I have come to proclaim the innocence of Jhean de Veard, hero of Atenia! Too long has his name been spoken in words given to you by liars! Here, on this day, the truth—"

"You shall be silent! Silent!" Sir Harras ripped his sword out of its scabbard and leveled it at her. "Guards!"

Unafraid of the steel hovering close to her face, she turned away and addressed the crowd, "Hear me, Atenians! Hear me! Jhean de Veard lives! He is innocent of the dreadful charges brought against him by his sister, who murdered your—"

Before she could get the next word out Harras dismounted, rushed toward her, and bashed her in the face with his steeled hand. Blood sprayed from her nose as she twisted to her knees, cradling her face. The guard ran to join the arrest.

Then, without warning, voices in the crowd called out.

"Jhean de Veard lives?" the first asked in disbelief.

Farther down the line on the northern side of the Franc, another spoke in memory, "Jhean de Veard lives..."

"Jhean de Veard lives!" someone finally cried out, captured by a long, lost hope.

Like fire spread from an errant spark, soon all the poor and oppressed of Atenia chanted the phrase as Harras and his men lifted the bleeding stranger off the middle of Entaris Bridge, binding her red-wetted hands and mouth.

"Jhean de Veard lives! Jhean de Veard lives! Jhean de Veard lives!"

An order given personally by the queen-regent secured a quick execution.

Dispersing the parade entirely, the whole procession instead ordered onlookers, servants, and solider alike to Gallows Square outside the citadel's gates. A post was erected where they bound the white-haired woman. Bundles of wood were piled around its base. A guardsman poured a bucket of stinking oil over her head, causing her to cough and gag past her stoicism.

The crowd, used to hangings as standard punishment for murder, rape, or theft, watched in quiet terror as Niklon made his entrance. Enlivened by the duty assigned to him, his broad smile grew as he walked before the condemned. He lifted his hands in a mocking display of wonder before the crowds and faced the poor woman.

"If you repent and speak the truth about your monstrous lover, you shall be spared the fire for a kinder, quicker method," he said. "Tell us where he resides. What will happen is the course of justice but think for yourself. Is your life worth that of a violator?"

The white-haired stranger needed no words where spit served. A howl of glee arose from the crowd.

"Jhean de Veard lives," she shouted them to silence. "He lives. And, one day, you will all die."

The true character of the sorcerer came out as he grabbed the woman by her throat. Incanting, his spell lit her entire body in magical flame without further ceremony.

What everyone remembered afterward wasn't how Niklon held her corpse by the throat, pinned to the blackened post as he was left unharmed. Nor did they remember, for those who dared to look up at the royal balcony, how Fransica watched in smiling satisfaction.

They did, however, recall the nameless Arbikkean, who they named the Burnt Lady, and how nothing about Atenia seemed real after her ashes flew off on the eternal winds.

1

# THE PRINCE OF TOLIV

Prince Aron Toliv of Arbikk had arrived. The land beyond the northern palisade rang joy.

The wraiths ordered the Children of Marta to brace throughout the horn song, never letting up the pressure on the gatehouse doors even after the Atenian guard ceased their attempts to break inside. All they heard as Black John ascended to the roof again were the foreign horns, light and airy compared to the hard, strong notes blown by the Veard's trumpeters. It grew closer and closer as the morning strengthened outside the arrow ports and fixed-glass windows, over the noise of the guards scrambling to man the walls, but no time to prepare in the chaos.

Then came a quiet, a shuffle of steel, horses, and a multitude of hurrying feet in retreat.

A horn sounded from the south, blaring five times to warn Atenia of invasion. Every rebel knew it came from the citadel. The Arbikkean horns with their gentle music continued once the royal drone ended.

Black John descended, stopping on the last tread of steps. "Do not let go of your arms, but do not attack unless I give the order," he instructed in his ghostly voice, burning eyes reviewing the survivors of the night's success. "Moon, Haidra, you're with me. Bon, stay here and remain until we return. Once we do…"

The eldest wraith paused. Tired to the bone and unwilling to do more than hold onto the sword she had somehow acquired in the melee, Haidra looked to his children for some indication for his lapse.

His face covered in red from a cut in the confines of his hood, Bon the Bloody smiled up at his father among the knot of rebels. "Go on. We'll know when to open up."

Haidra moved from her place beside the eastern door, where she had stayed behind two larger, stronger men who had held the oak slab shut even as wedges swung by the guard threatened to split their palms. Many made way for her, forming a lane to the descending stair. A few spoke to her in hushed, quiet voices.

"Thank you, Lady Haidra," one woman told her, touching her forearm as they scooted around each other. "Thank you for bringing sunset to our gray days."

"Thank you, Lady Haidra," Haidra heard one man ssay, nursing a bloody arm as he grunted his appreciation. He pressed himself against a wall, teeth bared and clenched as Aleaus worked bits of broken mail out of the open wounds on his shoulder. Blood drenched her hands, but undeterred, the blacksmith gave Haidra a small smile as she probed with stained fingers.

Beaming as she fell behind New Moon, the sorceress led the way, with Haidra in the middle as Black John followed behind. At the bottom they found the two wenches to raise the portcullis gate. Through the grid of steel and bolts, the day blazed in late-spring, the green hills teeming in a multitude of bright blue flags.

The first line of heralds marched over Atenia's northern hills with the sunrise, the rims of their horns shining bright as they bleated loud, low notes. Five thousand archers stamped through the burnt farmlands, never halting. Behind them, seven thousand spears and shields kept neat rows of men who swept forward, a bristling vanguard of steel before the great war machines crews of workers and herdsmen brought forth, lashed to the backs of horses, cattle, and the humped camels of the Arbikkean desert. Bright blue standards embroidered with a six-pointed star flew gallantly on the ends of cataracts' lances, the mail armors and needle-helms blazing by the time the sun freed from the earth. The calvary massed to a startling eight hundred riders, with multiple times the horses hauling their baggage.

Haidra watched this army approach with semi-joy, semi-terror, unsure about her role until Black John brought her back to attention.

Idrian Street lay deserted behind them. As quick as they formed, the Atenians had indeed retreated, taking their dead with them while leaving the pavement littered in broken arrows and scorched by the wraith's potent magics.

"Haidra, get on that one. Moon, there," Black John said as he walked under the center of the archway. "Hurry."

The sorceress heeded her father as she and Haidra assumed the opposing wenches. They worked well to a fair degree, only one or two fumbles of their tired arms stuttering the gate's creaking rise.

Alone and exposed, Black John signaled silently to New Moon with a point back up the stairs. He thumbed at both her and Haidra.

The sorceress let out an annoyed sigh as she passed behind her father. "At least let him know I'm okay."

"I will," said Black John. "You're the first person he sees after me."

"I'd better be. Come on, Haidra," said New Moon, nodding for her to lead the way up.

After they climbed to the gatehouse New Moon ordered the Children of Marta to secure the palisade. Sending runners to see to the status of the rebels who had manned the northeastern tower, she followed with a direction to move the wounded downstairs. She brought Aleaus to her with an inward wave.

"Yes, milady?" the blacksmith asked, a quick bow of her head added at the end.

"Don't do that. Whomever is left once the runner gets back needs to start recovering whatever weapons or armor the guards abandoned. We need to collect what resources we can to add to what the prince is bringing."

"Of course, mil…" Aleaus paused awkwardly. "We'll recover what we can."

"What of Ecktor?" New Moon asked next.

"He led the soldiers manning the northeastern tower's nest," Aleaus replied.

"Then we shall wait on him to decide where everyone goes once—" her expression hidden behind the ghastly illusion, she let whatever thought she had slip with an exhausted shake of her head. "I'll see him when I see him. Let's get the wounded moving, Haidra."

Those able to work, only about forty of the original three hundred who had shown that night, organized the least wounded around those with the worst injuries but a strong chance of survival, slowly working teams down in trios and pairs to carry the human load. Someone discovered a half-empty water barrel behind the stair, and tearing a piece of clean cloth into scraps, New Moon and Haidra went around cleaning off the faces of the fighters, removing grit to get a sense of the life in their eyes and examine any head wounds that might require a healer.

The very last and shy to be seen, Bon shirked his turn multiple times, ambling to a different part of the room before Haidra cornered him.

"Stop, Bon," she said when he caught her hand near the edge of his hood.

"It's not even stinging," he said, dodging from the wad of cloth she held up.

New Moon spoke from the top of the gatehouse steps. "Bon, let her! Stop screwing around and get downstairs unless you need someone to carry you."

"Quiet, you," he said back to his sister. "I can handle this!"

"Are you sure?" New Moon replied in half-mockery.

"Quiet, the both of you," Haidra said, sharp and fast. "Bon, please."

Sighing in defeat, the young warrior pushed his hood back. His face coated in a congealed layer of his own blood, a small nick near his hair line was revealed after a few stokes of the cloth on his forehead and cheeks. Needing little more than a fresh bandage, Haidra spotted some bruising puffing the lower lid of his left eye. She brushed it with her bare thumb, tracing softly until the rest of her fingers brushed his beard's rough edge. His hazel eyes hypnotized her.

Bon pressed his face into her palm, the flesh of his cheek hot against her clammy skin. "You okay?" he asked her as if they were the only ones in the world.

She did not pull away. "Are you?"

He nodded in her hand, smiling.

Breaking from each other, they helped bring the last of the wounded down to the entrance of the city.

The prince arrived outside of Atenia's northern palisade. Unlike the queen-regent who gloried in wealth, no carriage or cart ushered him, only a gallant charger he broke from his personal squad of cataracts. Upon the white stallion, his mail gleamed from years of polishing out blood, its patina oiled and bronzed. He pulled off his needle-helm when he and Black John saw each other, releasing a shock of dark hair which he shook out. The closer he came, the clearer his features, and to the shock of the Children of Marta including Haidra, this strange warlord could not have been older than twenty.

His lavender eyes, a highlight for his flawless brown skin, took in the walls with keen interest as he slid off his saddle.

Black John and Prince Aron eyed each other as they met. They whispered, sharing something only between them before the younger man launched forward, wrapping the tall wraith in his arms.

Working himself loose of his benefactor, the black warrior waved for the rebels, his children, and Haidra to approach. He and the prince came to meet them.

By Bon and New Moon's side, Haidra found herself ahead of the main group by several feet. Old anxieties the Veards had scarred into the life of every peasant reopened, averting her eyes to the dirt under her feet. As quick as the anxiety came it disappeared upon viewing the farmlands before the northern walls, reduced to the charred fields she had created.

This time the burnt, rotted wheat, wetted by at least one molding rain, awakened her. Remembering the destruction that had summoned three wraiths out of the night, of how she had fulfilled her father's ambition, unease sat like a rock in the bottom of her stomach.

How had she made it through all this? How was she alive?

Bon grabbed her hand, shocking her though she did not startle. Haidra looked to the ax-slinger.

"You're alive," he said, leaning closer, but not too close. He gently pulled her along. "It's all right, Haidra. It's okay to be alive."

Blinking away the tears as his words struck home, she squeezed his hand back. They let go as New Moon darted forward, arms out like a summer child flying after birds in a meadow. The demeanor of the prince changed as well as Aron ran to catch her. Their mouths smashed together in a long, fervent kiss.

"Eww," Bon said under his breath.

Haidra gave him a curious look. "Don't like kissing girls?"

"Not when you watch your sister do it."

Prince Aron let go of New Moon, who dabbed tears from her eyes, and went for Bon with his hand held out.

"Good sir," the prince cried.

Bon laughed, loud and hearty. "Good sir!" He took the offered hand and was pulled into a deep hug. The son from Toliv and the son of a devil broke, dusting each other's shoulders with a shared, small nod.

"How are you doing?" Prince Aron asked in a quiet, calm voice that made Haidra think of a gentle breeze. He smacked Bon on the side of his mailed arm. "Have a good morning?"

Bon looked back over his shoulders at the gates of Atenia and sighed. "It was a morning. Got wounded but nobody I think you'll need to worry about. Dad tell you yet how we're going to go in?"

"We've thoughts to that but," Prince Aron nodded to Haidra, "Who is this? Who am I paying now?"

Bon stood taller as the handsome prince paid his attention to Haidra. "Haidra, meet Prince Aron of Toliv, a beauteous kingdom of northern Arbikk. Don't let the armor fool you, he's a capable dandy."

Chuckling, the prince dipped his head toward Haidra, appraising the details of her face with his eyes. "Are you Atenian?"

"I am, my Lord," she said.

Bon's exhaustion returned in a somber expression. "Her grandfather was the man who found Dad. Her father led those folks," he said, nodding back to the Children of Marta lined up before the open gate.

Prince Aron's pleasant grin dimmed, but did not disappear, though it became sad. "Is Arverin here?" he asked Haidra.

"Not, my Lord," she said, teary and touched that a prince

remembered a peasant's name, and her father's, too. "He was killed before this started."

The prince reached forward and gently placed one of her hands in his, his gentle grasp warm and firm. She looked up at the newcomer—this invader—and was surprised to see him concerned with her and only her, as was Bon.

"Thank you for all you've done, Lady Haidra," he said. "I swear I've not come to harm you or your people. Thank you for believing in that. I'm so sorry about your father and all you have lost."

Beyond a thanks that was meaningless to Haidra, as she had not done any of it by herself, the acknowledgment of Arverin, of the shit and misery of her life, coalesced in a release of tears. She believed this man, like she believed the wraiths, and knew once and for all she had not betrayed anything good or decent.

She put her face in her hands, turning from both men in embarrassment. "I'm so sorry," she said, trying to wipe away the tears.

Having retained a hold on her, Prince Aron gently tugged her around again. He gave her hand to Bon and touched both of their shoulders.

"Don't apologize for freedom," he said. "Not before gods or goddesses, kings or queens. Bon, my bard is in the vanguard. Would you have him bring up the medical corps and field corps? I want these burnt fields flat before noon and the tents set upon them. The char will actually help the surgeons once they place their tables. I already asked Moon to gather the strategists, but we need to determine our command center."

"Of course," Bon said. "I'm sure my father already has thoughts to that."

"I'm sure he does." Prince Aron addressed Haidra again, always to her surprise, "Lady Haidra, may I ask a great favor?"

NOT ONCE THINKING she would return to the devastation so soon, Haidra steadied as she viewed the mouth of Idrian Street.

Bodies of dead royalist knights and spearmen lay in heaps, and anywhere she tried to find a space not filled by death. Blood puddled into boiled lakes of broken weapons and slain horses. Crows had descended from Bhadran's Wood, flocks of black feathers and beaks feasting on torn flesh. Too cold for flies, they had conquered the field.

From atop the gatehouse of the northern palisade and understanding what she had done, the weight of each and every soul below measured heavier by the number as she counted, knowing she'd never know the full number. The stench, too awful to describe, would have sickened if not for an empty stomach.

How had it come to this? Why was the world this way?

Black John laid his gauntleted hand on her shoulder. His hazel eyes full of tired sadness, he nodded to what she saw. "They'll be buried," he said. "We'll bury them. But are you ready?"

She considered this man she had seen on the side of her father's coin. "I am."

Black John glanced to Prince Aron. "So am I."

The lord from Arbikk, their third on the rooftop, approached its south-facing fence and cleared his throat. "I hope this goes well," he said, lifting his chin.

Black John touched two fingers to the apple of the prince's throat. After a few whispered words by the sorcerer-swordsman, he spoke out in his kind voice.

"People of Atenia. Good morning," Aron said, his deliberate words amplified by the enchantment. They rang out over the slums Haidra had called home all her life. Disturbed by the sudden boom of Prince Aron's voice, the crows scattered in every direction, a black shadow exorcised.

"Please, know you have nothing to fear from this voice

speaking. My name is Prince Aron of Toliv, a land on the shining northern coasts of Arbikk beneath the Southern Sea. I have not come to invade or conquer you. I do not intend to set up my father's caliphate in lands that are not born to our goddess. I have come at the request of your own to help you find your freedom from the tyranny you suffer."

Prince Aron paused and glanced to Black John.

The wraith stared off in the direction of Atenia's spiraling citadel.

The prince continued. "I do not expect Atenians to simply take the word of a stranger over their rulers, though I would ask you what sort of loyalty you owe rulers who abuse you? What I do ask is that for every person that seeks to be free of Fransica de Veard and her cruelty not take up arms against us. I'm setting up my camp outside the northern gates of the city. There will be medical tents and clean places for you and your children to sleep. If you are poor and in need we will help you. I have brought three years-worth of food for you, Atenians, to eat so you do not starve. We are not here to destroy your home. I leave you now, but before I do, I have brought a voice of your own countrymen to speak. Please consider her. She has been very, very brave for Atenia. Like Atenians will be again."

Prince Aron took a step back and lifted his chin for Black John, who did away with the magical amplification by a single tap and an arcane word.

Coughing after the touch, Aron rubbed his throat. "Your turn Haidra. Just say what's in your heart. That's all."

Understanding what she had agreed to, a strange ease in Haidra caused her to nod back. She stepped forward, and like Prince Aron, lifted her chin. Shocked by how gentle Black John's touch was as he incanted on her throat, she tried her best not to swallow a wet glob at the back. Failing, the wet sound resonated. Then she remembered nobody was there to notice save the dead.

She studied those bodies again, then the city ahead until she reached the top of Atenia's royal house. Too far to see if anyone watched from the balconies, she followed the prince's example.

"My name is Haidra. I am the daughter of Batitha and Arverin, menders of nets and cloth. I grew up in Low Corner, outside of Bhadran's Wood. I baked for my living. Three days ago, some knights broke into my family's home and murdered my father. Because he wanted better."

The scene before her washed away. Haidra sat at her kitchen table again, the man across from her slowly speaking about things like honor, courage, and kindness. His small chin like her own, the wave of his dark hair and tanned skin crinkled from days down at the river with the fishermen. His calloused, careful hands moved as he explained every intention.

"I grew up with a good man," she said, the sob in her voice echoing over the city. "He never hit me, never hurt me, and he always told me to tell the truth because that is hard to do in Atenia. He'd say that, sometimes, but I never knew what it meant. We all grow up scared enough not to ask. We all get out of the way of knights because we know, even as little children, those knights don't stop their horses. They didn't stop for my mother."

Prince Aron gasped.

"We know every three coins we make the crown takes two, one for them and one for the guard, though the guard will be by to take the last if you're unlucky. We know we only have the time we have and the rest of it goes to them. My dad started this because he grew up in a time when they couldn't take it. He grew up in a time where knights would have stopped for my mother, and not because the law made them, but because that was who they were. He wanted to live in those times again and knew we can't under the tyranny of Tobias de Veard. My dad was not alone in suffering. He wasn't alone in wanting to fight back. I'm not alone. Neither are you."

No sound arose from Atenia. Birds sang in the trees of the royal woods. Dogs barked in the slums, searching the daytime for lost companions.

"I'm looking at dead Atenians at the northern gatehouse. All of them were your neighbors. They were among your families," Haidra said. "But they are dead Atenians. We are killing each other for people living above us who don't care how we end up as long as they can live *high* above us. The queen-regent murdered her own mother. She murdered my father. What else has she done the we don't know about? Or aren't willing to look at? What else are we willing to let happen to those we love for her story nobody here is responsible for?"

She looked to Black John. The wraith did not break his concentration on the citadel.

Uncertain of her suspicion, Haidra spoke one last time,

"Please, don't fight us. We have not betrayed anything, or you, only the evil looming over us. We're the Children of Marta. We're here to put her spirit and the spirits of everyone taken to rest. Please. We're here to avenge Atenia."

2

## THE GHOSTS

Street by street, from the northern gates and spreading uphill to the Ursin Canal, the northern half of Atenia defected to the blue and white-starred banner of Prince Aron. The poor of Low Corner and Urghenna's Mall came easily in droves with their spouses and children, hungry and sick for care, followed by the dwellers in the abandoned hovels and shacks. Whole families filed into the food tents. Soon, every table and bench was packed by the hundreds. Those first seated were fed then moved to comfortable barracks, so the next group could be served.

Haidra saw neighbors among the psalm-seekers, but few paid her attention over an empty belly, often gorging themselves beside her at the tables completely oblivious to everything else. Another plate served among the dispossessed, she spent those meals in quiet wonder as people who grew up beside one another parted, taken to different camps with no guarantee of returning to their homes. By herself with no one to claim nor any to claim her, she retreated to the growing encampment the prince set for his retinue, including the wraiths.

The merchants of the Horras-Glory Market sent envoys in the late morning led by the heads themselves, each accompanied by their gang of roughs. Seeing the score for what it was, as they did the dead piled by the gate, they pledged to the blue banner in short succession. At noon, the priests of Hernos Court, long under the boot of Fransica's husband and his secretive cult, quickly offered praise to the Arbikkean lord in grand choruses, clouds of incense, and pledges of gold for protection.

To his credit, Prince Aron returned the gold and offered his kindness anyway.

Marching scouts up Idrian Street, the city's central artery, Prince Aron directed his infantry to the Ursin Canal. To the concern of the infiltrators, not a single spearman, knight, or guard had remained to defend the northern quarters, including the markets and warehouses laden with months-worth of provisions they immediately consigned to the rebellion. Bolstered by the calvary combing behind them, footmen searched out Atenia's alleys and squares for any hidden pockets of royalists waiting in ambush but found none.

Until they reached Entaris Bridge and the Victus Crossing.

Shocked by the combined effort of the wraiths and rebels in taking the northern palisade and the sudden appearance of an invading force, Sir Harras had ordered the guard over the canal and set his line at the southern mouths of both bridges, bowmen lined at the fencing. They fired the moment they sighted the Arbikkean's creeping line.

Infantry threw down their spears and swords, taking up shield walls they hooked together to protect legions of their cohorts lifting up sixty-foot-long pikes. The southern bank of the Ursin Canal bristled in steel shining under the daylight. Behind the line, the organized knighthood of Atenia rallied oncoming reinforcements called out of High Hill and the sellsword fortresses in the military district. Extra batteries of archers massed on the upward slopes on northward-facing streets, claiming the best angles for suppressing fire.

The horns of the royalists answered after the sun crested its noon apex. The pink and blue flag of Atenia flapped defiantly from the pinnacle of the citadel's highest spire.

"Thoughts?" Prince Aron asked in his war tent near sundown.

A cavernous covering held high by twelve stout beams and a twenty-foot-tall pillar at its center, he set his table between two braziers away from the main entrance. Seating twelve around them, mostly Arbikkeans save for Black John and a pale-skinned musician with red hair and a beard placed directly to Aron's right, he watched quietly as servants presented simple meals of roasted beef and garlicked rice along with helpings of black tea and cold water, and no wine anywhere. Stationed on stools directly behind Black John's seat at the table, Haidra, Bon, and New Moon observed quietly in a silent supper.

Nervous in the midst of so many strangers, she knew she had found, *felt* something different under that peaked roof, the swirling of power and conspiracy. The draw of another dish, her second helping of food for the day, kept her interest enough to focus away from her nerves, though she kept her eyes open and ear keened on the noise around her.

His generals and captains ate heartily, conversing with the prince and amongst themselves in Eaith. Each a disciplined warrior, they all thought deep upon their words before one of the cataracts spoke up, questioning Aron. His speech flowed natural in his answer, enunciated, to the point like his gesticulations on the table. He drew a line in front of him and dotted his side before he finished with an affirmative remark.

Black John responded in the desert rider's language, his face hidden behind illusion. Voice echoing, eyes aflame, he sat unmoving.

Undisturbed by whatever the wraith stated, the cataract gave a considerate nod and touched his forehead in salute. Black John maintained his silence but mimicked the sign of respect.

"Doesn't solve the problem of the line," the red-haired musician said in perfect Torsii, preoccupied with the eleven-string lute he had brought with him and its silver tuning knobs. "There's only two ways across. We'll have to take one of them."

"What about going up the Ben-Lomen?" the same cataract asked in equally fluent Torsii, drawing Haidra's attention and surprise.

"It's not frozen yet and many paths through the glacier will not be available until winter," Black John said. "Fransica is not surrounded by fools, and you are correct, Yamil, there is no punching through the pikes. I would not waste the horses either, my liege."

"Then what do you say we do, John?" the musician asked. "What about Bhadran's Wood?"

"It's already fortified along the Ursin's southern bank. One would have to march through the Veardens to make any real paths back to the city. It will take too long," the wraith answered. A statue breaking into animation, he leaned his head forward. "The path is over the canal and Harras sealed up the holes. Our only real chance will be found in monitoring his line for any openings. Likely, he will attempt to send his own scouts over the canal tonight either by rope line or a boat. Perhaps with a sorcerer. The channel runs deep and unless we send troops up with torches we will never see them until they are on top of us."

"Which means they can attack anywhere. Quite cunning." Prince Aron hummed as he claimed his teacup. "They know it is an uphill fight for whomever tries to cross over, but a small leap down for them, crushing wherever they land." He sipped intently as he plotted his next decision.

Permitted to their own meals, Haidra ate hers with extra zeal. Flavored with salt, a scant bit of pepper flakes, and a tangy-hot spice she had never encountered, the roasted meat and hearty rice was better than anything she had had in sixteen years of life. She and her father had lived on fish and gruel, spent grains and milk most of their lives, like many did in the slums. This taste of wonder almost made her murmur in happiness, but she chewed through, eyes shut to savor everything.

"We have to decide where exactly we want to defend and where we want to risk the battles that will need to be had," Prince Aron said after he called a servant to refill his drink. "They've already set up their siege weapons, yes?"

"They have firing lines for rotating teams of archers in the bazaar and will try to hit us from their elevation in High Hill, if they're foolish enough to incur the look of it," said another voice in heavily-accented Torsii. "It would help us if they were fool enough to fire on their own city. Probably make our volleys easier to place."

"Blunt as always, Ahmeti," Prince Aron replied in a dark but humored tone. "But the apologies should be mine. I set us a harder task. I promised I would not harm anyone in the city or their homes. Bringing siege weapons to bear on anything other than the citadel is impossible for us to do. Whatever solution, it must be done with minimal loss of innocent life and collateral damage."

"I have a suggestion," offered Black John in his resonate voice.

"Go on," said Prince Aron.

"Allow New Moon, Bon, Haidra, and I to attempt to cross the canal after midnight to scout the royalist artillery positions. It may damage buildings, but Arbikkeans are famed for the precision of their engineering and accuracy when throwing a stone. I will find out the positions we need to strike."

The mention of her name snapped Haidra from her food-induced meditation, her attention fully on the discussion. The rest of the men ate the table ate heartily, unmoved by the wraith's conspiracy.

"What can we do to support you?" Prince Aron asked.

Black John answered. "We'll need volunteers."

CLOUDS DRIFTED east to the Veardens, revealing a starry sky and cold half-moon, its twin's dark face obscuring itself. Leaned in the mouth of an alley, Haidra stared up at those faraway points before she brought her eyes level with the road uphill from her position. The weight of the mail given to her before the battle at the palisade gates sat heavy on her shoulders and back, the butted rings pressing through the fabric of the beige tunic underneath to chill her skin. She drew her new black cloak around her shoulders, bracing against the midnight air nipping at the end of her small, round nose.

New Moon stepped into the middle of the alley's mouth, at her side. The sorceress put a gauntleted hand on Haidra's shoulder. "Moving in two. I don't think that was a patrol we passed," she whispered, close to her ear.

Haidra nodded and followed behind the sorceress. They retreated deep into the lane until they came to the next intersection where the rest of the party waited. Along with Black John, Bon, New Moon, and her as their "sponsor"—whatever that meant when Aron's bard Valen said it—six more had joined their number, rounding out the group to ten members.

Drawn from the Children of Marta, the rebels had sent the former guard Talic, Aleaus the blacksmith, a young woman named Ada both Bon and New Moon remembered from the gatehouse, a cobbler named Gurshin, and finally the fisherman Adan and his son Clive. Chosen by Black John for their survival of the palisade battle as well as their native knowledge across the breadth of Atenia, he had armed and armored them like he had Haidra. Sword, arrows, and bows to each, black cloaks covered with studded brigandines. Matching black helms sat flush to the skull beneath their hoods.

Talic nodded from under his cowl to Haidra as she entered the space behind the sorceress. The former guardsman, still spry and able in his sixties, provided at least one friendly face.

Black John motioned for them to converge. "We are going to sneak to the southern bound of Urghenna's Mall," he whispered. "I do not expect us to run into royalists but keep low and alert. They will have sharpshooters on the lookout. One we get to the canal and check it we will move west toward Entaris Bridge. Stay together the entire way unless I give the order. Understood?"

His children and the volunteers muttered or nodded agreement. Black John marched forward and parted Adan and his son, who silently stood apart as Bon and New Moon followed. The rest waited on Haidra, already annoyed with such deference.

Sneaking through the alleyways, cats growled at the party from the gutters and atop fences, lazing in the dark since the siege had frightened the rats underground. Undeterred, they exited on the south end of Urghenna's Mall, the lower bank of the canal. A line carrying ice melt in from Ben-Lomen in the west, dumping the waste somewhere in the Veardens to the east, several ramps up to the southern reach of Atenia were guarded by pickets of royalists behind torches and lanterns. The expected lines of archers stood watch.

Silent as they observed from the safe vantage of an abandon shop's empty window after Bon broke the lock, they watched trios of knights escort units back and forth behind the line. Soon Haidra was able to follow the glow of their lights, somewhat surmising where they stopped or turned off in a different direction.

A half hour passed before Black John whispered. "Bon, Talic, and I will scout the canal. Moon, keep observing."

Neither sibling answered but Bon and Talic quickly fell in behind Black John as they retreated outside the side door.

"Psst."

Haidra furrowed her brow and glanced to the left, then the right.

"Psst."

She turned her head to the left and found Aleaus staring right at her. The blacksmith tipped her head up in acknowledgment.

"So, what are we doing here?" Aleaus asked.

New Moon answered before Haidra could, "Pardon?"

"I—" Aleaus silenced again as the three observed Bon and Talic scamper out of the adjoining alley toward the water. Fast to the edge, they stopped and scanned over the lower fencing, checking out both sides. Something caused Bon to jerk back. He signaled to Talic to follow, and they rushed to the safety of the shop and its dark, deep space, Black John not far behind as he appeared from around the corner.

"To me," the elder wraith called on his troops. "The royalists are trying to cross the Ursin to the east! We might catch them if we are quick!"

The ten filed out into the network of lanes before Black John broke them into a run. Weaving through, they stopped in a south facing outlet with a clear line of sight to the canal. High on the ledge of the opposing side a group of royalists had snuck down the slope, attempting to hide between a hedge and a row of buildings on the south bank. Carrying long, stout planks of bracketed wood, they slowly hauled the mobile bridge down the sidewalk for a point where the canal narrowed. Led by a knight without horse, a few carried pikes, but every single man had brought a longbow and quiver.

"Already infiltrating," New Moon said, following it up with an unknowable Arbikkean curse.

Black John motioned toward the three-story flats forming the alley's mouth, both having doors for side entrances. "Bon, I want you, Aleaus, Haidra, and Clive up on that roof," he said, pointing to the right. "Adan, Gurshin, and Ada are with me. Lay down suppressing fire on my signal. Kill the knight quickly before you worry about the rest. Moon, can you and Talic handle the bridge?"

"Think we can?" the sorceress asked the former guard.

"I'll follow you, my lady." He shrugged off his short bow and quiver before he drew his sword. "You lead, though."

New Moon laughed inside her hood. "Well, of course! I am a lady."

Not enthused by the banter, Black John's glower brought them to attention. "I'll signal the attack as well."

The sorceress sighed at her father. "No need. Just go."

Black John nodded to his son. The ax-slinger broke ahead, darting to the right side of the alley as his father went left. Wrapping her arm around her quiver so the arrows did not shake or rattle, Haidra hurried after Bon, behind the blacksmith and the older fisherman, who paused once to watch Clive enter behind the swordsman and disappear.

Bon paused at the door to the estate, flattened his palm against it, and spoke a quick series of words. Blue power, soft and hazing, pulsed from beneath his fingers. The lock on the other side of the entrance fell apart with a clatter of its wrought pieces. He forced the way into a short hallway which led to the thoroughfare of the complex. At the back was a rickety staircase to the upper floors, the hard bottoms of their boots creaking the loose boards. Rising to the third and highest level, the ax-slinger shoved open the unlocked roof hatch.

"String your bows and ready your arrows," he whispered. "Set up on the corner. Go!"

Stumbling as she cleared the top step, Haidra mimicked the rest and shrugged off her unassembled bow and quiver. Dropping the first at her feet, she gently placed the bundle of shafts to the side and retrieved the stave. Almost a foot shorter than the longbow she had struggled to draw on the palisade, its curve bent far easier with the help of her hands and a foot to anchor its low end. Hooking the bowstring, the arms bent inward as she looped the quiver back over her shoulder. Tiptoeing to the roof's flat southern edge, she knelt at the ledge beside Aleaus, ahead of everyone and at the ready.

A clatter caused them to look behind.

Bon tended to Clive, who had spilled all of his arrows on the ground. The wraith helped the poor boy gather them in an instant and nudged him forward. He knelt and whispered, his hands cupped together in front of his chest. A speck of dark red light blossomed in the pocket his palms. He blew on it once.

A small strain of green smoke lifted from the spark.

The illusion under his hood dismissed, he raised his eyes to Haidra, the glow of magic throbbing off his bearded chin. "When Black John calls, I'll throw this down at the target," he whispered to the three rebels. "Fire at whatever you see, duck back down, and nock your next arrow. Stay hidden unless I tell you to fire. Understood?"

Haidra nodded along with the blacksmith and the young fisherman, still heaving from his accident. Bon the Bloody knelt where he was, casting his gaze to the other roof in wait.

"For Marta!"

Black John appeared on the eastern side, wielding the same red evocation. Bon rose like his father and threw his spell down.

"For Marta," the ax-slinger roared.

Able to follow its path as she peeked over, Haidra caught the moment the fireballs slammed into the Atenian royalists crossing their portable bridge. The planks of bracketed wood caught, forcing the last few men off. They screamed as they plummeted into the water. The rest landed on the northern bank and scattered as Bon struck at their feet, the blast downing many of them.

"Bows!" Black John shouted.

"Bows!" Bon repeated.

Haidra sprang to her feet, raising her bow as she pulled back the arrow. Shocked by the little effort needed to align the shaft, she aimed at the burning men stumbling on her side of the canal. Aleaus loosed first, then her, followed by Clive after he righted himself. Three more flew from the adjacent roof.

Two of the royalists died, one toppling into the water after Haidra watched her arrow stick him. Too frantic to consider him anymore, she dropped hard to her ass and lay on her side behind the roof ledge.

Somewhere on the enemy side, horns blew over the growing fire's crack.

"Charge," Black John screamed into the alley between his and Bon's positions.

The familiar roar of the Burnt Lady split the night.

"Vengeance!" New Moon strode out of the alleyway, encased fully in the apparition of the infamous victim of the Veard's depravities. The illusion flung her blistered, desecrated arms about her head, a handful of her ruined hair grasped in both fists. She stomped forward, leaving footprints of flame in her wake. "Vengeance! Bhadran marches to eat your children!"

Rising behind the writhing, blazing woman towered a massive black bear. The standard of the Veards until the year Haidra was born, the beast of legend had roamed the wood in the east to the westward slopes of the glacier until a Veard chieftain befriended him, lumbered onto the embankment. He issued a bellowing roar as he stood upon his hind legs, clawing the air.

The royalists escaping the burning ruin froze in their tracks.

Capitalizing on their momentum, New Moon and Talic tore

into their disparate numbers. Stabbing her rapier into their faces and throats, she left survivors behind for the fading image of the bear to end by his sword. Bon leapt off the roof of their building. Landing with effortless grace, he went after his sister and her second.

"Abandon the roofs," Black John called over the crackling flames and dying foes. "Talic, grab that one!"

Talic hauled a prisoner away as Haidra popped to her feet with Aleaus and Clive. New Moon and Bon danced death among the remaining royalists. Killing the last, Bon the Bloody held the ground for his sister to leave first before he backed toward the alley with her.

"Retreat," Black John shouted. "Retreat!"

———

HAIDRA TURNED the corner in time to see Talic press the infantryman against the dingy wall, the edge of his sword on the man's throat. Black John loomed behind the former guard, staring down at the prisoner with his red eyes.

A royalist in an archer's gambeson, he clenched his tear-filled eyes shut and whimpered like a child. On closer examination Haidra saw he was only a few years older than her.

The other two wraiths and the rest filed into the empty alleyway, down the hill and in safer territory. The Children of Marta stood away, giving the swordsman and Talic room.

"Stop crying," Black John told the whimpering royalist. "We will not kill you, boy. Boy! Open your mouth and breath."

"Wait a second…"

One of the new faces, the honey-haired woman known as Ada leaned forward and peered at the prisoner in the darkness. She padded forward a bit, her eyes widening as she did. "Brotha? Brotha, is that you?"

The royalist slowly opened his eyes. "Aunt Ada?" Confusion

turned into recognition and relief, then desperation. "Aunt Ada! Please! Please help me! Please don't let them kill me!"

Ada rushed forward, putting herself between Talic and her whimpering nephew. "Stop it! Stop it! That's my sister's son!"

"Let him go," Black John said to Talic. The old man complied, happy to sheathe his sword.

Ada gathered the royalist in her lap and nursed the braying man against her, cradling him like a babe.

"Psst."

Haidra checked over her right shoulder to find Aleaus behind her.

The blacksmith, into her forties and wet with sweat, gave her a small nod.

She nodded back. "You wanted to ask me something?"

"Oh, right," she said. "Don't worry about it. I think I found out." She nodded at Black John. "See that sword?"

Haidra looked to the longsword belted at the tall wraith's side. Its waisted hilt forged of a bronzed steel ending in a hollowed, heavy ring, the diamond-sectioned cross ended in oak-leafed foils. Elegant as it was functional, the kingly blade fit naturally to its shadowy wielder.

"I've seen that sword before. All metalworkers in Atenia have," Aleaus whispered.

Haidra took stock of who stood around her. The wraiths circled Ada and the prisoner, guarding as much as they contained, while others had found spots to lean on either side. Exhausted by the adrenaline and a pounding chase spanning minutes, each second had been a year to the nerves.

Only she and Aleaus could hear each other, or the others were too tired to focus on anything else than the emotional center of the moment.

"You've seen his face, haven't you?" Aleaus asked.

The face on her father's coin.

"I don't know," Haidra said, almost protective of her foreknowledge. "I don't know anything about what happened. I was little. None of us grew up knowing what he looked like. I wouldn't know."

"Probably right," said Aleaus, distant. "It was a hard choice."

"What was?"

"Abandoning the idea. Who he was. Who we thought they all were."

"The Veards?"

"The goddamn Veards. Rapists and thieves with means," Aleaus breathed in a sing-song Haidra had heard so many times growing up but never understood. "Better hope it's not him."

"Why not?" Haidra asked. "Why does that matter?"

"Because Haidra," she said, "some people in this world think it's a person who is responsible for what they do, or what happens to them. Others think it's the fault of those who raised and kept them. The old nature-nurture, but who really knows? What causes one to kill or steal? What makes men violate and women hide it? What's true?" She let out a long exhalation through her nose, thin lips pressed in a hard line. "But nobody wants to remember what really happened. Who we were before all this. Why we let it go sidewise. It's easier for him to be dead."

"Do you hope he is?"

Aleaus mulled the question but never answered.

Ada had calmed Brotha, coaxing the lad to speak after regaining his breath. "I swear, no one will harm you if you come with us," she said to the side of his head, her arms still tight around his neck and shoulders. "You don't have to be scared of them or us, nephew. I swear it."

Lips quivering, the young soldier gazed up at the hidden face of Black John, eyes wide in horror.

The wraith spoke, his droning voice gentle despite the darkness inflicting every word. "Your aunt is right, soldier. You don't even have to come with us. We will escort you to Entaris and let you go over to your comrades. I'm sure they will be lenient after you give them an explanation. Either way, we will not harm you. But you can make a better choice: Tell us what you were doing tonight and where the others are planning to cross."

"But I'd be betra—"

"It's not betraying anyone to allow innocent people to remain alive," Black John interrupted. "The only way I can do that is by taking away the opportunity from the queen-regent to fire on us downhill—on your people. What's your greater duty, son: to Atenia's crown or her people?"

"By the gods," Aleaus commented to Haidra under her breath. "Let's hope."

The royalist guard gave up his loyalty and the movement of the queen-regent's artillery for a chance to leave with his aunt.

Later, as the wraiths and their dark troop marched downhill, new volunteers in the rebellion heard the whispers of what had happened at the Ursin, of what had been done, and spun their own tales. The next day, after a much needed sleep in their new cots, those chosen awoke as the Ghosts of Solomon, named for a damnable past many hoped would have justice brought to it.

# 3

# BRIDGES

The first sorties on the banks of the Ursin Canal began when the royalists pressed on Entaris Bridge at dawn. Pikes led the advance under silver horn calls, backed by a line of knights in fresh, gleaming armor to inspire their resolve. Archers lay in wait behind them, clustered in banks one could only see from the bridge when approaching the south-rising slope.

Aron met them with his infantry's long spears, broad-headed and tearing compared to the sharp, narrow points of the Atenians. No horse followed, but behind them came uniquely armored dervish dancers, all chains and blue ribbons, flashing long, thin blades that curved and wrapped like whips attached to glittering staves. They hopped and spun in place, always behind the pikes in eager wait.

The two sides edged toward the other until lances touched.

A fury of stabbing commenced, useless thanks to the brave soldiers on both sides wielding man-sized shields to defend their fellows. They came together, bashed and batted, and came apart four times before the royalists sounded for the artillery.

From the south side of the Ursin a volley of arrows flew up

from hidden positions, centered on the Arbikkeans. The skirmish shields proved effective, allowing the fighters in the back places to hide while those at the front continued to fight. As soon as the Atenian rain ended the forces of Toliv signaled their return.

Shocking the royalist on the bridge who braced for the showers of arrowheads, the artillery from the north aimed their mangonels on these hidden pockets of archers behind the enemy line. Dropping large chunks of rock dug from the foothills of the Veardens, chaos spread from the rear to the knights leading at Entaris Bridge, forcing a halt to restore discipline. Great cries followed in the distance as frantic horn signals were blown.

The Arbikkean pike pressed again. This time the invaders scored on the royalists, an infantryman downed by a thrust through his unprotected throat. The sight of blood stoked the monsters in all men. Both sides unleashed their full furies. Lances stung as dead fell upon the pavement, leaking over the sides of the bridge and staining the Ursin crimson.

Daring greater acts of savagery, those who lost their pikes drew swords and dove under the mass of poles, crawling ahead in mad abandon. Soldiers from both sides grappled upon meeting, wrestling until one fell atop the other, piercing or slashing whatever they could, before crawling to the next opponent if they weren't skewered by an observant pikeman.

Unassisted by the certainty of suppressing fire to support their position, the royalists dug their heels. The Arbikkeans peppered them with arrow fire from the rooftops of empty estates and warehouses, but the knights' leadership and the defender's toughness did little to shift the engagements.

The opposing forces skirmished six times over Entaris Bridge in the first few hours before noon arrived. In the lulls the Arbikkeans sent special teams of runners, unarmed and in white turbans to designate their nonviolent intentions, to remove their dead and injured. To the invader's vocal disgust, the Atenians did not make the same effort.

The reason why was revealed when a white-robed figure appeared at the front of the Atenian pikes. One of Nikon's sorcerers intoned high on the winds whipping cold across Ben-Lomen's glacier, his voice carrying.

To the horror of everyone watching, the corpses on Entaris Bridge combusted. They burned for hours past sunset, the white and blue flames diminishing sometime before midnight. The next morning those corpses still smoked within their magical conflagrations. Any attempt to pour water on them or smother the endless heat failed, refueling them, often leaving those who attempted with horrible injuries to their arms and hands. Many attempts trying to provide dignity to the fallen ended up in the medical tents right beside the war-wounded.

Unable to cross the burning field, the two sides relegated themselves to useless arrow fire. An attempt was made in the western reach of the city at Victus Crossing, but the result repeated.

The royalists' magic ground the Arbikkeans and rebels to a halt.

———

"Psst."

Shoulders burning from hard sword-swings minutes earlier at a pell, Haidra looked up from her view of the canal at Aleaus. Back from Talic's breakfast fire in a nearby alley, the blacksmith offered a small plate of toasted bread smeared with a soft, tangy cheese and a cup of black tea. The sight of food issued a low, rumbling cry from her stomach, which made the older woman smile.

"Something for those weary arms?"

Accepting them before her stomach growled again, Haidra

sat beside her new friend and watched the royalist troops transfer new detachments along the Ursin's high sidewalks, running to and fro to avoid arrows everyone knew weren't going to be wasted. The tea tasted deep and thick, almost too smoky if it didn't provide the hot, soothing warmth to ease the dryness in her throat. Haidra took small bites of the toast, the substantial slice filling with every chewy mouthful.

"I keep seeing Black John go out with Prince Aron a lot, just by themselves," said Aleaus, nursing her cup. "Think we're moving soon?"

"I hope not," Haidra said, staring down into her own tannin sea. The steam off the top obscured her elongated reflection but captured the clouds scattering across the warming sky. Around a campfire dotting one of the forward camps on Lilias Road, the lowermost boundary of Atenia's northwestern districts that included the temples at Hernos' Court, Horras-Glory markets, and the surrounding bazaars, they rested after a hard morning on one of the newly established training yards. The warehouse quarter provided headquarters for the Arbikkeans and Children of Marta, as well as ample space to toil in wait for whatever orders arrived, if any with the continuing standstill at the Ursin.

Outside of an old smokehouse, they finished their breakfast while watching the growing throng course around them. On the makeshift training pitch Arbikkean commanders cursed their Torsii translators, who in turn were cursed by the rebels not understanding anything anyone else was saying on the topic of swordsmanship. Already one or two of the men on both sides of the dynamic had bowed up, chest to chest and face to face, before cooler heads ended it.

"Think we should get over there and have them yell at us some more?" Haidra asked, the experience at the gatehouse still fresh in her mind. "We maybe should. Might help later."

"I think we showed our proficiency at the gates and no smart-mouth is telling me otherwise," the blacksmith answered, taking another dose of tea to finish the cup. She licked her yellow teeth. "And I don't want to carry a pike. You?"

"No," Haidra answered, scoffing at the ludicrous notion though she thought nothing less of those who did. Shoving the last bit of crust into her mouth, she watched anyone who listened follow their instructor's lessons on the sword. Interested in the weapon the wraiths had provided her earlier in the day, she paid keen interest to a desert infantryman practicing on a pell. The way he stepped into his strike hypnotized her after a while, the edge of his scimitar to the target before he stepped out to parry the invisible repost. Almost meditative, she studied the movements until her mind wandered to other things.

"Can I ask you something, Aleaus?" Haidra asked.

"Sure, kid," the older woman replied, setting her cup on a retaining log around the fire. "Don't have anything else to do."

"You knew my father. I know why he did all this. Why are you?"

"Same reasons he probably gave you. Same reasons you gave us a few mornings ago," she responded after a thoughtful pause. "My husband died in the last worker riots a few years back with the famine. He delivered carts of food every day and not a coin he earned could pay for the healer he needed for his lung-sickness, but those lords and ladies could afford to keep him working. He died hard, right in my arms." Aleaus bit the inner edge of her lip and shrugged. "I got tired, too."

Haidra hummed in understanding. "A few nights ago on the roof, when you said it was better that Black John was not who you hope he isn't—why?"

"You got a lot of *whys*, Haidra."

"I have a lot of questions."

"Some things are best left unsolved, then." She gazed back, her focus somewhere else other than Haidra, but deeply rooted with her at the same time. "It's just hard. What if someone murdered your daddy and you saw them do it?"

The question irked Haidra. "I did see them do it."

"I'm sorry, dear, I didn't—" Aleaus sighed and waved whatever else away, her expression aggravated. "You saw what you say. You were there. Arverin is dead, and there's no question what happened. The guard killed dissenters all the time, they just did it behind our backs when we were too tired to look, or too worn to care. Did it before the Children and will keep doing it if they come out of this on top. But that's easy. Arverin worked against the crown, the crown killed him, and here we are. Easy. What lead us here isn't."

"The accusation."

"Aye, that *accusation*." Aleaus spoke the word with heavy irony. "Who knows? Who's to say that the prince we don't talk about didn't do it? It wouldn't be the first time a man did something awful or for everyone to say nothing and look away. The guard does worse to us, after all, and not a speck of royal blood is in them."

Sighing at a well-worn truth, Haidra knew the validity of everything Aleaus said. Growing up as the only daughter of a single father in the midst of poverty and corruption, she had learned long before her first blood how to measure every man she met, whether what they held in their eyes and actions promised peace or harm. The fear of it had been so severe her father had forbidden her from the company of other boys in her neighborhood, but given the risks lived every day in Low Corner, few ever paid her much attention to worry over it.

"But what if he didn't?" Aleaus asked, almost whispering the question.

Haidra shrugged in confusion. "Then he'd be innocent?"

"No, no, girl, think! It'd mean all of this since old Solomon was a lie. Tobias, Fransica's regency, the brutality they paid us building their wealth and opulence—all built on the idea someone had done her wrong and to make it right we said nothing as she ruined Atenia. What's worse? The truth of her claims, or the possibility your daddy died over a lie? Think about what it would mean for us women. Never get a word in again that mattered, truth or not."

"Everyone would suffer it."

"Everyone's suffering it right now. What we're not dealing with are the rules."

"And those are?"

"Gods if I know." Aleaus combed her uneven salt-and-pepper bangs out of her eyes. "I was lucky to find a good one and not have to worry it unlike Fransica considering the devil she beds. But if someone told me my Lirik had done to someone what Fransica said happened to her, I wouldn't know what to think. I don't think any of us do, still."

"Do *we* even want to?" Haidra echoed, as much to herself as the blacksmith.

"Aye," said Aleaus. "Now you get it."

Before the conversation continued Talic walked up to their fire, his mail tinkling with every step. He wore it and the Atenian helmet with its outward sweeping cheek guards like a true veteran, any evidence of age cast off the soldier before them. Surprised at the transformation made from the old man she rode beside to the southern fields, Haidra was glad to still find kindness in those gray eyes.

"Black John wants us," Talic said in his gentle voice. "Ada's gone."

"What do you mean 'she's gone?'" Aleaus rose first, putting aside her cup. "She was the first to volunteer!"

"Changed her mind after she found Brotha. Boy's quitting the royals but not joining up, and she's feeling different about it all now there's someone alive."

Haidra dusted the front of her leggings then stood, letting the skirts of her mail shirt fall about her knees. She laid her teacup down for the sword beside it. "Makes sense. I'm sure the rest of you have someone somewhere in this city." She sighed hard as she belted it on like New Moon had taught her. Their quiet caused her to raise her eyes from the knot she tied, curious by their silences. "Don't you?"

"Not me." Talic glanced to Aleaus. "You?"

The blacksmith shook her head as the three started toward a tent closer to the camp's center, its white star banner snapping in the morning wind. "No, not me. I think all Adan and Clive are all each other have. I know Gurshin's a widower, too."

"Shit," cursed Talic. "I guess that's why we're here, isn't it?"

The blacksmith grumbled at his response, which Haidra understood when she remembered why she was there, and the things she had already done. Left with nothing, those like her, Aleaus, Talic, and the others had simply shown up and not died, which she learned was valued in battle more than anything—until that value vanished upon the field, in an alley, or on some bridge. Finished girding her sword and herself with these those grim musings, she joined the two older ghosts in a brisk march, eager to do more than wait in a camp before another decision was made about her fate.

Outside of Prince Aron's blue-and-white checkered tent, the three wraiths stood together with Adan and his son Clive, as well as Gurshin. The five turned on the three, the rebels waving to their comrades. Reunited, Black John motioned toward an empty paddock nearby, the horses already taken for the day's duties.

Unlike other times, the swordsman did not raise the illusion to hide his face, letting his hood cover his head and most of his nose. He spoke through a fine mouth bordered by a thick mustache and beard, combed to a simple fall. "We're splitting up tonight. Bon, New Moon, and Haidra will sneak across the Ursin to the royalists' camp set up on the low side of Gharm Hill. We have reason to believe the sorcerer assigned to Victus Crossing is there. He's to be dealt with."

He shifted his head in his children's direction.

They returned a solemn nod. Haidra stared, surprised she had been chosen for such a task, and less than thrilled about fresh danger. The drive to include herself, to take part in determining her days, dulled in an instant. She considered probing the question of why she had been chosen but an ineffable hesitation held her words. Whatever they had meant to say, they were replaced by flashes of Arverin's face. Vexed and brow furrowed, she warred with the notion of *wanting to be chosen*.

Black John failed to notice her awkward expression. "The rest will join me on the north side of Victus with Aron's troops. Once we know the sorcerer there has been dealt with, I will lead the charge."

"And then?" Gurshin asked, a man of medium height but strong, thick proportions. The expression on his pockmarked face intense, he bowed his head and leaned in Black John's direction. "What happens then?"

"We'll know when it's over," the tall wraith answered.

4

FASTER, FASTER

New Moon patted Haidra's shoulder. "Go!"

Head down, she ran out of the alley for the fencing between her and the canal. The two wraiths followed at her back. The throat of her sword's full scabbard held to her left side, her bow and quiver of arrows clutched tightly in the right, she tried to steady her breath as she closed on the barrier.

Adrenaline and fear pushed everything else away as Haidra jumped as high as she could.

Both feet cleared the iron barrier. Landing hard with a jangle of her mail and the smack of her boot soles, the momentum carried her forward. Faster than her in full armor, Bon and New Moon blew past her and leapt the canal. They crossed in a single bound and halted to wait for her.

Determined not to be the weak link, Haidra willed herself to run harder. Bile bubbling at the back of her throat after an ill-timed meal, she jumped a second time. The air rushed under her hood to blow it back, and surprised, she pulled her attention away as her feet caught mid-sole on the embankment's concrete lip. The sudden sense of falling was stopped when Bon and New

Moon snatched the front of her cloak and hauled her onto solid ground.

"Keep going," New Moon said in a hushed whisper, ushering her toward an access stair that climbed up the stone walls keeping them from Gharm Hill. The lower side of Atenia's wealthy quarter, a high retaining wall over the Ursin Canal separated the different worlds of north and south, poor and rich. Along it pairs of guards patrolled in constant rotations.

Pitch black by the molding water, the two wraiths and their ghost ascended slowly, rising to the first bluff. Wedging themselves through a hedgerow to avoid a checkpoint, they penetrated a small alley behind a series of lavish townhomes facing the water. A small path led to the allotments in the back. They sheltered in one of the overgrown yards, safe for the moment in its perfumed lot.

Bon extracted a square of vellum from the secret folds of his cloak. "Gimme some light, Moon."

The sorceress muttered an arcane word and snapped her armored finger and thumb together. The latter caught a sudden flame, bright yellow as it revealed the lines of the freshly drawn map in Bon's hands. Scrawled in firm strokes, a red line through blocks of the neighborhood ended at a base circled red in the west.

"The sorcerer has been seen with at least three knights, so it will be safe to assume they'll be close when we get there. He'll probably have archers and guards locking down the site, too."

"Probably?" New Moon teased. "I can't use the Burnt Lady anymore and Ursin won't do."

"Well, Dad yelled at you," Bon said, teasing back.

New Moon tapped the space south of their target, less amused. "Let's go in here."

"The deeper we go the more royalists there are," Bon replied. "Let's go from the northeast. We can run the roofs and provide a distraction while Haidra does it."

"Does what?" Haidra asked. "What am I doing?"

"You're going to take care of the sorcerer," Bon said. "He should be asleep."

"Are you all right doing this, Haidra?" New Moon questioned, more concerned than doubtful.

Haidra exchanged glances with the two wraiths. "I guess I don't have a choice."

"She's got it," Bon said to New Moon. He folded the map back up and replaced it in its hidden compartment, next drawing out the dagger she had used to kill Lerrod. Flipping it over in his steely fingers, he offered its cleaned hilt to Haidra. "Here. Better than a sword."

"Right," Haidra said as she accepted the old tool. The silken press of its point through Lerrod's chest woke the night in her head, but she didn't hesitate. "Right."

New Moon wrapped her gloved fingers about her thumb, killing the magical flame. "Little more time to catch our breaths and we'll go."

Bon led the way, taking the underpasses of the high streets in Gharm Hill. Under flowered bridges connecting row-home neighborhoods with cellar duplexes that housed the wealthiest among the Oyster Bazaar, the hub of commerce, culture, and trade for all of Atenia. Many born in Low Corner dreamed of walking the pristine streets, but running them in the dead of night, sucking the cold air of their emptiness, Haidra found them to be like the rest of the world she knew, consumed by conflict.

The three hid in a garden and two alleys to avoid patrols before they reached the point Gharm Hill met the retaining wall running west to east as its avenues opened for Victus Crossing.

The royalist's forward post was exactly in the spot Bon's map predicted it would be, barricaded by a small fence of broken spears. Established in a spacious square, snipers perched on the corners of the surrounding roofs while infantry circuited the grounds, always passing outside the entrance of the red-and-white striped tent in the camp's center. Four guards sat before its flap on little stools, warming their hands in the light of a small brazier.

Crouched behind the fence of a bridge overlooking a walking path to the square, the two wraiths and Haidra counted their number in the fifties.

"So, no Burnt Lady, huh?" Bon whispered.

"He didn't yell," New Moon said, kneeling to the right of him. "And he liked Ursin."

"They'll pin me up with arrows if I walk in like Ursin," the ax-slinger said dryly.

"I've an idea," New Moon said in accented Torsii. "Clear those snipers. I have something Haidra can use to get into the tent, but once she's in there I'll give a count to a minute. After that, I'll cause a distraction." She looked to Haidra. "And you get out of there."

"We're all splitting or are we meeting someplace?" Bon asked.

"Probably have to play it by ear," his sister said.

The ax-slinger shouldered his double-edged weapon and sighed before he took a step back and headed north, along one of the sidewalks. New Moon and Haidra continued their observation of the camp, searching for any gap or space to penetrate the defenses.

"So, how are they not going to see me?" Haidra found the nerve to ask. "I can't just walk in there."

"Oh, yes, you can," New Moon said.

The sorceress pulled open her cloak and poked through a series of hidden pockets sewn on its inside, her armored fingers deft in the flaps used to secure her load of trinkets, bottles, and components to spells. Out of one specific pocket near her left armpit she pulled a small bottle of cobalt glass, corked and sealed in purple wax. The top was stamped with the same white star that flew on the sky-blue banners of Prince Aron.

"When we're ready I want you to drink this. It's going to taste terrible, but it will do the job," she said, handing the potion to Haidra.

"What will it do?" she asked, palming the little blue bottle in her bare right hand. The glass cold, the wax seemed too thick around the cork. She feared having to use her teeth without knowing what would end up in her mouth.

"It's a potion of invisibility. Aron brewed it in case of emergencies." She favored the bottle Haidra held with a small smile. "He'd be furious if he knew I was using it this way, but the situation calls. Also, he's a prince—he can afford me the ingredients to make another."

"Are you sure you don't want to use it?"

"Do you want to let the guard chase you and I go into the tent?"

Haidra shut her hand to a fist and put the bottle to her chest. "No, Moon. No, I don't."

Minutes passed as new units of infantry rotated through the perimeter, always armed with pikes. The boys in the stools dozed in the firelight.

"So," New Moon said in the silence. "My brother and you get along."

The observation froze Haidra on the spot.

"I can ask him to leave you alone, if you want," she continued. "I'd understand if you wanted to be left alone."

"Why?" Haidra asked, confused on many fronts.

The question to the question caused New Moon to turn her head in Haidra's direction. Her beautiful, narrow face pointed to a delicate chin, her rich cheeks and smooth forehead framed the hazel eyes she shared with her brother, but infused with deeper, more luxurious lines of gold and brass. Yet, they were sadder, sharper, so keen Haidra could not help but feel the sorceress measuring her in ways beyond current comprehension. Only two years older than Haidra, great gulfs of knowledge and experience separated them.

"I thought that with the death of your father you would not want men prying your attention," New Moon answered. "I'm sorry if I misinterpreted."

Haidra studied the sorceress a second longer before she checked ahead again. None of the snipers had moved. "Is your brother trying to get my attention?"

New Moon chuckled. "He doesn't open up easily. Never has."

"Why?"

"Why what?"

"Why me?" Haidra asked. "What makes me so special?"

"I don't know what makes a man's eye catch to one star versus another, but…" The sorceress sighed on the question. "You've lost something. Someone. I think that makes you easy to understand."

"Doesn't that mean you lost someone, too?" Haidra rebounded. The idea that she and the rest of the ghosts had been selected simply for their lack of family and no risk of deeper loss, at once mean and reducing them down to fodder, tore away to expose a far different possibility. "You're brother and sister, after all."

"But, unlike Bon, I'm not alone." New Moon's attention raised to something out of view.

Following her eyes, Haidra looked in time to see one of the snipers on a nearby roof jerk back, consumed by a sudden patch of darkness. No screams, no clatters to break the night, Bon appeared in an instant, his ax bared.

In the next blink he was gone.

"Don't stop going until you're inside that tent," New Moon said. "Get the cap off!"

Heart racing, Haidra remembered the potion. She used her left finger and thumb to break the blue wax. It crumbled under the pressure and the cork slipped free. The liquid sloshed inside, a few drips escaping the minute mouth and landing on her knuckles. Trying to keep the bottle steady and track the snipers, both tasks seemed at odds until New Moon's hand clapped her right shoulder.

"Now," the sorceress said, hurried and hush. "Drink it and go!"

Haidra lurched forward as she put the potion to her mouth and slugged it back. It came out, sweet, syrupy, but with a heavy medicinal flavor on the back of her tongue before she swallowed. Out in the open, she spotted the guards ahead at the barricade. None scanning the corner of the rooftops surrounding the square, she almost laughed aloud when not a single sniper remained. She sped across the pavement, her boots knocking loud.

One of the sentries at the fence looked in her direction. "You hear that?"

Haidra slowed to a stop.

"Just our lord inside his tent," one of the seated guards beyond him said. "I heard it."

"It sounded like boots," another man said.

Shocked none of them saw her, Haidra viewed her hands. Completely invisible, not even her own eyes found any discernible outline or shape in the space of night.

"Well, I don't hear anything," one of the royalists voiced. "Can I get back to my snooze?"

Haidra paced forward at a steady clip, slower than before, but passed by the two sentries at the fence, walked around the four men in front of the tent, and ducked the flap with little noise. Not a single man had seen or sensed her.

Ensconced within a cloth chamber supported by a central pillar and retractable roof grid, the candles within the tent cast a cozy illumination. A small table in one of the corners was heaped in correspondence and a large map of Atenia.

Atop the mess the sorcerer slept, face down in the letters as a simple wooden chair supported his forward lean.

Golden-skinned like Haidra, with soft brown hair cut close to his scalp, he snored loudly as drool seeped from the corner of his mouth. His dragon mask on the floor where it had fallen, the white snout gleamed a dull orange. Haidra clutched the dagger Bon had given her, her right knuckles tight as she squeezed.

No emotion crossed her face as she stepped behind the sleeping man, fixed on the back of his unprotected skull. With strange effort, she reversed the weapon for an easier strike, an icepick grip.

Who was this man? She glanced to the mask on the floor a second time. Fanged, horned, and scaled, it glared in silent warning.

He didn't kill her father. A knight had, and who knew if she would see that bastard again in this life? Royalist or not, this man was an Atenian like her. How had they ended up here?

The royalist sorcerer stirred on his desk. Posting on his hands, he lifted his nose off his table. Haidra looked down at the dagger in her hands, which had reappeared, full and fleshed. She gasped when he raised and twisted around.

She launched toward him, the point of the dagger in the right side of his neck while she grabbed his left wrist with her free hand. The point sunk, inches of clean steel driven deep. The sorcerer jerked, a mortal spasm that shuddered through the hilt. Haidra pulled him off his seat and flung his stumbling body onto the flagstones. The blade tore free, another ghastly wound.

One hand out to protect himself, the sorcerer grasped his bleeding neck with the other, already whispering a spell.

Haidra knocked the offending limb away and stabbed his back, ribs, and neck, scoring hits each time. She thrust into his temple twice before he fell limp completely, legs shaking under her. Blood flowed everywhere, hot and iron-smelling.

Sick and exhaustion grabbed hold, the dump of adrenaline

brought a swoon. She heaved atop the dead, trying to steady the tremor in her body.

"Ben-Loman's spew, what the fuck are those things?" one of the guards shouted.

"Holy—move! Move!"

Pealing screeches erupted throughout the camp. Awoken to the fact the sorcerer's warm blood soaked through the leggings covering her knees to the shin, Haidra rose with a disgusted half-moan. The man's life ran into the front of her boots, her skin crawling as she limped through the gross cascade between her toes.

At the flap, she lifted the left half high to the side.

Gigantic serpents slithered everywhere as clusters of infantry attempted to press them into the square's corners. One group of five had broken off from the rest and attacked New Moon. The sorceress flipped over the shining barbs of their spears, launching onto the shoulder of one man. Atop of him like an acrobat, she slashed down at the royalists around her, opening heads and blinding eyes. She skipped behind their knot, turning on the spot to skewer one of them through the back.

Haidra stepped out of the tent, gory dagger in hand.

One of the snakes, scaled in pale plates of armor running the entire length of its body, hissed its fangs and screeched as three spears rammed under its chin. Shedding no blood, the serpent exploded in strobing light. Her vision stolen in a brief second, it came back in time to see a black shape run to her from the right.

Bon jerked Haidra alongside him, headed for the square's northern exit.

Another dying screech preceded the next set of flashes, stretching their silhouettes ahead of them. Desperate to keep her feet beneath her, Haidra allowed the wraith to lead them deeper into the city's oppressive midnight. They dodged briefly to the east, into the alleys, then north again at a headlong sprint.

Emerging on the southern bank of the canal, the royalists blasted their signal horns behind them.

Others answered, close to their position.

"There!"

On one of the high streets an archer pointed his short sword at Haidra and Bon.

Bon shoved her ahead of him, putting his body between her and the royalist. Bowstrings twanged. An arrow zipped over his shoulder, slicing a rent in his cloak.

Haidra ran for the high ledge overlooking the canal's black flow and leapt. By Crook's hand she landed hard on the other side. She tumbled onto her chest and stomach with smacking force, lucky to miss her chin or face. Crawling until her hands and knees were under her, she dared to look back.

Bon leapt the edge of the retaining wall, his cloak full of arrows. He fell short, splashing into the water at the bank's edge. His ax smacked the side, ringing as he disappeared into the murk.

The royalist archers mounted the top of the wall.

Haidra flew headlong for the water, diving forward to get her arms in the Ursin's cold flow. Bon had already popped up, gasping, and caught one of her hands. The archers fired from their high position, their shafts clattering in the unlit darkness.

She pulled with all her might, hauling the wraith's heavy weight out with his help. Dripping wet, he stumbled to his ax and retrieved it. Blood dripped from within his hood, and he staggered. Haidra ducked under his left arm, her right wrapped around his strong midsection, and hurried them as fast as she could.

A second volley of shafts struck, scattering around their feet.

"Move, Bon," she yelled at him. "Come on! Come on!"

Able to walk on his own strength, they cleared the block and turned into a barn at an empty horse market, somewhere in the warehouse district. Slipping inside, Haidra pushed on the door and leaned, her back braced against it.

"We need to—" Bon slumped against the door and slid down, breathless from exhaustion.

"Do that—" Haidra caught her breath in the complete darkness. "Can you light your thumb?"

He laughed lightly at the question and whispered the words she had heard New Moon say earlier. Flame wrapped his thumb, the light banishing shadow to reveal the green paint of the doors and the yellow hay under them, dry and dusty, all the way to the empty stalls in the back. Long out of use, manure had hardened on the packed dirt floor, reduced to a sweet, subtle earthiness.

Bon groaned as he braced. "I think Moon got away. I saw her running as I tore past you," he said in a low, nasal tone.

"Moon?" Haidra asked, the next wave of exhaustion arriving. The sight of his bloody nose kept her awake. "Let me look at you."

"Why?"

"You're bleeding." Not giving him time or space to argue, Haidra dropped to her knees and pressed her hands into his hood. She lifted it off his mane of honey hair. Red ran from Bon's left nostril in a gelled mess, mixing in the hairs of his mustache and beard on the left side. The bridge unbroken, neither of the high cheeks to match his sister's had swelled. His face, warm to her touch, was smooth as she pressed her thumb along his nose.

"I'm okay," he said, wincing. "It's just blood."

The kind note in his voice, the manliness of his response elicited a thrill in Haidra. In the next second she touched her forehead to his, their eyes open to each other and nothing else. They shut them to center on the delight of their lips as they met.

"Hey," he said when he broke away to breathe. Red smudged his cheek.

"What?" she asked, the same warmth on hers. "It's just blood."

———————

Bon and Haidra arrived not long after New Moon reported their success. The pair, close together as they wove through the camp bustling in the dim hours of the morning, entered Prince Aron's tent to find the sorceress, Black John, and their benefactor pouring over the map of Gharm Hill and the greater High Hill region quarter of the city. The bridge of Victus Crossing pinned by a bronze casting of a griffin clawing forward, it faced the south, up the ascent.

In the corner of the tent sat the bard Valen, playing a gentle melody on his lute. He paid no attention to the proceedings, his full focus to his songs.

"There wasn't any great resistance we met," New Moon said, her hood pulled back to free her blazing white hair. She leaned forward by Aron's side, a slim, mailed arm over her lover's shoulders. She pointed a taloned finger at the renderings of Victus Crossing and Entaris Bridge, tapping the former hard. "They were only playing at pickets. I think they expected to keep us with the sorcerer lighting the dead."

Valen's playing remained smooth, the melody steady.

"Niklon's cultists won't be eager to come out today for war," Aron said. Once more in his steel and leather riding harness, his curved sword hung from the side of a jeweled, glittering girdle. His brow knit in thought. "We can push now. I can call forces."

The tempo increased, the notes reverberating as the bard plucked.

"Do it," said Black John, cold behind his demonic guise. Haidra wondered, as he surveyed the map from his upright and ridged stance, what she would do when he found out about her and Bon. Beside his son, who watched with quiet concern, she questioned what happened there as well.

Not her first kiss, but definitely the best, its buzz had yet to wear off.

"Where are we pushing?" Aron ripped a pair of fine leather riding gloves hung from the top edge of his girdle and inserted his strong hands in their sleeves. "Entaris Bridge is easier to get my riders through, but I would understand if you wanted them at Victus."

The bard's tune carried, strong and charging.

"No…" Black John kept to the map. "No, I want them at Entaris. My troop and I will rally the forces at Victus. I need you to make it look like the pressure is down the center on Idrian, but if this works, we can have Gharm Hill and a cleaner firing position for the citadel by this evening. Take Moon with you. She can assist with her illusions."

"Oh, now they're fine," New Moon said in a chiding tone.

"Nothing revealing," Black John responded.

"Come, love," Aron said to the sorceress, taking her gauntleted hand in his gloved one. "Let's go yell at Yamil about making room in his tactics for your immaculate art. John, Valen, with me."

The wraith and his ally gave each other curt nods of assurance. The bard ceased his playing, leaving his lute by the stool, picking up a flanged mace on a side table by the tent flap as he waited on his liege.

"Finally, someone speaks to my station!" the sorceress said to her prince but stopped beside her father. No words, no final goodbyes. Instead, New Moon laid her hand over his heart. His hand over hers in response, they parted. On the way out she spotted Haidra and Bon, as well as the matching smears on their faces.

She looked at Haidra for an extra second, her smile growing in each passing step.

"Eww," she said loudly as she and the prince passed them.

Black John cleared his throat.

Her attention returned to Bon, who popped his brows, deadpan as he addressed his father. "I'll have the ghosts ready in a few," he said, at ease no matter the evidence on his and Haidra's faces. "Pikes?"

"Pikes," Black John answered after a beat. "Put Aleaus, Haidra, and Clive behind the shields. The rest of us will do the other work."

"She did well. Haidra," Bon said. "Walked right into the tent and did in Niklon's man. We all did well."

"I know," Black John said as he faced them and paused.

And paused.

"Huh." The wraith's burning gaze centered on his son. Then her. "Huh."

"Father..."

"You're both injured," Black John replied. "Go get checked by the medic and get cleaned up."

5

# OF HONOR

Haidra laughed at Black John's lack of concern until the royalist formation marched toward her, understanding fully why he hadn't taken the time to address her and Bon's shared smudge. The edges on their spears glinted in the morning light, pointed at her, her face, her heart.

They did not stop no matter how many times she wished, trembling behind the tall, thick slab of iron-backed oak they had called a "shield." A curtain of chain pinned to its stout corners, there *in case* one broke through, jangled in her face as she tried to peek around it. Behind her, hundreds of rebels and Arbikkeans pushed, their long pikes rested atop of the responsibility she held up.

To her right braced Aleaus and, to the left, the fisherman's son Clive. Lined up alongside their fellow rebels and Arbikkean allies, they provided the foundation to the advance over Victus Crossing.

The Atenian royalists were already arrayed when they arrived, spears at the front and only the knights to command the rear. Conspicuous in their absence, no archers lined the Ursin Canal's high retaining wall.

"Forward," Black John bellowed behind Haidra.

The wraith stood amid the pikers cobbled from the Children of Marta, swollen from their hundreds to tens of thousands of new volunteers in the preceding days after their victory, armed and armored in steel gifted by their foreign allies. He brandished his longsword upon his shoulder, its hilt gleaming bright as dawn crested the Veards on a cold morning. Bon waited beside his father, black ax foisted as his black coverings writhed and smoked.

The rebel pikers pressed in behind her, taking a full step. The royalists responded.

Every order brought their points closer and closer, until wielders on both sides thought themselves close to brave decisive hits. Faces tore and throats were pierced as wood batted back and forth, back and forth, a cacophony of mistiming in the chaos of death-curdling screams.

"Holy shit, holy shit, holy shit," Clive, short and skinny, shrieked in his cracking voice. "Stop! Stop! Stop!"

Haidra could only hunker down and pray Crook spared her a skewering. The buzz from the kiss with Bon a happy memory, it dimmed as a corpse dropped on top of Aleaus. A dead Atenian who's severed throat sprayed the blacksmith's face red, she screamed until she shrugged him off. The heat of his blood ruined the cold, clean smell of the morning.

The lines separated to breathe and reset before they edged closer again. Somewhere in the instance, in the bodies vanishing under stomping feet, Haidra was certain among the dead had been Gurshin, one of their own. Jabs from above as the battle rejoined, punctuated by squeals from Clive, shut her eyes to the fact.

"Forward!" Black John shouted, his voice haggard behind the ghostly echo.

Aware of the order, Haidra tilted her shield and lifted the bottom edge over the next set of the Victus' paving stones, keeping pace with the everyone else who inched forward. The line of shields came down in a thunderous clunk. Spears bounced and scraped on the other side, always aimed for the gaps.

"Press that hole! Press that hole," Black John said behind her.

"To me! To me," Bon the Bloody called over him. His black figure appeared over Aleaus, swinging heavy blows that shattered pike-shafts by the swipe. The canopy disappeared, the broken spear heads falling down behind her and Haidra. The rebels shouted in ravenous, hungered joy, focusing their efforts on the hole he created.

"Go! Go! Go!" Black John repeated. "Keep pressing! They're thinning! They're almost—"

In the next moment, the rebels broke the royalist formation, surging in a wave. Bodies heaped where Fransica's loyal stood their ground, scores of infantry overrun by the second. Knights charging to their defense were dragged off their saddles by the commoners they long oppressed, stomped and stabbed in their armors.

Caught in the stampede, the Ghosts of Solomon joined the momentum, freeing their swords along the way. Always in the rear of faster, hungrier soldiers insistent on reaching death first, Haidra allowed the tide of steel to rush over, a morbid witness to the terrifying route.

Fleeing royalists were cut down by the droves when an ear-splitting, bone-shaking roar quaked Atenia to its roots. From atop the dividing wall that separated High Hill, Torborough and half the Oyster Bazaar exploded in lines of stone and falling rock.

Then the homes on the south side of the Ursin blew apart. The entire district of Gharm Hill vaporized in fiery magic. A rain of shrapnel sent every single soldier, friend of foe, scattering in all directions. Hundreds dove into the canal, allowing themselves to sweep away in groups to avoid falling debris. In reach of a park bench near a piece of wall that remained intact, Haidra and the other Ghosts dove under it. Smoke billowed everywhere.

The blasts ended, leaving Atenia in silent shock.

By the time the dust cleared, a new wall ran from the entrance of the Colis, slicing Idrian Street and climbing west to cut off High Hill from the rest of the city. The rich, safe behind this barrier created of the lives they had ruled, reorganized their sellsword troops and moved siege engines into place. Entaris Bridge, once the lifeline of a legendary metropolis, was rendered a gateway to the ruins.

The Arbikkean drive to support a commoner's rebellion transformed into a rescue mission. Among the new wreckage, covered in dust like the rest, Haidra silently questioned if there would be anyone left to save.

"How can she be this mad?" Prince Aron raged hours later, knocking the small gryphon statue off his table.

It's heavy, broad wings skipped across the wood. His bard, the redheaded Valen, dodged it in his seat. Aron pounded his fists on the table, tears wetting his long, black lashes. Representatives of the rebels, now tripled by the actions of the Veards to defend the sovereignty of wealth, watched in wonder as this stranger seethed for everything they had lost. Given their own high-backed chairs on the dais the royal used to address the audience, the three wraiths reposed in the background. The Ghosts of Solomon, to the right of Bon's chair on the outside edge, waited in a dim corner of the tent, watching in quiet and recovering from the battle upon the Entaris and the royal bombardment afterward.

Still unwashed, Haidra dazed on a short, three-legged stool when a figure interrupted their brooding meeting, a rider covered in the dust of destruction. "My lord, the Veards! They have sent a white flag of truce!"

The prince of Toliv straightened as the three wraiths rose to the ready. "Breathe first, brother. Breathe, and then be heard."

"My thanks, my Prince," said the Arbikkean. "A knight on horseback and one of their wizards have taken the center of Entaris Bridge but advances no farther."

The entire court accompanied their benefactor outside. Having set his headquarters in Low Corner, the position provided an ample view of the city, its citadel, all the way south to the rich communities upon High Hill's southwestern ridge. In the middle of the small horde of armored Arbikkeans and tired rebels, Haidra pushed her way to a place where she viewed the cause of the commotion higher up the climb, the scene framed between the iron spaulders of two foreign cavalrymen taller than her.

A knight on a white charger had descended on a wooden platform suspended by ropes and pulleys, allowing him to ride forth in full regalia. His shining helmet, open to reveal his broad features and rough amber beard, was plumed in pink and navy feathers, and around the neck a scarf of pure white silk emblazoned with the bound petals of Fransica's emblem. Scale skirted to the knee shone along with the gold hilted sword on his saddle. He wielded an eleven-foot lance in his main hand. Strapped to the other arm was a broad, thick kite shield bearing the arms of the House of Harras, one of Atenia's most ancient families.

And by his side rode one of Niklon's dragon-masked sorcerers, enchanting the knight's voice so it echoed for all to hear.

"The Knight of Honor has come," Sir Harras declared in his mocking, nasal authority. "Under the flag to truce I bring challenge! Come forth, you wretches, and meet the satisfaction of your better!"

The bard Valen laughed aloud. "Now we're talking."

"I summon the wraiths of the Burnt Lady, those foul spirits!" The knight snickered in his amplified meanness. "Though let us be plain. They are not wraiths. That woman is dead. Whom I really call is Jhean de Veard, hidden by the shameful moniker of 'Black John.'"

A hush came over the prince's retinue, none deeper than the Atenians among them. Every single person turned their attention to the tall, dark warrior.

He raised no noise. Eyes of flame and torture gazed into nothingness.

"I thought you a coward, a pitiful one," Sir Harras said, almost friendly. "But I knew. I knew one day you'd come back here, angry and dangerous as ever. The name fits, by the way. Black John—a black mark on our days. If I had known, you rapist, I would have done what was right sooner. We all would have. Even before we knew."

"That bastard," Prince Aron cried. He started forward. "An archer! Ah, to Landro's hell, bring me the bow!"

Black John raised a hand in opposition. "Aron."

"Come and show yourself, wretch!" Sir Harras shouted. "You abandoned goodness for silence! You abandoned your lands for cowardice! You abandoned justice for atrocity! Come! Come and fight me, you damned coward! I've hated you all my life! All my life! Come!"

Black John lowered his hand. "My ghosts."

---

He walked ahead of the rest as they strode up the growing incline of Idrian Street. At the top of the ramp in the distance and the mouth of Entaris Bridge, the wraith unbuckled his scabbard from the sword belt on his hip, carrying it in his left hand by the throat. Shoulders squared, he marched undaunted.

Nobody, least of all his children flanking him, said anything to deter Black John's progress.

"Okay, fuck that," Aleaus said, stopping dead in her tracks.

The Ghosts of Solomon halted, as did the three wraiths at their head. Black John did not turn to face his troops.

Covered in dried blood, the world-weary blacksmith widened her stance. Eyes shut tight, the grime on her golden face from the city's constant dust raised the wrinkles in stark highlight. She threw down her sword.

Its clang reverberated on the pavement, drawing a gasp from Haidra.

"You can go," Aleaus said. "I just don't know if I can. I don't know if I can keep going knowing what lies up there."

"What do you mean, Lea?" Talic asked. "What's up there?"

"Fuck if I know, Talic." Aleaus pointed at Black John's back. "But I don't spend time thinking these days on what's up there. Only about how we got here and how we'll get past it. And I think about other things. And right now, I need to know if I'm going to get past this."

"Know?" Bon asked, the lone figure between the ghosts and his father. New Moon stood off to the side, her focus on Black John's stillness.

"Why in the gods' name are you three here?" the blacksmith asked. "And don't give me any shit about Arverin. I want to hear it from Black John. I want to know what I'm fighting for in all this. And for who."

"Would it matter?" the swordsman asked, his voice able to cut daylight. "Would it serve you something, smith, when you lie your head down tonight?"

"That *when* is a big *if* and, yes, yes, it would serve me!" Aleaus walked right up to the wraiths and stopped behind their leader. "And it will do for you to face me. After what I've been through today, you could at least bloody well do that."

Black John turned on the blacksmith, towering over her. He glowered, the illusionary mask housing his malefic glare.

Undaunted, Aleaus glared back. "It'd still work if I thought you were honestly like this. But I remember *him*, though we can't say it. He wasn't this, despite what those people up there said, or that lying fuck Sir Harras. But if you're *him*, be *him*," she said without pretense. "Let us decide what that means. Pay the price for it. So many need to know, and not just for your sake, or Fransica's sake, but to know there was a real reason to all this. To why we're losing so much for so few. But if you're not, put an end to it."

"What do you think I'm doing here?" Black John asked Aleaus. "What do you think all this is about?"

"Nobody knows," Aleaus answered. "That's the problem that's got me, sir. Every time it comes down to it, women and girls like me spend our entire lives worried about getting caught by the wrong man at the wrong time. The idea her brother did what he did? Wouldn't be the first, but in the face of all this?"

She motioned to the destruction around them. "Why was her violation so different that this is okay when it wouldn't have been for us lesser women, the ones without tiaras and titles? Why am I watching my home get torn to shreds while so many other girls were silenced, ignored, or never even allowed to bring their voice before a *queen*-regent's judges? Why did I suddenly have to believe *her* all those years ago when so many would have never believed *me*, or my sisters, or their neighbors unless we moved heaven and earth to prove it? Nobody destroys a city for us poor ones, but the moment a princess simply sniffs at her ruined honor?"

Black John offered no answer.

Frustrated, Aleaus grunted before she looked to the rest. "Well, you lot, what about it? Are you all just happy to go marching off to death not knowing why or if any of this matches up to anything else? That we just watched Atenia become rubble because others made the decision?"

Adan the fisherman spoke up, "You got a point there, Lea."

Bon the Bloody entered the conversation. "Folks, I do not wish to—"

"Then, don't, kid," Aleaus interrupted the ax-slinger. "We've spent our whole lives stopping on the order of lords and ladies, and I have no confusion what you and your sister are. We're here because of people like you. Shut up and let us little people talk this out for once. You mind?"

"Be quiet, Bon," whispered New Moon. "It is their home, not ours."

"I'd like to know." Talic weighed his gentle voice. "I might die in all this. Yeah, I'd like to know."

The other ghosts firmed alongside Aleaus, setting apart from the wraiths, and to her despair, Haidra as well.

Appraising them, Black John answered. "Then follow me."

He continued up Idrian Street for Entaris Bridge. At a loss for his brusque dismissal, Aleaus looked at Haidra in growing anger, who could only put up her hands and shake her head. The younger wraiths fell in behind their father, then Talic, Adan and Clive, and finally Haidra and Aleaus when the latter had no reason other than to witness the swordsman satisfy her demand.

Sir Harras waited on his white charger, pacing the beast back and forth across Entaris Bridge's wide way. He reined the stallion to a stop when Black John crested the northern mouth. Niklon's sorcerer had disappeared.

Haidra huddled beside Bon and New Moon. "Why is he giving Harras what he wants?"

"He has a reason," Bon said, chewing his bottom lip. His golden brow bright on his brown face, it furrowed in apprehension.

"And?" Haidra pressed the ax-slinger and his sister. Her frustrations with them, in addition to the murky nature of the ax-slinger's kiss, removed any politeness. "Aleaus is right—you both know it. By answering he's saying something. Is he? Isn't he? Why are you two so silent as all this happens to us? To my homeland?" An exhale of emotion, torments and questions sludged together, flooded out. "Isn't this yours too?"

"We knew this day would come," New Moon said. "But don't be stupid, Haidra. Nobody owns the earth. Not you, not me, not those fools up in the citadel."

"Then why?" Haidra demanded.

The sorceress turned on her in an instant. Bon did not stop her. Her hazel eyes glowed in wrath as she bore every ounce into Haidra, making her wish she hadn't said a damned thing. "Because despite your pontificating about the evils of the world, you let it happen. Power flows two ways. You don't deserve any more answers than you're getting because you're the people that set my mother on fire. Yes, Haidra, Aleaus, you and the rest. You let Fransica do it. You stood by."

"That's why you're here?" Aleaus asked, aghast by the sorceress' venom. "Old, mean vengeance for something no one could stop? Is that what we're doing?"

"Comical how the complicit decry justice and name it vengeance." Bon the Bloody's gaze cut her way. "And my father will answer you. And everyone else."

Black John had drawn his longsword from the scabbard and cast the cover to the side of the bridge. The bright blade shone in the noon sun above them, a silver torch dwarfing the radiance of Sir Harras' raiment. He proceeded with the point low at his side, his pace slow and deliberate.

Sir Harras reared his mount. The white stallion's hooves clawing the air as he thrust his lance skyward. "For the Veards!"

He fell into a heavy charge for Black John.

Both Aleaus and Clive turned away, but Haida watched in morbid fascination as the wraith dodged the spearhead, one step to the side as he slashed the stallion's forelegs. Cut off at the knees, the poor creature toppled face first into the bridge, snapping his strong neck as he threw his load from the saddle.

Sir Harras flew, but a deft rider, rolled through to his feet. He faced the wraith, the remains of his shield strapped to his arm.

Black John retreated with a fluid back step, the point of his shining sword high in the air.

Roaring in defiance, Harras rushed to his dead horse and drew the fine sword fixed to his saddle. Its steel rang against the brass chap as he leapt the large corpse and attacked, his violent slashes aimed for the wraith's head.

Silence fell upon Atenia, interrupted by the clash of steel and grunts of the knight as he chased the blackguard. Expert swordsmen danced in their thrusts and parries, cuts batted away in ripostes only a breath from the heart or face. His shield affording him a chance to bear the worst of Black John's powerful reprisals, the knight remained valiant.

Leaned back to avoid a backhanded slash, Black John cast his blade like a fishing pole. The tip whipped forward, slicing apart where Harras' broad brow and nose met.

His enemy dropped his sword and stumbled, hands to his face to staunch the bleeding. The wraith chased him, throwing a shoulder into his back. Knocked onto his stomach, Harras flopped over and raised his bloody hands in protest.

"Jhean, please," the knight screamed, his bravado trampled. "You're my best friend! Jhean, no! No, n—"

The length of Black John's sword rammed through Sir Harras' throat. The wraith withdrew and stomped forward, seething something mean and angry in his hood.

The rest of the ghosts, Haidra among them, stood petrified as the body of the royal's champion quivered in its final throes. On some weird hunch, she raised her eyes to the citadel looming to the southwest, its walls pearlescent under the sunny sky.

A pair of individuals stood on its grand balcony.

"They came out to watch," Haidra said, amazed.

Black John employed the sorcery needed to amplify his voice, free hand on his throat.

"Jhean de Veard is dead," the wraith declared. "You slew his soul without a trial. You darkened his sight when you allowed the murders of Marta and Solomon. You stabbed out his heart in allowing Fransica de Veard to burn his innocent wife. Jhean de Veard is dead."

6

# SALTING THE WOUND

The southern side of the Ursin smashed by artillery, uncountable dead buried beneath its rubble, the death of Sir Harras preceded five days of total exhaustion. The toll of the royalists' intentional destruction of its southern quarters held its victims mute, a palpable cloud of sorrow worsened by Black John's declaration. Refugees dug themselves out of their obliterated homes, caught between traitorous rebels and their foreign backers downhill in the north or their oppressors still, as always, high on the untouched ridge. The decision for survival, food, and the promise of Prince Aron's shelters ushered a migration across Entaris Bridge and Victus Crossing, the only paths away from everything they had lost.

A prince in more than name, Aron of Toliv earned his admirers that week. Ordering his troops to put down their weapons, he picked up shovel and blanket and pushed into the dead zone himself. Herding the starving to Hernos Square, the forested temples flung open their doors when their rescuer marched at their head. Along with condemnations of all and every Veard they revealed their hidden stores of food and medicine. Extra cheer was dolled, blankets were distributed, and every child was made certain they did not have to sleep under cold starlight unprotected.

The wraiths, now kept at a distance by most defecting Atenians save the highest officers in the Children of Marta, remained unattached from the work, often leaving in the mornings to scout the boundaries of the rubble fields and blasted buildings. The Ghosts of Solomon, reduced to Haidra, Aleaus, Talic, and the fishermen Adan and Clive, joined them in searching new routes to the royalist lines. The first few days ended in frustration and many dead ends.

Waking the morning of the sixth day in a tent rewarded to each ghost for their service, Haida was surprised to find Bon up before everyone else. He tended the campfire within their circle without his cloak, stripped of the chain and tunic beneath. Toiling bare chested, he piled red coals and fed them fresh kindling.

Brown like wet clay, his hair bordered his firm, fine face in small curls of golden blond, a contrast she noticed most acutely around his eyes and mouth. On his knees, he let his hazel gaze linger on the refreshed blaze until he lifted it and found Haidra spying from her tent.

His stoicism vanished in a small, secret smile that found its way onto her face as well. Pulling her blanket along to keep the pocket of warmth in the cold, crisp morning, she crawled out and stood.

"Morning," he whispered.

She paced to the fire between them. The burning scent of the wood pleased her senses along with the handsome view before her. "Hi."

Uninhibited in his half-nakedness, Bon tilted his head to the side. "Sleep any?"

Haidra bobbed her head, trying to remain stick straight as the cold finally shivered up her spine, her bare feet chilled by the hard earth. "Getting better." She shifted them wider, trying to catch the edges of her blanket to insulate her numbing toes. "Or the ground is getting softer."

"Maybe both." Bon drifted back down at the fire and swallowed, no longer smiling.

"Bon?"

He hummed at her in curiosity.

She dared. "What was her name?"

"Who?

"Your mother."

Bon blinked a few times at the licking flames in front of his knees, their scattering light caught in his pools of blue and green. Sad, longing pools. "Hibni."

Arms tight to her chest, Haidra exhaled through her nose and nodded. "Thank you."

His mouth quivered, withholding a sadness she understood too well and too recent. "For?"

"I've been thinking a lot about what he said. Your dad," she replied. "He's not right, but he's not wrong either."

"How so?"

"I mean it..." She sighed, frustrated by her sudden inability to speak the words in her heart. "I just wanted to know her name because all we've done is call her by what happened. *The Burnt Lady.*"

Bon almost flinched at the name. She wondered how many he had hidden over the days. "Yes. You have."

"I want to call her something else," Haidra said. "I don't want your dad to avenge on me. I would want to make it right. So, I thought if I knew her name, I could stop calling her that and just let her be her again. Let her be your mom."

"He's not going to avenge on you, Haidra," Bon said in a groan. "He—Black John—is... His reasons are different. His ends are different."

"Now, what does that mean?"

"He's here to kill Jhean de Veard," he said. "He's here to end it all."

"And you? Moon?" she asked, more perplexed than before. "What are you two here for then?"

"Because he's a good man. Before he's our father, he's that."

"And after?"

"I live here and now, Haidra," he said. "All I have is what lies before me. The people here. You."

They beheld each other, lights waking to what lay in the shadows of their souls. She stepped around the fire. He rose to meet her first.

Haidra had her arms around his neck, fingers buried deep in his hair as he lifted her by the waist. Their mouths touched, lingering longer than they did the first time. Perhaps the desperation of the times, the need to be close, or the simple adoration she had felt for this marauder drove her into him. Whatever the reason, she savored every touch, every brush of his lips. He did not grab her or force her but folded together with her in—

"Gross."

Startled, Bon broke the kiss first, but did not let go of his embrace as they found New Moon watching from inside her tent. Her chin rested on her smooth, dark hands, she could not hide the grin behind her scrunched expression.

Haidra blushed to a deeper golden color as Bon cleared his throat, slowly loosening himself from their embrace.

"Are they doing the thing, Moon?"

Haidra and Bon turned about the tent circle to Talic. The soldier had already crawled free of his shelter and wound his arms about to stretch his shoulders. He let out a long yawn. "That's a gold Atni, if we can find one," he said. "Aleaus isn't going to be pleased."

"Ah," New Moon said as she emerged in the morning air. Without cowl and barefoot, she stretched her arms and bent at the waist. "Well, Bon? Get breakfast going. Black John left and you know he'll want—"

From the southern ridges of High Hill and the military centers south of the citadel, and upon the heights of Atenia's royal house, the silver trumpets of the Veards belted out the national melody. Every bird hidden within the ruins, thousands upon thousands, flocked in clouds of rapid chatter and song, banking in their formations and fleeing.

The song rang for five whole minutes, drowning out every other noise until the horns quieted. In the space between, hundreds of men shouted orders, and thousands more voices protested beyond sight.

Talic spotted them first on the debris wall in front of the dead zone, right where the magical explosions had turned Gharm Hill into a cliff of broken foundations and rubble. Hundreds of captives, rebels and Arbikkeans, ascended to the uneven edge. Spurred onward by spears at their backs, they stood in stark quiet until a royalist stepped up beside them. Almost in practiced unison, every guardsman pulled their standard-issue dagger.

"By gods, no..." Haidra whispered.

Her hands clapped upon her mouth to hold back a terrified scream as those hundreds dropped into the unseen oblivion below with severed throats. One by one, another prisoner, whether a native rebel dressed in the green and black of the Children of Marta or a blue-swathed Arbikkean, died alongside poor vagrants and orphans unable to escape the city's sundering, all on the malice of a red edge. She turned into Bon as the second wave of bodies were shoved off, the ax-slinger wrapping her tight.

"What the fuck are they doing?" Talic cried in morbid confusion.

"What is going on?" Aleaus scrambled out of her tent, frantic as she pulled her undershirt down. She seized when the third line of victims climbed atop and were executed in brutal fashion.

Then like an eclipse of a moon on the sun, Black John appeared.

"Take cover," he bellowed at them in his distorted voice. "They're about to—"

Hundreds of counter-weights slammed down in the far distance. Out of the posh, wealthy communities of High Hill rose hundreds of human-sized boulders hurtling toward the northern boundary of the dead zone. The fall of stones issued a cloud of smoke and dust, pulverizing rescuers caught unawares in the onslaught. Positioned near an overland bridge that had held, thanks to Atenian ingenuity, the Ghosts of Solomon hid under its eaves.

The bombardment issued twice before the royalists launched hollow wicker globes covered in tarry pitch.

Arbikkean horns sounded the retreat as royalist archers on the debris wall launched volleys of fire-arrows, setting the field alight in an uncontrolled fire. Spurred by a sudden gust from the south and southwest, the fiery glow of death attempted to compete with the sun.

Black John ordered his children and ghosts to retreat to the banks of the Ursin Canal. Fleeing refugees and relief workers clustered the mouths of Entaris Bridge and Victus Crossing, already choking its wide lane and stoppering its frantic flow as debilitating dust and ash darkened the daylight. A few of the foreign soldiers, veterans of far-off campaigns, rallied together and commanded the masses over the water.

The conflagration spread under the unnatural winds. Smoke blackened the sky multiple times no matter how hard the breeze blew, whipping infernos of cinder and ash into small cyclones. The eating, chewing fire raised the heat of the city, and even after the last allied forces crossed Entaris Bridge the scorching

scents of boiling metal and charring wood chased them wherever they went.

"Moon," Black John called to his daughter over the fiery roar.
"Do you hear them?"

Between Talic and Adan, Haidra mashed into Clive
constantly during the mad escape, hooking her arm to the
young teen so he did not fall behind the rest. The entire group
froze on their commander's halt. Each tried with the wraiths to
listen above the growling destruction.

Voices droned in the firestorm. No words, or anything to
distinguish the intention, but they were there. Long and
melodic, perhaps even syllabic to Haidra the longer she listened,
every refrain ripped the breeze harder, faster than before.

"They're stoking the fires!" New Moon motioned to her
father and brother to close in tighter. "Shield me!"

"Ghosts, a wall!" Black John bent down and lifted a shard of
wood, thick and half as tall as him, to block his daughter from
falling debris. "Find something and form in front of New Moon!
Quickly!"

Everyone sought their own protection then manned the line
to defend the sorceress. Aleaus took position in the middle of
Bon and Black John as Clive, Adan, and Haidra formed the rest
with Talic on the end. Scraps of doors, walls, anything they
could raise and lean against the strengthening currents, formed
a ramshackle shield. Stones battered the fronts.

New Moon intoned, waving her hands in wild gestures as the
words echoed. She sang in a language Haidra had never heard,
the evocation fast and flowing in long, hanging vowels. The
sorceress' hazel irises faded to pale rings of silver as she chanted,
jabbing her fingers toward the sky beyond the smoke-layer.

On the corner of the northwestern horizon, surging against
the spell-made wind, black clouds pregnant with rain raced to
her summons. Like waves of the sea, they flowed upon Atenia,

blotting what remained of the sun that Fransica's fires had not covered.

Thunder boomed on high. Drums of deluge rattled in the depths of the eerie downpour. Wind and water whipped into Haidra's face, shutting her eyes multiple times when her hair massed into her lashes or crowded her mouth. Bracing as bits of metal and wood knocked all around, she wondered if Clive had started screeching again when Talic nudged her.

"Hold, Haidra," he screamed. "Hold fast!"

"Hold!" Black John echoed. "Hold! Hold!"

The wraiths and ghosts stood unified, shoulder to shoulder, unrelenting as the water pounded fire back into the earth, snuffing a cruelty born from the hate in a ruler's heart. The rain flagged from a driving, endless sheet, smoothing into a shower. The choking ash cleared.

New Moon's evocation slowed to gentler, kinder tones as peeks of morning light shot through the clouds. The dead zone lay inert in a fresh layer of blackened loss, the burnt stench intermingled with the rain's freshness. Niklon's cultists silenced by the sheer force of her deed, the sorceress ended her song in a gasp.

Haidra dropped her shield and caught New Moon as she toppled. Black John quickly swarmed them both, gathering the sorceress in one arm while gently passing Haidra to Aleaus and Talic. The giant warrior cradling his daughter, he carried her into the refreshed daylight, down the slope toward the rebel positions. To the relief of the ghosts and Bon, she quickly roused in the swordsman's arms, writhing in surprise.

"P-put me down!" New Moon chided Black John, kicking herself onto her feet. She wobbled on unsteady legs and reached out. He grabbed her whole upper arm in his hand, assisting her balance.

"Better than last time," the wraith-lord said behind his magical mask, the pride clear in his voice.

New Moon leaned, her face coated in sweat as she rested against his chest. "Thank you. I thought it sounded better. Could have—" she swallowed hard. "Could have firmed up the end."

Black John addressed the ghosts. "We need to retreat now. Go and try to recover what you can from the camp. We need to find Aron and—"

The royalist horns sounded upon the southern ridges. Swing-arms slammed into crossbars, ringing the metal supports on their beams.

Artillery answered New Moon's storm, hailing the dead zone until sundown, then at dawn again, and then four days after.

Nobody in the north knew how much they lost, or if anyone they had known escaped the rubble beneath the layers already piled atop the dead zone. What had once been Gharm Hill and the Oyster Bazaar, vestiges of when Atenia grew in bounty instead of briars, disappeared like every other happy memory.

# 7

# THE RAIN

I t's hard," Talic said, leaning back. His uneaten bowl of soup in his lap, he searched the opposing wall of the barrack tents. A small snub candle rested on a discarded shield defined his square jaw in its tiny light. His legs over the side, he let his head follow his gray eyes. "But I'd vote for it at this point. They fired first, right?"

"Easy for you and me to say," said Aleaus, seated on her cot beneath the spot where he gazed. "We've been out there while the rest of them been marching and moving, eating well and sleeping every night." She dipped her heel of pale flat bread, thick and doughy, into the lentil-onion soup. She swirled it around, soaking it in the savory paste. "They probably think they're going to end up living up there."

"But you're all acting like Prince Aron can even reach them. Nobody is tossing any rock across that dead zone any more than I could have fished the Franc end to end," Adan said as he pounded his spoon on the side of his wooden bowl, calling for attention the first two rarely allowed once dinner started. An illiterate but wise in the ways of the city, and more than capable in battle, the fisherman scooped a spoonful of the green gruel into his wide mouth, staring at the rest of them with heavy-lidded eyes. Clive sat on the end of his father's cot, arms cast over his knees as he curled into a ball. His bowl of soup and share of bread lay on the floor, untouched and steaming.

Haidra focused on the fisherman's son as she chewed through soft, silken onions, the better part of the equation against the gluey lentils.

"It's not about hitting us," Talic responded. "It's like what John said: Fransica just needs to keep us from entering that dead zone, and as long as she does she's fine. Can't reach us farther than that, though, and who knows? We might be able to get through Bhadran's Wood."

"But we can't reach that position on High Hill from there either. And fuck all for the woods," Adan retorted. "If she hasn't packed that place full of those damned sellswords I'll be king tomorrow."

"I know," Talic said with a huff, the older guard not favorable to debate.

"What do you think, Haidra?" Aleaus asked. "Any insight from Bon what the prince and Black John are thinking up?"

"We're not like—" Haidra grimaced at the blacksmith, who paid her a teasing smile. She leaned into the fact. "In fact, I don't think anyone knows because nobody has any place to go. I might as well take Bon and go play house in Low Corner before all this clears up. Might have you all over for dinner where we can actually eat something."

"Gimme some time and I can rustle up some fish for a pie," said Adan, far more pleasant when speaking to Haidra. "I bet the fish are eating well in the canal. Real well."

They all joined in a dark, morbid laugh broken by the arrival of Bon at the entrance of the barracks. Hood raised, he waved for them to follow with a serious expression. "Get your gear. We're probably going."

Putting aside bowls and the leftover crusts for the camp

attendants to tidy, the Ghosts of Solomon hauled their weapons out, belted and slung their armors, and reentered the world. Mails and helms covered in black tunics and cloaks, they trailed Bon to Prince Aron's tent at the intersection of north Idrian Street and Roromheta Road, overlooking the sections of Urghenna's Mall where he had stationed friendly artillery.

Cavernous in its blue trim and white checking, it seemed more populated each time Haidra passed under its gilded lintel. The usual council was already arrayed around his twin braziers, now sandwiching a table holding a large map of Atenia. New faces massed at its edges eager to have their voices heard.

Like all rebellions built on the backs of the few, the number of those who called themselves leader had multiplied, each with unique concerns and arrogances to think they could impress solutions. While the cobbler Ecktor continued to represent the interests of the Children of Marta, several representatives of several sub-committees rabbled over the wine and bread their host served, never once peaceful until the prince appeared at his stool.

"Silence," he shouted over their din. "Silence so I may be heard!"

Loyal or leeching alike quieted on the demand.

Plopped down on his seat, Aron surveyed the people around him until he centered on the red-haired bard to his right. "All right, Valen. What do you have to say in all this?"

Strumming the eleven strings of his wood-bodied lute, the bard, an odd confidant to the prince, let the last note hang at the end of his stroke. "My dear and wonderful prince," he began in smooth, elegant Torsii, "it is unfair of you to ask me that. You know what must be said and what must be done. The question is whether or not you have the courage. And it's not on me to answer."

"Nor me," said Black John, the haunting guardian stationed behind the prince's chair.

The young prince of Arbikk worked his tongue in his mouth as he measured the rebel Atenians under his tent. Clearing his throat, his sat up, trying to bear the burden of leadership as he spoke. "I swore when I came here that I was not here to invade. I hope you all have seen my sincerity in this. I also know the horrors you have been living under now, shown to all of us in stark detail by the Veard's cruelty."

"Damn the Veards," one of the rebels shouted in the back. Her fellows clapped and cheered.

Aron swallowed his way through their dark mirth. "And their cruelty continues. Any attempt we make to move forward across the Ursin Canal will be stopped by their artillery, spells, and bombings. We could scout the dead zone quietly, thoroughly, in a few days, only for it to be reduced to rubble again and all for naught. And more lives lost."

The last point sobered the rebels as he desired.

"We have reached the hardest impasse of any siege: they have fortified their position in punishing ways we cannot afford to throw ourselves fully at. Given our intelligence of the royal stores, the queen-regent can sit in her palace while her forces in High Hill use the southern highway to replenish their numbers and supplies. My advisers have instructed me that my only option to press forward would require me firing upon them."

The cobbler Ecktor stood at the opposing side of the table to be heard. "My Prince Aron, I see what you are asking. To advance our rebellion you would have to break one of your kindly promises not to destroy our homes. While we are once again awed, sire, by your kindness, let us be fair to you. I have gone to sleep in my house for the past two days, able to rest my head in my own room. I have taken meals in the homes of my friends, who have in turn opened their doors to our brothers and sisters who lived south of the Ursin. We need no further sweetness to know you speak with truth, just like we have no concern about firing on a place already dead."

The rebel Atenians murmured their agreements.

Prince Aron's Arbikkean commanders reciprocated with eager nods and thanks, but not their leader. He sank on his throne, gazing down upon the map of the city.

"Start calculating our placements," he ordered Black John. "Gods damn Fransica for putting me here, but I shall answer. With clarity."

————————

ON THE SIXTH day after the dead zone's creation deployments of rebels and Arbikkeans drove forth catapults and dug stones out of the Vearden's foothills. Set along Lilias Road and hidden behind a row of buildings smashed by royalist shot, Black John situated the firing crews out of the Veard's range, sending the ghosts to escort every convoy to their positions one by one until the strategy was set.

Two days later the morning broke with the sound of stones shattering roof tops, but not in the north of Atenia. Weighted with special counterweights and a modified swing-arm Bon explained was created by a race of beings called 'sirtyas,' the catapults tossed missiles far past the Ursin, leaving dents in the bluffs of High Hill before the first horns of the royalists signaled a counter-response.

The entire north face of High Hill was obliterated in minutes. The royalists' artillery halved, their bombardments lessened in frequency, though their accuracy remained potent at distance to the Entaris Bridge and Victus Crossing.

"He tells me they're going to pool forces and move things back around the top of Idrian Street, where it meets the end of Victus. They can't stop us from crossing Entaris now, so the concentration is on them," Bon said as he poured a light, milky tea into Haidra's cup. He put down the blued steel teapot, his gaze to the south and the booming echoes beyond.

She grinned despite the dour subject, enchanted by a second serving of the sweet-spiced brew. "Pass me some of those biscuits?"

"Oh." Bon searched around where he sat on the blanket they had laid out in the middle of an old public square Haidra played in as a little girl, nestled on the only remaining patch of grass in its center. A deep blue rectangle of silk backed in leather, red vine-work and white roses patterned its borders, providing ample place to sit and stretch without worry of the mud underneath their shifting weights. He lifted a small basket of butter squares Aleaus had baked for their scouting trip, soft flakes that melted perfectly with the tea she suspected New Moon had packed alongside it after Bon expressed surprise at the flavor.

Cozy despite the late-morning cold, and a chance to be alone with him, allowed Haidra space to breathe. "Who'd think Aleaus would be such a good baker?"

"She's a smart old crow," Bon said, tearing his attention away from the bombardment to answer her. A switch happened, the frigid distance of battle vanishing as he admired her quietly.

"What?" Haidra asked, breathing the blushing heat in her cheeks.

"I wish..." Something deadened his smile, but not completely. Exhaustion reweighed his eyes, a quiet tire outside of body and mind. He hurt again, no matter how hard he tried to hide it from her.

Haidra picked up his blue steel teapot by its black handle and refilled his cup. "So...Moon. She's a princess, right?"

"Yes?" he answered, puzzled away from despair.

"Are you a prince?"

"Ah," he concluded with a suspicious smile. "No. I'm not."

"But she is?"

"By my mother...Hibni," he said, nodding to her as if for her permission. Haidra nodded in return, smiling at his comfort around her. "She was the Shahira of the Northern Sands. A priestess of Uma dedicated to Arbikk's wind, water, and dunes."

"Sounds important."

"Very. The Shahirs or Shahiras of the Four Points of the Great Desert and the Forty Clans they serve assist in the taming of its winds, bringing rain to fuel the crops, and let us husband the beasts of the wastes with gentle hands instead of steel. They are our healers and our leaders. Rich or poor, from queen to peasant, all seek their council."

"Why did she leave then?" Haidra asked. "It sounds like she has so many things to be there for I can't imagine why she came all this way."

"Because we are Arbikkeans," Bon said between sips of tea, "we're not bound to our homes like you Torsii. Sand shifts under foot and hoof alike and with it we go. My mother expected things of my father living on those sands, and being who she was, took more things on herself after what happened."

"I was too little to remember when I lost my mother," Haidra said. "But, somehow, you grew up knowing."

Bon set his tea cup down, trying to smile past the tears. "I've known since I was four."

She mustered on, "I remember the day Hibni died. I saw her on Entaris Bridge, standing there. I couldn't hear her, but whatever she said to Harras was enough to change the day in ways I remember more than what Niklon did. It didn't matter the words—whatever they carried scared those that scared us. But I wonder, Bon—"

"Yes?"

"Moon shifted the heavens and brought the rain down. If she is so powerful I'm guessing your mother was, too?"

"I don't know. When you see the rain summoned every year power has a different meaning. I guess what you're asking is why didn't she save herself?"

Haidra nodded.

"I've asked myself that question every day," he replied. "If I knew I'd tell you."

"Does Black John know?"

The ax-slinger scoffed at the question. "My father knows which way the wind blows a week before it arrives, but like it, he makes no announcements."

"Lucky when you need allies who are like sand," Haidra said.

"You know, for a poor girl you're really smart."

"And you're too sweet for that thing," she said, nodding to the black ax that lay in the grass past their blanket. Its dark edge gleamed where bloody effort had worn the bluing.

"I'd rather have that than be a prince," he said. "Less stress."

"So, again, how are you not?"

"The people of Arbikk will always need their Shahiras, but the world doesn't need more princes or kings."

"How can you have a world without kings?" Haidra asked.

"By our better graces," Bon said. "Or at least that's what my dad says. And where I'm from we get on without them better than not."

"Maybe one day I can see someplace like that," Haidra said. "Being a poor girl and all, I doubt it."

Putting down his cup, Bon reached across and cupped Haidra's face in his tanned hands. His calloused fingers warm, his skin smelled of the vanilla cream she often watched the wraiths applying to their skin after removing their armor. The scent drove her mad.

"Sand carries a lot of things with it when the wind blows," he said.

Haidra forgot about her tea and the pounding echoes in the distance as she sought his kiss.

"Seriously you two, stop it."

The romantic moment shattered by New Moon's arrival, the sorceress walked toward them from the mouth of a northern alley. Her white hair free, she seemed every part of an elemental goddess without her hood and gloves, the cloak replaced by an ankle-length black shift and a scarf of blue silk Haidra recognized from Prince Aron's own shoulders as he patrolled his campsites, taking the duties of his soldiers as his own. Her rapier, belted to the side in an intricate belt formed to her shapely hips, stretched the soft muslin where the handle caught.

Bon grunted, withdrawing his hands from Haidra's face. "You can't keep doing this. It wasn't funny when you were little, it isn't funny now. And you're a grown woman! Does Aron know you're just following me around, bugging me like this?"

New Moon loosed a bright cackle. "Of course! But I'm not here to spoil your date. We're called."

The loveliness of the day was sucked out by the announcement, but like the wind stealing the heat of the tea and the sun's warmth, the three accepted the summons. The aches of the last march, the anxiety of racing headlong into death again, instilled Haidra with an immediate lethargy.

"Where to?" Bon asked, slowly letting his gaze trail back to the dead zone.

Visible from their position in the square, the broken slopes of High Hill stabbed the shortened horizon. Smoke trailed as boulder-sized chunks of rock were volleyed from behind its edge.

"Not there, thankfully," New Moon said. "Bhadran's Wood."

Finding the handle of his ax, Bon levered it to his shoulder. "To the tombs, then."

8

# SCION

Striking high on the pink and navy pennants, morning burnished the alabaster walls and spires of the fortress bright atop of the twisting rise of Snail's Way golden. Birds broke from hidden eaves with the breeze's shift, taking to the sky in dancing clouds, spiraling toward the smoking city below. No matter the blackened hills battered under it, the elegance and majesty of the Veard's home glistened, a spirit of a past forgotten.

Clive stood atop an old, overturned oak, awing up at the citadel. Clear as the daylight and full in its looming, he shook his head at it. "Never been this close. Have you, Haidra?"

"No, not me," she said, breathless. "They closed up the gates before my ma and dad could ever bring me in here."

"Yeah, me, too," said the fisherman's son. Almost a head taller and rail-thin compared to his overweight father, he pulled off his helm and freed his shaggy shock of brown hair, his tawny eyes blinking as if seeing for the first time. "Why did they close this off? Nothing's out here."

"This is Bhadran's Wood, Clive," Bon said, standing next to

the young man. "Don't you know the stories about this place? It's sacred ground."

"Why's that?" asked Clive.

"Old Bhadran, great-great-great-great-great-great-grandfather to the Veards lived in these woods before there were Lomens, let alone the kingdom," the ax-slinger said, motioning his cup of tea around at the surrounding forest hiding them from the lookouts upon the citadel's precipices. "Slew the griffins until they were driven into the Veardens. His descendants kept this place for him and his spirits, found in the old bears and lions that once roamed. They say those bears and lions used to come to a true king of Atenia's call."

"You know a good bit of history for a foreigner," the boy's father said from a rock behind his son. Adan blew the steam off his cup, switching hands when the clay grew too hot. "But nobody has been allowed in here since those towers up there were built and the ol' queen-regent kicked out the crown's beneficiaries."

"Beneficiaries?" Haidra asked, looking over her shoulder at Adan in confusion.

"Once upon a time, when things were kinder, the Veards used to let travelers, the homeless, and even vagrants camp here if there was no place in the city to rest their heads, and many of the workers who built up there used to camp over yonder. Fine nights, those were. Just cooking, camping, and getting up the next day." He nodded to Clive and grinned. "Before I met your mother that is."

"Did you work on those buildings, Pa?" Clive asked.

"Sure did, son," Adan said, chancing another sip of the sweet brew. "Right, Talic? Aleaus? I think we all worked."

The old guard and the blacksmith murmured agreement, dark looks on their faces over the reminder.

"All we ever done is work," Clive said under his breath.

Camped behind a cluster of ancient trees, the ghosts and

younger wraiths waited on Black John until he returned from the base of Mount Ectis. The second highest peak of the Vearden's southern spurs stabbed up past the citadel's defensive wall, connected by a thin ridge of rock to the royal mound.

"How bad was it up there?" Bon asked the elders in their troop. Leaned on a trunk beside Haidra, he stared directly at the highest of its two spires.

"Bon," New Moon whispered, "they might not want to talk about that."

"Been years now, Miss Moon," said Adan. "I took food up there when the knights allowed. Eels out of the canal and some puff-breads. Almost drained the canal of the speck-bellies for all the stews made in those days."

"My mother had a recipe," Aleaus chimed in. "I hated those eels by the time I was done with my tour up there."

"We all did," Talic said. "I had to eat them, too."

"Oh, bullshit, Talic," cawed Adan. "You guards got chicken. From them southern farms—"

"No, no," Talic was quick to respond, shaking his head vigorously. "That went to the knights like Harras. We just went where we were told and got eels too."

"Damn," Aleaus said, sympathetic, "I'll be damned. I wonder what they were eating up there, then? Remember when they told us that the crops in the south blighted, and we'd worked three days before they could bring in trade food from Horras? Were they telling the truth about that?"

"I don't know," Talic said. "They ate well enough, though. I guarded the carts they brought in for Tobias's larder every week. The boy never went without, and I doubt his pappy or those damned white masks did either."

"You know, I'm real glad your dad killed that Sir Harras," Clive said to the wraiths. "Right one, he is, despite the things he said after."

"You have nothing to fear from me, child."

The whole troop startled, dropping their cups and plates of runny quail eggs Adan had whipped up alongside the sweet, soft tea the wraiths carried. Black John stood tall at the top of the knoll, reviewing each of them in passing as they calmed.

"Bloody hell, John," Talic shouted back as he bent over to gather his cup. "You know you can stop that now, right?"

"Gather your gear," the swordsman said. "We're not far."

The Ghosts of Solomon packed their mess, belted their weapons, and half an hour later trailed the swordsman downhill on a narrow but even path to the bottom. Through the glades of ancient elms and beeches, their dark trunks speckled by the scant light filtering through the boughs, the quiet of the shadow glade was uninterrupted by birdsong or animals skittering about. In the rays touching her face, Haidra smiled in this pristine domain, thankful to be alive and breathing after so many moments that should have gone the other way.

This joy multiplied the few times her and Bon drew close on the journey. Fingers tangled, fumbled together sweetly, before space or New Moon's teasing pushed them apart.

On the slope of Mount Ectis they traversed along a twisting among the pines. A mile up Black John deviated from the meandering hike and skirted them along a narrow path slowly pushing out of the hill, more carved than natural the farther they tracked into the glens. Into an old ravine clustered by oaks and brambles, he filed them onto a goat's trail that thinned as the earth rose on both sides, ancient hills built by centuries of packing and repacking the dirt by hand.

At the end a large entrance cut into the berm, gray and flat.

"Is this it?" New Moon asked.

"It is," said Black John, shocking the group a second time that morning by speaking in his natural voice. The timbre of his baritone, firm but warm, surprised Haidra. It felt so long ago, in that warehouse, listening to him lecture his daughter about her illusions.

"What is this, John?" asked Talic, on the swordsman's left.

"It's their tombs," the oldest wraith answered. "My family's tomb."

Every single Ghost of Solomon froze on the confession, but none dared the question.

The towering warrior unbuckled the straps of his spiked-steel gauntlets, passing them to Bon. His golden hands, the color of rebel flesh, pressed against the slab. "I speak the name of Solomon, who came after Rennar, who came after Solemo, and a Solomon before him," he intoned. "As the rightful king, I open the last land and the first home of my ancestors, laid in their wasting bones."

The door shook under Black John's touch, vibrating a weird sound before the entire hill quaked. Dirt and loose pebbles tumbled down the ravine. A grinding noise under their feet buzzed into Haidra's knees as the stone door receded. It turned on an unseen hinge and flattened against the wall.

A torch-lit passage into oblivion had opened.

Glacial like Ben-Lomen, Black John moved one step at a time, bending his head to clear the portal. The steel edges of his greaves rang on ancient rock, fading, fading into the broken darkness. Eternal lamps fueled by some unknown source lit the gentle steps smoothed by the wear of time. Warm and dry, Haidra was the first to doff her hood and leather gloves, happy to work feeling into her clammy fingers. The rest followed on their own, as did Bon and New Moon.

"This place is legend," Adan said from the rear of their queue.

"Nobody is supposed to come in here unless they have the blood," Aleaus said, behind Haidra and in front of New Moon. "*Royal* blood. The only way we get in here is with a member of the family."

"Keep marching," the sorceress snapped.

The stair ended in a high-ceilinged vault stretching far into the perfect dark, where no light touched its corners. From the illumination within the passage radiance gleamed off the polished corners of two sarcophaguses sculpted in white marble veined with pink. Haidra spotted them over their leader's shoulder. More long, high boxes sprouted in the gloom the longer her eyes adjusted.

Black John sang aloud into the chamber. "Upon the spirits of the bear, waken, waken! Upon the spirits of the falcon, waken, waken! Upon the spirit of the Veards…"

The final note of his dulcet voice reverberated. Instead of quaking and falling dust, a voice on the edge of perception answered, rousing and complete.

"We waken. We waken."

Starting from the doorway Black John filled, a series of small candle-like lamps ignited, one by one, crawling from his end all the way to the other side of the underground mausoleum. The walls shone, spotless in the intense glow.

"Enter quietly." He made way for the rest of them. "You walk in the halls of Atenia's honored dead."

Struck dumb by the revealing pronouncement, the ghosts complied, then his children. He kept New Moon last, whispering in her ear.

The sorceress nodded slightly and took point. "Everyone with me, please. Let's get to where we need to get to and set up camp."

Haidra looked to Bon, but the ax-slinger waved her forward.

Black John stayed behind.

They passed by rows of coffins, their shapes and sizes shifting the deeper they went. The first boxes were simple, hand-carved marble before they gave way to a later period, the ornamentation chiseled into the shapes of bears and falcons. These designs reached their zenith through full depictions of the dead within, kings and queens of legendary lore Talic, Aleaus, and Adan pointed to and mentioned. Neither

Haidra nor Clive knew any old tales to the dismay of their elders.

"What happened here?" Adan asked, pointing to a flat square when the coffins disappeared.

"They stopped burying long ago and started burning them on pyres in front of us, remember?" Aleaus said. "Looks like we're close to the end anyway. Bet the damned cheap bastards didn't want to use up the space."

"Or they didn't hold value in the body anymore," said New Moon, "for what is a body when our souls pass beyond it, and sometimes can see a future not yet here? In fact, they started burning them when—"

The sorceress stopped dead, a hand up to halt the rest of them. Hands shot to the hilts of their weapons.

New Moon waved her hand. "Bon."

The ax-slinger joined his sister at the end of the final crypt and froze as well. "Oh… Is that…"

"Go warn him," she said. "I'll make it presentable."

Haidra came around as Bon left and gasped.

On its side, the corpse of an old man that had long lost its flesh, liquefied to stain the fine garments he wore in huge splotches of dry brown. Clear wounds in the leathery remains of his back and chest, a wicked cut severed the front of his throat. He had grabbed at the wound in his final moments, a victim who died in terrible agony.

New Moon squatted quickly at the body's bare feet, its stench soft but gross. "Haidra, help me. The rest of you give us space."

"Who is it?" Aleaus asked.

"My grandfather," New Moon answered. "Solomon de Veard III."

The revelation shocked the native Atenians. Aleaus covered her mouth, tears already in her eyes as the next gasp sank her. Adan was by her side immediately and Talic on the other. A generation forever alive to the horrors after the last good monarch's disappearance, Solomon's ultimate fate gave the final stab to their hearts, pinning the fullness of the queen-regent's falsifications on grander, brighter days they all remembered no matter how silent they kept them.

"They murdered him," Talic said, aghast and emotional. "They murdered him and just threw him in here. Like trash."

Haidra knelt at the corpse's side. "What do you need of me?" she asked the sorceress.

"He's been in this position a long time," New Moon said, nodding as she surveyed the body of her slain grandfather. "I want to turn him onto his back together so he's laying correctly. Be careful because his spine might break. We'd cause worse damage."

"All right," said Haidra, taking a deep breath as she shook out her hands. Blood gathered in her fingers. "Ready."

"Slowly…"

Haidra grasped the top shoulder and Solomon's neck, surprised when the mottled, too-soft flesh held against her touch. The smell harsh and immediate, no matter how long time had worn at it, under the sorceress's guidance they repositioned the dead king upon his back. Head firmly connected despite attempts to saw through the vertebrae in the front, Solomon's eyeless skull absorbed his subjects for the first time in fifteen years.

Talic did not shy from those voided sockets. "Shook my dad's hand once. Told me he was proud he helped him keep Atenia safe. My dad told that story when he went in his bed." He screwed a wrinkled, tired face, one eye shut by tears. "Ol' Solomon didn't get his bed."

The three older fighters broke down. Adan covered his face in his hands as Aleaus wept a second round, holding Talic in her strong arms as he sputtered, wiping his eyes no matter how useless the effort. Their emotions loosed upon the old king's death, the crimes of Atenia, of their complicity, assailed in fresh sorrow before that dreaded voice stoppered their mourning.

"No. No, no, no, no!"

Every soul turned to find Black John standing beside Bon.

"Moon," he called to his daughter, staggering. His son rushed to his side, picking him up. "Is it…is it?"

"I'm so sorry, Daddy." New Moon's steely façade shattered, despairing like the rest. "It's him. I f-found our—"

The outcast collapsed to his knees, overtaken by a scream. Bawling by his side, Bon held the giant figure as he writhed, twisting and pulling in his child's hold.

The truth of everything she had been told, founded on lies, caught Haidra. She fell back on her bottom, weeping for reasons she could not explain other than a gut-sense everything was wrong. Now, everyone knew it.

Everyone had known it.

Arverin had told her as much, she had seen as much, but bearing the brunt of the long-lost son confirming the worst, her crying captured her. She tried not to look at the dead man near her, nor his broken family.

Black John came and knelt beside Haidra. By some skill beyond her, he focused to the task of meeting his father. The wraith reached up and pushed back his voluminous hood.

The weight of the cowl, worn days at a time for periods few could guess, had thinned the long dark hair atop a well-formed head. The prince's hazel eyes went wide and locked upon the body, unable to remove his growing anger. A rough, long beard covered his lower face containing features, which made his parentage to Bon and New Moon unquestionable.

For Haidra, there was no mistake: This was the man from her father's coin.

She failed to withhold a gasp. "It is you," she said first, the truth clawing out. "It's been you all along."

Jhean de Veard exhaled through his clenched teeth. "For this moment."

"But you're Jhean de Veard!" Talic dropped to a knee first, his head bowed to the floor. "By Crook... By the dark hills!"

"Don't, Talic," the prince growled, and it was a growl, wounded and fierce. "None of you start that. Not here."

Aleaus spoke almost in child-like wonder. "But, Sire, we—"

"Not that either." Teetering between sadness and hate, Jhean de Veard shook his unruly mane. "That all died with that man. It needs to stay dead."

"But you are the king," Aleaus retorted. "The truth! The truth lies before us! The days of glory may b—"

"I ordered you quiet, woman!" Jhean de Veard roared to his feet. "The *truth*! Pah! Where was the truth when he vanished and not a single damned one of you dared to search? Where is my mother? Have you all found her body in this horrid place? This hell? You say *truth, truth*, but what have you found, Aleaus? What the fuck do you think you have now?"

"Say it, and we will know, my Lord," the blacksmith responded shrilly. "Simply say what we all wish to know! Wish to hear! Proclaim, and we shall exalt it from the deepest wood and one day to the very tops of that bitch-monster's towers! But say it, our prince!"

"Say it, milord," Talic pleaded. "We would hear what we know in our hearts!"

"Even now?" the prince responded, incredulous. "Even now? After what she has done to you? To your homes?" He stepped out of the way, so the rotted body of his father was reviewed. "After him, you still need for someone to say it?"

The subjects of Atenia, Haidra included, shuddered on the question.

When Prince Jhean de Veard spoke again ice edged in every word. "No, I will not give you something you took from me. I have nothing to say to you, who believed when you should have questioned, bowed when you should have investigated, and idled as tyranny fell upon you. No, I do not have to say it because nobody informed me of what my accuser said until it reached me through the words of merchants. Merchants! The mouths of strangers!"

"Then why come back?" Clive asked, mustering courage to speak.

His father, Adan, groaned. "Please, forgive him, milord. He's young and a bit of a dullard."

"That boy has had more courage and guile than generals thrice his age, and you will treat your child with such respect!" the returned prince boomed at the fisherman, shrinking him under the admonishment. "Don't you dare look upon one of your children and shame them, you little, little man. Bullies like you think they can simply say something about someone and nobody is allowed questions, assuming themselves above *everyone*. I came back because *no one* should be able to make such pronouncements, let alone act upon such power. I'm here as I said, to take vengeance upon the Veards! On the story we've wrought. But truly, fisherman..."

Their lord, their king, he turned to face the body of his dead parent. "I wanted to find my father." The anger stripped away, word by word. "I want to know what happened to my mother."

"I'm so sorry, milord," Adan said. "I didn't mean to—"

"Quiet, man," Jhean de Veard commanded. Not tearing his gaze off Solomon, he clapped Adan on the shoulder. "Remember, a son is his father. The courage and guile came from somewhere."

The fisherman sniffed, sharing a smile with his boy. "Yes, sir."

Jhean de Veard pulled his hand away. Breathing deep to steady his shivering, the emotions vanished. "Bon, go open the balcony and set camp in the old guard station. The sun should be out by now and we can start making counts."

"Aye," the ax-slinger said, thumbing the last wet from his eyes. "Fall in."

The Ghosts of Solomon gave the prince and sorceress a wide berth, leaving father and daughter behind to tend the dead. At the furthest wall Bon crouched, reaching into a hole in the low right corner where the forever-candles had gone out. Two fingers in the fissure, he pushed inward.

A latch clicked.

The bottom of the wall unsealed from the floor, letting in fresh sunlight to ease the stuffy darkness. The section's candles snuffed in unison as the slab ascended and locked in a recess, the bottom the new lintel for an exit to a sprawling balcony fenced in a long stack of ancient shale.

Bon went through first, peering both ways before he gave the "clear" signal. Haidra was the first out after him, inhaling the cold mountain air to rid her lungs and mouth of the tomb's mustiness and the corpse-stink. Fresh oxygen reinvigorated her as the chill breeze seeped through her coverings and armor and goosed her skin. She joined Bon at the edge of the short wall that reached her mid-thigh. They dared to look over the vastness of southern Atenia.

The farmlands stretched from the palisades to the Franc River, running west to east as the melt from Ben-Lomen's glacier fed its network of creeks and flood plains. Smack in the middle of a field near the gates, a black spot remained, as did the husk of the burnt wagon. Not far behind those fields of wheat the camps of the Veard forces dotted the banks of the river in hundreds of tents. Thousands more people milled about. Horses dragged wagons full of supplies back to the city as knights watched the roads.

In the distance, on the backside of High Hill, crews pushed catapults higher toward the peak, clustered among the posh manors out of range of the Arbikkeans firepower on the Ursin's northern bank. They could not see, from the high vantage, the military districts past the southeastern wing of the palisade but could view the full scope of Atenia's royal citadel.

Haidra marveled at the expanse. She reached for Bon's hand, hoping to snare it for the moment.

"Holy shit, they didn't even move it," Bon said, chuckling at the discarded wagon. "Lazy."

The mood dampened, she grabbed it anyway with a sigh.

The ghosts searched out the guard station at the far end of the balcony. A small but cozy stall to brace against the worst of the wind, bedrolls and gear were broken out. Charged with carrying the firewood cut from Bhadran's, Talic and Aleaus unloaded their hauls.

"Bon, go get your pad and pen." Jhean de Veard exited the tomb. New Moon came behind him, scrubbing her cheeks of any leftover sorrow. The prince joined his son and Haidra at the wall, reaching his bare hand inside his cloak. He pulled out a brass cylinder.

Before Haidra studied it farther he pulled it apart, smaller tubs sliding from the largest until its length locked in place. One end wider than the other, she noted a glass plate in its large mouth.

"What's that?" she asked.

"A spyglass," the prince replied as he brought the smaller end, another lens sealed in soft leather, to his right eye. "Now be quiet, Lady Haidra. We've doom to plan and I'm having the worst of days."

# 9

# FRESH HELL

Before the next dawn Jhean de Veard placed Solomon III on the exposed balcony looking down from Mount Ectis' southwesterly face, in full view of the city, and the land they once called theirs. His children waited in the guard station with the rebel subjects of the old realm, still dumbstruck as they witnessed a son pay his father the final rites.

In a dignified pose on his back, the assassinated monarch had his hands folded on his chest. Unable to keep from sobbing through arcane words, Jhean de Veard wept as he looked on his father's emaciated corpse, a sight that made Haidra cry when the true prince of Atenia pressed glowing lips to the dead man's forward. A magical fire covered the body.

A morning gale whipped the bluing flames high. Solomon's smoke, black but with a roasting savor, tore off to an eternal road beyond dawns and dusks.

The three-day journey to and from the tombs coincided with three days of continuous bombings within Atenia's proper, the rain of stone layering the slope until what remained of Oyster Hill blocked sight of Victus Way, the southern curve among the mansions and low-laying estates. Restless, rebel and Arbikkean alike waited in tensing anticipation, opposed by the worst foe of any siege—boredom. By the time the Ghosts of Solomon returned to the prince's tent at the fork of Idrian and Roromheta a lethargy had spread among the desert veterans, fueling the frustrations of the native Atenians watching the destruction of their city to replay for hours on end, day after miserable day.

Their return elicited an excitement among the refugees. Not bound to either the rebellion or the royal past, they gathered on sidewalks to watch the eight black figures plod to the center of Idrian Street, the tallest swordsman at the front of their pack. Children, stitched in garments gifted by the prince shaded in blues, whites, and golds waved and cheered no matter how deeply Black John's eyes burned. Their parents, still reminded of the elder wraith's promise after the slaying of Sir Harras, offered less enthusiastic responses.

Arbikkeans ushered their Shahira to Aron's tent, emptied of all save him and his bard. Supping on a plate of rice and simmered vegetables, the son of desert kings rose instantly the second he spotted New Moon.

She nudged ahead of her father to meet her betrothed as the rest slowly trickled inside.

"Come, my friends," Prince Aron said. Holding New Moon tight, he released her to wave the rest inside. "Please, please! You're all welcome at my table. Valen, tea."

The bard, road-worn in a muddied riding harness over his hunter green trousers and tunic, put the lute he had been tuning on the table to meet the call, less energetic than his liege. "Don't hurry to help. I got it."

The ghosts assumed the stools and benches around Aron's table, dropping their gear and weapons on the cobblestones of the street serving as his floor. The bard came around with a tray of eight small cups to supplement the pair he and the prince already used, along with a carafe full of a dark, steaming brew. Poured in concentrated doses, each of the fighters sipped or turned it away, exhaustion suppressing their hunger.

Aron and New Moon sat down at the prince's spot, hand in hand. Pulling her hood back, she slowly unbuckled and removed her gauntlets as he retrieved his own cup, lifting it before them.

"To your efforts," he said, gentle and sincere.

Heartened by the toast, every ghost followed the gesture, downing a mouthful of dark, biting tannins. The blot of caffeine in Haidra's skull left her with a dull headache. Bon fetched them a larger cup of water to share as his father, hooded and mantled, reported their grim adventure to the tomb of the Veards.

Another layer of truth was revealed as the disguised prince produced the notes he had written on sheets of paper, not as a subordinate submitting a report to his better, but two equals in a constant exchange of power. She wondered how these two polar opposites—one scorned and embittered, the other kind and gregarious—had come together in such a wide world.

"Whomever is in charge of the knights now has them coordinating the encampment behind the southern palisade," said Black John as he directed Talic, then Aleaus, to pass the papers forward to Prince Aron. "All of their artillery is rotated on a three-hour cycle and are repaired after sundown. They have dug shot out of the Lomen's foothills, but they will run out of pitch soon. We saw more riders headed out on the western highway than we saw wagons coming in, and there were no discernible outliers."

"Nobody has come to help her?" Prince Aron asked, astonished. "What about her sellswords companies? We counted her forces as having ten thousand extra-reserve."

"Sellswords only stay when there's a battle to win," Valen said, adding his voice to the conversation.

"Do we think that is how they feel?" Prince Aron asked, "Or what we know?"

"What we do know is their artillery positions," Black John interjected. "We could neutralize High Hill if we pushed our artillery into Hernos' Court and up the hidden paths of the Ben-Lomens only the wise-whisperers know lay in the west. If we reassemble atop the glacier's falls feeding the Ursin, we can finish them in a day. I've already charted routes to maximize the cold mornings, so the ascent will not be as arduous."

"But these positions will open us up to counterattacks at such a distance," Valen whispered to Aron as he pulled one of the hand-drawn maps the wraith had provided. He raised his eyebrows as he scanned between it and the fixed map of Atenia at the round table's center. "But John's right. If we're quick, we could do this—"

"Jhean! Jhean de Veard!"

The ghosts seized the same time Black John did.

A voice none had heard in years echoed outside the tent. "Jhean! Jhean de Veard! I know you're there, big brother," the queen-regent of Atenia spoke in her amplified soprano. "I know you wouldn't resist. Couldn't resist. You never could."

"In the Uma's name..." New Moon clutched tight to the arms of her chair. "That—"

"Come out, blackguard! Come out of your foreign hole and take off your silly little costumes. Come out and face your crimes."

Almost serpentine, Black John lifted out of his chair and headed straight for the entrance of Aron's war tent. The rest fell into his long shadow cut by the sun through the flaps.

He burst into the central camp where most of the soldiers, rebel and foreigner, had halted in place. All eyes were on the citadel in the southwest, and as suspected, a lone figure had taken to the royal balcony.

At distance, Haidra surmised some detail about a figure she

had only heard spoken of in terror or disdain, but had never actually heard, let alone witness in the flesh. Tall like the rest of the royal family and her brother, a gaunt women bent at the white fence, dressed in a white sleeping gown stained in filth.

Her attention went from the queen-regent to Black John.

The disgraced prince, in the presence of his accuser, remained silent.

"I saw the smoke from the tomb. Smelled its ichor. You had to go there, didn't you?" Fransica whispered, her enchanted voice bitter and tight. "Do you think it matters? Do you think it changes what you did? I will go to my grave proclaiming against you, Jhean de Veard!"

The sudden rise in volume crackled in Haidra's ears. She winced along with everyone else in immediate sight.

"How can you traitors, you thieves, actually follow a monster like this? He is a bloody murderer who killed your families, brought terror to your lands, but it is I who is the enemy? I am your villain? This man who impregnates foreign teenage girls and—"

"You bitch," New Moon shouted up toward her aunt. "You damned, dirty—"

Black John barked at his daughter. "*Shahira!*"

The sorceress silenced.

"—cavorts with mercenaries! He's a fool and a dullard! I brought you art! I brought you design! I brought Atenia love of the highest order, but you throw me away? To my grave! To my grave, Jhean de Veard!" Fransica ranted. "I will go to my grave proclaiming what you have done to me in these wretched halls! You shall stand in the shame of everyone! Everyone! Shame! Shame, shame, shame..."

Her voice projecting into the unseeable distance, she whined something unintelligible, muttering too fast to understand. Bent at the balcony, a whimper became sobs, then grunts until she unleashed a piercing scream.

"Mad," someone said in their native Torsii. "We were ruled by the mad. All of them. Just mad."

Hearing the admonishment spurred Haidra to step forward, but Bon grabbed her hand. She tried to jerk away. He shook his head at her intention, as if knowing, and held tight.

"How can you not want me?" Fransica whispered, reverberating. "My way is the way of love. I brought you all love…" Her rapid breathing broke into despairing insanity, moaning and long before she bit the air. "Why aren't you helping me? What aren't you thanking me? I gave you love—"

Someone in the camp shouted. "You're killing us! You were killing us!"

Summoned from years of anxiety, walking every day with her head down, always worried a knight might run over her like they did her mother, urged Haidra to speak. She wrenched her hand free of Bon's.

"She murdered Solomon," Haidra screamed at the absolute top of her lungs. "She killed the king! Threw his body in a hole! Her knights murdered my father! My father! Killed him right in front of me—"

New Moon and Bon rushed her at once, pushing her back into the prince's tent. The ax-slinger and sorceress crushed her between them as she descended into a panic, images of her father dying, the light leaving his eyes as she dropped from a window. Stinging tears blinded as New Moon's arms pulled her in close. Thousands of voices called out against the queen-regent, everyone with their own story unable to be stamped out.

"I know. I know. I know. I know," New Moon whispered into Haidra's hair, stroking the back of her head. A true princess tightened her embrace as her vagabond-brother kept guard.

Able to peek over New Moon's shoulder, she spotted Black John's hooded outline through the tent's opening. A statue of grim reprisal, the rightful king remained unmoved by his sister's ranting.

"Show yourself, you disgusting coward!" the queen-regent screamed. "Come forth and face your accuser! I dare you!" A mad laugh conquered her rage. "To the high gate, big brother! The high gate! If you are a man, if you are brave, or any of those silly things all men aren't, ascend! Ascend, ascend, ascend! Walk up Snail's Way! By some cruel jest if you remain unharmed then I will silence my tongue upon your name! I will silence truth for the 'sacredness' of claimed innocence! But I will stand in judgment! I will hate you! I hate you, Jhean! I hate you! I hate—"

Several more figures appeared on the balcony behind the queen-regent. White masks clear in the unhindered daylight, they tore at the wretch half-hung over the fence, frantically kicking and screaming in the final seconds of her enchantment. So far to be silenced by height and distance, the cultists dragged Fransica inside and slammed the doors shut.

An act seen by those able to view the citadel, the frightening scene left the destroyed metropolis in a grim, foreboding silence.

Haidra could hear Prince Aron outside the tent speak first. "What does that mean, John? What is happening?"

"It means this siege lasts until it ends," said the wraith, unaffected by familiar slander. "For one of us, at least."

10

# THEY SAY

The morning's madness subsided to war's constant grind. Both sides sunk deep into their entrenchments, stirred by the reminder of how their ruin started.

Tasked to move the artillery west, the Ghosts of Solomon lead the heavy work crews through the empty streets of the warehouse district, past the stone and mortar palisade that separated the wooded temple quarter from the rest of Atenia's once-forested city. Named after a famed bear possessed by spirits of the land that worked in harmony with the native Lomens who settled after fleeing the sorcerous north of Torsdaina, hundreds of small huts and shrines nestled inside oak tree-hollows, under overhanging rock, and by the multitude of small, trickling falls to be found among the vines and thickets. In the greater groves of ash and pine, tall wooden buildings constructed of sticks and stones, not iron beams or nails, held effigies and altars to the greater gods of sun, moon, and stars.

Born to dingy alleyways full of rats and scraggly trees, not beautiful greenways and towering giants, Haidra often dallied during the long, slow trek to the fragrant foot hills. The air, never dirtied by soot, drew a dose of waking she found thrilling and strange to her lungs. At the back of the ghosts' cart parked on the upward curve of a cattle trail climbing the canyons beside the glacier's roaring falls, she stood on the edge of a grassy berm and gazed out over the city, smiling for simply being as the sweet breeze combed her soft brown hair.

The rest of the troop busied up ahead with a crew of Arbikkean siege-engineers arguing with the Atenian rebel-laborers, more than a few already irked at having to listen to foreign voices berate them in ways few understood beyond the intent. Already Aleaus and Talic had stepped in to serve as liaisons between the two parties while Bon and New Moon quietly castigated their countrymen for their lack of gentility. Adan and Clive, both smart enough to watch the gear and peel the potatoes for supper later on, mused quietly at the small scuffles and fisticuffs that broke out along the way.

Wandering past the convoy of mules, men, and machinery dragged uphill, Haidra meandered ahead of her friends, the opportunity to be alone and unnoticed too enticing to let slip. Jogging ahead, the muscles of her tight, athletic frame moved in a harmony she had lacked weeks ago, the weight of the sword on her hip and the bundle of bow and arrows on her back an almost negligible burden. The grime on her face and hands, not to mention the sweat almost crusted and caked in places she ignored beneath her layers of black, battered mail, felt almost a second skin. She raced up the side of the rebel artillery march, catching the attention of many when they saw her dark cloaks and hood, the slight rust of her armor mottling the steel.

Free, fearless, she slowed when the weight of the chain drained her stamina. Gaining her bearings she saw she had reached the top of the next natural ramp. Brawny men and hard women hauled a forty-foot catapult, loudly straining but never complaining while under the blazing watch of Black John.

The wraith observed from the edge of the rise. His sword's point in the earth, he rested his spiked hands on its pommel, the length of steel reflecting the passing noon. Always in his mask, he let the fiery gaze roam before it shifted upon Haidra. Black John raised a gauntleted hand to wave her over.

Caught unprepared, she marched for her commander, head up and her gaze never leaving his. Though she knew no malice waited behind those points of fire the dramatic effect of them had yet to vanish, always renewing her sense of the eerie.

"Come to report?" he asked in his ghostly monotone.

"Uh, aye—" she said, stammering. "Aye, Black John."

The wraith pulled his stare off her and onto the nearest crew. "Go on."

Back to reality, she involuntarily shook her head. "We're making steady time, sir," she answered, which was the truth. "The ghosts are on the next ramp down. Some of the Arbikkeans are having trouble with the Atenians."

"Do they require me?"

"No, no," she was quick to reply. "The others have it."

"Good. Carry on."

"Yes, sir," she said, turning down the hill. The line of men on her left, struggling to heave steel and beam over the fresh earth, seemed like they would take forever. She faced the wraith again and cleared her throat.

"Yes, Lady Haidra?"

"Why don't you say anything?"

The wraith regarded her. "What is life like looking up?"

The question interrupted her thoughts, skewing every other apology she had planned. "Pardon?"

"I saw you running up the hill," he said. "I saw you smiling."

The way he said it, almost an accusation, shrank Haidra. "Yes, sir?"

"Did you get to do that every day when you were growing up?"

She wrinkled her brow in thought. "Well, of course I smiled."

"But did you look up, in the streets, and smile like you did when you ran up this hill?" the wraith asked again.

"Not every day." Plumbing the depth of his question, she let out a small grunt of recognition. "No, I did not."

"Not a single person your age has lived a day able to look up under a Veard. It no longer matters who they were before. The world is measured in what it is now."

She tilted her head slightly in confusion. "Milord?"

"Replacing one Veard with another Veard, or the relative of one, or new king, or a new queen, or however winners come about their game of thrones, results in the same problem."

"I'm not sure I follow," Haidra admitted.

"All of them believe they have the right to command you to look to the ground. Or command you to look the other way. Or disbelieve your ears. That will come to an end."

"But then how will Prince Aron—"

"It does not do to worry about a time and place we have yet to reach, Haidra," the wraith interrupted gently. "Who knows what may happen on the way there?"

The hard-won wisdom had her nodding. "Aye, sir."

"Is there anything else?"

"No, sir."

"Lady Haidra."

Haidra forced her feet in place, refusing to flinch as Black John turned in her direction. Taller than his son by almost a head, and her by two, he maintained his watch on the convoy. She attempted her best to follow his example, reviewing the workers or the equipment for something she had no clue about.

The wraith had barely moved a muscle until he removed his hand from the hilt of his ornate sword and touched his illusionary mask with his sharp fingers. The layer of darkness and the two floating eyes fell away, vanishing below his bearded chin in a fading dust.

Able to make out the hard line of his sad mouth, Haidra craned forward. "Milord?"

Those green-blues mixed in flecks of gold petrified her. He beheld her the way Bon did, by measure of his expression, but not in the amorous manner of the younger. Jhean de Veard appraised her as one soldier to another, one Atenian before the next.

To her surprise, Haidra spoke first, "My dad told me stories about the Wolf of Cyhra in the southern fields. They say you soothed her when everyone else wanted her dead, and that's why our herds stayed safe for so long. Is that what happened?"

The prince nodded, his golden face easing at the old memory.

"He told me that story over and over as a child. Told me there were people who did do right. But you took so long to come back. Why did you take so long?"

"Shame."

"But you didn't do—"

"Nobody knows the shame of a lie's acceptance until a lie is accepted about them. None of you—"

"We were scared," Haidra said. She shut her eyes tight, headlong into daring. "Everything changed."

"Everything always changes," he replied with a touch of the sardonic. "Are you still scared?"

Haidra shook her head.

"If one of you, then another, then another," the prince said in a leading tone.

"But we had no leader," she retorted.

"You can lead yourself, Haidra," he said. "That's what I mean. The idea you cannot, that you must resort to seeking someone with some gold on their head, must end. Each and every person is endowed with the spirit of freedom. The only time they lose the latter is when they bend to people like me."

"But you're a hero."

"I'm one man in a line of selfishness parading as virtue. The only way to rule is by dignity. I have seen heroes. They do not exploit power."

"But if not gods and kings, then who?" Haidra asked. "What other way is there?"

"A way that gives you, Aleaus, Talic, and every single Atenian their voice. In the square, in court, and before those they have chosen to serve them."

"The people served by those that rule them? Nonsense."

He glowered at her. "Only for those unwilling to fight for it."

"But you've lost your wife. Your parents," Haidra said. "Why didn't you fight before?"

The return to the core irked Jhean de Veard, firming his jaw. "Because it would have done more harm than good. It might now."

Haidra shrugged, at a loss again.

"You make different decisions when you love someone. When you have children," he replied. "The moment I found out what had happened, what Fransica..." he sighed, "I tired of war. Of fighting. I didn't want to tear Atenia apart just to punish a mad woman."

"But isn't that why you're here? To punish her?"

"I'm here to make right what was wronged. My wrongs," Jhean de Veard said. "I thought if I stayed away, if I simply let the world go on without Jhean de Veard in it, Atenia would continue as it was—in peace. Free. I placed my sister's life and her son's life, as well as my children, higher above a worthless seat. And I shouldn't have."

"Did Hibni?"

"No," he said within a deeper, heavier sigh. "She wanted to fight the moment we found out. Aron would have followed her. As the years went on, the more we heard about what was happening to people like you and your father, the more she urged me to return. I held when I should not have and, in doing so, she—"

The revelation ended as explosions rocked Atenia's citadel. The whole convoy stopped at the peal of magic explosions. Too bright to register the flashes, plumes of smoke spouted from multiple points behind the white walls, somewhere at the base of the two spires high above the palace.

"Oh, no," the prince said. "He's done it. He's turning on her."

"Who?" Haidra asked. Already, horns blasted in the royalist camps beyond the charred expanse of the dead zone. "Wait, look!"

A volley of arrows rose in a flock from the ruined quarters of Low Hill, but not aimed northward across the Ursin but immediately in the direction of the citadel's lower gate. Lime balefire mushroomed at the site in five distinct pillars. The force of the impact shifted the dust in Atenia's air, even to the slopes of the glaciers.

"To me, Haidra," Black John shouted as he charged down the grassy ramp. "Niklon betrays her!"

Ordering the convoy to continue their climb to the chosen positions atop Ben-Loman's falls, the Ghosts of Solomon called horses and rode hard to the city, the journey dominated by the cacophony of furious sorcery.

## 11

### ALL THINGS EQUAL

Prince Aron of Toliv, lacking in any outward cruelty, could not fail to hide the sinister smirk he shared with the other native Atenians in the tent. In the company of his Arbikkean countrymen, looking on with passive interest, dozens of rebels gathered under their benefactor's blue peaked roof to surround the prisoner on his knees, his blood speckling Idrian Street's cobbles.

A communal growl, eager and thirsty, grew in every corner of the warm enclosure.

"You know," Aron began, "since I came here, I have attempted to meet every single person I can and hear their stories so I know what will be left when all this is said and done. The farmers said the things I expected: taxed too much, worried for their daughters when you and your ilk visit for those taxes, but in general left alone. I worried there for a moment because that speaks of a sound ruler at least. The fields come first. But, my dear guest, the moment I entered the gates of this city two names were repeated again and again and again. One of them, surprisingly, was never the name of your son. *King* Tobias. No,

212

every tongue speaking Torsii speaks two names: Fransica and Niklon. Fransica and Niklon."

The prince lost the levity in his voice. "And I heard more about you, sorcerer. There are so many stories about you."

Haidra focused on the round-headed man centered in torchlight.

Face and hands pale and sallow from years in smoking dens, Niklon shivered on the street's stones. Stripped to a white linen robe and his underclothes, his captors had bound his hands and feet together at wrists and ankles. Someone had blackened one of his eyes and tore the corner of her upper lip, leaving his chest soaked in his own blood.

"Please," Niklon begged, gurgling from a broken nose stuffed in gauze. "Please, my Lord. Mercy!"

Aron leaned slightly to the side on his stool, almost in fascination. "Tell me, sorcerer, and I might consider it: Why were you and your cohorts fleeing the citadel?"

"She's gone mad," he cried out. "She's always been mad! Mad! Mad! Mad!"

"Stop shouting," Aron said, unmoved by his prisoner's outburst. "Answer my questions honestly, and I will have my healers tend to you. Do you understand?"

"Yes, yes! Please, milord, mercy!"

"Just answer," Aron repeated in Torsii. "What do you mean she's mad? What happens in the palace?"

"What has always happened! Darkness and chaos! Long after her murder of her father Fransica insisted on heightening her glory, almost forcing the priests of Hernos' Court to install a temple to her and her 'gods of love and new tradition'! The sacrilege would have thrown the people into rebellion, but the more we spoke wisdom against her inane plans the deeper her evils grew!"

"You speak as though she's been doing it all alone these years," said Aron. "Come now. I said I wanted honesty."

"I tell you no lies," the sorcerer whined. "The court of Atenia and I have spent years attempting to keep the kingdom together against her notions of conquest and worship, to spread her 'religion of love' across the south of Torsdaina! She thinks herself the mother of Hernos in the grandest of her delusions! She thinks herself the mother of bears!"

"What she thinks matters little to what she does now, Niklon. Why did you flee?"

"I told you!"

"No, no," said Aron. "Telling me she's mad doesn't explain why you blew up a part of the citadel. Telling me what everyone already knows doesn't explain to me why you risked arrows and swords when you were in enough control to pull that mad woman off the balcony a day ago. You're not telling me what I don't know. What don't I know, Niklon? What is she doing up there?"

"Power," the sorcerer rasped. "She gathers what power she has left. Feebler and feebler. Atenia is lost."

"To what end, then?" Aron asked. "Does she intend to maintain her defense?"

"She intends to kill you all."

"How? With what numbers?"

"You keep asking questions and I already told you," Niklon howled. "She thinks she will kill you. She has killed everyone else, but even on the verge of ruin, she persists!" The sorcerer twisted, teeth gritted as he tried to muster beyond the excruciating pressure his bonds placed on his limbs.

"He still hasn't answered your question," Aron's bard called from the prince's platform. Posed upon a small chair beside the prince's stool, the strummer Valen had come without his instrument to the proceedings. "And he's not sworn to any gods of love we know of, my Liege. But I know one god he does worship."

One of Aron's servants handed the prince the infamous

white dragon mask, symbol of the secret cult the sorcerer had failed to hide through his reign as the queen-regent's consort. Niklon detached from his discomfort, his full focus on the scaled oval.

Aron held the mask in both hands, staring into its fearsome eye holes. "Tell me what this is," he said. "Do otherwise, and you will be resigned to your proper fate."

"There is only one fate, and it lies with Dhir," the sorcerer said in a clear, serious monotone. He stared through the Arbikkean prince, red-eyed in defiance but unemotive.

Aron checked over his shoulder at the bard. He held the mask up. Valen thought deeply on the item before he nodded.

"One last time," Aron said. "What is she doing up there?"

"Burn," Niklon answered. "We're going to burn you all."

The prince raised his eyebrows and sighed. "Funny you mention that."

On cue, Haidra stepped out of those gathered together, quickly beside Clive and Aleaus as they laid hands on Niklon. She pulled the dagger Bon had given her to slay another sorcerer not long ago. Instead of a jugular she sliced the cords around his wrists, freeing his arms.

Screaming a shrill sound, the blacksmith and fisherman's son unceremoniously dumped Niklon onto the cobblestones again. One of the wads of gauze knocked free of a nostril in his rough roll, fresh strings of red leaking on his cheek and jaw.

The Ghosts of Solomon pressed, backed by two wraiths without their hoods. Bon de Veard's face, leonine like his father's, could not hide his hatred. New Moon simply looked down at her uncle, her expression unreadable. Huddled on his knees and hugging his body to relieve the pain in his back, shoulders, a creeping familiarity widened Niklon's eyes in terror as their father loomed behind them.

The husband of a murdered wife snatched the sorcerer by his skinny throat.

"I'll be ready for the signal," Prince Aron called over the screams as they dragged Niklon away.

---

THE SUN DIPPED BEHIND BEN-LOMEN, drawing the blue out of the sky until only fire and purple clouds remained. Twilight had fallen on Entaris Bridge, and barren of any life save a few birds hopping along its stone rails, only the drag of the log's end marred the quiet.

Black John bore the other end on his shoulder, hellish eyes ahead as he marched upon the bridge's midpoint. Gauntlets removed, his bare hands dug hard into the grain.

Behind the swordsman came his son, bearing a sack, and Moon with the first armful of kindling. Haidra led the rest of the ghosts after them, each of them with a load of firewood except for Talic and Clive. The two men strained under the weight of two seventy-pound stone rings, the base supports needed to keep the stake upright.

After they raised the pole on the flattest part in the center, Black John nodded to his son. "Let me see him."

Unbinding the sack's ties, they dumped the broken, beaten form of Niklon in front of the swordsman. Coughing from the smothering burlap, the younger man by a few years wretched on his knees before his guts steadied thanks to the fresh air. Eyes shut tight, he collapsed onto his side.

"Rise," said Black John. "Rise."

Niklon trembled on the rough cement of Entaris' path.

"Get up," Black John said. "Get up and look at me, you damned cur."

The sorcerer remained inert.

The wraith dashed forward, kicking Niklon hard in the left side. The blow brought a low, whooshing moan. He bunched in a ball, his knees close to his chest to guard his face and organs.

Black John grabbed Niklon by the back of the neck and wrenched him to his feet. The other steeled hand closed around his prey's throat. He lifted the human load backward until they met the pole in the bridge's center.

"Look at me!" Black John roared in Niklon's face. The wraith's floating, fiery eyes flared a harsh green color, no longer red and smoldering. He pressed the sorcerer's throat, squeezing harder and harder. "Look at me."

Niklon opened his undamaged eye, the other swollen red and bulbous.

Black John used his free hand and touched his illusionary mask. It disappeared in an instant, the screen of shadow dissipating to the hard, handsome features of Jhean de Veard.

Eye to eye with his brother-in-law, Niklon shuddered before a slow, weird laugh overcame the pain of his wounds. Resolute against the mad sorcerer's cackle, the rightful heir of Atenia braced his arm, cutting the mirth off at the source.

Niklon gagged until the choke was released.

Jhean de Veard closed on him, noses almost touching. "I should have known the moment I saw you. The hesitance, the tone you took. There was never a thing honest or real about you. Just a sad little boy vying for power among other sad little boys."

"Better than a man who beds his sister!" Niklon proclaimed in an oozing-red smile.

"What did you do to her? What did you do to my sister?"

"Nothing that you hadn't."

Jhean de Veard smacked Niklon across the cheek with the back of his bare hand. He followed it up with a solid right to the stomach. Unable to fall down, red-tinged vomit exploded out of the sorcerer's mouth and nose. He spat it to breathe and suffered another round of hacking for the effort.

"Did you place a spell on her?" Jhean asked.

Haidra whispered to Bon, tugging on his hand. "What is he talking about?"

The ax-slinger gave no response, focused on his mother's murderer with a morbid fascination.

"Tell me," the prince of Atenia said. "Tell me the truth."

Wheezing through his chattering teeth as he tried to suck air past the prince's grip, Niklon banged his cut-up fists on the armored arm of his captor, feebler with every pound.

Jhean de Veard jerked the man closer. "Say it," the prince said. "Say it out loud. The truth. All of it."

"I didn't need a spell when the lies and cunning did the work for her," Niklon gurgled, able to speak. "It's all lies. She lies, she connives, she schemes. She said it because you didn't—"

"Of course, I didn't," Jhean de Veard screamed in Niklon's face. "I never gave her what she wanted! Is that why? Is that why she did this? Or did you make her? Did you make her kill Solomon?"

"Make her? You damned fool," Niklon said. "She planned it!"

New Moon called to her father, "Focus."

He stared at the sorcerer for a long moment, weighing each other for the inevitable. "Where's Marta?"

"I don't know," Niklon said. "Stopped caring once we locked her upstairs—but I won't tell you where."

"And your son?"

"Which one?"

Jhean de Veard drew back, aghast at the response. "How many have you two—"

"As many as I put in her."

"And Tobias? Where is Tobias?"

"How he fared was up to her." Another wave of misery ran through Niklon. He failed to swallow, wheezing before it cleared. "Spare me, Jhean. I hate the bitch as much as you do. Let me go and I will tell you what she plans."

"I'll end it."

"But—"

"My ghosts," said the prince, barring no interruption. "Bind him."

Passed a six-foot-long piece of hemp cord by Talic, Haidra advanced with the rest. The son and daughter of Hibni remained where they were. Crystal trails escaped from corners of New Moon's eyes, flowing down her dark cheeks.

Niklon fought against Jhean de Veard's might, gibbering as he cursed the prince to his face. He clawed at the mail arm until Haidra and Clive, responsible for his hands, wrestled the sorcerer under control. Aleaus tied their prisoner to the smoothed stake at the ankles and knees as Talic and Adan held his legs straight. Clive struggled against the sorcerer, who kept throwing his weight forward.

"Hurry, Haidra," Clive said, grunting. "Bugger's coated in oil already, the fiend!"

"Curse you, you dimwitted boy—"

Jhean de Veard's other hand capped Niklon's mouth. "Quickly, Haidra."

"I'm going, I'm going, I'm going." She cinched two loops around the sorcerer's wrists and secured a haphazard knot, thick and ugly. She stepped back, dodging Niklon's winging elbow. "There!"

Fixed to the stake, Jhean de Veard motioned for his troop to give him space. Tearing a baleful glare off the sorcerer, he checked on his children.

"Last chance," he told them. "One of you can do it. Do not fret if you do not wish it. All is as I promised."

"And you have kept your promise, Father." New Moon studied her condemned uncle, addressing him. "Uma forgives all sins, and I hope that in your night you find the way to the stars again. I forgive you, Niklon."

"As do I," Bon said. "Let's be done with what needs to be done."

"Practically saints, you lot," Adan murmured under his breath.

"Their goddess is kinder than our many." Jhean de Veard grinned violence at his wife's killer. "They're kinder than me. Your hoods—take them off. All of you. I want your faces to be seen. I want her to see."

"Who?" Aleaus asked as the blacksmith unleashed her salt and pepper locks, matted and tangled with sweat. "Who are you talking about?"

"Her." Jhean de Veard looked up toward Atenia's citadel, his lost home, for the royal balcony. Too dark in the evening to make out if anyone guarded its unlit rise, he ripped his sword from the scabbard on his hip. "Her."

Bare in the dying daylight, the ghosts and his children watched in grim wonder as Jhean de Veard incanted. The long steel blade of High John the Conqueror caught the flame of the sunset, but as the fallen prince evoked his magics, the length glowed brighter. From yellow to red to gold it grew in heated intensity, until the moisture in the air sizzled around the brand of Atenia's ancient line.

"No! No!" Niklon shouted at the man he had made a widow.

The flashes of light in every stroke boiled the blood from wounds so terrible much of it never hit the pavement. The smell of scorched viscera and sizzling fat nauseated Haidra too much before she turned away, unable to bear witness to the butchery.

Jhean de Veard thrust his sorcerous blade into the seared remains of Niklon, fixing through to the wood. The entire post flared alight. He stormed past the flaming stake, his full face exposed as he unleashed years of withheld rage.

"It ends, sister," he screamed up to the darkened citadel, the declaration lost beneath the loud crackling of the burning effigy. "It ends!"

Upon the immolation of Niklon the artillery positions atop Ben-Lomen's glacial lakes fired in unison. Stone and fire bombs streaked the darkening sky as the sun disappeared, but not before the impact razed the crest of High Hill in a curtain of dust. The horns of the royalists blew but quickly fell silent under the relentless battering.

Prince Aron's forces crossed the dead zone the next day, conquering the rest of Atenia's metropolis. Rebel forces surrounded the citadel.

PART III

———

# THE SUNDERING

Haidra knew he had something planned the moment she woke up that morning.

"Be home for dinner, Haidra," her father said before he left, off to haul dung and unload Ecktor's bins for extra coppers. "I'll be working on Iner's nets all afternoon so I'll be here. Don't be late."

Left to fend for herself every morning since she was eleven and could work her own jobs, Haidra paid the order what she usually did, nothing more than her father's usual stress peaking as the monotony of life continued for another day. Busying in the kitchen with the leftovers, she trimmed the mold of the cheese block, matted some clean slices on a piece of crusty bread, and quickly dressed in her brown hose and underclothes before throwing on a red woolen dress and apron dusted in the front with faded splotches of dough. Binding her hair in a bun she covered with one of her mother's old scarfs, Haidra marched out into the streets of Low Corner, eastbound for Idrian Street and one of the many bakeries along the thoroughfares.

Head down, eyes to the path, Haidra traced her way through the alleys, cutting across old public squares overgrown in weeds and overpopulated in stray animals, children, and poor too lame or sick to work. She ignored the pans thrust out in front of where she walked, made way for the roving bands of grubby boys and girls searching for food or stealing it, and more than few noted the flour stains on Haidra's apron. A few of the older boys and a rough-looking girl a few years younger followed her down the block, but she escaped them at the next corner at a guard station manned by a full accompaniment.

Not that it made things better.

She quickened her pace as one of the spearmen spotted her on the sidewalk.

"Hey, girl," he cried. "Hey, girl, look here!"

"Oh, come on, sweet tits," the soldier beside him brayed. "Headed off to the kitchens? I got something for your oven!"

"Something with a nice filling," the first spearman added. "Come on, sweetheart! Where're you goin'?"

Haidra paid them no attention, eyes straight ahead until the catcalls faded.

Not far from Roromheta Road, a few blocks north on the east side of Idrian, she signed her name on a ledger to check in at the bakery, the rough letters unique among illiterate marks. One of the few women her age able to read and write thanks to her father's diligence, she reported to Tanny, the old woman in charge of the storeroom in the back. Tasked to manage a crew of twelve laborers picked out of a crowd that clustered every morning for a loaf of rye and a few coppers, the lot spent the whole day piling sacks of flour brought in from the fields in the north and south or delivering to the kitchens to feed the always-roasting ovens. Every single item used was counted in exact quantity so the taxers didn't punish them for being in error at the end of the month.

Apprenticed to take over the role of stocker which Tanny

had filled since before she was born, Haidra shadowed the heavy-set woman across the floor multiple times as she took notes dictated into another ledger she hefted in one hand, scrawling with quill in the other. Balancing a small bowl of ink in the crook of her elbow, the day ended over a wash basin full of cake-y water and strains of black, which always took longer to get out than the flour.

The sun was setting when she escaped the bakery's yeast-stink, armed with two fresh loaves, one of whole wheat and the other blended with chives, and the silvers needed to help pay rent for the month before old landlord Jasper pounded around with his cudgel, threatening and leering until her father shooed the man away with coin.

The guards at the station near her house in Low Corner didn't notice her, another weary worker shuffling home in the dim. Thankful for the peace and relative quiet as cats chorused in allies, she gave wide berth to the rats infesting the gutters and under the overgrown trees, already on the hunt for dinner. A few people she knew from the neighborhood offered a kind smile here, a nod there when she saw them, and like the day before she was certain to repeat tomorrow, Haidra arrived at a lit hovel and the warm smell of boiling barley on the hearth.

Loaves clutched to her chest, she used her hip to push the door open.

Her father toiled over the pot hung on its stand above their stone fireplace, an open rock chimney they had rebuilt a few years ago after the old one collapsed and Jasper refused to replace it. Flush to the wall of the apartment they rented but would never own due to Fransica's favoritism to deeds and landlords, she grinned her and her father's achievement. Theirs or not, they had done it together.

"Bar the door when you're in," Arverin said. "Make sure it's tight tonight."

"Storm coming?" Haidra asked as she laid the bread on the dinner table first. "It looked clear out."

"Just bar the door, Haidra. Now."

The edge in his voice stole her smile. She slowly paced to the door and set the stout oak bar on the brackets riveted into the frame. She re-faced the room of the house she had been born in, watched her mother die in, and made every day the one single place in Atenia she knew was safe. Her father's nets, long and thick with green cord to catch the rock backs and silver-streaked bass thrashing through the glacial streams in the west or the Franc, were tacked by the windows. The dishes lay ready on the table.

So did the coin.

Haidra sighed at its place by Arverin's bowl. Small, round, and gold, it was stamped with the old royal seal of Atenia on its backside, the one with a dancing bear nobody was allowed to depict. Why he kept it, she couldn't guess, but on the nights it was brought out, the mood of the only man that mattered to her soured. Never fearing an angry hand or unjust word, only brooding and dark thoughts, she hummed a note of acceptance and returned to preparing supper. Along with the barley porridge he stirred she cut thick slices of the chive-bread she patted with cheese and toasted on a brick by the fire.

They sat for a quiet meal, spooning the hot mush with nibbles of bread and sips of day-old water. Arverin studied the coin, the amber eyes he shared with Haidra full of hard memory.

"Get the net done?" she asked in one of the long lulls.

"No," he said, swallowing when her voice broke his fixation. "I'm not going to finish it."

"Then how are you going to get paid by Iner?" Haidra asked. "We need that money, Dad."

"Don't worry about Iner. Iner's fine with it." He raised his gaze from the gold to her. "Haidra, we need to talk about something. Something that's not going to be easy."

"You're marrying me off to Joachim, aren't you?" Balling her fists, Haidra tightened her face in growing anxiety. "I knew you were—"

"No, Haidra," Arverin interrupted. "Listen!"

Haidra clammed up in her chair. She watched in growing concern as her father kept looking at the coin. The depiction of a man she had never heard about on its gleaming face, polished velvet by many rubs of the thumb, glittered on the spot it rested.

"I have to go to Ecktor's tonight," Arverin continued in a low, whisper-like monotone. The tension in his brow subsided, his mouth relaxed, but the odd glint in his eyes remained.

Haidra feared the glint. "Why?"

His eyes with hers. Then it vanished for a second, the loving expression of the man she adored appearing in tears brimming his eyes and a wain, detached smile for someone else.

"You look like your mother. I know I tell you that a lot, but you do. You know it's been really hard since—"

"I know," Haidra said. "We don't have to bring it up again, Dad. I miss her. I remember her."

"Oh, little, I know," he said, caught between laughter and weeping. "I know you do. And you've been so, so strong through it. Stronger than me. But, uh..." He wiped both eyes with calloused fingers. "It's time for me to be strong for you back."

"But I don't—"

"I need you to go to Tanny's tonight," he said. "Right after we're done here. I need you to go and stay with her until I come find you."

"But why, Dad? What do you mean you have to be strong?"

"I..." Arverin gasped with emotion, clapping his hand on the coin. Anxiety shuddered the net-maker in his wooden chair. "You won't understand it because you were too little when it happened, but there was a point when I didn't have to worry about you. I didn't have to worry about not owning my home, or that the law wouldn't protect me. I didn't have to worry like I did in those days before she—"

"Before?" Haidra asked. "Before what?"

"Before the queen-regent. Before old bastards like Jasper could walk around with a cudgel just because nobody would stop him. When old Queen Marta was around, Haidra, there was no worry of what would happen if a knight ran into a woman in the street. Bastards like them wouldn't have been given a sword, let alone allowed to gallivant around like pomp cocks, running innocent women under hoof while they're walking home from the goddamned market!"

"I know." Haidra repeated her constant response every time he started on the Veards. "But why do you have to leave? Why tonight?"

"Because tonight can be the end of it all. Tonight will be the end of it all."

The certainty of the last sentence froze Haidra. "What are you going to do?"

"I'm going to light the queen-regent's fields on fire," he answered, as if possessed by someone else. He grinned once more, but this one was mad and broken. "After that?"

Haidra slowly rose from her chair. "Dad, you can't. Th-that's food! People need that food."

"People need freedom, Haidra," Arverin retorted. "There's no bread in the belly when you're always hungry. There's no wheat when you never see a harvest. And what happens to you? What happens when it comes time for you to lay down and die, and someone takes your spot at the bakery? Well, Haidra? What would have bread done for that?"

Every question a nail hammered in, not only for the truth, but for the possibility of what he was about to do over them.

"But what about us? What about our home? What happens if the knights or the guard—"

"If I'm successful tonight, you'll never fear them again," Arverin said with bravado. "When the ghost of old Marta rises and the sun comes tomorrow, none of Atenia will."

The front door of their hovel burst apart, the oak bar splinting into two as a ram smashed through the panels and bars. The blunt end withdrew as mailed hands reached in, punching and smashing the remains still fixed to the frame.

"Make way in the name of the queen-regent," a booming voice called outside. "Prepare to surrender!"

Arverin was around the table before Haidra could see him, the old carving knife she used to cut the bread in his main hand. He snatched her by the arm and pushed her toward the lone window of their home, behind his nets. Unable to fight back against his size or strength, Haidra whined as he forced her on the sill.

"Make way!"

"Run, Haidra," Arverin shouted as the door broke apart.

Men in helms and mail covered by pink-and-navy checkered tabards flooded in, led by a knight bearing a longsword.

"I love you! I love you!" Her father turned, raising his knife up as he charged the lead warrior. "For Marta!"

In a stroke, blood flowed, his body dashed to the boards of their home.

It was the last thing Haidra saw as she dropped out the window. Landing hard on her feet she toppled forward, bruising her knees. Adrenaline pushed her past tears she couldn't contain. She ran as hard and as fast as she could. Everything disappeared in an instant, from tomorrow's shift at the bakery to Arverin's illicit coin on the table, stained dark like the floor of a home she'd never return to.

Despite every yearning, every want to save her daddy, she never looked back as the night swallowed her.

1

---

# THE SIEGE OF THE SHELL

The Arbikkean artillery atop Ben-Lomen's glacier leveled High Hill's position, obliterating the only impediment blocking the rebels and Prince Aron from crossing the Ursin Canal in full force. The moment the shelling and firebombs ended one of the watchers along Lilias Street spotted a white flag at the dead-zone's edge, held high by a singed man on a horse.

Riders were sent to meet the surrendering knights fronting a horde of refugees, royalist prisoners, and the dead of those who had cared enough to keep them through the destruction. The prince of Toliv accepted their surrender, feeding and sheltering the lost as his agents and functionaries slowly worked out the events of the last few hours.

To both the delight of the Children of Marta and Aron's retinue, the informants yielded news of Fransica's sellsword armies. All paid on a coin quickly running out, many quit her ranks not long after Black John had immolated her husband for all to see. Leaving in waves of hundreds, their immediate dispersal once High Hill fell coincided with the remaining royalists fleeing for the citadel.

From the northern walls where they first fed the spark of rebellion to the southern palisade beyond the charred dead zone, horns blasted in triumph as great cheers resounded. Those sworn to Marta, many of them older in years and weathered by Atenia's violent decline, dropped to hands and knees in racking sobs, thanking or cursing their gods for what they had done. Every scrap of pink-and-navy heraldry to be found was cast into burn-pits. Old statues of the Veards across the metropolis toppled under the yank of the lash. Stone shattered on the stained roads and streets as torches, swords, and fists speared the air in teary relief. Families, huddled in their homes through the song of war and death, emerged to reunite with loved ones who gave so, so much.

Whispers spread as well. The sight of High John the Conqueror and the mad declarations of the queen-regent had placed the name of Jhean de Veard in mouths that long wished to say his name in blessing or scorn, debating the cause of their turmoil.

As the exiled prince feared, calls to find him or his heirs spread.

When it came time to approach the citadel's lower gate at dawn every single man, woman, and teen able to carry torch or spear fell in with the Arbikkean vanguard as they marched across Entaris Bridge and up the Colis. Cries for Fransica's death, the death of her son Tobias, rang up at an empty balcony.

The royalist stationed at the lower gate emerged along the battlements, a column of three archers going as far back as the first ascending curve. They drew arrows under the command of a lone knight at the rear, who quickly gave the order.

Veterans of the siege raised their shields or stepped behind cover, but a few unfortunate newcomers fell, unable to cover themselves in time. The Arbikkeans called a short withdraw, setting Prince Aron's forward camp in the middle of the Colis, in clear sight of the enemy stronghold.

"You worked up there, right?" Bon asked the next morning as they stood under a tree line east of the gates, giving them a good vantage of the royalist archers nestling behind the barrier. "Talic?"

"Aye, sir," said the old guard, his gray gaze forlorn. "During the construction of the second tower. I was in Horras for the rest of it."

"What made you leave?" Aleaus asked. "You joined the Children relatively late."

Chewing on the end of a piece of grass he had plucked off the berm they stood on, Talic glumly eyed the challenge ahead. "Same thing that led us here, Lea. Just got tired."

"John says they have enough stores in there to last a full two years on their own," Clive said, sitting lower on the ditch next to his father as they trimmed pieces of leftover bread for their lunch. The cooking fire behind them was tended to by Bon and New Moon, who had made a fine meal of chicken, rice, and sweetened curds beside the bottles of wine the former had "borrowed" from Prince Aron's tent.

"She doesn't have that time, son," Adan said, his head in the grass. "It's all a matter of time."

"What do you think is going to happen, Bon?" Talic asked. "I'd fucking bring the damn gate down with artillery and that magic you all have and call it a day. Let them starve up there while we get to cleaning."

"I wish it were so simple," the son of Atenia and Arbikk answered in fluent Torsii. "We'll see what the ups have planned. Haidra, let's get the horses?"

"Right," she said, offering him a warm smile he returned.

She jogged into the trees where they had tied two strong black stallions for Bon and Talic, who had experience in the saddle, while the rest had been given dark ponies to weather the first weeks of horsemanship. Bringing all by their bridles using an Arbikkean horse-charm one of Aron's instructors had berated them to learn, the Ghosts of Solomon moved as a unit, clopping down the hill. Decked in their black clothes and mail, they brought a reverent attention as they passed by recently constructed horse pens and the outlying tents for the vanguard, most of whom rose to their feet and saluted.

Prince Aron's headquarters rose out of the clusters of wagons and carts cluttering the Colis' midpoint, leaving a single way in and out of the large tent guarded by a dozen spearmen knelt in the entrance. Dismounting, the ghosts were given way. Bon entered first, followed by Haidra before Aleaus and Adan, then the rest.

As always, the war-tent was packed around the table and two braziers, forever in the middle of the next conspiracy. This time one voice held sway, projecting naturally above the grumbles of both natives and foreigners.

"—the issue is not whether I'm willing to commit the forces I've brought to this siege, my prince." The bard Valen leaned on the prince's round table, facing Aron directly so one half of the room was forced to see his back. "I'd simply implore you not to waste them until the high gate had been breached. When that happens I'd be more than willing to send them forth, but you both know what an uphill battle that will be. Please, something else."

"What else is there, Valen?" Prince Aron replied. "Your forces, my forces, the end result will be the same. Any attempt to reach the citadel will be met by heavy resistance. The royalists have the advantage of both the high ground as well as their ability to hem us on the path. Nothing we do will mean anything until we reach those gates."

"There were explosions seen when Niklon tried to escape," Black John said from his seat, holding his own corner of the table. "There's no way to enter but Snail's Way—that is why Atenia's ancient chieftains first settled and carved the hill. Underneath the citadel itself are many basements and sub-basements converted from the ancient caves. There is no doubt those remained sealed from the lower passages, and likely packed with Fransica's larders."

One of Aron's cataracts, the horseman called Ahmeti, leaned forward to gain the prince's attention from the bard. "My lord, why do we simply not destroy the gates with our artillery? Batter it down and we can pick our way through dead archers after."

"It's not designed that way," Black John said with confidence. "Snail's Way was rebuilt three centuries ago under the rule of Argenia II, who had the ramparts designed to collapse inward and block the way in case there was an invasion by one of the sorcerer-nations in the north. There were fears of them marching southward in those days, hungry for slaves and spoil needed to spur their petty wars. Before Atenia had spellcasters of their own the only way, it was thought, to stop their advance was by cutting off the way forward."

"And if they flew?" Valen asked the elder wraith. "What if they sent dragons?"

Black John's fiery stare shifted to the pale, handsome bard. "Then the Veards would have fought a dragon. Right to the bitter end."

"It seems, despite our best intentions, all roads lead that way," Prince Aron remarked with a heavy sigh.

"I'm not so sure," New Moon said from her seat beside her father. The Shahira of the Northern Deserts had removed her hood, her dark beauty and silver locks a vision of confident grace among the hardnosed, battle-scarred warriors. "Has anyone here ever considered scaling the walls?"

Her father responded first. "We discussed this."

"I think we should discuss it again," New Moon pressed the men at the table. "We just handed these people their lives back and their land. We cannot ask them to throw that away for the chance at Fransica when they are tired, homeless, and hungry."

She engaged her father. "She has a smaller force up there, correct?"

The two points of flame slanted in her direction. "Yes. Most are massed at lower gates."

"So, who is left above?" she asked. "Those who watch the rampart, but you can't fit more than three men shoulder to shoulder if we forget about the main path. If we can get up there—"

"But there is no way to get up there," Ahmeti interrupted. "Pardon, milady, but we are not birds."

The inanity of the response made Haidra speak up. "That's not fair."

Thinking she had said it low and whispered so that no one heard her, the entire tent—princes, warriors, patrons, Children, and her friends—paused to place their attention on her alone. A rat caught by a cat in the bin, she froze, open-mouthed.

"Do you have something to add, Lady Haidra?" asked Prince Aron, smiling from ear to ear as he looked away from Valen. The bard's expression rankled as he did so.

Unable to breath, she grunted when Bon nudged her on the left side. "I meant only to say—"

"I mean no disrespect to Lady Moon with my comment, girl," Ahmeti said, dismissive. "Now, what I think—"

The words of the horseman disappeared behind the belittlement, but the days had worn her, the miles straightening her stride and hardening her hands to the hilt of a weapon like his.

No longer a baker, let alone a shivering girl on the edge of a field, Haidra spoke louder. "What I meant to say, milord," she said in clear, concise Torsii, regaining the tent's attentions, "is that you don't have to be a bird if you're not blind."

A roar of laughter erupted from the Children of Marta and disparate quarters of the rebel cause. The foreign fighters with a sense of the native language broke in fits, a few of them slamming the table with their fists.

"Pardon me, girl?" Ahmeti asked, stunned by the pointed rebuke. He fixed on her with those mean eyes, a growl curling his hairy upper lip. Neck to ankle in scale cinched with a girdle carrying two curved swords and a dagger, he stood from his chair and leaned both scarred fists on the table.

Never leaving her behind, Black John and New Moon bolted to their feet, matching his posture to the rising cheers.

"Quiet, quiet," Prince Aron said. "I will have quiet!" The roar of the smiling prince calmed the rabble. He waved down the wraiths and his rough riders. "Lady Haidra, if you'd please."

"The Tomb of the Veards," she said, not wasting words she might stumble over. "There is a ridge connecting the tombs of the royals with the citadel. It's not impossible to cross—"

"For birds," Ahmeti interrupted.

"And perhaps the brave!" Haidra shouted back, drawing a hard laugh and clap from Aleaus. "Do not forget, we have one more duty to do for Old Atenia. We must restore J—"

"That is enough," Black John said, cutting her off. "The ridge is high and easily viewed from the top of the walls day or night. Thank you, Haidra, but the way is unsafe. We must devise another means of breaking in."

Defeated by her captain's proclamation, Haidra receded back among the ghosts, eyes averted to the patterned carpets the servants had thrown down on the Colis' road. Gentle pats of affection and confirmation on her shoulders by Talic and Adan and a gentle squeeze of Bon's hand did nothing to diminish the embarrassment reddening her face. Daring to look up again as princes and lords planned days of death, she hesitated too long when she caught New Moon half turned in her chair, staring dead at her.

The sorceress smiled without a care for who saw it.

# 2

# HAIDRA BLOOM

**W**ake up," Bon whispered in her ear. "Haidra."

She stirred on her cot, sliding her feet under the edge of the wool blanket as the morning chill found her bare toes.

"Haidra, honey, wake up," he whispered again, planting a warm kiss on her right cheekbone. She smiled through the light of a summer dream as she lay in hot sands, baking beneath the sun beside him, naked and free. She patted the place she expected to find her uncrowned prince, groping the air as the blanket was pulled off her.

The sudden shock of the cold woke Haidra as she seized on her cot, yelping as she realized multiple people stood around and above her.

"Gods damn, Aleaus," Bon said. "She was waking up!"

"Well, now she's up," the blacksmith said, taking a step back to allow Haidra room to rest her feet on the ground. The communal tent the ghosts shared, not far from the blue fortress Prince Aron called his and lent rooms to the wraiths, lay in the half-dark of an early morning. The fire in the brazier was down to its ruddy coals, moved about by the poker in Talic's hand as he dropped one handful of kindling after another, slowly refueling the flame. Adan and his son Clive posted by the entrance, already in their mail and sharing a pipe full of wort and stinking hashish an Arbikkean apothecary issued for a persistent headache both suffered every morning and night since the first shelling. It put calm in their eyes and posture. Seated not far from them on her own cot, Aleaus had plopped back down and held her hand out, waiting for the smoking bowl.

Bon and Moon had arrived, their hoods cast back to show their faces.

"Haidra," New Moon asked, not waiting for her to rub away the last dregs of sleep, "what didn't you get to say in the tent?"

"What did I say in the tent?" she asked, confused as she massaged her eyes using the pads of her chilled fingers. Already they hurt from the growing fire in the brazier.

"Something about restoring my father," the sorceress said plainly. "That's what you were going to say, isn't it?"

The sincerity of the question, almost like New Moon had caught her, brought Haidra to full wakefulness. The ghosts and Bon watched, waiting on her answer.

On her plan.

"Well," Haidra said, looking up at New Moon, "It's what Fransica said—if Black John made it to the gates, then he would have proved his innocence by right of deed. I was thinking of him at the moment. That's all. I know I shouldn't have—"

The sorceress dropped to one knee in front of Haidra and wrapped her arms around her neck and head, pulling her in a deep, long embrace.

"I knew you had it the moment I saw you," New Moon whispered in Haidra's ear, deep with emotion. "Now, get up. You and I have a lot of people to talk to."

"To do what?" Haidra asked as she was freed.

Bon bent down at the foot of her cot and lifted the black boots someone had given her back before the palisade fell, stained and road-worn from marching from one end of Atenia to the other. "We're going to bring a man back from the dead."

"Getting horses, gear, that's all well and good," said Bon as he marched ahead of them ten minutes later, his ax low in his hand as he turned and walked backward. "The problem is going to be getting past him."

"Your da's got to sleep like everyone else, Bon-boy," Clive said, not hesitant to address the older comrade so casually. "Right, Da?"

"I once heard Jhean de Veard fought off a pack of wolves by himself, dagger in hand, for two days while on campaign in the wastes of Golghra." Adan shrugged his stocky shoulders. "I wouldn't put it past a sorcerer. Begging your pardon, Lady Moon."

"No, no, you're not wrong," New Moon replied. "He's devilishly persistent and disciplined, made all the worse by a penchant for brooding into the wee hours and lonesome patrols in the city. There's no way we leave him conscious."

"So…" Clive asked in a leading tone.

"So, Clive-lad," Bon said, facing straight ahead, "we'll have to incapacitate him."

"This will not go well," said Talic at the rear of their cluster. "Not well at all."

The children of their intended target led them to the apothecary tent, one of the tall, wide canvas shelters housing the many sundries and services Prince Aron had brought to Atenia's oppressed, requiring none to pay a single cent for care or personal need. New Moon pulled Haidra inside, leaving the rest out in the cold, sunny morning.

Beeswax candles on multiple shelves, stands, and stools, illumined a table segmented into multiple compartments stuffed to the brim in herbs, roots, resins, small bottles of tinctures, packets of all sorts of seeds, sachets, incense both in cone and stick, and a dizzying array of items smelling of every corner of the continent and farther abroad. The heady odor, strong and spiced with a small hint of dank on the back of her tongue, made Haidra press her lips shut, not wanting to inhale invisible fumes or particles in the hazy air.

An older woman waited behind the main bar. Her long black hair bound by a headscarf dripping in rhinestones and precious gems, she raised her hands and cried out in joy. Draped in lengths of silk over fine, form-fitting robes, she embraced New Moon in a lavish display, both of them pecking the air in front of each other's cheeks. They quickly fell into a fast, happy dialogue Haidra could not follow in Eaith, her attentions torn as they gossiped in front of her.

"Haidra," New Moon said at a brief pause in the conversation. "Come and meet Auntie Sakinah. She's Prince Aron's aunt by his mother and—"

"Haidra? Haidra Bloom?" Auntie Sakinah launched into another litany Haidra did not catch as the figure of shadowy beauty rushed her, pulling her into her bosom with a tight hug and pecked two more of those invisible kisses by her cheeks. She talked and talked and talked to Haidra, running through several sentences she only caught snatches of, littered with the odd Torsii name or phrase.

New Moon halted the apothecary into the second full minute of her one-woman festival, snatching a painted hand and planting a kind kiss on the back of it before she said a short sentence.

Auntie Sakinah's entire demeanor changed as she squinted conspiratorially back at the sorceress. She asked questions in Eaith, low and whispered, directed only to New Moon.

The Shahira of the Northern Sands answered in calm, affirming words.

Tapping her dark, full lips with a finger, a knowing smile spread across the apothecary's face. She skirted around her tables, disappearing behind a wooden partition.

"What just happened?" Haidra asked after the whirlwind.

"Oh, she's just going to go get the potion," said New Moon.

"The potion?"

"That potion," said New Moon. "The potion for Black John. The potion chosen especially for Black John. Black John's potion. That potion."

"No, I understand," Haidra said in a withering tone. "What's Haidra Bloom?"

"Oh!" New Moon shook her head with a half-smile, somewhat surprised. "You didn't know?"

Haidra shook her head.

"Haidra," New Moon said, almost as if she was stunned. "I don't want to sound rude, but you're really an innocent, aren't you?"

"What does that mean?"

"What I mean is…" The sorceress sighed, half-closing her hazel eyes. "For someone so determined and strong, you really aren't aware of how much you affect the world around you."

Blinking a few times, Haidra could only shrug.

"You're the daughter of a rebel leader. You set the fields on fire that exploded the Veard dynasty of Atenia, ending the tyrannical reign of its queen-regent. You summoned the wraiths of the Burnt Lady. You're the first *bloom* of hope people heard when help arrived. You're the first Ghost of Solomon. You slew the wizard that halted us at Victus Crossing. I don't know if you know this, but just about everyone adores you and my brother, though I cannot stand it for the life of me. Aron and I are much cuter."

"But I didn't do those things for attention."

"It doesn't matter," New Moon said, checking on Auntie Sakinah as the Arbikkean lady rummaged through the back of her supply area. "Well, it does. I can't say it doesn't matter because how people view us and what they say about it after has a huge impact. More than I'd like to accept."

Haidra shifted her stance. "How so?"

"Well, you're not the only one who's come out of this different," New Moon said. "They call Talic "Talic Gray-stare," able to seize men on the spot with his fearless gaze and cut them down, but you and I know better. They say Aleaus Hammerstrike cackles every time the stones of our catapults fell on royalist heads, but you and I know better. Adan and Clive, two simple men with good, heroic hearts, are known as the 'Fishers of Souls' because they think we gave them the power to pluck the life from their foes at a distance. But you and I know."

"Then, why do they do this?"

"The truth is too simple, too complicated, and far less exciting. And terrifying, if I'm honest with myself," New Moon said. "But I'm rarely that on purpose."

"I suppose I can see why," Haidra said. "I'm sure things have been said about you."

"Oh, just imagine," New Moon said with an ironic smile. "Then imagine being his daughter."

"It's not just helping *him* to the high gate, is it?" Haidra asked.

She smiled at the question. "No, it isn't."

The weight of the confirmation planted Haidra where she stood, her expression flat in contemplation until Auntie Sakinah returned, bearing two small vials of cobalt glass. She placed them in New Moon's palm and said another long series of sentences, patting her hand over the little bottles after every period. She repeated the last sentence twice, and made the sorceress do the same. A few more air-kisses for her, a few more for "Haidra Bloom", and they were quickly back outside.

Emerging into stronger daylight, the world seemed recast in Haidra's eyes. Now she noticed how people stopped and looked their way, refugee or rebel, or how their children had been following them through the camp, packed together several yards behind the ghosts. She scanned a few of those faces, catching unexpected nods from the adults and waves from the little boys and little girls. Deciding not to draw attention, she considered those fierce souls around her.

Talic Gray-stare, the kindest man in Atenia she had ever known. The Fishermen of Souls, father and son bleary-eyed from smoke. Aleaus Hammerstrike, who always offered that kindly, sisterly grin to put Haidra at ease.

Then she saw Bon, beaming at her in the brief moment before the march. It wasn't passion, or the moment, she decided then and there.

She loved this man.

"Ready?" Bon asked New Moon.

"Haidra and I will head off and see Aron. You and the rest go get these handled." The sorceress passed the blue phials to her brother. "I think you have to speak to Hamzhat. He might be the current cook."

"Not. Well. At. All," Talic declared as Bon led the other ghosts into the camp built on the southwest corner of Idrian and Roromheta. The pack of children chased after the majority of the heroes headed up the hill, though a few of the older girls stayed with the littler ones who had to be carried and escorted. Not fearing the eyes of the strong, armed men always upon them, they watched Haidra and New Moon from their distance.

"Haidra," the sorceress whispered.

Her concentration broken, Haidra nodded back. "Yes?"

"You see?" New Moon said, remaining at a whisper. "It's hard. Some of it is wonderful. Most of it isn't. But that's the cost of making real change: you can't hide anymore, no matter how much you want to try."

"What do we do, then?" Haidra asked, focusing on the sorceress and not the children staring at them.

New Moon spoke at her normal volume. "You make the best

of it." She smiled and waved at the little ones before she knelt down and beckoned them. "Come here! Come on!" she shouted in clear Torsii. "All of you! All of you com—"

A great cheer exploded from the throng, charging headlong into a wave of screaming adolescents and toddlers, the squalls of the babies in their arms pitched in delight. They swarmed before Haidra or New Moon moved, dozens of voices and hands held up for attention, and some even holding up the babes.

"Haidra! Haidra Bloom," one golden face would shout.

"This is my little sister Haidra! My momma named her Haidra! She went off and fought, too! Isn't she nice?"

"Look at me, Haidra, look at me!"

Having lived a life never wanting to be looked at by those armed and armored, Haidra grinned her widest, held back tears of a lost youth, and did her best to give them a moment she never had. Children able and unable to speak, some barely a few months off their mother's milk, whined and wriggled in her arms as she tried to unload the burdens of so many little ones who weren't getting their chances at a child-hood like she did, as bleak as it may have been. She wondered how many had lost their fathers or their mothers, or if she had served beside a brother or sister in the gatehouse, or Victus. Each question flooded her with emotions she restrained to pay attention to those mattering most in this grim, dark world. She was thankful she had given whatever she could.

Like Arverin had. The pride she had earned kept those tears at bay.

She and New Moon answered every happy question with a smile, every serious one with concern and a promise to ask Prince Aron, and in the constant rebellion about her knees it suddenly halted in front of prince's tent. The two guards stationed at the open flaps tensed where they stood, putting practiced smiles over concerned frowns, though neither broke discipline to address the loud horde.

"Okay, okay, okay," New Moon said in a motherly tone, "I want you oldest ones to wait out here and watch your little brothers and sisters until Haidra and I get back. The two guards here—"

She gave both a charming grin,

"—will keep watch. Once we come back let's all go get something to eat, huh? Is anyone hungry now? Well, if you are, just ask one of these guards. Their future queen is certain they will be happy to get you whatever you want."

"Of course, Shahira," the guard on the right said behind a tight grin. He surveyed the children along with his partner, the corners of his mouth blunted. "Of course."

"Perfect. Be right back," said New Moon. "Haidra."

"Be right back," Haidra said to their departing admirers.

Barren of the usual crowd of political figures and fighting men and women, the round table near the blue tent's center seemed so much larger without the full capacity trying to gain notice. The usual war council sat in their chairs and seats, save Black John. All spoke in turn to Prince Aron. The new King of Atenia, his head bare of wrap or crown to designate this ascension, listened intently until he saw New Moon enter.

"All of you out," the sorceress shouted first in Torsii, the required language of the table. "Wait, wait, wait! Ecktor, you stay. Valen, you stay. The rest of you can get out!"

The collective uproar of the Arbikkean contingent in their native Eaith was met by a glum prince, who returned his lover's entrance with an expression of annoyance. "My Moon, does this really—"

"Yes, Aron," she said in a tone disallowing any protest. "It's about him."

Prince Aron paused, his bright brown eyes glinting with curiosity in the ambient glow of the braziers on both sides of his table. He shared something with the sorceress in their gaze before he turned to his advisers. "Everyone, go. I will call you back soon to continue the council."

The Children of Marta rose and left with a nod from Ecktor, the simple cobbler from obscurity to represent the common voice of most Atenians. The riders and knights of Aron, the mustached and glowering Ahmeti among them, filed out of the tent while grousing, strapping curved swords to war-girdles and tugging on their gloves. The cataract among cataracts did not hesitate to look right at Haidra, but buoyed by the understanding of her role, she did not avert her eyes or flinch.

"Where is he?" New Moon asked, cautious to search the tent for her father.

"I sent him to review our forward positions in the dead zone with some of Valen's specialists this morning. I was surprised you were able to talk him into keeping your ghosts behind, my love."

"I convinced him they needed a much-deserved rest," New Moon replied, nodding to Haidra as if she was in the know. "But I have to admit that doesn't fully expound on the fullness of my intentions, my dear. I had reason to keep him separated from us for today."

The bard, reclined sideways in his chair and his feet on the table, strummed his fingers down the strings of his lute in a lovely cascade of notes. "I believe she's up to no good, my prince."

"A meddler would know," New Moon said in faux-cheer, "but I assure you, Aron, our intentions are purely for the best."

The prince crossed his arms, shutting his eyes as he nodded. "But will require nefarious means to obtain, I imagine."

The sorceress nodded sweetly. "Yes."

"And what is your part, Lady Haidra?" the prince asked. "How has my wife-to-be roped you into this?"

"It was actually Haidra's idea, Aron," New Moon chided their host. "Tell him Haidra."

"I..." Haidra saw Ecktor gazing at her in honest confusion. "Wait, who here knows?"

"Knows what?" Ecktor asked.

"Who Black John is," Valen concluded.

"Oh," said Ecktor, before the weight of the topic struck. "Oh!" He gripped the curve of the table, braced. "Well?"

Prince Aron sighed at his lover, the Shahira of his homeland, and waved at her. "It's up to you."

"If this plan is to work..." New Moon faced the cobbler, studying him under her silver brow. "My father, the witch-king Black John, is Prince Jhean De Veard VI, the right and true king of Atenia."

"Oh," said Ecktor. "That's a bit anti-climactic."

"You knew?" Haidra asked.

"I supposed," the cobbler said simply. "Many thought old Solomon, we had betting, somehow slipped out his daughter's grasp. Some of us thought he might actually be the ghost of your granddaddy, but for it to be Jhean de Veard is something else." A small smile crept onto his face, like a good but forgotten memory. "You know, I saw once the prince joust with some Mesca herders driving their cattle and were-goats out of the east. Back in the good old days when they let us buy their meat and trade for skins, but Jhean de Veard—" he knocked the table with a knuckle. "He laid them off their horses without a hair harmed. Lot of things make sense now, Miss Haidra. All those things Arverin hoped. He knew."

"He did?" Haidra asked.

"Well, like some," Ecktor replied, "he hoped. It is a chance for the truth, whatever it may be."

"Is there a question?" New Moon asked in a hard manner.

"That will depend on what is being asked and how," said

Ecktor. "Every Atenian, nay every person, has an inalienable right to the truth. We must know why these things happened."

"That only occurs once we break the queen-regent's defense," the sorceress said. "But I believe we can serve multiple ends. Now, tell him Haidra."

"Oh," said the prince. "This."

"Listen to her," New Moon ordered her husband-to-be. "Without Ahmeti, or the riders, or the men bound to fight one way because it is all they know. Be wise, Aron."

"Then let her speak," the prince jabbed back, grinning at his betrothed's passion.

The eyes of the powerful and empowered upon her again, Haidra breathed through her first unsteady words. "Your advisers are wrong, Prince Aron. There is a way to break the siege of the citadel. It will require great daring, but it will also require tricking Black John. Moon and I have—"

"You had me at 'tricking Black John,'" said the prince of Arbikk.

Valen strummed the strings of his lute. "But of course!"

# 3

# KINGS AND QUEENS

Bon came to the edge of the tomb's balcony and scanned the distance. He leaned over, the weight of his hood obscuring the back of his head so Haidra could not see his expression.

"It's high enough," the ax-slinger said. "But I can't really see."

"Use the spell, dummy," New Moon said from behind. "It's midnight. Of course, you can't see."

"This is why we have Black John here, ain't it, Talic?" Adan asked, his face caught by the starlight as he chewed on the last bits of a bread crust.

Talic shushed him, lost in the folds of his hood and the lower half of his face masked by a scarf to protect it from the bitter wind whipping the night. The Ghosts of Solomon sans their leader had made the mad dash across Atenia's north and northeast to arrive at the Tombs of the Veards not long after sundown, ferried on the prince's wagons while their supporters remained behind to contend with the more terrifying half of their conspiracy.

Haidra pulled the edges of her hood down around her face, hoping the wool against her cheeks brought some warmth. Her back and legs ached from the furious pace their carriage-drivers had set, the Arbikkean steeds pounding up and down hills of jarring pavement and broken, battle-torn earth, but none of it hurt worse than her feet.

Until the cold touched her nose and cheeks.

Wanting to tilt forward and bury her face into the back of Bon's inert cloak, she waited with the rest in misery.

"All right, all right." Bon clapped his taloned hand over his face and intoned. *"Edjo."*

Small sparkles appeared in front of his eyes, silver-dust dotting his cheeks. "Ah, there," he said. "See them much better now."

"How many are up there?" Talic asked. "I can't imagine they have a full watch."

"I see a few, but they're crowded around braziers. They're not expecting us." Bon slipped his bow and quiver over his head and shoulder, handing it back for someone to take. "I need a driver, Moon. It's a far shot wherever I place it."

"What's the plan?" Aleaus asked as she grabbed the ax-slinger's gear and passed it to his sister.

"Well," Bon said as he measured the vast, "Haidra was right, there is a ridge we could pick our way across, but we really don't have time and the noise would draw attention. So we're going to fly."

"What the fuck are you on about?" Clive asked. "We've not got wings."

"Our language has a word that yours doesn't so it's lost in translation," New Moon said. "An arrow, Aleaus."

"Yes, milady." The blacksmith slipped a shaft free of Bon's quiver.

"Don't do that. And, please, string his bow."

Aleaus grumbled as she pulled the compound bow out, its length taller than her. She pressed her foot down on the lower arm and held the upper in one hand. "Here, Haidra. Help me."

"Right," she whispered to the blacksmith, holding the quiver of arrows tight to her chest.

As Aleaus strung the sorceress whispered to herself, the latter's gaze on the arrow intensifying. She rolled her fingers along its shaft. The chant strengthened in Eaith until she squeezed it tight.

Green energy pulsed from the sharp steel head to the fletchings, popping silent emerald bubbles. Grunting as a matching light bled out of her eyes, New Moon lifted the arrow up. "Only Bon can take it," she said, out of breath. "Hurry. It wants to go."

"Here, here," Aleaus spoke, lifting the bow over Haidra's head.

The ax-slinger pulled it forward and extended his right hand back, waiting for the arrow. "I think I see a good spot. Everyone's hunkered down."

"But what the hell are we doing?" Adan asked, impatient. "We didn't bring any rope so we weren't going to climb up or down nothing. If this has all been a waste you can leave me and my boy here. I don't want to go back and see what Black John's going—"

"Oh, hush, Dad," Clive said, shaking his father by the forearm. "I want to see."

New Moon thrust the arrow toward her brother's hand. "Bon!"

"Okay, sister," he said, laying hold of the shaft. He nocked it and straightened, one foot on the balcony's stacked-stone fence as he aimed and loosed. The arrow flew forward in a straight, fast trajectory. The streak ended where the rising, twisting rampart of Snail's Way touched Mount Ectis's ridge, but to the awe of the ghosts the emerald line of light remained!

Hung in the night air like a beam, its angled toward their destination.

Haidra understood immediately. "In the gods' name, no."

"It's the quickest way and the spell itself will keep you up,"

Bon said, hooking his bow over his shoulder. He took his ax and laid the handle across the top of the light beam, and as promised, let his feet dangle. "See? You can even grab the light if you want."

"You two are mad," Adan said, backing away from the edge of the balcony. "Bleeding, blinding mad!"

Bon scoffed. "Come, Adan. Is this any worse than—"

"It's not a drop over that," Aleaus spoke over the ax-slinger. "You come on, Bon!"

Bon grunted and waved them off. "We do this all the time at home!"

"Bon," said New Moon, exasperated, "just show them."

"All right, but she goes next," he said, pointing at Aleaus.

"Fine by me," said Adan. "Fuck all that."

"Just..." Haidra covered her nose and mouth in her gloved palm, half-stabbing Bon with her eyes. "Are you sure?"

"Of course," he said with that heart-melting smile. "Would I endanger any of you now?"

"Not a great question, Bon-Boy," said Clive. "Dad, if he goes, I'll go. If I go, you'll go too, right?"

The elder fisherman's stony countenance softened. "Always, my lad. Always."

"Fantastic, the spell only lasts so long," New Moon said to end the debate. "Bon, now!"

The ax-slinger exhaled loudly, gripped his ax at both ends, and kicked off. Like a leaf during autumn's shed, he started away from them at a slow, almost lofty pace, before momentum and a few kicks sped Bon into the night. His black shape disappeared along the beam's glimmering length.

"Crook shepherd me, I didn't say I was going next," Aleaus said.

"I said I'll go." Clive stepped forward and drew his sword. He glanced toward New Moon with clear concern. "No worries?"

"Absolutely none," the sorceress said with a disarming smile.

"Just hold the hilt of your sword and the end of the scabbard and the magic will do the rest. Trust me, we use this spell in Arbikk to bring home waylaid shepherds lost in sandstorms. You will be safe."

"Yes, ma'am," Clive said, bracing as he put one foot up on the fence. "If you say so."

Adan darted forward and was stopped by Talic. "Clive!"

"Careful, Dad," the younger fisherman said. "If she says, she says, right? Now…" Clive unbuckled his sword from its harness on his right hip, rehoused it, then mirrored what he had seen Bon do. He pulled down a few times on the magical line, which never budged. He puffed his cheeks and exhaled as he kicked forward.

As before, the weight of his body gathered momentum. He slid into the starlit expanse above Ectis' connecting ridge.

"Gods damn that boy," Adan said in half-pride. "Braver than me."

True to his word, the elder fishermen went next, then Talic. All the men vanished, leaving the three women in the group alone for the first time.

"So, you do this a good bit?" Aleaus asked New Moon as she freed her sword from her belt. She used one hand to mount the ancient balcony's mortared fence.

"Every summer and winter when the winds whip the deserts and the dragons make their migrations," New Moon answered. "It really is safe, but we also need to move quicker. I'm going last and I would rather not have to pull myself out of a fall because we took our time."

"Okay," Aleaus said, anxious. She barred her sword atop the shaft, inhaled once to calm the tremors in her feet, and bunny-hopped off the balcony's edge. A second later, the darkness consumed her.

"Haidra," New Moon asked, "have you thought on what you'll do after this?"

"After I get down there?" she asked, focused on placing her sword across the beam in a perpendicular line, her hands squeezing the hilt and the scabbard's chape. To her curiosity, the leather-encased wood did not slide, slippery and free, but forced against a rough texture, like overgrown grass. She huffed to banish the tingle of fear in her face.

"No, after. When we've won," said the sorceress.

"Aren't we getting ahead of ourselves?" Haidra asked, incredulous. She tore her attention away from the gap.

New Moon smiled up and shrugged. "You're right, sorry. Silly goose moment. Hurry on."

"Me hurry on?" Haidra mumbled against the wind as she faced forward. No longer willing to wait on it, she kicked off. She gripped hard on instinct as the wind and weight zipped her forward. Expecting speed, a scream, or the pressure of her entire body hung in her hands, instead she felt almost framed upon her sword, weightless but fully aware of herself and her position. The greater surprise came as the darkness peeled away from her sight, leaving the city below and the citadel brightened by stars.

Almost breathless from Atenia's nocturnal glory, the gentle descent to the wall ended quickly. She found her friends waiting at the bottom, hands up to catch her when her sword slid off the magical beam. She landed in Bon and Talic's arms, who bore her gently to her feet.

"By the gods," Haidra exclaimed, giddy. She caught sight of Clive, sharing child-like giggles as they caught their excited breaths.

"Get your asses in line," Talic said to them. "We're in the heat!"

The joviality ended with the reminder, and cultured to danger, the two youngest rebels re-buckled their swords. New Moon dropped down among them a few seconds later, grasping the beam with a bare hand. Her rapier out in the other, she signaled them to disperse. The Ghosts of Solomon moved as one, searching out every threat.

Depleted after weeks of pummeling siege, the royalist numbers had divided the remainder of their forces in two. Behind the high walls of the citadel plumes of campfire smoke obscured the two spires beside the main palace, and once Talic checked below from the vantage of an empty way station, discovered their archers behind the low gate. Few sentries patrolled the parapets above Snail's Way, broken into clusters centered around lit braziers to find warmth in the chilly night.

The seven approached one of the main wood and iron bridges connecting the parallel parapets, offering a view below to the main walk. More barren below than above, the lack of guarding eyes provided New Moon the moment to draw them to her.

"Here's what I have off the top of my head," she whispered to them.

"I thought you said you had a plan," Bon chided, raising every nerve.

"No, Haidra had a plan, and then we all had a plan to get up here," she replied to her brother. "The rest of this is what it is."

"Great," Aleaus said, almost at full volume. "Time's a ticking, lass."

"Here's what I have in mind," New Moon continued, "Haidra, Talic, and Adan cross the bridge. Clive and Aleaus will keep this side of the ramp down. Bon and I will go below and take the center."

"And do what?" Adan asked. "Clear them out?"

"Indeed," the sorceress replied. "Don't worry about them coming back at you. I'll have it covered."

"Oh, well," said Adan. "Come on, Haidra, Talic! They got it covered!"

"Empty your quivers at them first," the sorceress said. "Trust me. They will be far more frightened of you than you are of them."

"They better be!" His broad shoulders rising and falling as he sighed through his nose, eyes shut, Bon the Bloody nodded. "Oh, hell. Just pure hell."

Haidra could not have said it any better.

She ended up beside Talic as they ran toward three royalists huddled over the brazier a minute later. Adan had halted behind her, drawing back on his first arrow before he loosed. Trusting the fisherman, the shaft flew over her left shoulder and struck in the nearest man in the back of the skull, toppling his corpse into the bowl of smoking coals. The other two fell back, one of them losing his balance completely.

Her sword already drawn, Haidra had no choice but to charge the standing guardsman. She cut for his head and a jet of blood sprayed as he twisted onto the ground. Talic knifed the other man in the side of the neck. On the other side of the bridge Aleaus and Clive had similar success with a pair of sentries.

Descending a stairwell set inside the outer wall, the combined voices of the youngest wraiths echoed along Snail's Way, arcane words haunting on a roaring breeze.

"Keep going," Talic said over the chanting. "They'll catch up to us!"

The constant downward curve of stone and concrete, endless sets of steps, and another small grouping of guards lay ahead. This time Talic stopped to the take his shot, killing the closet of the pair. Adan and Haidra smote the second together. Losing sight of the other side of the rampart, they stormed its inner edge, the spell of the Veard's rightful heirs growing in intensity until, after a third run slaughtering unaware royalists, a blanket of brief light phased out her vision.

When it cleared, Haidra found herself standing still. Yet, somehow, she had grown several feet taller.

Recalling the first time she was clad in illusion, she looked herself over in wonder. Her mail skirt, already down to her knees, had gained spectral links to reach her ankles, the feet below heeled in shining dark steel. The sword in her hand had transformed into something longer, more wicked, as had the gauntlets gripping its coal-back hilt. Unaware of how her helm's face guard had shifted into the visage of a gaunt, haunted woman, she almost reached up with her free hand to make sure the flesh and blood behind it remained when Adan caught her attention.

"No time to loiter," he said, shifted into an eight-foot-tall wraith armed in his sword and shield. Crowned in a diadem of rusted arrows and broken crossbow bolts, the disguised fisherman halted his fury in relation to the ghastly figure she had become. Likewise, Talic had turned into a wraith of a bygone era. Their armors matching the royal bear of Atenia, Ursin's ancient seal inscribed the front of their breastplates and pauldrons.

Haidra looked southward to the other parapet and found two more ghostly giants marching up the slope.

Then, as if memory plucked out of sudden remembrance, a face appeared in the bare skies above Atenia. The burnt, blistered face of long-dead Hibni, grimacing as the agony of her death built to a havocked cry, spewed flame between brittle, blackened lips.

"Again! Again!" the apparition screamed. "Again, High Atenia comes to claim its ghosts!" Unbidden, the mouth of Haidra's illusionary visage moved in perfect time with the steps she took, each footfall punctuated by Hibni's death chant.

"Death!"

Every single wraith chanted as they descended. "Death!"

"Death!" Hibni screamed. "Every step toward a traitor brings death!"

"Death!"

"Death!"

The howls echoed in the night, far into the distance to where no one missed it even if they could not see the dreadful face above the stronghold. Running along the walkway, Haidra dared its edge and looked down. Side by side, New Moon and Bon the Bloody marched together on the central path, their eyes blazing as their cloaks writhed in all directions.

The effect on the war-worn guards, many hungry and sleepless, won out on any notion of defense. The eight figures, kings and queens of Atenia's legendary past, advanced on the opposing forces clustered inside the lower gate. The infantry on the ground threw down their spears while archers abandoned their bows.

Only three knights had been assigned to command the remaining artillery forces. Foolish notions of honor refused them the right to surrender as they freed their swords.

Raising her bow as Urghenna the Swift, Haidra and Adan under the guise of King Kolmec II downed one of the knight's horses. Disrupted by the failing, flailing beast bucking its spasming legs, the knights wrestled their mounts out of the way before the next one was brought low by Aleaus' keen arrow. Bon dragged the final man, allowing the visage of Solomon III to have his time on those who betrayed him.

The rush of broken soldiers to the lower gate coincided with a horn blast from the rebel line on the other side. Arising from the picket, the Children of Marta stormed out of their camps without their Arbikkean allies. Thousands of swords and axes claimed by pickers over the ruins of the city, many of them stolen from the dead, thrust skyward. Hundreds reached the portcullis in an instant.

"Marta! Marta! Marta!" the rebels of Atenia chanted in unison as they beat down the iron gate.

"Marta!" screamed Hibni.

"Marta! Marta! Marta!"

The conjured illusions answered from their haunted mouths. "Marta!"

In the fray Aleaus and Clive reached the winch on their side first. The giant specters lifted the gate in tandem, shouting the holy name as the true souls within did the human labor of raising the entrance. The first foot allowed space for those desperate enough to dive under, but as the portcullis smoothly clicked upward, the truth of the royalist surrender became obvious. Less than twenty minutes later the prisoners were quickly marched off by surprised Arbikkeans, only now showing up to the fracas.

Up above the royalist horns, diminished in their resound and numbers, blew the notes of alarm as the rebel forces flooded through the lower gate and ran with all their efforts to the very top of Snail's Way. The older fighters, long to the cause of freedom and survivors of the brutal construction schemes Niklon instituted, grew stronger every step they took toward old places class and cruelty had kept them from after they had laid blood and sweat in the mortar. They led the young to the places where so many sacrifices were made for that bowl of food on the table, or the chance of a roof over their head.

A dignity none of them ever thought to reclaim was theirs.

Watching all of it from her place high in the heavens, the face of Hibni smoothed. The blisters faded, the grimace ended, and the likeness of a forgotten mother vanished with a happy smile.

The Burnt Lady was never seen again.

Before dawn peaked over Ben-Lomen more horns called under an open sky. Not the tinny, sharp notes of the royalist silver horns, or the brass booms the Arbikkeans used to signal movements. A native of Low Corner, old before *the old days*, produced an ancient civita. The clay horn produced a moaning, longing note.

It was blown as the Ghost of Solomon retreated down the

ramp of Snail's Way, headed for their camp along the Colis. The entire city had awoken to the miracle of their deed, the raucous cheers breaking out from the slopes of the glacier where refugees camped, to the prince's central stage on Idrian Street, and finally the high gates. Rebels clustered at the silver fence holding them back from the final battle. Beyond the forces of the queen-regent, a contingent of spears and knights on horseback, enclosed behind a wall constructed of debris and stone.

One more line set, the children of the shamed prince went in search of their father.

# 4

# THE FALL OF ATENIA

To the surprise of everyone, it was Prince Aron who met them at the entrance to Black John's tent. A three-posted covering of canvas and hides native to the continent below the Southern Sea, the inner reaches of its long chamber was lit in a ruddy light somewhere out of sight.

"He's inside," he told Bon and New Moon, a worried expression on his face. "Valen's in there with him after he swore to never speak to me again."

"Does he have his sword?" Bon asked.

The rest of the ghosts, including Haidra, cringed at the question.

"Does that matter?" Aleaus had the bravery to ask. Haggard from the nighttime descent, she leaned on Clive and Adan, braced between the fishermen.

The prince, the sorceress, and the ax-slinger's expression answered for them, their severity in the affirmative.

"I'm shocked Valen's in there," Bon said. "Dad and he don't get on."

New Moon and her betrothed scoffed.

"Knowing that meddler they're probably best friends," New Moon said. "So, do we wait?"

"That supposes one of us isn't going in," replied Bon.

"Well," Haidra asked from his left, "isn't someone?"

The hesitance hung thick among the ghosts, the wraiths, and their host.

Then Clive raised a soot-smeared hand. "I'm not volunteering."

"Then why did you raise your hand?" Aleaus asked.

"It's polite to raise your hand before you speak," he said. "Right, Dad?"

"Quiet now, Clive," Adan said.

Haidra pinched the bridge of her nose, stopping a runny flow brought about by the cold. The tension of the huddle, the buzz of the adrenaline finally flowing out of her nerves, broke the last care she had. "I'll go."

"You?" Bon asked.

"Gods, people can hear you," said Valen as the bard exited Black John's tent. His lute clutched by the neck in one hand as always, he surveyed the entire troop. "And so can he."

"How's it?" Prince Aron asked his closest and most secretive adviser.

"Oh, good and mad. I tried to tell him this one story, but it didn't take too well. Surprising because it usually lands," the bard answered with a thoughtful shake of the head. "Whatever you all did, it better be good. Real good. Men like him with two-handed swords and anger? No thank you."

"I'll go," Haidra reaffirmed before anyone else spoke. She raised her gaze to Bon, who tilted his head toward her.

He studied her for a long moment. "He's going to yell."

"But why, Haidra?" New Moon asked.

"I started this," she said as she stepped forward and forced Valen to make way for her. She lifted the flap to the tent. "Might as well own it, right?"

She waited for her friends, Bon, or her hosts to offer some sort of affirming sign of encouragement. The lot simply stared back in worry, some in wonder. Aware of how alone she was, she gripped her sword by her scabbard's locket and entered the tent.

His hazel eyes locked onto Haidra the moment she breached the dim compartment, the canvas walls dyed navy to trap a deep gloom. His features cut from the unsteady coals in a small brazier at the foot of a long but spartan cot, she shied away as soon as she could to take in the rest of his abode. Blankets and threadbare pillows had been tossed near the entrance, as had his gear, cloak, and cowl. One boot lay by his hip, the other almost in the brazier if not for the angle it had landed on the edge. The smell of warming, singing leather wafted with the meager heat.

Discarded like some meaningless thing, High John the Conqueror lay half-askew under his tent's hem, its gilded hilt free to grab for any thief wary to notice an easy prize.

Jhean de Veard sat shirtless and barefoot, fists balled on his knees as he stared at Haidra.

Unable to avoid his gaze or its potency, she dared to meet it. Instead of wrath, she found something else in his pools of fury, a broken sadness running down his cheeks to the golden beard sticking out at odd angles.

A broken glass bottle sparkled at the head of the cot, Haidra noticed, its red pool already soaked in the mattress.

Understanding, she nodded at the age-old crutch. "It was me."

His eyes narrowed at her confession, pinpoints of dire anger.

"You left me no choice, sir," Haidra said, suddenly infused with courage she didn't expect to appear. "It was either sit here and wait or do something, and all of you seemingly wanted to do the former. Especially you. I think I know why, but I didn't agree with it."

He grunted a dark noise in the back of his throat.

"Oh, to hell with you," Haidra snapped as she stepped toward him. Shocked by her own aggression, she jerked to a stop.

Jhean de Veard tilted his head, a lion measuring a mouse. "Pardon me?"

She dithered, too stunned by her gross mistake. "What I meant to say—"

"You said to hell with me," the prince of Atenia cut her off. His glare deepened. "Be brave."

"Oh, me?" Haidra asked. "Fine. Yes, it was me. You left me no choice."

"Is this where you truly wish to start?"

"There are so many places I wish I could go back and start again with all this," Haidra said, stripped of pretense. "But that's not why I am here. Where I am is right here, and—"

"You're babbling."

"Stop interrupting me," she shouted at him. "May I speak or are you so high on that damned blood of yours a voice like mine only really matters when its saying 'yes, sir', 'no, sir', 'ready to face death for you again, Mr. Black John, sir!' Which is it?"

The stinging rebuttal sealed the prince's mouth, his jaw clenched.

"It's time to put this to an end. You said so," Haidra stated in the face of Atenia's destiny. "We can sit here and yell. You can get up and beat me like your sister says you would, but I don't think you will or ever did. And that's it: you don't get it because you're too wounded to see you're not what she says you are."

"I never was, but what you all—"

"That's not true either. Not completely," said Haidra, cutting him off this time. "We didn't know. We do now. We won't betray you again—not if you stop acting like such a damned coward and walk up to that gate. Meet her challenge."

"It's not so simple, Haidra," said Jhean de Veard. "The moment I do that, it's over for her."

"For who?"

"Fransica."

His answer brought the entire world on her head and shoulders, as if a whole new heap of history lost in dim corners had dropped atop of her. The mere mention of the queen-regent in such sympathy, and who spoke it, almost caused Haidra to laugh.

"What?" she asked. "Just... What?"

"We don't know if she's guilty," he said. "She might be sick or Niklon might have—"

"We're not doing this either." A headache formed behind her eyes, worsened by the throbbing coals in his fire bowl. "Look, I understand. I do, and from where I stand, I would appreciate it. But what matters now is the truth. And the only way that happens is by you going up there and finding out what it is."

"It's another march," he said. "It does nothing to prove my innocence."

"It does for us," Haidra replied. "It does for all the people who have fought and died to know."

"To know what?"

"Whether or not all of this mattered," she said. "This isn't about just you, you foolish prince. This is about Bon and Moon. It's about me and Talic and—"

"How?"

"Because of all the shit we've gone through," she barked.

"I am not—" The rage fled to the natural sorrow he carried every second of his days. He heaved on his pallet. "I'm not deserving of it. And I never wanted it. I just wanted Atenia free."

"Then walk the damned way," Haidra said, pounding a closed fist on the skirt of her mail shirt. "Do it for me."

"You?"

"You're not here without me, Jhean de Veard," the mender's daughter snapped. "And don't you forget it. You owe me. Me."

"But—"

"Do it for your children," Haidra persisted. "Do it for Hibni.

266

Let her rest in a real way and not just as some smiling face in the clouds, quick from the memories of people too ashamed to want to remember her."

"Don't do that." Tears brimmed his eyes in the half-dark. Jhean de Veard grimaced and put his chin to his chest, a dog's whine rising out of him. He sobbed once, more emotion than she had seen in her entire time as his witness.

"Don't do this, then," Haidra said. "If not for them, or her, or me, then do it for Marta. We need to find her. Don't we?"

Through shadows and sorrow, the question instilled a different sort of glint in Jhean de Veard's eyes. He drifted his attention to the sword on the floor, half out of his tent, then the boot on the brazier. He sighed loudly and wiped his eyes with a nod. "Send my daughter in. And bring me that sword before it rusts. Damned thing."

---

BIRDS SANG in the morning when New Moon ducked out of the tent first, stepping to the side so the figure behind her could follow. Every single soul not positioned along the sinuous path up to Snail's Way lined the streets from the entrance of Black John's tent, Atenian and Arbikkean alike. Yet to the shock of each person, prayers answered for some, it was not the wraith who emerged.

The collective forces of Prince Aron Toliv, prince of the Northern Deserts, had spent decades in their homeland fighting alongside the legend of the black-clad mystery and demonic heroics, the wave of his sword and sorcery legends to fighters among the dunes of Arbikk. Many of them had known or heard of the rumors, but never questioned out of the same discomfort any felt around a condemned man, unable to measure truth beyond the actions they see by their eyes alone. No matter the fealty they swore to his benefactor, nor the distance in blood and birth, the cataracts and infantry removed their swords together and offered upturned hilts.

The sign of royal respect, paid only to sultans and the sons of sultans like Aron, slowed Jhean de Veard but did not halt him.

Walking without his hood, the forgotten prince kept his gaze ahead. As leonine as Solomon III had been in his golden countenance, and affected by the kind beauties of his mother, he kept his stoicism before his march like a shield, paying no acknowledgment to his son and the ghosts as they fell behind him along with New Moon, the prince of Arbikk, and the red-headed Valen.

The native Atenians, however, unleashed upon him.

The first voice, belonging to a rebel garbed in mishmashes of armors he had picked up along the way, dragged his fellows to the right and left into the street by their shirts, forcing them to their knees as he fell upon his own.

"High John the Conqueror! High John the Conqueror! The king lives!"

Almost struck, Jhean sided away from them, aghast at their adoration.

Next was a woman who dropped her baskets of bandages and cloth, heavyset with her hair covered in a soiled wrap. To Haidra's shock she barely recognized Tanny, her old baker and boss, layers of dirt and blood on hands long divorced from white flour.

"Jhean de Veard," the poor lady cried, pounding her chest with her fists before she threw them up, almost in a swoon. "Jhean de Veard! Jhean de Veard!"

"The king! The king! The king!"

"Atenia is saved! Atenia lives!"

"The king!"

Caught in a tidal wave of adulation, the prince of their past hopes and future dreams pressed on, unmoved by their gratitude.

Save for his face.

To the shock of everyone able to see, tears welled into those angry hazel eyes. The proud mouth split in a quiet gasp of pain. Jhean de Veard bowed his head and plodded forward, the march of the damned rather than the proud. Entrapped by their celebration, the chants of his name were soon backed by raucous applause and cheering, bombarding a poor man poisoned by it.

"The king! The king! The king!"

Haidra saw him in full measure. Unable to stay back as he paraded against his will, and fully because of hers, she dashed forward.

Bon tried to catch her hand as she passed but failed. "Haidra! Haidra!"

She ignored him and the warning glare from his sister, but New Moon did not stop her as she reached the prince's side.

"The king! The king! The king!"

"My lord," she said. "My lord, what's the matter? Are you hurt?"

"Get back, you little fool," he seethed at her. "Look at what you've heaped upon me. Look at everything I've never wanted."

Stunned by the rebuke, Haidra kept pace with his slow march so as not to cause a greater scene. "My lord?"

"No, no," he said, almost spitting at her as he finally looked her way. He tore his attention off her for a second, roaming the crowds of screaming, excited faces. "No, stay right there. Right beside me, Haidra. I want you to suffer this with me."

"I..."

"The king! The king! The king!"

"March, girl!"

To the order out of deference and honest fear, Haidra fell into lockstep beside Jhean de Veard as he straightened before the audience, grasping his longsword as he set a warrior's gait, proud and confident. His strength no longer concealed stoked the citizens of the ruined city-state into a frenzy. Women held up their babies and toddlers, hoping he would come over and bless them. Men, beaten and battered by the war on their doorsteps, cried openly in joy.

"Do you see?" Jhean de Veard asked Haidra. "Look at them."

Everywhere Haidra looked, she did so at happiness, and then at him in confusion. "They're happy!"

"For what?" he almost barked at her. "Tell me."

"The king! The king! The king!"

Someone in the crowd thrust a lit torch in the daylight, a sword-salute to their returned champion. "Death to Fransica! Death to the liar! Death to the bitch!"

Haidra searched those faces again after she heard that, this time locating the trouble.

The men on their knees still gripped their weapons like the torch-wielder. Women and children cognizant of events pleaded past their smiles, begging a restoration she now understood never existed as an option. The fervor, the need, blended in ecstatic thirsting no amount of royal blood could provide, reared its evil face.

Every single word, demand, and admonishment the prince had made clicked together.

"The king! Death to the bitch! The king! The king!"

Death, death, and more death.

Bringing her eyes forward in shock, she swallowed a horrified gasp. "You..."

"You're all fools," Jhean de Veard said aloud. "You'd go right back to the thing that caused your problems in the first place."

Her anxiety flew skyward with Atenia's damaged mania. "But what else is there?"

"The king! The king! Death to Fransica! Kill the liar! The king!"

Coming to the lower gates of Snail's Way, the Children of Marta held the entrance and corralled their supporters away from an aisle their captains and commanders had formed for the prince. Clay civitas blew in discordant strains, attempts at old anthems rousing the elders. Many of them sang old songs few remembered.

"Stay with me," the swordsman told Haidra, steeling himself for the climb.

"The king! The king! The king!"

Jhean de Veard passed through the aisle, Haidra on his left heel. Every single man and woman, all of them having served on the northern palisade, dropped to a knee as he passed. To their credit they did not chant or beg his attention. Prince Aron ordered his own followers to support their line, receding back so only the ghosts and their captains continued. The eight ascended the path alone with the cheering populace at their backs.

Not paying them any respect for their homage, Jhean de Veard kept on until the voices faded from sharp clarity to muddling roars.

"The king! The king… Death to the… The king…"

The quiet provided no solace. He no longer stalked forward like a confident monarch, but neither was he weakened. Often, he would take time to stop and study the ramp and the parapets to both sides. The white walls enclosing Snail's Way were stained in sections from age and disrepair, the details of such things stark in the growing daylight. Banners and standards of Fransica's failed reign, pink upon navy, hung tattered from age. As with the illusion of grandiosity and wealth, careful examination the higher they went revealed worsening decay.

"It wasn't any better before," Jhean de Veard said.

Aware he addressed her, Haidra cleared her throat. "It wasn't?"

"It's all trappings and white paint," he said. "That's the trap. That's what those poor idiots back there don't understand. Kings and queens aren't there to solve their problems. Or save them. Or avenge them."

"Then why are you here?"

"I came to give every single innocent a choice none ever gave me." Jhean de Veard craned his head up, the citadel's pinnacles always in sight.

From thereon, he did not speak another word to Haidra. Step after slow step she followed behind him as he arose, but the long minutes expected by the prince's pace quickly ended before the scratched gates of Atenia's citadel. The contingent of rebels who held the position outside of the inscribed panels of oak and bronze paid their respects as those below had, respectful as they maintained a quiet watch of the queen-regent's remaining forces on the inside.

"The gates are unlocked, my Lord," one of their captains told Jhean de Veard. "Fransica's men are beyond a debris wall, but they've made no move to attack or advance. They've seen us and we've seen them. It makes no sense, my Lord."

Absorbing the information, the prince glanced at his troops for a moment, his impassive expression unreadable. His hand had not left its hold of his sword. "Stay your position."

Bon resisted, moving from their cluster of black warriors. "Father, I think—"

"Quiet," he snapped at his son. His glare roamed from the ax-slinger to the sorceress. "You want me to have my moment, children? Then let me have it."

He nodded to the rebels and the gate. Pushing it open on their power alone, the heavy slabs swung inward and slammed into the frames. He strode forward and drew his weapon. Huddled with the rest on the threshold, Haidra watched as he put his back to them.

No more than two hundred men braced behind a debris wall made of stones taken from toppled buildings. Planks from the frames of her subject's ruined home heaped in a line that separated the citadel's upper entrance from the palace and spires. Some raised spears immediately, but no arrows flew for a lack of archers. Knights manned the two entry points, a bristling wall of swords and spears accompanying them. No sorcerer or watcher was stationed upon the thin, tall spires.

Every single soul defending the last of the Veards saw him, alive and hale, armed before them to claim his rights.

Jhean de Veard disallowed any awkwardness in the moment. "By the word of your queen-regent, my innocence…" he said the word bitterly, "has been shown. I am Prince Jhean de Veard, rightful heir to Solomon III and son of Queen Marta of the Lomen clans. I bear the beater of ills, High John the Conqueror!"

He lifted the glittering longsword high in one hand. Whispering incantations in quick succession, a white flame emanated from the ancient steel. A great gasp rumbled through the royalists. Dozens of spears pointed in his direction dipped.

"I have come to set right the wrongs that have been done here," he declared, squinting under the magical fire and the sun. "But no man willing to lay down his arms and walk forward in surrender need be part of that anymore. The battle ends for you if you wish." He cracked a sinister smile. "Except the knights. You all can go home once you turn them over to me."

The demand brought an immediate response. Shoved or prodded forward by the rough hands or points of their subordinates, the armored knights at the portals of the debris wall were herded forward, cast out of their protection. Stumbling and shocked, they pulled their swords and wheeled, coming together against all sides.

Cackling a low, awful sound, the prince advanced upon them.

The first man dropped his sword and begged. "Jhean! Jhean! We were friends as children! Friends as—"

Silenced by a slash to the side of the neck, Jhean de Veard wasted little time ramming his point through the second knight, who died staring in disbelief at his rightful king. The prince shoved the man onto his back, put a foot on his bloodstained chest, and yanked the sword free. The brand dripping in gore, he stalked forward but stopped in his tracks.

To the last men, the remnants sworn to Fransica, had thrown down their arms and knelt in surrender.

# 5

# LEFT AT THE TOP

The debris fence separating the citadel's high gate from the palace, and its spires was transferred from its former defenders to the conquering forces of the rebellion, the last fight boiled down to two estranged siblings and the animosity that had rent a nation apart. The last royalists released to their families among the refugees in the city below, the Children of Marta and Arbikkean allies left the last of it to Jhean de Veard's Ghosts of Solomon. Privileged with the choice of any soldier, unit, or legion to bolster him and his seven companions, they waited to see who would be allowed to take part in the final act.

To the shock of everyone, save Prince Aron and the bard when called, Black John requested the services of Valen Goldentongue.

The bard, magnanimous to the request, blew a pink conch shell upon the next dawn.

Across the Franc River in the south a contingent of black-armored infantry marched out of the wooded hills, clad in different armors and weapons from all over Dovhain's blue-green globe, from every corner of Torsdaina and Arbikk's continents, and lands far beyond the seas that surrounded them. No matter their arms, their ethnicities, they marched through the southern palisades together. Immediately members of the old royalist guard recognized a few of the captains among the queen-regent's abandoned sellswords forces, and many were stunned to see rough and familiar faces pass under the arches on Snail's Way. Unexpected in their discipline and orderliness, they arrived at the top and lined up in front of the Ghost of Solomon's tents.

The bard and Black John summoned the ghosts when they went to inspect the new troops.

The first to emerge out of the tent with Bon, Haidra awoke to a bright, cool morning, one of the few in a long time when she hadn't started with some sort of ache or worry. The reality of an end, of a victory she never imagined in life but craved, emboldened her as she pulled on a woolen tunic, some soft hide trousers, and her marching boots before belting on her sword. Its weight, once awkward on her hip, felt at home more so than any other thing she had possessed in her short life. Its single-lobed pommel provided an easy place to rest her off-hand as she meandered around her and Bon's shelter before they joined their friends at the cooking fire.

Talic busied about chicken eggs in a hissing pan, trying to employ the fat leaking from the streaky bacon beside it. Aleaus sat in a chair to the right of him, watching from the confines of her blanket. In the background the two fishermen tarried near the debris wall a few meters away, examining its haphazard construction as they smoked their blends. Bon and New Moon convened with their father and the mysterious bard as their new band of supporters broke out in their own camps against the citadel's southern wall, settling tents and fires before the final assault began in earnest.

Aleaus saw Haidra first, offering a smile and a nod. "Tea?"

Haidra came to the fire, nodding as she placed her cold

hands in front of its radiance. She cast her focus on the sellswords building the lean-tos, already exceeding the organization of her and her friends. The black-helmed warriors serving the bard ran back to three tight columns formed before Black John and the red-headed singer when they finished. Arrayed in perfect formations, each had brought a matching spear and shield.

"They're good," she said.

Talic lifted his steaming skillet and dumped the heap of yellow eggs into a clay dish by his right knee before he scrapped out the last bits of bacon with his knife. "Breakfast." He wiped his hands on the front of his trouser-legs before he looked to the sellswords as well. "And yes, they are, despite the look of them. Different."

"How would we tell?" Aleaus pressed her feet out of her blankets folds, leaned to the side in her chair to take up the carafe of leftover tea. Fishing a cup from a bin where the ghosts kept their mess, she poured a steaming serving for Haidra.

Talic shouted to Adan and Clive. "Boys! Breakfast!" He glanced to Aleaus and back to the sellswords. "You can just tell. Real clean. Cleaner than any sellsword I've ever met."

"I wonder how good they are if we beat them," the blacksmith responded.

"Wrong idea, Lea," said Talic. "That's the problem with sellswords: just when you think you've met them all more come along and surprise you. Right bastards, but one of the reasons the good ones make the gold they do is because they can turn around after a loss and find a win. And these aren't any swords or axes bought off some highway. They all work for that bard, no doubt, and if a wank like that can get the respect of fighters like them? I bet all of them are real trouble. And mind! We beat the ones that we beat. These may have survived us."

Aleaus hummed in understanding and some worry.

"Well, good they're on our side. This time," Haidra said

before she sipped. A thin brew of lemon grass and a headier hop-flavor that made her small nose twitch, the hot liquid roused her from the last dredges of sleep. The fresh taste caused her stomach to rumble. "Let's eat before the food's cold."

They ate the quick meal of eggs and bacon before they finished their arms and armoring. The five converged on the wraiths and the bard at the end of their scheming.

"Perfect timing," Valen said with his typical joviality. "A grand morning, my friends. It seems we are the first to be the last. Clear on what we're doing, John?"

The prince beneath the hood answered in his enchanted baritone. "Just keep the sorcerers off our backs, bard, and we shall do the rest. Remember, nobody enters the palace or the spires first but me. It must be me."

"As you will," said the bard before he addressed his contingent of sellswords. "Shed the blood!"

"Save ourselves," Black John intoned with the sellswords before they parted. He faced his children, who had stood at his back and listened the entire time. He acknowledged the ghosts behind them and making sure to see Haidra last. His gaze lingered on her as if he planned something.

"Good day," he said in unexpected warmth. "The end of this nears. As you see, we only have the two spires and the palace before we can be certain the reign of Fransica ends. Watchers and a few of the wall climbers were able to report movement from inside the palace and surrendering royalists informed us the remnants of her court have retreated inside. Our mission is simple: clean out these buildings until she is captured or dead."

"Won't one end in the latter anyway?" Adan asked in his grousing manner.

Haidra elbowed him hard in the side, knocking a hard grunt out of him and a glare.

"That remains to be seen," Black John said, impassive to the fisherman's rudeness. "There is also the issue of the queen-regent's children. There has been no confirmation of Tobias or his siblings being seen for some time, but we have been told that one of these spires contains them."

"And the other?" Haidra spied on the two spires behind the debris wall. Their crenelated nests empty, no pennants or banners flew from their needled tops, nor did any one patrol the compass-balconies.

"The remains of Niklon's cult of sorcerers," Black John said. "The devils in the dragon masks."

Adan blew a long note this time. "Well shit, boss."

"Do we know which one?" Aleaus asked, less than enthused as she crossed her mail-ringed arms and studied their destinations.

Bon chuckled. "Of course not."

"Valen's forces will observe unless we call. The door of the eastern tower is unlocked and unguarded." Black John pointed to structure to their left, furthest from the palace.

Unlike the other spire, which bridged to the second floor of the royal house, it stood disconnected and alone.

"We'll breach there first."

---

New Moon stared at the door of the far spire for long minutes, repeating multiple spells that glittered and sparked in front of her face, sometimes in repeating patterns. At a loss after long minutes, she retreated to where the rest waited.

"No, I'm pretty sure," she told her father, "There's nobody on the lower level waiting for us. Nobody with magic, anyway. I also don't detect anything hidden on the doors."

"See?" Bon said to Black John's left. He shouldered his black ax. "Maybe it's as easy as it looks."

Masked in fire-eyed illusion, Black John fixed on the spire's double doors. "Bon, Talic, Adan, Clive, and Aleaus will ready their bows upon the top of the tower. New Moon, Haidra, and I will open the doors while they cover us. I will give a signal once the floor is cleared for everyone to enter."

"Right," said Bon, laying down his main weapon to drag out the quiver and bow slung on his back. The others heeded the order as Black John signaled his daughter and Haidra to him.

"Stay behind me," he said. "Haidra will keep the rear. Be ready in case something springs out, Moon."

"Yes, sir," the sorceress answered.

Haidra copied. "Yes, sir."

The three drew swords and walked to the doors. He signaled to Haidra first, who implicitly understood her role. Positioned on the hinge of the right door, she leaned and grabbed the handle. New Moon stationed herself on the other side, prepared to do the same.

High John the Conqueror in both hands, the tall wraith nodded once. "Now."

Both Haidra and the sorceress wrenched at the same time. The doors gave with little effort. Stopping the thick slab of oak and iron before it smashed her against the spire's smoothed stone, Haidra held it in place as Black John charged, his blade coursing with white fire. She pivoted out from behind the door and trailed behind him with New Moon, her rapier angled up toward the ceiling. Resting her sword on her shoulder, Haidra padded behind them.

The first floor, a long hallway divided into two rooms to the right and left, ended at a fenced-off stairwell in the rear. Not a single person, guard or servant, answered the trio's intrusion from the unlit chambers.

Black John took to the left, his shoulder along the wall as he signaled New Moon to the stairs and Haidra to the room opposite of his choice. The sorceress ran forward without hesitation, whispering a spell to bring a blue light from the tip of her long, slender sword. Its point forward like a torch, she strode confidently to the end as her father pivoted into the first chamber.

Left in the hall, Haidra gripped her sword by the hilt and held it up to her left ear, ready for a backhanded swing or a block if someone attacked once she entered the door to the right.

To her relief, Black John reappeared the next second. "Clear."

New Moon, a black silhouette under her sharp weir-light, answered in kind from the other end of the passage. "Clear down here."

Unwilling to be late or lacking, Haidra stepped full into the remaining unlit room. An empty chamber with two plush chairs facing each other, corresponding bookshelves filled with dusty tomes loomed behind them. A few more stools and seats cluttered the corners.

And nobody to worry over.

"Clear," Haidra said with more relief in her voice than she wanted.

"Go get the rest," Black John ordered her. "On the double. Meet us at the foot of the stairs."

"Yes, sir!" She raced for the open entrance, breaching the sunlight long enough to wave to Bon and the other ghosts. The five dropped their bows and arrows on the spot to draw swords and axes.

Gathering at the bottom of the stairwell to the spire's next level, the troop followed Black John's orders to slowly ascend. He and Bon led the way. Up a dark, dusty corkscrew of black marble foot boards and black iron runners, they met a lone door at the top.

Black John murmured the same spell Haidra had heard Bon employ at the tombs of their royal ancestors, and by his daughter before they breached the spire. His eyes lit by the same gold-silver sparkles, he edged toward the door. He touched the point of his longsword to the slab and pushed.

The unlocked door creaked inward.

The eldest wraith marched forward, lowering his blade. "Weapons down. Keep your hands out where they can be seen."

They stopped just beyond the threshold.

A lone figure stood in the middle of an empty room lacking in furniture, rugs, curtains, anything to make it seem anyone lived there, though people certainly did. Two more figures cowered in the shadows beneath the next set of steps built against the round walls, leading up to a ceiling hatch and the spire's apex. Stained black around its mouth and cold, the stone hearth was heaped in old ash.

Two small boys clung to each other in fear, their hazel eyes fixed on the fire-eyed figure in black. Unarmed, tears ran down dirty, un-scrubbed cheeks. Gowned in old threadbare tunics, they shivered on the spot.

The young man standing before them bared an old kitchen knife, holding it high in a foolish pose which left him open to easy attacks. He shook as well but bolstered by a familiar bravery Haidra caught within the first minute of studying his face, he was resolute to defend the little ones.

The hazel eyes. The brown-blond hair, naturally streaked in places.

The fierceness.

Black John scabbarded his sword and drew back his hood. The burning eyes and constant shadow vanished, revealing features akin to the teen's. He held out his hands to both sides, palms up to show his lack of threatening intent.

When he spoke, he did so with a soft, gentle tone. "King Tobias de Veard?" he said, lowering his head to the young man.

The teen started where he stood but kept his knife high. "Who are you? Who comes?"

"Show no fear, young king, for you have no need of it," said the long-lost uncle to his nephew. "My name is Jhean de Veard. I have come to set you free."

BLACK JOHN SENT HAIDRA, Aleaus, and Talic to the kitchens on the first level while Adan and Clive retrieved their supplies of food and drink. The larders of the spire long empty, they relit the hearth and set the pot over the fire, the water inside sloshing before it settled for the boil. Talic diced carrots, old bits of garlic, and a full onion that left him in tears before he roasted them on a clay stove with some oil. The heady smell of the simple vegetables seeped throughout the entire spire, snaking into the upper level.

Aleaus butchered the rest of the conies they had from their previous dinner—whenever that was when they all stopped for a moment to acknowledge exhaustion—and some salt pork into Talic's frying pan, letting it simmer together before heaping the mix into the boiling water over the hearth's fire.

Haidra and Talic plopped down on the corners of the brick fireplace, letting the heat ease the cold out of them while they trimmed mold off their cheese and old loaves.

The blacksmith wiped her hands with a towel and leaned against the counter. "Well, we went from three to six."

Talic half-scoffed, half-chuckled. "Nothing surprises me anymore. Not now at least."

"Poor boys," Aleaus said, a frown wrinkling the corners of her small mouth. "Just left up there like that. Barely a thread on them. Veards or not, none of them deserve that."

"We shouldn't be so forgiving so quick, Lea," Talic replied. "That boy up there is old enough, after all."

"Aye, you're right," she said. "What do you think, Haidra?"

"I think I'm happy we're in here and they're up there," she said. "Just imagine the sort of things that are to be discussed."

Talic sucked his teeth and nodded as he wiped his cheese-crusted knife on the left leg of his black trousers. "I'd rather not."

The conversation ended when Bon pushed open the door into the spire's kitchen, unarmed and unhooded. His expression despairing, he worked to decide whether or not he would speak until he found Haidra.

She put aside the remains of a half-loaf of rye to cross the tiles. "What? What is it?" She extended her hand.

He accepted it without hesitance, their fingers laced tightly together. "I… came down because they need to eat. They haven't eaten in a long time. They're…"

"We have something right here," Aleaus said in a high voice, snapping the attention to her. "Talic, the bowls. Quickly."

The old guard and the blacksmith sped together three trays recovered from the cupboards and some clay cups, which they filled with a good serving of spiced ale. Dolling out the rabbit stew, Aleaus assumed a meal in both hands while Talic balanced the other two on his palms, making a quiet dash out into the hall packed full of Valen's sellswords. Allowed in not long after Adan and Clive returned with the bard conspicuously in tow, they clogged the route.

Alone in the kitchen with its savor and silence, save for the fire's crackle, Haidra drew close to the ax-slinger's face. "Bon."

"They're so little. So hurt," he said, breaking in a full cry. From there he descended, blubbering so deeply his breaths came staggered.

Unaccustomed to seeing this champion of her heart diminished before her, Haidra pulled him close, the top of her head in the hollow of his throat as she clung tight. An oak, he wrapped his limbs about her, both of them sharing his misery before it trailed off into the dim warmth of the room. Bon reached up and wiped his eyes with a knuckle, rubbing deep until they were red.

"I'm sorry," he whispered, elbows up as he kept his hands over his face.

"Shhhh," she said, listening to his heart through layers of chain and cloak. "How is your father handling it?"

"Oh," Bon said, exhaling. "In his typical fashion. Boiling."

"At least your sister is—"

That exact moment the sorceress entered the kitchen, nowhere near her brother's torment but obviously disturbed. She stopped the second she noticed Bon and Haidra but said nothing as she glanced toward the fire.

"Any food left?" she asked. "I think the boys will want more."

"Of course," said Haidra. "Let me get some more bowls, and I'll—"

"No, I'll get it," New Moon said. "My father asked for you, Haidra. And Bon and I will need a minute."

"All right," Haidra said, always wary when the eldest wraith called on her. She checked Bon one last time and received a gentle nod before she left.

Bare of her mail and cloak, and stinking of stale sweat under it, she carried her sword and dagger on her belt as she pressed into the hallway. As before, the tough and diverse crew of sellswords under Valen's employ crowded the passage, a feat in itself considering how wide it was. Where she expected leers, maybe catcalls from the rough-looking fighters, instead men and women alike offered nods if they deigned to look up from card games, polishing their weapons, or the daze of waiting for the next order. Pipe smoke ruined what breathing room remained. Like her, they stank as well, paying no mind.

Clive stationed at the bottom of the steps, his father positioned at the spire's entrance to the south. He leaned against the left banister and nodded to Haidra. "Bon okay?" he asked as she raised her foot to the first black marble step. "He was crying when he came down."

"He will be," she said. "Have you eaten yet?"

"Not yet."

"Moon and Bon are in the kitchen. Go get your dad. There's plenty of stew in the pot."

Only a few months younger than her, the young man plucked up his long-handled ax, gripping it at the throat. "Thanks, Haidra."

She climbed to the tower's second level. The door had been left open, and the closer she came the clearer Tobias's voice was, distinct in its cultured tone.

"—and we did not see her after that. Niklon went down into the city and never returned. We've been in this spire since."

Haidra entered though neither rulers at the table paid attention to her. Past them, near the cleaned and replenished fireplace, Valen delighted the two youngest Veards with his lute, leading them along the strings as he plucked the notes of a little song. Aleaus and Talic tended to the blaze.

"And nobody came to check upon you?" Unmasked, Jhean de Veard looked across the long table. He did not offer a comforting expression.

A year older than Haidra, perhaps around the same age as New Moon, the long-unseen king of Atenia paid his uncle the same, sullen and emptied by the fresh tears on his cheeks. Neglecting the half-eaten bowl of food in front of him, he splayed his fingers on both sides of the dish, matching Jhean de Veard's posture, or attempting to. Long bereft of sunlight or proper nourishment, the gaunt figure was a pitiful caste of his uncle, his head large like his sorcerous father's with a mouth that seemed duplicitous even at rest.

"No, nobody." Tobias shifted his focus to Haidra.

Jhean de Veard's gaze followed his, and sighting her, signaled Haidra to his side. "Sit beside me, Haidra."

She pulled out the wooden chair next to the wraith's, negotiating the length of her sword so it did not knock against the table's bottom.

"Who's she?" Tobias asked, indicating her with a flick of his head but not taking his eyes off his uncle.

"This is Haidra Bloom," Jhean de Veard answered. "She was one of your subjects and a hero of Atenia. Perhaps it's first."

Haidra could not help but look at him for the statement, touched by his regard.

"I've never heard of her," Tobias commented, a cocksure arrogance in his reply. "And I know all the heroes of our line."

The towering prince laughed at his nephew.

"Pardon me, sir," Tobias said, his voice cracking as it rose. "You laugh at a king."

"No, I laugh at a fool." Jhean de Veard's grin, neither kind nor warm, instilled a fresh tension. "But be certain, nephew, she is as brave as any knight, far more cunning than your bastard father ever was, and full of a kindness you should not take for granted. Truly, she might be one of the few to give you a fair consideration."

"How so?"

"First, I think you should consider things differently now," his uncle answered. "You and your little brothers days as royals are done, so I would cease using terms like 'prince' or 'king' or 'I'm the son of a tyrant.'"

Tobias gasped at the insult.

"Please," said Jhean de Veard, "you just finished explaining to me years of abuse, neglect, and have completely done away with any guilt over how I ended your father. In fact, I can say without hesitance that your days, as hard as they have been, are about to be much, much harder. You are about to live a true life, one where you aren't handed it all. You see, boy, the world outside thinks you and your mother are the cause of their suffering."

"What suffering?" Tobias protested. "The Veards have given their entire lives to—"

"You will be silent and not repeat such falsehoods," Jhean de Veard said, each word a dire promise that shut Tobias up in his seat. Even Valen, Talic, Aleaus, and the two younger boys stopped their distractions at the rumble in his order.

Haidra cleared her throat. "My Lord, if I may?"

The rightful king beside her half-glanced, half-glared her way.

"You called for me," she said, unable to be frightened by him. "How may I help you?"

He ground his teeth before he returned his dagger-stare onto Tobias. "My nephew here has been explaining to me the circumstances of his predicament. It has been a very sad and very telling account, but he seeks to maintain that this rebellion —in fact, my return—is all part of a continued conspiracy against him and his mother reaching back to his grandparents. As you can imagine, he's had a few choice things to say about me."

"I can," Haidra said.

"I have given no defense, no answers, or any explanations." Jhean de Veard backed his seat out and stood, plucking High John the Conqueror off the table where he had rested it in plain sight. "But you will."

"I will?" Haidra asked in confusion.

"Her?" Tobias echoed.

"Her," Black John repeated as he raised his hood over his head, covering his golden mane and bearded face. He whispered a word and the veil of darkness raised. As he spoke the hell points emerged out of the illusionary void, strengthening the effect of his vocal enchantment's low howl-hiss.

"Because, my King," the wraith rumbled, "I despise you and have no need to waste my labor explaining to you anything. Certainly, you have suffered the same abuses all have been treated to under my sister, but unlike the rest of us, she raised another greedy little monster unable to see outside himself. Not once did you ask about your people. Not once did you ask about the innocence of your grandfather or grandmother. Yes, I see you and your suffering, but I also see someone ignorant of the greater disaster outside his gilded cage. I'll let Haidra tell you, from beginning to end, and you shall judge me off those. How you respond will dictate what happens to you next."

He left the table, headed for the door.

Tobias rose at his end. "Jhean de Veard," the prince cried. "Stop!"

His uncle halted but did not face the pompous wretch.

"What about Fransica?" Tobias asked. "Say what you will about your mercy for me or my little brothers, the rightful sons of this land. I watched what you did to my father. What of her?"

The wraith walked out without an answer or promise.

# 6

# TOWER OF THE DRAGONS

T hen what did he say?" New Moon asked, her silver brows pinching together.

"Nothing," Haidra said, stressing the word before she raised her teacup. She sniffed the brew, its tannins deep in her nose and little else. "He just sat there until he told me, Aleaus, and Talic we could go. Valen was still there after I left."

"Good, I guess," said the sorceress above her own cup. She stared into the campfire before them, ruminating. "My father will be sending Tobias and the boys away tonight. They'll be taken to a safe place."

Haidra side-eyed her. "And then?"

New Moon stared into the flickering campfire, lost on the question.

"Moon." Haidra set her cup down on her knee. "What happened in there? What did they say before I walked in?"

"What my father expected." The answer deepened her gloom. "Not what I expected. It's easy to expect gratitude from those you rescue and much harder when they don't give it. And, of course, he was raised by my aunt."

"I don't think it's all his aunt," Haidra said. "He seemed

honestly surprised when I told him what I had seen. I don't think he ever knew about Hibni or your grandmother. He didn't even know the name Marta."

"But he knew my father," she said. "He hates my father for something he isn't."

Haidra measured her response. "I think it's less hate than distrust. He doesn't trust anyone save his mother and now we've put that into real question. What I told him may change it, but it didn't change the fact no one has ever truly been there for him. Worse, he thinks his is 'the due of all kings.'"

"He said that?"

"Of the little he said. He made it as some weak reply about the suffering of his subjects over the years."

"How? How did he say it?" New Moon questioned.

"Like suffering was a natural course for him. His brothers. I think they were raised to believe the entire world purposefully neglected them. Only their jailers loved them enough to keep it away. Or so they thought." Haidra raised her cup with a nod and took a sip, the caffeine a needed perk to keep her awake. "To his credit, he apologized for Arverin. Didn't have to do that."

The gloom thinned but did not lift. New Moon hummed a mysterious response. The sun set in the west above the world, the sky cascaded in rippling sheets of cloud obscuring a pink sky fading into a pleasant shade of navy bolstered by a bright half-moon shaded green and the other, red and full.

It was a few more sips before the sorceress broke the peace. "Did my father say anything about Fransica?" she asked, clearing her throat. "Or mention his plans for her once we find her?"

"You don't know?" Haidra asked.

The daughter of Atenian royal blood, mistress of the winds and sands of Arbikk, shook her head.

"How in Crook's name do you all live like this?" Haidra asked.

"From one daughter of a conflicted man to another I could

ask you the same about how you endured this place," New Moon responded. "Couldn't I?"

Haidra considered the question and a smart answer when Talic walked out of the twilight and in front of their fire. Fully dressed and armed, his black cowl and mail coif obscured everything but the aged features of his hard face. His gray stare absorbed them both. "Ma'am, Haidra. Time to go."

"Right," New Moon answered, the first to stand after she set her teacup down on the cobblestones of the courtyard. "Anyone up top yet?"

"Apparently," Talic said as Haidra rocked forward onto her feet and off the stool she had occupied before the bonfire. She bent to the side to collect her sword and knife, but left behind her quiver and unstrung bow behind.

The three marched to the eastern end of their encampment, putting the last of the daylight behind as night conquered the sky. Held back by dozens of torches lifted by Valen's black-helmed "Grinders", as the ghosts had learned they were called, a brazier set directly in the yard's center burned as well.

Flanking its flame was Black John and Bon, faced toward the second spire and its bridge connected to the palace. The other Ghosts of Solomon formed a line behind them.

The windows of the thin tower lit with lights all the way up to the apex, none guarded its height, but more than one shape peeked over the small wall of its compass-balcony. The ports set apart in an ascending corkscrew pattern to match the internal infrastructure of what Haidra guessed was its stairs, heads clustered to look out. A few white dragon masks, smooth and white, stuck their snouts out in the open.

New Moon stepped beside her brother. "How many do you think?"

"Almost two dozen, unless my eyes are failing me," Black John said. The sparkles of the vision spell, which Haidra was beginning to understand, danced a few inches in front of the opening of his hood. "None of them are very powerful, though. They've thrown several spells at us since we stepped to the light, and none one of them has reached far enough to even harry us."

"They have?" New Moon said, surprised. "I haven't felt a thing!"

"I don't think they're very good at this," Bon said. "But can't you hear them now?"

Haidra and the rest watched in confusion as New Moon bent forward and tilted her head, trying to hear something none of them could.

The sorceress started. "A lot of that is clearly wrong."

"Again," said Bon. "Not very good."

"Don't dismiss them. The closer we get the stronger their spells will be," said Black John. "We're going to do this in stages. Valen is willing to press his men on the door. I will go with them. Talic, Adan, and Haidra will be with me. New Moon and Bon will bombard the nest while Aleaus and Clive guard them, just in case."

"In case?" Clive asked. "In case of what?"

"In case these damned sorcerers try to bomb you out of existence," Adan admitted to his son. A hard man, he kept his face void of worry. "Best hope we get up there first, right, Boss?"

"Right indeed, Adan," Black John said as he waved with sparkles away with the pass of an armored hand. "Let's go."

"Fireballs?" Bon asked his sister.

"Fireballs," New Moon answered in full confidence.

"Do not burn the tower down atop our heads," Black John said as he diverted for the bard and his contingent. Haidra hurried with Talic and Adan, falling into an easy pace behind the fallen prince's long strides.

The singer and one of his captains met them first. "John," said Valen before he gave a small salute to Haidra and the rest. "About twenty-two, you think?"

The wraith grunted. "Twenty-four. Either they are

holding their best spells or there are very few among them worth worrying over. Whatever their skill Niklon was a competent sorcerer and I do not expect him to have left the possibility of his work or the cult to be taken without a fight. They haven't surrendered, and we shouldn't expect them to. Not after they know what awaits them even if they escape."

"One way in either way."

"Where do you want us, bard?" The wraith asked his shorter, slimmer co-conspirator.

Valen smirked. "Help me batter down the door and we'll get the rest done."

Black John nodded and faced his ghosts. "Go with Valen and follow his orders. I will signal Moon and Bon. Once you start, do not stop until one of us gives the order. Understand? Talic? Adan?" He looked square at her. "Haidra?"

"Aye, Black John," the two men said, echoes of each other.

"Aye, Black John," she said with steady confidence.

He signaled the three to join the sellswords. Folded into their numbers, closer proximity to the mix of warriors from lands Haidra had never heard of revealed they all spoke in her native Torsii, leaving no confusion to what the plans were for the night.

"Right, lads and ladies!" A mace in one hand and a small buckler on the other sinewy forearm, Valen used the flanged end to point at the long ram at the sellsword's feet, roped for nine carriers on each side. "New friends in the front, a few of the pups in the back. Seems fair. Hattie, you have the call."

A second woman bearing an ax, but a much larger round, stepped forward. "Three by three in front, back, and the rest cover the kids. Shed the blood!"

"Save ourselves," the sellswords intoned together, their booming voices startling Adan.

"Holy fuck!" the fisherman yelped.

A few of the rough killers laughed, but in a kind way as they clapped his back and shoulders.

Haidra half-walked, half-herded to the long length of oak, both ends shaved flat and blunt before fire had blackened them hard. Holes drilled through the center and strung with thick hemp allowed a solid but biting handhold as she and Talic assumed the ram's front, Adan behind her, and the youngest among the sellswords hauled the rest. Lighter than she expected and thankful for her leather gloves, Haidra waited in a turbulent mix of anxiety and anticipation.

"Fucking fuck, Talic," said Adan behind her.

"Fucking fuck, Adan," Talic responded to his compatriot.

Valen and Hattie closed their ranks around the ram as Black John's voice called out, heightened by a vocal enchantment.

"The flames of vengeance will claim the dragon!"

Upon the declaration Bon and New Moon appeared from the right and the left, carrying the blood red diamonds they had not summoned since the battle at the northern palisade. The younger wraiths launched the fiery magic as high as possible. Bon's fell short by a foot, setting the south-facing side of the spire's apex ablaze in unnatural flame, while New Moon's scored the parapet wall. An explosion of concussive power spread the conflagration, immolating Niklon's cultists in hiding.

Black smoke filled the night sky instantly.

"Oh, fucking fuck," Haidra had her turn to say.

"Charge," screamed Valen.

Brought along or trampled if she failed to keep up, the extra weight of the ram found her knees in every jarring footfall. She sped, unable to slow, toward the burning, smoking point ahead. She couldn't see over the taller warriors in front of her, the night led by the bard and his second setting a growing pace.

"Red mists!" Valen screamed. "Run! Run and don't stop! Don't breathe!"

Haidra understood despite the conflicting directions,

gripped her length of rope tighter, sealed her mouth, and held. The whole troop powered into a sprint. The glare of the burning spire, the black-blue night with its clinging shadows thrown away, caused her eyes to water as hot cinders soaked the air. Somewhere in the mad dash she thought she saw a bloody mist around her knees but cleared its bounds in seconds.

"Shields up," Hattie shouted. "Flasks!"

The warriors raised shields of every size over the heads of Haidra and the rest, covering them in darkness. Lost in a forest of strong arms, glass broke above her. The quick stink of oil was engulfed in sulfurous blazes of lime and yellow.

"At the door," Valen declared. "Ram! Break down the door!"

Nine sellswords parted in front of the ram, raising their shields to form a short overhang. Another flask dropped from on high, but deflected with a batting move, exploded in blue fury a few feet away.

The rammers mustered speed. The spire's door appeared out of the murk, unbarred in the front.

The ram's face collided with the loudest crack, deafening Haidra as the shock of the impact jolted her entire body. By some grace, she kept the strap in her hands, the weight of the oaken pole born by the others. They swung again in unison.

The second *crack* thudded more, and the third smashed apart the growing crease. Cultists in their masks and robes buzzed in the space behind it, arming themselves.

Hauling backward, the ram crew let out a heave as they broke the entrance on the forward stroke, snapping the lintels and iron hinges. The splintered doors landed with resounding booms.

Their foes, caught in scramble, raised their steel.

Before Valen, his sellswords, or the ghosts advanced a black shape flew over them, bearing a line of white fire. Black John alighted on the floor past the doorway, tearing forward with his longsword. The cultists in their white dragon masks died by the stroke.

"After him, after him, you gentle sort!" Valen cried to his Grinders.

Forced inside by the rushing tide of sellswords, Haidra had drawn her sword in time and kept the point high, leaving her room among the crush to make space with her free arm. Trapped but flowing with the rest, she passed under the cracked lintels as a great light issued from above.

Two voices clashed in a language she did not know, but recognizing the voice of the wraith, she opened her eyes and suffered the glare of seeing.

A giant among the sellswords and cultists alike, Black John had raised High John the Conqueror to form a concealing dome of illumination, pure and bright. Blocking a gout of fire aimed directly at him, she followed its blazing line to a furious sorcerer at the top of the curving steps to the next floor. Flinging his hands in all directions, his words and gesticulations made the ring of fire in front of him spin faster, its projected line of destruction never-ceasing.

Haidra saw a path through the fighting. Able to break out of the cluster of bodies, she dashed for it. She dodged past a sellsword in the midst of spilling a cultist's guts, stomping on fallen entrails as she ducked and crawled under another set engaged in a fatal knife fight atop a table. It toppled over the second she cleared its corner. At the foot of the steps she tripped but, ending the fall with a hand, she recovered.

Fixed on frying Black John's magical shield, the masked sorcerer's field of vision left her out of view. She stormed up the steps, teeth gritted to forbid a roar as she let her sword do the work.

The wide point pierced the cloth of his white robes, an immediate splotch of red growing where the steel sank past ribs. The breath stolen out of him, she drove the length through his lungs. The evocation snapped out of reality, leaving the room lit by the wraith's shining defensive cone.

The body at the end of Haidra's sword toppled headfirst off the landing.

The last cultist fell, shrieking as a Grinder cut the sycophant from throat to sternum, the killer's self-disgusted screams a final punctuation before his friends gathered to console him.

Black John lowered his longsword, dismissing the bright shield to leave them in the darkness of the steaming, bowels-emptying room. He quickly recalled the white illumination to the blade, revealing the fullness of the ruin.

Bodies of dead men, all of them masked in the guise of white dragons maned in black fur, lay in gross states. Certain after she took stock from her high vantage point, not a single Grinder had added to the mortal tally.

"Valen, the fire," Black John called over the groans of fighters collecting themselves. "Tell my children to put out the fire!"

The bard, emerging from the din covered in blood from head to toe, his buckler lost, stumbled toward the entrance. One of the sellswords chased after Valen, ducking under an arm to lift the man up. Haidra noticed how every one of the sellswords placed their full concern on the singer, and despite the boorish-ness in Aron's tent, understood a depth of love shared between their captain and his command.

The same pride, though brief in the midst of corpses stewing in red lakes, spread when she found Talic and Adan picking their way past the horde to reach Black John. She descended the steps back to the bottom level.

The wraith king raised his free hand. "Brace."

A new groan rose outside the spire, sudden gusts of wind ripping past the broken entryway. It carried for sustained minutes and, looking above, Haidra watched in wonder as the smoke spilling through the cracks of the ceiling receded. The gales ended a few minutes later, and though the smell of burnt wood haunted, the crackle or chew of flame no longer troubled their ears.

The wraiths and sellswords collected together, checking their minor injuries. Bon and New Moon found their father, and waiting on him, followed up the steps to the second level. The ghosts trailed after as quickly as they were able, as did Valen once he recovered his stamina.

They entered a large altar room on the next level. The walls painted black like the floors, small tables built under the ascending stairs lay cluttered in wands, staves, bowls heaped in powdered incense, cases of imported herbs, and the many books and tools sorcerers needed for their experiments. In the center was the altar slab, wide and heavy at its base, but clean of any sign of use.

"Valen," Black John called out.

Armed only with a cloth to wipe the crusty red mask on his pale face, Valen's bright blue eyes absorbed the scene as he nodded. He stuck out his hand toward the elder wraith. "Pleasure doing business, Jhean," the bard said as the masked prince accepted with a firm shake. "Mine can handle this room."

"If you find any sign..." Black John started.

"I'll come running," said the bard. "There's one more level before the roof, right?"

"Yes," the swordsman said. "My ghosts."

From the brave many, they became eight again, the Ghosts of Solomon heeding the call of the three black figures. Unified and uninjured, a feat both Clive and Adan reveled in when father and son reconnected, they marched the steps up to the next door. Confirmed by both Bon and New Moon after they employed their vision spell—a few more words of which Haidra caught—they pressured open the unlocked portal.

Black John entered first, as always, but halted. His son scooted past before he stopped as well.

"What's up?" asked Aleaus, at the rear of their line.

Death. Sweet, stinking, rotting, wafted out of the doorway.

Haidra entered third, after the swordsman and ax-slinger. She understood their silence when she saw the corpses.

Lit well by several small oil lamps set in the pocks of the mortar wall, their perpetual enchantment set a rosy haze ill-matching for the chamber's contents. Five bodies, thin and emaciated beneath brown-spotted sheets, stared into the gables of the spire's burnt roof. A desk covered in correspondences and more tomes was set against the northern wall, and atop the grand, high-backed chair before it, a shrunken skull rested in its seat.

Bon neared his father. "Dad?"

"Go...go look," the lost prince whispered to his son. To anyone. "Three of them are women... One of them might be..."

New Moon strode into the room, full of the courage her father needed. "Haidra, Aleaus."

The three women among the Ghosts of Solomon removed the sheets from the men. Their faces had been harvested, along with their eyes and ears, sliced away to reveal the dried muscles and ligaments attached to the skulls. Patches of tissue from all parts of their body were missing.

The third woman had been murdered, stabbed multiple times in the heart before her killers dug routes along every major artery with a razor, mapping the body from throat to ankles. Well preserved with salts and tinctures New Moon identified in small bottles rested on the corners of her slab, it had nonetheless leaked ichor and green after weeks of improper care.

By the time they found the will for the third body Aleaus broke off and wandered to the desk, in search of a clean breath of air in the abattoir. New Moon and Haidra prepared themselves.

A keen reader and quick eye, the middle-aged blacksmith skimmed the documents. "These are Niklon's," she announced.

"They have his signature. Some of these are orders to the guard, the knight's council—one here is to Fransica—and—"

New Moon interrupted. "She's here," she said, almost sounding surprised. "I found her."

The sorceress had approached the third table by herself while Haidra had been listening, trying to keep focus beyond the grossness they uncovered. She had removed the cloth to reveal the hollowed, drained face of an old woman.

Black John rushed to the side of the third corpse, looked down upon her, and howled in despair. "Mama! Mama! No! Mama, no!" the son underneath repeated over and over, hugging the decayed body of Queen Marta to his chest no matter how hard his children tried to pry her away. "Mama, please! No!"

Pieces of the missing queen sluffed off the body, splotching the grimy boards.

"Let her go," New Moon sounded as Bon rushed to join her. They fought hard, prying at his arms. "You'll damage her!"

"No!" Jhean de Veard screamed again. "Mama, no!"

Haidra would never forget his words until her dying day, or how they had reduced a king to a common orphan like her.

# 7

# HOW TO MEET ARISTOCRATS

Father," New Moon shouted as she threw herself forward, wrapping her arms around his strong middle. "They'll hear us!"

Haidra tried catching the prince by his arm, but moving too quickly, he tore the limb from her hands to pound his fist against the door. Almost wrenched off her feet, she kept balance and clawed at his cloaked shoulder again, failing to grab one of the guards underneath the black cloth. Off the main chamber of the spire's third level, which held the slain Niklon's personal laboratory and morgue, a single door led to an interconnecting bridge across to the palace, built by the queen-regent's husband for convenience.

Jhean de Veard attacked it with all his might, beating High John the Conqueror's pommel against the ironwood. Scoring jarring blows that rattled the door in the frame, he gouged chunks, but to no avail.

Standing in terrified awe of the roaring, towering prince, the rest of the ghosts split their attentions, caught between his rage and the mummified remains of Marta de Veard, the long-lost queen left on the floor where her son had dropped her the moment despair subsumed to wrath. Aleaus and Adan especially seemed concerned with the corpse, hovering over it as they tried to cover her in the muslin New Moon had half-pulled away in the discovery of her murdered grandmother.

Bon grappled for the elbow of his father's off-hand, grabbing it tight with both arms. "Jhean! Jhean! Stop! It's not going to—"

In a snap Jhean de Veard dropped his royal blade and snatched Bon's black ax from him, battering the door in a renewed attack. Better suited to the work than the small, blunt point of his pommel, the wedge was only a little more successful on the banded wood.

Enraged by the theft, the younger man threw himself on his sire, as did his sorceress-sister who snatched the haft.

Foolish but fearless, Haidra tried for his waist. She pressed her head against his back, the layers of cloth and hidden armor making her hold difficult as he twisted. She struggled to keep her legs under her, whipped in every direction.

"That does it," said Talic as he leapt in.

Timing his approach, the old guard threw himself in front of Jhean de Veard when New Moon was able to pull back the ax. He shoved hard, and the full weight of four bodies against one man won out. Stumbling back a few feet, his daughter's pull on the weapon in his hand and Haidra's awkward burden faltered his steps. Downed to a knee, the prince grunted as his son assisted his daughter in tearing the ax from his possession. Haidra pushed to keep him down.

A talented wrestler, Talic dragged the prince forward instead of up or back, breaking his posture. He rolled the prince onto his side and mounted, pinning a knee on his chest.

"Stop it!" he shouted in Jhean de Veard's face. "She's watching! Marta watches!"

Seizing under the man's weight, Jhean de Veard cursed in Eaith before, as it happened to every broken child, the despair reduced him to emotions and nothing more. Bowled on her side with her hands linked on the other side of his body, Haidra lay there and hugged instead of braced, letting the muscular form melt into an inert state. New Moon knelt beside her father's head, cradling him as he sobbed.

Adan, Aleaus, and Clive tended to the queen's body, lifting its withered mass back onto its proper slab.

When he calmed and was released to stand, the hulking image of grief attended to his mother's side. The three who had restored Marta to her place cleared the area as Jhean de Veard looked down, studying the hollowed eye sockets where the orbs had been stolen, the lines of half stitched scars and places the sorcerer had written notes upon a design never finished. None of the hair had survived, or the teeth, the latter pulled from gums long receded.

New Moon joined him on his right, and then Bon on the other side. Withdrawn and cold to the sight of a grandmother neither had known beyond stories, they paid their father's sorrow with the respect of their silence.

"We go now," Jhean de Veard said to everyone and no one at all. He refused any other image but the morbid one before him. "This ends. Now."

"Us three, then," said Bon in a soft tone. "The others need rest. We need rest. Dad—you need to—"

The glare the avenger gave his son ended that argument.

The fray of nerves and the shock of the battle they had endured cascaded for Haidra, unable to keep her peace out of impatience and frustration. Her shoulder hurt from where she had fallen with the former monarch. "Fuck the three of you, then."

Bon and New Moon shifted to have their turn at a glare, but she beat them to it. The elder wraith was unmoved by her rebuke.

"We're not going back to camp," Haidra said. "We're not going to let you three go off alone. No. No."

New Moon started, her tone hard. "Haidra, this is a family—"

"No, it isn't," said Clive. "Haidra's right. Be wrong to let you—"

Bon interrupted the younger fisherman. "Adan, tell your son—"

"You tell him, you blower!" the older fisherman scolded. "Don't you go telling us about the evils of crowns and titles, and then try to throw yours around. You know, I've been meaning to tell you—"

"Shut up!" Haidra shouted this time, silencing the growing arguments. Again, the entire room turned on her, the target of focus and growing ire. "All of you be quiet! There's no debate on this! If you three go then we're all going. Talic?"

"I'm with her, Sire," Talic said.

Aleaus spoke next, "As am I."

Both Adan and Clive agreed with clear nods.

The two children, beaten back and unable to answer this certainty, offered no more resistance as they waited on their father.

He did not look at them or the ghosts. Rising from his hunch, he gazed at his mother in sad bitterness and held out his right hand. "My sword, Talic."

<hr>

THEY LEFT Marta de Veard behind with Valen and explicit instructions to bear her to the city below. After a quick trip to their camp past the debris wall to eat a meal and reorganize their gear, the eight black shapes moved in the midnight hour, straying far from the torches the sellswords had lit to reveal the courtyard. No balconies available for men to guard and the windows boarded, the three wraiths arranged before the palace's double-doors.

"Aren't the rest of them knights?" Clive had the sense to ask as New Moon evoked powers of air and light first, followed by Black John and Bon.

"You said 'we're with 'em,' Clive," Aleaus said, a round shield in front of her and a sword rested on its top rim. "Too late to wonder about that now."

Haidra paid none of them attention, intent on listening to the words the wraiths spoke in unison. A familiar delta of energy pointed toward the gilded palace doors, burning bright but somehow constrained to bubble against the flagstones. The lines they spat on the nighttime breeze, long and melodic, grew in volume with successive choruses, until suddenly their waving gesticulations synchronized. Flat hands pointed high, the three chopped forward at their destination. The wedge of magical light sped, smacking into the palace entrance.

The illumination absorbed into the doors.

Everything exploded outward in a hailing shower of splinters, stone, and mortar.

The cloud it produced was quickly banished by a simple wind charm New Moon conjured, leaving a gaping hole to the grand foyer within. Knights in armor backed over themselves in escape, up a set of damaged steps.

Black John led the march, longsword rested on his right shoulder. He used the two fingers on his left to trace an enchanting rune. He pressed it against the apple of his throat.

"It ends," he shouted, his demonic voice amplified and resonant. "It ends! It ends! It ends!"

They tore out of the night, spirits of Atenia's vengeance outlined against the warm lights outside. None waited in the foyer, or on the carpeted path to the throne room tucked under the split-staircase leading up to the second floor. The first occupants they met were the servants and staff of the palace, sent to stop the prince with whatever crude weapons the fleeing knights left them.

"Not one," Black John ordered. "Not one royalist leaves alive!"

Black John cut down the first butler, then the next footman, then a cook that screamed out the prince's true name in pleading. Not a single one of them were spared the swordsman's sweeping furry, their lives ended in slashes and stabs. A few dodged around his charge but fell to Bon's ax or New Moon's cruel rapier.

"Gray-stare! Hammerstrike! Hold the steps!" Black John bellowed as he, his children, Haidra, and the Fishers of Souls continued into the throne room.

Past another anterior chamber lay the great hall of the Veards. Elegant in its high-beamed gables and immense columns lining a red runner to the royal dais in the back, upon the three-tiered rise rested the oaken seat of kings, gnarled and knotted in places where ancient knives and files tamed its wild shapes. It bore a green pillow in the hollow where the monarch sat, but the cushion lay un-warped.

Arrayed in front of it stood the final twelve knights of Atenia. Owning only their swords, they had lost their armors, their wealth, reduced to the plain clothes of the servants they had sent to die before them.

Haidra knew none of their faces, but Adan did.

"That's Sir Alwyn," said the fisherman in open mockery. "Sir Pierce! Look, son, Atenia's heroes."

To the shock of the ghosts, the twelve knights dropped to a knee and offered their swords by the hilt.

Sir Alwyn, a lout with lank brown-gray hair spoke as he fearfully gazed at the floor. "Mercy, Prince Jhean! Mercy!"

"Yes, prince, mercy!" shouted another knight, voice frayed by fear. "We have thrown up our swords to you, knowing full well our betrayal and crimes against Atenia! Against you!"

"Mercy, lord, mercy!"

The knights begged, Alwyn and Pierce the loudest among them.

Their scorned king, the fallen prince, glowered at the mewling lieutenants. He checked over both of his shoulders until he found Haidra and signaled her to his side. She came, quiet as a few of the shamed men dared to raise eyes at her.

"Haidra," Black John said, "These men have beaten, terrorized, and savaged the citizens of Atenia. I am in no place to rend judgment, but you are of the people. Would the people spare them?"

She shook her head.

"I thought not," Black John said aloud, looking upon the dishonored knights. He leveled the royal blade of the Veards from his shoulder and re-homed it in its scabbard. "I spare each of you. I will grant you the mercy of your lives."

Sir Alwyn, a long-known miscreant who performed his chivalry to cover grosser misdeeds, lifted his head with a smile already smug at the edges. "My lord, thank you! Your kindness is—"

Black John raised his steeled, spiked hand. "I said I will grant mercy, Alwyn. But I'm no longer king, and my judgment bears no weight next to those you spurned."

The Ghosts of Solomon drew their weapons, Haidra pulling her sword first. Without hesitation she charged Alwyn. Hungered and exhausted, he was too slow to bring up his sword in time. She batted his blade off with a glancing blow before she wound around, the edge angled at his ribs. The blade cut flesh and bone, driving deep. He gasped, choking as blood flooded from his mouth.

The champions of Atenia's common folk set upon the kneeling aristocrats, Bon and New Moon included.

Their father maintained a full view of the slaughter.

# 8

## IN THE HALLS WHERE THEY LIVED

The ghosts followed the three wraiths to the stairs of the palace's second level, and through the second to the third, until finally to the shock of every member expecting resistance, they entered the royal residences on the fourth floor. Void of any life or noise-—even a stray cat or rat— the long halls lay empty, the doors of the apartments shut.

Jhean de Veard removed his hood as he stood at the top step. The rest halted with him, keyed to every movement or emotion.

And for long moments, in the halls where they lived, the remains of a dynasty stared into the yawning passage. Finally, without any warning, he sighed.

"I must..." He searched the carpeted floors ahead, the lattice-design of pineapples, angels, and gold-spun stars pounded into mushed outlines of what they once were. "I must confess."

The ghosts, especially the oldest three, turned in shock.

"I did not violate my sister or abuse her, nor she did grow up in a den of incest or abuse. But that is not to say we grew up perfectly." His mouth tense as he worked at something in the front of his thoughts, Jhean de Veard ground his teeth. "My father neglected us for his reign, and more than that. You all know before his murder knights were not pure of heart, nor 'the scions of peace' Fransica tried to recast them as—but they were better. My mother did control us, down to the word and thought, save the ones we kept to ourselves."

He paused for a long time, his eyes roaming between the apartment doors that lay on each side of the hall.

"But what is your crime, then?" the young fisherman had the bravery to ask. "You said you wish to confess, but Lord—"

The prince glared at the proper title.

"—Jhean de Veard," he continued, sharp in his correction, "I have not heard a crime."

"Because there was no crime. None save giving her every reason to hate me." He flared his nostrils in a quick, hard sigh. "What I say now I do not say as a prince, nor do I say it as your leader, nor as your comrade, or anything. I speak only the truth as I know it and expect you to make of it what you can. My sister Fransica loved me deeply—too deeply for a boy born to swords and expectations of battlefields, but also in a way a brother cannot, should not, love his sister. It grew worse the more we matured, to the point where I sought quests in the name of Atenia and my father. The things she tried from her budding even to the day she married the sorcerer, I—" he shuddered in clear disgust. "I fled Atenia because I sought to flee her. My crime was refusing to face the truth of what was happening. Or tell it."

"But we were always told you were sent," said Talic, fourteen years old than Jhean de Veard, "that some great monster or beast assailed the farmlands, or bandits, or how you staved off wars with the tribes of Mesca by helping them battle the Ohars in the north! All of that was a lie?"

"I did fight the Ohars with the Mesca, and there were beasts throughout. My father made up the bandits," the prince replied, unvarnished in his honesty. "All of which to cover my refusal to return. Even when she married and I thought myself safe to remain, the ceaseless hunt started again, lewder and more provocative. I thought a final distance would wither her fixation, but it became more. She wanted all of us to give her things, things meant for my father, myself, and by law the people of Atenia. I left for Arbikk as a diplomat, seeking the distance once again."

"Until Hibni," Haidra said, glancing at Bon and New Moon.

The ax-slinger and sorceress bared little more feeling than their father, sullen as they stared into the dead space of the hallway. The hands of her lover tight to the handle of his black ax, the way his sister curled her fingers into claws, paid heed to the turmoil within them.

"Until Hibni," their father confirmed. "I thought to remain in Arbikk as long as I could, happy with my life and leave my sister with hers until my ascension. Not until I wrote to my father announcing the Shahira of the Northern Desert's pregnancy and the assurance of Atenia's heirs did she make her claim."

"All because she couldn't have what—who—she wanted," Aleaus said, almost at a whisper. She faced away from the entire party, caught in the dismal truth. It spread among the ghosts and reinfected his children, petrifying them where they stood.

"One of the many things I learned in Arbikk was the uselessness of kings. The perverseness of queens," Jhean de Veard said, "but she never had the chance. Not outside the lives we lived, here in these halls."

"What does that have to do with anything?" Haidra asked.

"Everything," the proper ruler of her homeland replied. "I ask none of you to come with me, for you have gone farther than required by anyone. What remains is between her and I, my son and daughter, who will come with me to meet the aunt that shaped so much of their lives. If any of you wish to help see the end of this, however, you may. You have earned that."

All explained, all revealed, the Ghosts of Solomon were reduced to their normal selves, citizens of a fallen land where all they had were the steps they took, one by one and day by day. Talic, Aleaus, Adan, and Clive remained where they stood as the wraiths walked forward, shoulder to shoulder.

Haidra followed behind them, for she did not know who she was before this rebellion, or whom she might be after, but determined to see the end of what she had started. She owed it to Arverin to know.

Down gilded halls and murals depicting the long history of Atenia's hero-kings and gallant queens, Jhean de Veard passed the first two portals on both sides. He stopped at the second set of doors on the left and glanced at the three young companions. He viewed his children longer than he did Haidra, studying the face of his daughter more than Bon's.

Slowly Jhean de Veard reached down and unbuckled his longsword from its harness. He handed it to Haidra.

"She expects me to be violent, to storm in there in a rage," he said as he removed his gauntlets next, slipping his hands free of the protruding steel. Bon offered to hold them, but his father shook his head, dropping them on the thick carpet. He rubbed his heavy, calloused hands. "I will not give her the satisfaction of it. She will say many, many things you've heard, but she'll also say what she needs to keep herself where she thinks she is strongest. Do not answer her if she speaks to you. Wait for me. Understood?"

Tucking the long blade of kings under her arm, Haidra bowed her head one more time.

"Stop that," he chided her directly before he turned the gold-wrought handles.

The stout door covered in pearl lacquer swung inward, revealing an apartment larger than the house Haidra grew up in, but to her surprise and the obvious surprise of the prince, it lay completely bare of furniture, decoration, any sign of habitation. Looking around as if confused, he hurried to its central nexus.

Finding no one in the un-dusted bathing chambers with a

tub basin of hammered gold Haidra noticed longer than she should have, or the immense wardrobe full of empty closets able to hold every loaf of bread she baked Tanny in a week, or the north-facing balcony Haidra recognized from the few times the queen-regent had appeared outside, their joined confusion grew by the second. To her dire worry and expectation, the prince went to the fence and gazed over in search of the worst possible outcome. She gave a conflicted but thankful sigh when he turned to signal otherwise.

"Where is she?" New Moon asked.

Giving no answer, Jhean de Veard motioned for the retreat back to the central hallway on the fourth floor. He stopped in its center and stared at the door across from his sister's apartment. "Bon, Haidra, go check the apartment at the end. It was my parents'," he said. "Return back here if you find anything."

Weapons in hand, Bon and Haidra quickly jogged to the end of the floor, and like the apartment of the absent queen-regent, discovered chamber after chamber bereft of any accouterments. They returned less than ten minutes later, the ax-slinger giving a silent shake of his head to his father's questioning look.

"This was yours?" New Moon concluded as the four faced the last room.

Saying nothing, Jhean de Veard turned the gilded handles down, freeing the bolts. He pushed the doors open.

In the central sitting room, a fire had been built in the stone hearth, blazing bright to spread its warmth on the scuffed floorboards, though it quickly became the only civilized detail. Strewn on every surface, scattered on every inch of floor, was every bit of clothing, trash, wasted food, dried puddles of wine, and clumps of ash emptied from a pipe. Glass glittered in the corners where goblets had been thrown, and across the portraits of old Atenia's glories someone had taken a dagger to every canvas or tapestry. A smell of rot, feces, and cinders pervaded.

Jhean de Veard entered his former abode.

"I'm waiting for you, Jhean," she cried from somewhere beyond the nexus. "Always waiting!"

The prince shuddered, a quiver un-befitting of a brave warrior. Fists closed tight with tension, he nodded for his children and Haidra to follow. "Draw your weapons but stay behind me," he whispered as they crossed the sitting room for the hall. "If she's armed, disarm her, but do not kill her."

New Moon spoke, "But if she—"

Jhean de Veard's look warned his daughter against it.

The short hallway ended at an intersection blocked by two broken doors left in a makeshift wall. The way right opened to the prince's part of the grand balcony at the top of the palace, the left his personal wardrobe and study, ruined by years of intermittent trashing.

But forward was the grand bedroom, lavish in its proportions. Unlike the rest of the apartment, it was spotless, the boards scrubbed, and the giant four-poster bed remade with fresh linens and embroidered covers. Soft candles burned on the long dresser under the galley window overlooking the citadel's northern walls, sweeping eastward to the Ben-Lomen glacier. The daylight bright to dull the beeswax's columns low light, their points of fire still provided a weird, lurid haze, made all the stranger by the single figure standing in front of the bed.

Queen-Regent Fransica de Veard was where she had chosen to meet her estranged brother, gowned in a simple white dress of a gauzy material. It exposed the thin, skinny body underneath in full detail, scarred in places with burns and small mutilations. Tattoos, high in color and detail, patterned one side of her hips, her inner forearm, and foot, facsimiles of the old Lomen designs used by the native clans before she and Niklon had purged them from the glacier's slopes. No crown netted the thick blond mane, and if not for the madness in her hazel eyes, she would have been beautiful to behold.

If not for the madness.

She stared hard at her brother, eyes wide with pure hatred.

The exiled stared back, stoic to her presence.

Fransica exploded, breaking into tears and sobs. She backed towards the windows, kicking and thrusting her hands out. "He's here! He's here! You let my rapist in!" she screamed as loud as she could as she spasmed against the glass panes. "Stay away! Keep him away from me! Please!"

Unfazed, Jhean de Veard watched in complete detachment.

"You've helped my molester, my torturer!" she squealed at the hooded figures flanking him, paying no attention to Haidra, dwarfed where she stood behind the prince. "You stand with a murderer! A killer! A scourge of women's chaste virtue—"

"Quiet," Haidra said as the defeated ranted.

"—this villain, this monster, and you would defend him?" Fransica hissed at his children. "Defend a violator of women? A murderer of cities? A wretch who dresses like a devil and has never done anything more than be a violent, toxic ma—"

Tossing down the royal blade of Atenia's ancestors, Haidra stormed around Jhean de Veard, who the first and only time startled at her entrance.

"Shut up! Shut up," Haidra screamed as high and manic as the woman three times her age. "Shut up! Shut up right now!"

Simple, punctuated, the scorn thrown at the queen-regent by the outburst produced the desired effect, snapping the mad matron to silence. Enraptured by the effect of a serf telling her lady what every serf wished to say, Haidra did not allow the awkward quiet to carry.

"I've seen your father's body. I've seen your mother's." Side-eying someone who had become her worst enemy as well, she swallowed the curses she wanted to spit, settling for cold, honest truth. "I watched your men kill my father. You will be quiet, your highness, for you've lost all room to talk."

The weight of simple, hard facts, along with many more

Haidra had had ready without ever speaking of them to Bon or the others, deadened Fransica's demeanor. The mania once present in her eyes, cheeks, and mouth left, replaced by a haughtiness natural to her pretty face.

"Who dares speak to me in such a way?" Fransica asked aloud as she looked to Jhean de Veard, almost as if Haidra was not there.

"That is Haidra Bloom," Bon said, his enchanted voice full of passion behind the burning mask of darkness and the illusions. "The true holder of Atenia and its hearts. Don't forget it."

"She a wretched little thing," the queen-regent spat back. "Who is she to address her proper—"

"She said shut up and she's right," New Moon interrupted. "Stop, Aunt. It's over."

The sorceress' address woke the obvious within Fransica. Still ignoring Haidra, she looked to Bon, then to New Moon. As with the first outpouring of madness to the cold fury of her silencing, Haidra witnessed the contrived shifts in Fransica's expressions. She wondered how the woman suffered until, once more, she took on a new aspect as she scanned her niece and nephew.

One of smug satisfaction as she realized who addressed her.

"I guess it is, isn't it?" Fransica said, a smirk parting her thin lips to reveal her teeth. She straightened on her bare feet and smoothed the front of her transparent shift, running her hands sensuously down the front. Clicking her tongue against her teeth, she chuckled, completely reveling in her sanity.

Haidra couldn't help but shake her head at the beast before her.

"Well, well..." Fully relaxed as she crossed her feet at the ankles and reclined against the wall again, Fransica swayed her hips as she peered at her brother. "I guess it's all done. All out. Everything."

The prince studied his sibling like a stranger.

His inactivity spurred a spike of anger, dispelling her cock-sure façade. "Say something."

Nothing.

She leaned in his direction, teeth clenched behind tight lips. "You ruined me. From the very beginning. All I ever wanted was for you to love me. Me, Jhean—your little sister. I just wanted to be loved by you like I love you." When he did not respond, nor react, she hissed, "Speak to me damn you! Say something, you terrible bastard!"

"You made your choices," the prince replied.

"No, you made them!" Fransica jutted her finger in his direction. "You made them! You made them when you left on the first quest! You made them with your coldness and your neglect! You made them when you married that foreign bitch who—"

"I said enough!" Haidra shouted again from his side. "Don't you dare say another word about her. Not in front of her children."

"Little girl, I burnt their mother," Fransica said, immediate and without thought of who she said it in front of. "Don't act like I care about them anymore than I do you."

"You said enough," Jhean de Veard warned Fransica.

"What then, Jhean?" she asked. "Are you going to cut me down?"

Glowering at his sister, without the satisfaction she had found in harming him, he took one step toward her.

The queen-regent flinched. "You'll stay back."

"I will," Jhean de Veard responded. "In fact, I'll leave you now, Fransica. To go to prepare the way."

"The way?" Fransica asked. "The way to where?"

"To your *rescue*," he answered, adding renewed emphasis to the word. He put his back fully to his sister as he strode from the bed chamber.

"Wait! Don't you turn your back on me," Fransica protested. "Jhean! Jhean! You will look at me!"

He lifted his hood, obscuring his face as he stopped beside his daughter. "Haidra, with me," he said before he glanced to the sorceress. "New Moon, you and Bon get her ready. No broken bones."

Black John walked out.

"Ready for what?" Fransica shouted. "Ready for what? What worry should I have about my bones?"

"I'll show you right now, bitch," New Moon said. "Close the door, Bon!"

The ax-slinger shut the door behind Haidra and his father. A few seconds later, Fransica's protest turned to screams among the noise of breaking furniture and New Moon cursing in Eaith. None of the intent was missed, nor were the resounding smacks that finally quieted their aunt.

Almost halfway down the hall Black John put his hand in front of Haidra. He turned her about by her shoulders to face him and crushed her against him in a powerful embrace.

"Thank you," he whispered into her dark hair. "Thank you. For my children. For my mother, my father. For my Hibni. Thank you, Haidra."

Lost in the unexpected show of kindness, his complete vulnerability, the memory of Arverin's hug, released the long-held sorrow she had dammed up the moment she fell out of their old window. Before her friends, in the halls of a dead dynasty, she cried alongside its remaining spirit over everything lost.

# 9

# THE FINAL VILLAIN

They heard the crowds long before they departed the palace, the courtyard packed from the broken entrance's last step, and beyond. Every soul that could inhabit the top of Atenia's grand hill and citadel clogged the upper reaches of Snail's Way, crowded to see, hear, and witness the rise of their rightful king. Adan and Clive exited first, hoping to make a thoroughfare in the throng but to no avail. The resounding cheers for the Fishermen of Souls soured any attempt, leaving them with inert smiles and an unwillingness to argue. They paid the same to Aleaus Hammerstrike and Talic Gray-stare, who flanked the opening to the Veard's dim halls.

Haidra came next bearing High John the Conqueror. Flooded with undesired adoration, she understood Jhean de Veard's endless dilemma. The sword she cradled in the crooks of her arms, the scabbarded blade snug to her chest and point reaching past her shoulder, gained attention and anticipation the longer she remained with it, all to her growing dread.

The crowd roused to a raucous pitch when New Moon passed out of shadow, her hood drawn back to reveal a dark face streaked in tears. She seethed under her disheveled silver mane, more her father in appearance than ever before. Her brother, tall at her side, simply looked impassively forward. Not to Haidra, not to the ghosts, not the people.

Nothing.

The arrival of the prince drove his subjects into a frenzy. From pockets of the thousands rose smatterings of an old song, too garbled and disjointed to be understood fully, out of place and time those after Fransica never knew. Civitas blew, the clay horns deafening in a discordant mass. The anthem to the Veards, to their Atenia, resounded in a cacophony.

The prince raised his hand, re-sheathed in its gauntlet.

The gesture brought silence, all eager to hear the words of their restored champion.

A great horn blew at the citadel's high gate, the note loud and long across the cloudless blue sky. Raising pennants and flags to match the glory of heaven above, the procession of King Aron Toliv I of Atenia broke through the masses into a renewed cascade of adulation. Atop a gallant camel brought across the sea from Arbikk's deserts, he rode side-saddle, gowned in a long dress of blue and white to match the winding turban on his head. His facial hair trimmed to a delicate mustache and beard oiled to a black sheen, he also paid no emotion to the celebration. A cavalcade of his cataracts followed behind, sharp-pointed helms and mail glittering in the sun. An aisle formed, grateful citizens parting to allow the reunification of their saviors and heroes.

Aron slid off the great mammal before he reached the foot of the battered steps. He yanked off the curved sword at his side and immediately knelt at Black John's feet, to a joyful, almost maddened response.

Lifting the hilt toward the wraith, he raised his head to look at the Atenian eye to eye.

Jhean de Veard nodded down to his benefactor, future son-in-law, but did not take the sword.

From bended knee, Aron ascended to stand beside the tall figure, equal in every respect. He raised his weapon before he spoke in his rich, kind voice.

"People of Atenia, your homeland is yours. You are free."

Haidra wondered for a moment if she had gone deaf. The exhalation of sixteen years of tyranny and its liberation loosed in a wild, uncontrolled fervor. Men wept and pounded their chests as much as they sang to victory, the women wailing amid the songs to cover blighted childhoods full of nightmare and doubt. Only their children, running about legs and hips like ants in the hills or perched on shoulders to see, found a purer contentment. They cheered on and on for ten minutes before passion ebbed enough for Aron to regain order.

"Long was the time of grim suffering, but longer will be the time of kind healing, a time needed to restore Atenia to its vital essence. There will be questions of its fate and who it will fall upon to determine it. With the end of the Veards, a decision must be made on who is to rule, what is to follow, and more importantly, the spirit in which we attend to it. I have been made king by you through deeds of grace and valor, but these are not the only things that make a king: he must govern with the consent of his people. I am not of these lands, no matter how close you hold me to your hearts, and though you granted me sway it is not for a Toliv-man to rule an Atenia-woman, or anyone here. Today I have brought my sword, which I have been blessed to carry through this conflict without marring its edge upon a foe's steel or tragic flesh. For a true warrior there is no greater desire. But I have not shed the blood you all have shed. I have not taken the risks you all have risked. Who am I?"

Aron maintained the height of the golden weapon. "I am lord of one land, far from here, by the right of blood. But here, now, stands a man of blood and deed, who paid both to return Atenia its soul. Who am I to call myself king when a rightful one stands beside me?" He turned away from those he addressed, to

Jhean de Veard. The wraith did not face his benefactor. "Therefore I, Aron Toliv, abdicate the throne of Atenia and return it to—"

The second round of deafness made Haidra's head ache. The audience shook in anticipation. Able to strain out their words here and there, the refrains echoed.

"Raise the flag of Jhean de Veard!"

"The king! The king! The king!"

"Hang Fransica! Raise Jhean de Veard!"

And then, more horrific than anything, after everything she had heard, they chanted, "Give us her head! Give us her head! Give us her head!"

"The Veards! The Veards! The Veards!"

His face concealed by his hood, the prince scanned the storm of worship and fealty, his mouth a hard line. The rest of the ghosts, Haidra included, looked to each other in wait, their combined worry gathering as the horde of his would-be subjects closed, leaving little room for Aron's camel or the cataract's horses. No matter how well trained, the animals fretted, forcing the prince's mounted horsemen to force a calm.

"Give us her head! Give us her head!"

"The Veards! The Veards!"

"The king!"

Jhean de Veard silenced the day as he put his right hand out. Without needing an order, Haidra bore forth High John the Conqueror. He grasped the hilt, the leonine pommel flush to the crook of his elbow and the oakleaves at the ends of the guard shining. The long steel blade, blemished by centuries of use, flashed brighter than starlight as he drew it out.

He reached up with his free hand and pulled back his hood to show his full face. Placid, he brought the sword into his full grasp, fists clinched tight to its long, corded handle. He took a few steps forward and stopped.

Sated by the moment, the people of Atenia cried out again in disparate unison.

"Hang her!"

"Raise the Veards!"

"The king!"

Sudden rage lanced across Jhean de Veard's handsome features. He took one brief step and raised High John the Conqueror, as if to hold it aloft like the trophy, sign and office of everything deserved about the man.

"The king! The king! The k—"

Adoration stuttered to silence as he brought the sword down with a clang, its edge flush to the stone courtyard. He screamed with every ounce of might as he brought it up and whipped it down. Fissures spread on the holy steel.

He rained it upon the ground his mother's ancestors had made, on the stones his father had trod, until the sword shattered. Shards flew in every direction, causing those around to panic and cover their faces with their arms.

Jhean de Veard spiked the remains of the hilt at his feet, the punctuation to a stunned, disheartening act. Unarmed, unbridled, he glanced over his shoulder at Haidra. The rage remained, but his mouth peeled back in a lion's growl, revealing his teeth.

Incapable of processing the moment, she mouthed back the one sensible question, "Why?"

He faced the audience, away from her, empty hands out to his sides.

"It ends," Jhean de Veard declared. "It ends. I told you from the moment I came back to this miserable kingdom that I wasn't here to take the throne, nor was I here to end my sister's reign. I'm here to end it all. This. I came to end Atenia."

The gasps were as loud as the cheers.

He dropped his arms and heaved, blinking as sadness stripped away the anger. "Do you not see yourselves? Do you not see who put you here? You cheer, so quick to forget why you were assailed in the first place—and by what. And yet the moment you place down your load you'd take it back up, fools broken by their masters."

The mood of the crowd transformed, no longer joyous. He sensed it, his dark expression deepening as it combined with clear, uninhibited sorrow. "No, no. Don't you dare. You will look at this. You will look at yourselves. You revel with no mind for your past and no concern for your future. You would crown me, the brother of a sister who tore at your souls for more than decade? You would crown me, the man who has slain your sons and brothers who bowed to her? Have you no honor to yourselves, or any sense of shame?"

Prince Aron spoke, gentle but serious, "My Lord, please—"

"No," Jhean de Veard said. "No! I will not have what has happened here be forgotten so quickly for the sake of comfort! Damn your comfort and damn your rescue if this is what you have planned with it!"

The condemnation coalesced in the crowd in varying ways. Many simply listened, their brows heavy in worry, while others who had fought and lost only to win ground their boots against the stone, bound their fists, jaws tight as they stared evil at the man reminding them of its origins.

"This happened because of power and the contest of crowns," Jhean de Veard said, undeterred. "This happened because scorn and rejection birthed hatred and madness. The choices of a few—my few, me and my family—brought ruin upon you. Do not bow to kings undeserving of your fealty when you are born to be ruled by none save you and your choices alone. Do not fail the dead because you refuse to see who made them."

"Who made them?" a voice in the crowd dared to ask.

"You did," Jhean de Veard shouted, pointing at the grime-covered man. "We all did! We made them when we put up gods and then let those gods pick kings! What have you gotten from your gods? What have you gotten from kings and queens? The same things you will always get when you place power into the few instead of yourselves and each other: the brutality of the undeserving! The despotic!"

His voice elevated to an impassioned plea.

"You can have it differently. We all can, together. Never enthrone the few when you can vote up the many. Choose the power of the vote before a ruler's right to violence. Choose your children as I wished someone had chosen mine. Choose their mothers..." He broke down, the tears flowing. "As I wish someone had chosen mine! Choose your wives and husbands, brothers and sisters, but gods help you, choose anything else but kings or queens! Then, you will never have to be here again —nor I."

10

# MEMENTO

King Aron assumed rule of Atenia, but after the abdication and scolding by the last Veard, agreed with its citizens to form a council to take possession of the kingdom in fifteen years, rebuilding before they established a new city-state without kings, queens, or a lone ruler in full control. The time of Atenia was given away to history, and in its place the Children of Marta were given the choice of a new name.

The days of Lomens, Veards, and Atenia passed on, leaving the newborn country of Veardia in its place in the southwestern reaches of Torsdaina, one of Dovhain's four great continents. When asked why later by scholars and storytellers, natives of the land would say it was called so to remind them of what they had been, as well as a dire warning of where never to return.

Three days after the fall of Fransica, whose body was unable to be found in the citadel, nor her children's, the three wraiths met at a farewell party at the northern palisade. Arrayed alongside King Aron, the newly-elected Governor Ecktor, and the bard Valen, Haidra waited with the Ghosts of Solomon. From young Clive to the eldest, Talic, every one of the five survivors had brought their gear and belongings they thought sensible for a long journey ahead. But instead of the ghastly figures who had appeared out of the night weeks ago, the three who emerged to meet them were as strange as their previous selves. Their black horses the only darkness they bore out into the wider world, the son and daughter had put away ax and rapier, mail and leather, to dress in gentle cottons and colors.

Bon in particular caught Haidra's gaze in a silken thawb of honey gold to match his hair, bound in a black turban. The long dress' sheen provided a wonderful contrast to his blue-green gaze. Leading his black steed to where she stood, he beamed brighter as they came face to face. He leaned forward, without word or greeting, meeting a kiss which served well for both.

"Ready?" he whispered.

Haidra lifted her forehead from his and bent to the side, raising the bundle of new clothes and the cleaned bits of armor tied around her sword. He took it and secured it to his fine saddle on the right side, his horse's glossy left flank already claimed by a bag and the black ax wedged under it.

Gowned in a flowing white caftan she weighed with a belt of gold plates and a large pendant of an inverted half-moon, New Moon went immediately to Aron, as enthused to greet her husband-to-be as Bon had Haidra. The quick kiss ended as the rest of the ghosts loading their bags into a troop wagon, already hitched to a team of four geldings arranged two by two.

Last was Jhean de Veard, bare of any royal trappings. His chin and cheeks shorn of the beard that once reached to his collarbone, the full lips of a proud mouth remained a hard line of worry, his tanned brow never truly easing. He went to Ecktor and Valen immediately, dressed in little more than fresh riding trousers, a shirt under a thicker tunic, and a simple longsword belted to his waist. Though now equal to him in the ways that mattered, the bard and the rebel-cobbler both bowed before they talked among themselves.

Always in firm control of her gigantic horse, New Moon broke from Aron so her love could join the council of leaders and came to Haidra and Bon. She offered the long leather reins to the former. "Here," she said. "Hillary should be much more fun than a wagon ride, and she's gentle."

The gigantic mare bore a hard gaze at Haidra as she took the reins. Trying not to focus on the dark brown eyes fixed on her face, she looked to New Moon in surprise. "Me? But where will you... Wait." She looked from Bon and to his sister, both expressing an unvarnished sadness. As if sensing the unease in Haidra, the other four ghosts halted their packing.

"You're not coming?" asked Aleaus, her salt-and-pepper hair recently shortened close to the scalp after so long under helm and under-washed.

"Aron must remain and rule Veardia," New Moon answered. "I will remain here with him for a few months while he appoints his court and afterward travel to Arbikk to prepare for our wedding." She glanced to the king speaking to her father, the pair engrossed in a short conversation with Ecktor, though the bard paid little attention to. The handsome ruler of two king-doms separated by an ocean caught her glance and smiled back. "We've been waiting, but we can wait a little more."

"But, my Lady..." His dark brown hair finally combed out of his face which had been scrubbed clean to reveal round cheeks covered in peach fuzz, Clive hopped down from the wagon. "Will we ever see you again?"

"What a silly question," New Moon replied, leaving her horse with Haidra to go and embrace the young fisherman. His father embraced the sorceress as his own daughter before Talic and Aleaus had their turn. More than a few tears were shed between Aleaus and New Moon, the older blacksmith and the younger mystic having found a kinship separate from the rest over the long battles. To the shock of all Talic loosed a few drops of sorrow over their parting. But before they embarked in the

long, covered wagon taking them and the last Veard to wherever fate waited, the three leaders of the past, present, and
unknown called them forth.

Jhean de Veard spoke first, solemn in his bearing. "All of you
have chosen to come with me. I understand. I could not remain,
no matter how—" He glanced up to the left, and they all
followed his gaze to the gatehouse of the northern palisade,
manned and kept by the rebels, now a militia with his mother's
name. The old banner of Ursin at the river, guarding it from
beasts from the north so his kin and those southward slept well,
flapped on a gentle wind.

He roused himself. "Though there is no longer an Atenia, it
will always remain at its best in you," he said, nodding at Haidra.
"And you, and you, and you, and you," he said to Talic, then
Aleaus, then Adan, then Clive. "And they who remain wish to
say something of it as well, if this be the last time we see this
place we once called home. I beg you give them your attention."

New Moon joined King Aron at his side as the gallant young
man approached. Letting go of her hand, he reached up and
slowly unwound his turban. Both Valen and Jhean de Veard
moved at the act, as did the others, for among the warriors of
Arbikk their head-coverings were considered the sacred wrap
of Uma, their singular goddess the tribes of the desert continent
believed birthed the world out of her nightly shroud. He pulled
the dagger in his belt and took its keen edge to the sky-blue silk.
Slicing five equal portions, he came to each of the Ghosts of
Solomon, ordering them to raise their right hands.

"A king of my lands does not do this," he said, laughing as
tears ran. "We are trained to be hard. We only do this for our
family that rides with us into the defense of justice. You all have
no families yet gave so much to your people. To each other. To
me." He tied them to their wrists, looking the hero or heroine
square in the eyes when he finished. "Do not forget, now and
forever, the house of Toliv is your family. Thank you, you

blessed, blessed souls. I will pray every day Uma takes you to her heavens if your gods will not."

Valen broke in as Aron retreated to his place beside New Moon, who's tears had overtaken her. The bard played a long, beautiful song on his lute, needing no words added to birth in them something they would cherish and seek to remember, note by note, in the coming years. Whatever magic held in the performance finally broke Talic, who dropped his head forward to bawl like a child before Aleaus collected him.

Ecktor came last. The governor of the city, thinner and far more aged in the face than Haidra remembered, surveyed some of his oldest friends and neighbors. He hooked his thumbs in his wide girdle and sighed. "Little to be said after all that, least of all by me. To you this may be a farewell, but I will leave it as a goodbye for now. You are always welcome in the land that is yours more than anyone else's. You will always have a vote in Veardia."

Well enough to part on, the final hugs and kisses were exchanged, especially among Jhean de Veard, Bon, and the third of their constant, lifelong trio. Promises for later were whispered into wet cheeks and gentle shoulders, many knowing some were only said in passing. Helped onto Hillary, Haidra was surprised her feet fell into the stirrups as she balanced on the fierce but kindly mare, peaceful despite her constant shifting. Bon brought his black mount beside hers and took the reins, guiding both.

Whatever was left to say by Jhean de Veard he said to Aaron and Valen alone, then bidding his daughter a final kiss and long, hard embrace, he ascended to his gallant warhorse. One short but sworn to see again, the seven companions who had endured war and worse set off, northbound to one of the many frontier highways eastward curving over the Ben-Lomen's sparkling glacier before it turned south for the sea beyond.

Until they heard shouting behind them.

"Haidra! Haidra! Haidra, wait!"

She turned in the saddle as the rest did in their places on the wagon, surprised to see Ecktor running hard to catch them. Rushing up to the right side of Haidra's horse, by the curb of the road, he grabbed her hand.

"Haidra! I'm so sorry, I forgot!"

"Forgot, Ecktor?" she asked, confused as she pulled back to stay in the saddle.

He turned her hand over and pressed a small, hard round into her palm. "I found this when I went to look on him. Someone had done the decent thing to bury him, but this was on the floor. I just knew—" He released her hand and let the horse carry on, holding his own to his heart. "I knew you had to have it!"

Haidra opened her hand and cried out every bit of happiness and sorrow in her.

The face of a wraith who kept his oath looked forward in golden relief on the coin's face, carrying more than one satisfied spirit into a better future.

# THEREAFTER

A morning wind swept down the grassy cliffs overlooking a sparkling ocean, the sun enflaming its light in sheets upon the surface. Eagles lofted on the sweet air, riding the currents far away, only to come back the next day from their distant sojourns to hunt with the gulls. Cattle grazed on the sloping plains ending at Torsdaina's edge, a five-hundred-foot plunge to the rocky shore where waves gnawed the upshot earth. Their lowing calm as their demeanors, they hoofed along the meadows, chewing where they wanted.

Bon led Haidra and Jhean de Veard through a thin herd, giving them no more attention than the bovines paid them. Their blacks cloaks, hoods, and armor discarded, Jhean carried his simple longsword on his shoulders and wore a pair of trousers, a cream shirt, and his dark riding boots. The former prince had combed his hair free of the tangles the years had put in, and his washed face and skin made him seem almost as young as his golden son.

Unarmed, Bon matched his father in dark riding breeches, deciding to dare the field barefoot.

In the four months since leaving Veardia, Haidra would have considered the sight of herself mad if not so comfortable with it. In leather-ghillies tied up to her knees, she traipsed over cow-pies, her blue dress hiked up in both fists though her sword's scabbard always caught the back hem. Her weapon, unused in as many days, was more for decoration between her and the ax-slinger when they scampered into the hills for play and love-making. Around her neck hung her father's coin, punched at its edge and tied in black cord. Her hair free, it had grown long and light in the unspoiled sun. Now used to country fens instead of squalid urban streets, she formed a fine place in the family, even starting to soften the dethroned prince.

Not far behind them, on a smooth path cutting down into the hillside, one of their wagons driven by Talic disappeared behind the berm.

The mood was settled and carefree until they crested the next hilltop.

An old outpost raised itself on stone and mortar at the edge of the bluffs. The top of the tower domed in copper and glass, the observatory once belonging to the Atenians had lain dormant until a recent occupant had taken residence. The isolated station had been repaired a few years before when King Aron made Jhean de Veard promise to restore it and claim a few hundred acres of western Torsdaina's coastal countryside—in Veardia's restored territory, of course—where the beaches rose and plummeted in a rocky border between the land and the world. A few miles away, northeast in the hinterlands, the prince, his son, and Haidra made their space in a well-appointed cabin in the piney heights.

"Are you ready?" Bon asked his father.

Jhean sighed deep as he levered his sword off his shoulder and handed it to Bon. "Never. But wait for my signal."

He descended the hill, taking it slowly to avoid any hidden roots or dips in the earth below the grass.

Haidra watched from her place beside her lover, hands clasped in front of her. An anxiety she had not felt since entering the citadel, still stark in memory with its empty shadows and bloodletting, gathered a stone in her stomach. She reached with her right hand and found Bon's searching for hers.

"Is this the last time?" she asked.

"I don't know." Bon searched the sea beyond the observatory. "Maybe if we go back to Arbikk. Maybe." He squeezed her hand in his. "I want it to be."

"Should we?"

"Oh, of course." He cracked a sardonic grin. "Lead me through it."

"All right," she said, letting go of his hand after a short squeeze.

She balled her fists at her sides, took a deep breath before she unclenched them, and exhaled. Shutting her eyes, Haidra imagined the world beyond her eyelids, the beautiful hills, the countless sky, and the endless horizon of the Southern Sea with its sparkling waters brimming with life. Trying to gather it all, she melted into it, skin and muscle dissolving before her bones gathered into the dust of the world's winds.

But Haidra remained, her gross body banished for the mental one beneath, as Jhean de Veard had explained it, giving access to a greater source of power. Her mental self and the ineffable as one, every word uttered was magic, wielded for means only Uma truly knew.

Haidra spoke the goddess' will, power thrumming through every atom of her being, *"Edjo."*

As she opened her eyes, she concentrated past the sparks manifested in front of them, a reaction of manifest energy. Smart now not to let the glow of them blind or distract her attention, she gazed out on hazing, glowing, revealed land. From the tallest pines full of needles to the blades of sweet-smelling grass whispering, the whole hillside danced with the wavering ocean. She sensed all of it, and when fixing on the prince plodding down to the observatory, heard his footfalls in the rocky soil.

"Good," said Bon.

She glanced to the ax-slinger, her spell firm as she held its thought-form in place. He had evoked the same enchantment, his eyes decorated by a dusting of star-specks. Smiling together at a repeated but important achievement, their mirth waned as they returned to his father, witness to one more march.

Before Jhean de Veard found the bottom she appeared, in the entrance of the tower's timbered doorway. Fransica had dressed in a gown of bright blue cinched around her shoulders, letting her long blond locks go free. Years of make-up, sleeplessness, addiction, and madness, washed away by the healing waters her greatest foe had provided, only revealed a deeper layer of defeated scorn beneath.

He halted within a distance so they could hear each other, stationed on the grass.

She opened her mouth first, shut it, then spoke simply. "What is there left to say?"

The breeze shifted the honey-dark locks of Jhean's mane as he gritted his teeth. "You'll see I left my sword behind, but you have a dagger. No need for it. I've not come to claim vengeance."

"Have you not?" She tensed, refusing to move her hands from their place behind her back. "You have proven your point very well."

"This wasn't about proving points. The crimes you placed upon me were so heinous, Fransica," he replied. "Things none questioned because honor demanded it, and rightly so, but the sins you laid upon my head, upon our parents, were lies. You knew it. I proved it." He let out a mean, sad sound. "And yet you still have no idea what kind of suffering you put me through. Or others."

"You wouldn't have left me alone," she said. "You would have come back and ruined my marriage to Niklon. Made me look like a bad mother. You would have turned my sons against me as you became king. You would have—"

"I would have done none of those things! None! Nor did I ever want to come home," he said, interrupting. "I didn't want anything to do with your—"

"I'm not finished!"

"Look around you, sister!" Jhean roared. "You are."

Bon squeezed Haidra's hand tightly, fidgeting on the spot next to her. She gripped tighter.

"It's all right," she whispered, mind set on the thought-form, the word of the spell, and the wholeness she felt. The stone in her gut had been banished, leaving behind a warming, healing spot.

Exhaling through his aquiline nose, Bon nodded.

Down the hill, Jhean de Veard turned away first with a grunt of frustration and anger. He studied the sea to calm his wrath.

Fransica pressed her advantage. "You couldn't leave me alone to deal with my destiny as I wanted to. There was always some little word you shared with Father that I could not, or something Mother discussed with you which she thought applied to something that was mine not yours. Everything was his, hers, or yours. Never mine. They allowed you to murder and quest while I worked harder than everyone else and achieved so much more, and yet they were telling me what *you* thought?"

"They saw *your* character."

"You should talk, *Black John*," she said. "You were a bully and a braggart. The only good thing you did was marry well, and she would be ashamed of what you've done."

"Ashamed?" Jhean de Veard asked, galled. "She and I never tied our son to his bed when he wouldn't sleep on command. I never abandoned him in spires because he did not fit my selfish expectation or grandiose visions even when they were falling down around your own children! Dress me however you want, sister! I am a murderer, bloody and awful. There's no excuse for why I did it other than the same reason you did what you did—because we hurt each other. But I haven't done what you have and the slain never stop whispering. Have they started whispering to you yet?"

"You suppose we both care to listen." She laughed, a cruel sound. "Or worry for those dead and gone."

"We were raised to. We were raised to be better."

"And they didn't live it any more than the rest of us. Neither of them," she said. "Solomon never let the crown off his head enough to be a father, but we felt the anger of the king, didn't we? Didn't we, Jhean? Didn't you get tired of Marta trying to control every thought, every word you had?"

"I don't blame our parents for my choices any more than you can put your atrocities on them, or Niklon, or whoever you'll push your evil onto. Solomon was no great man, but he loved us and his people. So did our mother. She loved you more than anyone else, and you blew us all up because you wanted attention."

"You would have made me your subject," she said without any sign of regret. "I did what was best for me."

"You aren't some victim, Frannie," he said, turning his back to her. "Just little and wicked."

"Only because of the great and vicious," Fransica retorted at her brother's back. "I'll always be sick to everyone, Jhean, but no matter what you do or who you free, you'll always be my molester to someone—whether true or not! You took Atenia away from me. So? You took it away from you, too. Slaughtering my army? More dead to whisper at you. Whatever I did changed you for the worse. Who really won, brother of mine? The day is still sunny and nice for me at least."

A clatter and roll of the wagon's wheels as Talic reached the observatory interrupted the argument. Crested on top of the last lump of earth overlooking the sea-side tower, its red cloth was bright under the clean, clear day. The driver dismounted from the bench and went around the back as he waved at Jhean de Veard.

"You're right," Jhean de Veard said, his voice hollow as he watched Talic open a door out of Haidra's line-of-sight. He wiped away the tears from his cheeks. "There will be people who will believe the worst about me forever and ever, no matter how others tell it. Some will paint this as vengeance and imagine the worst outcomes of what I will do to you, thinking I'm simply finishing the damage I started."

"You ruined yourself at word one," she said, smirking. "Dig your hole deeper."

"You burnt the mother of my children. You killed our parents. You murdered hundreds of thousands through starvation, cruelty, and war because you didn't get your way. The problem wasn't with me, or you, Fransica, but the idea our crowns gave us the right to think ourselves worthy of such choices in the first place. Nobody should be on a throne. Not me, or you—anyone. I am leaving you here because you will have to suffer it."

"Suffer?" she asked. "How is this peace you've given me suffering?"

"Because you're just you now, Queen-Regent, and not even that. You don't have your royalty to hide behind or meaningless smears. All you have is you."

He signaled to Talic, who unlocked the door of the carriage. From the darkness within arose Tobias. Amber-headed and rounded in the face like the slain sorcerer Niklon, the young man froze when he saw his mother before the tower's door. His mouth fell open in shock.

Fransica started down the steps, the expression on her face between awe and joy when Jhean de Veard stepped in her way.

Frightened by his simple movement, she seized, bringing up

the dagger held behind her back. Pressed to her ear, she hissed like a cat, almost daring him.

"But why?" she asked, her confusion aroused by her panic.

"All you have now, Fransica, is you. You." Not taking his focus from his sister or her weapon, he threw his head back in his nephew's direction. "Remember this moment. Remember that while you took and took and took from me, I gave you back your son when I didn't have to. The other two will be on the way when and *if* they want to come. While my son lives without his mother but knows enough to make peace with it, your children will spend the rest of their days trying to have you explain what you did to them and to others. Tobias knows. The others will, too. I've spent years learning to live with a shame that was not mine, but now you will live with what you did every day when Tobias looks upon you. Perhaps you did ruin me at word one, but once he finally sees what the world sees, I will have defeated you beyond that."

Jhean de Veard turned to start back up the hill.

"You bastard!" Fransica cleared the last few steps and tried to run after him but was stopped by some thought. It brought her to wrathful tears. "How could you just—"

"Because for all you did to me," Jhean de Veard shouted, not taking the effort to look back, "You live. I live. And we'll have to live with the world we've made. There's no better ending than that—at least for me!"

The house of Veard died on a windswept stretch of cliffside, buried in its final moments by the silence of its ruin.

THE END

# ACKNOWLEDGEMENTS

I do nothing without the grace and support of my wife and partner, Margo. To my child, Ben, who raises the sun and sets the rest of the stars for me.

This did not happen without Tim Marquitz, Simon Underwood, Tom Mock, Lucy Gray, and John Hartness. My deepest thanks to each and every one of you.

And to Aaron Toliver, a prince among men.

# ABOUT THE AUTHOR

Jay Requard is an author of Epic Fantasy and Sword & Sorcery located in New York City. The winner of the 2016 Write Well Award for his novelette *Mask of the Kravyads* and a runner-up for the Manly Wade Wellman Award for the novella *War Pigs,* he also helped establish Falstaff Books as one of its original authors and, for a little bit, an acquisitions editor. His most recent series include A WAVE OF LIONS and the upcoming Urban Fantasy series, THE BLESSED & POSSESSED.

He is also the host of PONDERING THE ORB, a YouTube show dedicated to books, music, and more, as well as WHERE NO BUBS HAS GONE BEFORE, a Star Trek: The Next Generation podcast.

He walks the roads of adventure with a wonderful wife, a son he adores, and a star-cat named Mona Underfoot.

## ALSO BY JAY REQUARD

*A Wave of Lions*

*Death & Dust: The Pale Sand Adventures*

*Thief of Destiny*

*War Pigs*

# AFTERWORD

Sign up for my monthly newsletter and get two eBooks full of new adventures and intrigue!

https://www.subscribepage.com/booksforthemarchprime

Safe journeys!